New York Times and *USA TODAY* bestselling author **Heather Graham** has written more than a hundred novels. She's a winner of the Romance Writers of America's Lifetime Achievement Award, a Thriller Writers' Silver Bullet and, in 2016, the Thriller Master Award from ITS. She is an active member of International Thriller Writers and Mystery Writers of America, and is the founder of The Slush Pile Players, an author band and theatrical group. An avid scuba diver, ballroom dancer and mother of five, she still enjoys her South Florida home, but also loves to travel. For more information, check out her website, www. theoriginalheathergraham.com, or find Heather on Facebook.

Debbie Herbert writes paranormal romance novels reflecting her belief that love, like magic, casts its own spell of enchantment. She's always been fascinated by magic, romance and gothic stories. Married and living in Alabama, she roots for the Crimson Tide football team. Her eldest son, like many of her characters, has autism. Her youngest son is in the US Army. A past Maggie Award finalist in both young adult and paranormal romance, she's a member of the Georgia Romance Writers of America.

DISCARDED

OUT OF
THE DARKNESS

HEATHER GRAHAM

APPALACHIAN
PREY

DEBBIE HERBERT

MILLS & BOON

First Published in Great Britain 2018
by Mills & Boon, an imprint of HarperCollins*Publishers*
1 London Bridge Street, London, SE1 9GF

Out of the Darkness © Heather Graham Pozzessere 2018
Appalachian Prey © Debbie Herbert 2018

ISBN: 978-0-263-26556-9

39-0218

MIX
Paper from
responsible sources
FSC
www.fsc.org
FSC™ C007454

This book is produced from independently certified FSC™
paper to ensure responsible forest management.

For more information visit: www.harpercollins.co.uk/green

Printed and bound in Spain
by CPI, Barcelona

OUT OF THE DARKNESS

HEATHER GRAHAM

For Saxon and Joe, two of the nicest
and most talented young men I know.
May their move to New York be filled
with dreams—and, of course, all kinds of
visits from West Coast friends!

Prologue

What Davey Knew

The Bronx
New York City, New York
Ten Years Ago

The eyes fell upon Sarah Hampton with a golden glow; the woman's mouth, covered with blood, split into a diabolical smile as she cackled with glee, raising her carving knife and slamming it down on the writhing man tied to the butcher block in the kitchen. Blood seemed to spurt everywhere. Screams rose.

And Sarah, laughing at herself for her own scream, grabbed Davey's hand and followed Tyler Grant out of the haunted house.

"Fun!" Tyler said, laughing, catching his breath.

It was fun. Though Sarah had to admit she was glad she was here as part of a party of six. Fun? Yes, sure…

And creepy! The weapons had looked real. The "scare actors" could have passed for the real thing quite easily as far as she was concerned.

"Ah, come on, the guy on the butcher block—his screams were nowhere as good as they should have been," Hannah Levine said. "He must be getting tired of screaming—long season, long night. But I guess it is Halloween."

"Yeah, I imagine that the poor kid has been at it awhile," Sean Avery agreed. He looked at Sarah's cousin, Davey. "Then again, this place opens for only four weekends, with Halloween weekend, the last, being the boss. Coolest thing ever, Davey!"

Davey gave him a weird little half smile.

Suzie Cornwall—Sarah's best friend—frowned. "What's the matter, Davey? Was the haunted house too scary for you? We were all with you, you know."

"That one was okay," Davey said.

"But now…drumroll! We're moving on—to the major attraction!" Sean said.

"No, no, no!" Davey shook his head violently. "I'm scared!" He clearly didn't want to go into Cemetery Mansion, another of the haunted houses; he seemed terrified.

Sarah looked at her cousin with dismay.

She loved Davey. She really loved him. She had never met anyone who was as kind, as oblivious to what others thought, as willing to help others.

But Davey had Down syndrome. And while most of Sarah's friends were great, every once in a while they acted as if they didn't want to be with her, not if she was bringing Davey along.

And tonight…

Well, it was almost Halloween. And she and her friends had scored tickets to Haunted Hysteria in a radio contest. It was the prime event of the season, but one they couldn't actually afford. Well, to be honest—and they all had to agree—it was Davey who'd won the tickets. They'd asked him to dial the radio station number over and over again, and Davey hadn't minded.

The place itself was fabulous. Decorated to a T. Bats,

ghouls, ghosts, vampires, witches and more—young actors and actresses, of course, but they walked around doing a brilliant job. The foam tombstones looked real and aged; the makeshift mortuary chapel was darkened as if older than time itself. Lights cast green and purple beams, and fog machines set in strategic places made for an absolutely immersive experience.

And now they were all here—she, Davey, Tyler, Sean, Suzie and Hannah. Suzie, tall and well-built, perfectly proportioned to be dressed up as Jessica Rabbit for the night, was her best friend. Tyler was the love of her life. And most of the time, both of them were truly wonderful friends. Tyler had even told her once that he knew right off the bat if he'd like people or not—all depending on the way they treated Davey.

Hannah was a stunner, olive skinned and dark haired—and as an evil fairy, she was even more exotically beautiful than usual. Sarah was pretty sure she'd caused one of the "scare actors" to pause—too startled by her beauty to scare her!

Sean… Sean was charming, the old class clown. Apropos, he was dressed up as the Joker. Every once in a while, his wit could be cruel. Mostly, though, he was a great guy, and the five of them had been friends forever, even though Sarah and Tyler were the only duo in their group.

She had come in steampunk apparel; Tyler had matched her with an amazing vest and frock coat. Davey had come as his all-time favorite personality—Elvis Presley.

They were all nearly eighteen now. Come October of next year, they'd be off at their different colleges, except she'd be at NYU with Tyler, as they'd planned. But for tonight…

It was fricking Halloween. Aunt Renee had asked her to take Davey with her. Yes, of course, Sarah was very aware the tickets really *belonged to Davey.*

Sarah always tried to be helpful. It was easy to help care for her cousin.

Aunt Renee wasn't in any kind of financial trouble—she had a great job as a buyer for a major chain store—and she had household help and could afford to send Davey to a special school.

But Aunt Renee wanted Davey to have friends and spend time with people his own age—Sarah's age. Aunt Renee wanted a wider world for Davey; she did not want his mom to be his only companion.

Sarah's friends were usually happy to have Davey with them.

But now Sarah could feel that Davey was holding them all back—and they were kids, with a right to be kids. The others were looking at her. Sure, they loved Davey. They were good people. But she could see them thinking *screw it!* They'd come to Haunted Hysteria; they were going in the haunted houses, and Sarah was welcome to sit outside with Davey.

Tyler, of course, had the grace to look guilty. He wasn't eighteen until January, but he was already over six foot three, heavily muscled in the shoulders and extremely fine in the face. Hot, yes. Tyler was hot. And he loved her. He really did. Then, she hoped she wasn't exactly dog chow herself. She was, she admitted, the typical cheerleader to his football hero. Yes, she was blonde and blue-eyed, the fault of her genetics. She was a good student and coordinated enough to be a great cheerleader. She liked to believe she'd been taught by her family to be a lot more, too—as in decent and compassionate and bright enough to see and understand others.

She thought Tyler was like that, too. No matter how cool he was.

They were just right for each other—and their group of friends was nice, too! Something she considered extremely important. Tonight, they wanted to be seniors—they wanted to be a little bit wicked and have a great time.

But being Davey's cousin had long ago taught Sarah about the importance of kindness in the world. Patience, sharing, caring…all that.

All that…

Seemed to go out the window right now.

"Davey, I know you were scared in the first house, but we're all with you," she said.

"Hey, buddy," Tyler told him. "I'm bigger than the damned ghosts!"

"You can go between Sarah and Tyler," Suzie said. "They'll protect you."

"No! No—the things in this house—they were okay. They weren't real. But that house…that one, there. There are things in it that are real. That are bad. They're evil!" Davey said.

"Oh, you're being silly," Hannah said.

"It's true," Davey said.

"How do you know?" Sean asked him.

"My father told me!" Davey said. "He helps me see."

Sarah bit her lip. Davey's dad had died over a year ago. Aunt Renee was alone with Davey now. Davey's dad had been a marine, and he had been killed serving his country. Her uncle had been a wonderful man—good to all the kids. She'd loved him, too, and she'd known he loved her.

"Davey, your father isn't here," she said. "You know… you know your dad is dead."

Davey looked at her stubbornly. "My father told me!" he insisted.

"Davey," Sarah said softly, calmly, "of course, the point is for it all to be very scary. Vampires, ghosts—but they're not real. It's a spooky fun place for Halloween. There are all kinds of made-up characters here."

"No. Real bad things."

They all let his words sit for a minute.

"The actors in there—they're not evil, Davey," Suzie said. "Come on, you've seen creatures like that before—and the ones who walk around, they're high school kids like us or college kids, and now and then, an adult actor without a show at the moment! You know all about actors, buddy. There are pretend vampires—and werewolves, mummies, ghosts—you name it."

"No. Not werewolves. Not vampires," Davey insisted. "Bad people. Like my dad said!"

"You love actors and movies," Sean said. Sean knew Davey had a skill for remembering everything about all the movies and, because of that, he always made sure Davey was on his team for trivia games. When they weren't playing trivia, however, Sean had a tendency to ignore Davey.

Sean seemed to be trying with the rest of their group to engage Davey, but he kept looking at his watch. He wanted to move on.

"You shouldn't go in! You shouldn't go in. It's bad. Very bad," Davey said.

"It's just a haunted house!" Tyler said.

"I love you, Tyler," Davey said. "Don't go. My father... he was next to me. Yes. He was next to me. All the things he taught me. He's dead, I know! But he's with me. He said not to go in. He said there would be bad men and you have to look out. He was smart. My dad was a marine!" he added proudly.

"That's kind of sick!" Hannah whispered to Sarah. "Does he honestly think…"

"Davey," Sarah said softly. "Your dad loved you—you loved your dad. But he's gone."

"I'm not going!" Davey said stubbornly.

"He should come," Tyler told Sarah. "If you give in to him all the time…it's not good. Don't make him into a baby. He's several years older than we are." He turned to Davey. "You know I love you, buddy, right?"

Davey nodded. "We don't have a weapon. I'm not going."

"Davey, I'm begging you…please?" Sarah asked.

Davey shook his head, looking at her. There were tears in his eyes; he was obviously afraid she was going to make him go into the haunted house.

"Just go," Sarah told the others. "Davey and I will get a soda or…hey, there are a bunch of movie toys over there. We'll go look at the toys."

Tyler sighed. "I'll stay with you."

The others had already fled like rats.

Not even Suzie—some best friend—stayed behind.

Just Tyler. Staring at her.

"Go," she told him, suddenly feeling put-upon.

"Sarah—"

"Go!"

He stiffened, squared his shoulder, shook his head— and walked on quickly to join the others.

"I'm still so confused. What scared you so badly?" Sarah asked Davey, leading him to a bench. At least she could sit. Her steampunk adventurer boots were starting to hurt like hell. "You were fine when we first got here. The haunted house we went in was made up to look like that one from the movie—you know, when the kids get lost in the woods and they find the house, but everyone in it is crazy! The father likes to hang people, the brother plays with a Civil War sword, the sister sprays poison and the mother chops up strangers for dinner. It was creepy cool—and they were all actors."

"Yes, they were actors," Davey said.

"Then why are you afraid of that one?" She pointed to the house where her friends were now in line, Cemetery Mansion. It was a good, creepy representation from a horror film where people had built over a graveyard and the dead came back to kill the living for disturbing them.

"It's evil," Davey said. He shoved his hands into his pockets and shivered. "I saw them. Dad told me to watch—I watched. That house is evil."

"How is it evil? It's honestly much the same. The themes are different. There are a lot of fabricated creatures—some cool motion-activated stuff, like robots—and then more actors. People just pretending. We went through the one house—it was fine."

He nodded very seriously and then pointed at the Cemetery Mansion.

"That one," he said. "It's wrong. I'm telling you, Sarah—it is wrong. And I like Tyler. And Suzie," he added. He didn't say anything about Sean or Hannah.

"You mean—you've heard they got the characters wrong somehow? We haven't been in it to see what the house is like, Davey."

"No, we can't go in," he said insistently, wetting his lips as he did when he got nervous. "No. It's wrong. You can feel it. It isn't scary—it's bad. Evil."

She looked at the house. It *was* spooky—the theme park had done a good job. Images were hazily visible in the windows: creatures that had just crawled from the grave, bony, warped, black-and-white, like zombies or ghosts, horrible to behold.

"You should stop your friends from going in there. Make Tyler come back. He wanted to stay with you. But you were all stubborn and mean."

Sarah heard the words and spun around to stare at Davey. But he didn't even seem to realize he had spoken to her.

He was looking at the stand where there were all kinds of toys.

Sarah suddenly smiled. His eyes were wide; he was happy to look at the toys. Davey loved the movies and he loved toys—that made movie-inspired props and toys extra special.

"Let's go see what they have," she told him.

"This is wrong," Tyler said as he got into the line for the haunted house with Suzie, Hannah and Sean. What was one more haunted house? he asked himself, irritated that he had let Sarah push him away. No matter if it was their idea or not, Davey had gotten them the tickets. He'd been patient enough to dial his phone over and over and over again.

And Tyler knew that Sarah was feeling alone—as if Davey was her responsibility, and she wasn't about to burden anyone else.

Tyler loved her. He knew they were both lucky, both blessed. People referred to them as the "Barbie and Ken" of their school. He liked to think it wasn't just that he played football and she was an amazing cheerleader—for any team the school put forth. He tried to be friendly, kind, sympathetic—and he worked hard in class.

Naturally, he and Sarah had been intimate—though not in a way that would give others a chance to tease them. They were discreet and very private; Sarah would never do anything to disappoint her parents. But in their minds, marriage was a given. Sometimes, in the middle of a class, Tyler would smile, imagine being with her in such an intimate way again, when they both laughed, when they grew breathless, when the world seemed to explode. She was an amazing lover and he hoped he reciprocated. Sex was fireworks, but life was loving everything about her—her great compassion for others, her integrity. He liked to think that he was similar in his behavior.

Leaving her on her own tonight hadn't been considerate in any way.

"I'm going to go back and wait with Davey and Sarah," he said flatly.

"Go back where?" Hannah asked him. "They're already gone. And besides, Miss Stubborn Pride isn't going to let you stay with her. I'm sure you already tried to and she sent you after us. She doesn't want you to have a lousy time just because she has to."

Tyler gritted his teeth and looked away. "She isn't having a lousy time—and neither am I, Hannah. I love Davey. No one out there has a better heart."

It was true, though, that Sarah and Davey had walked off somewhere.

He should have firmly ignored Sarah when she'd pushed him away. She was usually bright enough to be angry if someone didn't understand that hanging out with Davey was like hanging out with any friend...

And Tyler was suddenly angry himself; they wouldn't be here at all without Davey. Davey had won the tickets.

"Oh, come on, Tyler!" Hannah said. "It's okay! The retard is *her* cousin, not yours."

He wanted to slap Hannah—and he was stunned by the intensity of the feeling. In his whole life, he'd never hit a girl. And Hannah was a friend. She was usually...fine.

"Hannah, you know calling him that is not okay. Not cool. He's just like you or me," Tyler said.

"Maybe like you!" Sean said, laughing. "Not me. Hey, come on—this is supposed to be the coolest thing here, ghosts coming up out of the ground from all over. They say the creatures—animatronic or whatever—are the most amazing, and they put their best 'scare' actors in this one. Tyler, come on, we take Davey with us all the time. But this is our night. It's our last Halloween together. If he doesn't want to come in, screw it!"

"Not to mention that, as I already pointed out, we don't even know where they are anymore," Hannah said.

"Yep, well, I do have a cell phone," Tyler said.

"Tyler, leave it," Suzie said. She looked guilty, too, he thought. But maybe she was right. "We have VIP tickets—we get to move into the express lane up there. We'll be out soon and then we'll explore the food booths—Davey will like checking those out! And we'll hug him and tell him that he was right—we should have stayed out. It was really scary, so now we're all hungry!"

An actor in some kind of a zombie outfit came toward them, using a deep and hollow voice to ask for their tickets. They showed their passes and were moved up quickly in the line.

They entered the mudroom of the Cemetery Mansion. Bloody handprints were everywhere. They were met by a girl in a French maid outfit—with vampire teeth and blood dripping down her chin.

"Enter if you dare!" she said dramatically.

A terrified scream sounded from within. And then another. And another.

The place had to be amazingly good.

"Ah!" said the maid. "I say again, enter if you dare!

Those who have come before you seem to be just…dying to get back out!"

She opened the door from the mudroom to the foyer and stepped back.

Tyler thought she looked concerned. As if…

As if people actually were dying to get out.

"CAN WE GO look at the booth over there?" Davey asked Sarah.

He gave her a smile that made her ashamed. She had been secretly bitter; she'd wanted to go with her friends. It wasn't terrible that she should want to; she knew her feelings were natural. But she felt guilty, anyway. Davey wasn't being mean, she knew. He wasn't hurting her on purpose. He had his irrational fear set in his mind.

"Come on!" She caught his hand and led him to the toy stand. This one was stocked with prop weapons.

There were all kinds of great things: realistic plastic ray guns, gold-gleaming light-up lasers and much more. There were fantastic swords, like from some 1950s sci-fi movie, she thought. They were really cool—silver and gold, and emitting light through plastic blades that shimmered in a dozen colors.

They were cheap, too. Not like the licensed merchandise. It was called a Martian Gamma Sword.

Sarah smiled, watching Davey's fascination.

She worked three days a week after school at the local theater and could easily afford the toy sci-fi sword. She paid while Davey was still playing with it.

"Okay, good to go," she told him.

He looked at her, surprised.

"I bought it, Davey. It's yours."

His eyes widened. He gave her his beautiful smile again. Then he frowned, appearing very thoughtful.

"Now we can go," he said.

"Pardon?"

"We have to go," he insisted. "I can save them now—Tyler and Suzie. I can save them."

Sarah couldn't have been more stunned. She smiled. Maybe they could catch up—and if not, well, she'd still be able to say she'd experienced the most terrifying haunted house in the city—the state, maybe even the country!

"Come on!" she said. "Sure, I mean, it will be great if we can save them. So great."

"I have to go first. I have the Martian Gamma Sword."

"Okay, I'm right behind you!" Sarah promised. She hurried after him.

"They don't like this kind of light, you know."

"Who doesn't like it?"

"Those who are evil!" he said seriously.

He had his sword ready and held in front of him—he was prepared, he was on guard!

Sarah smiled, keeping behind him. She hoped he didn't bat an actor over the head with the damned thing.

TYLER DIDN'T KNOW when it changed.

The haunted house was incredible, of course. He knew the decorations and fabrications, motion-activated creatures and the costumes for the live actors had been created by some of the finest designers in the movie world.

The foyer had the necessary spiderwebs dangling from the chandelier and hanging about. As they were ushered in—the door shut behind them by the French maid—a butler appeared. He was skinny, tiny and a hunchback. Igor? He spoke with a deep voice that was absolutely chilling.

Tyler had to remind himself he was six-three and two

hundred and twenty pounds of muscle. But just the guy's voice was creepy as hell.

"Cemetery Mansion!" the butler boomed out. "The living are always ever so careless of the dead! Housing is needed…and cemeteries are ignored. And so it was when the Stuart family came to Crow Corners. They saw the gravestones…they even knew the chapel housed the dead and that a crypt led far beneath the ground. And still! They tossed aside the gravestones, and they built their mansion. Little did they know they would pay for their total disregard. Oh, Lord, they would pay! They would be allowed to stay—forever! Forever and ever… with those who resided here already!"

Suddenly, from thin air, haunts and ghouls seemed to arise and sweep through the room. Suzie let out a squeal. Even Hannah shrieked.

Good old Sean let out a startled scream and then began to laugh at himself.

It was done with projectors, Tyler realized.

"To your left, ladies and gentlemen, to your left! The music room, and then the dining room!"

They were urged to move on. The music room hosted a piano and rich Victorian furniture. There was also a child sitting on the sofa, holding a teddy bear. She turned to look at them with soulless eyes—and then she disappeared. A figure was hunched over the piano. Suzie tried to walk by it; the piano player suddenly stood, reaching out for her.

She screamed. The thing was a motion-activated figure, one who would have done any haunted mansion proud. It was a tall butler—blond and grim-looking, with a striking face made up so that the cheeks were entirely hollow. It spoke with a mechanical voice. "Come closer, come closer… I can love you into eternity!"

It was nothing but a prop, an automaton. But it was real as all hell.

Suzie ran on into the next room.

The dining room...

At the head of the table was a very tall man—an actor portraying the long-dead head of the household; a man in a Victorian-era suit, wearing tons of makeup that had been applied very effectively. He was sharpening a knife.

There were dummies or mannequins or maybe animatronics slumped around the table. At least their bodies were slumped there. Their heads were *on* it. Blood streamed from their necks and down their costumes.

"One of them is going to hop up, I know," Hannah murmured.

She bravely stepped closer to the table. No one moved.

Tyler noticed there was a girl about their age at the end of the table. She was wearing one of this year's passes to Haunted Hysteria around the stump of her neck.

Good touch, he thought.

The bodies around the table did not move. The master of the house watched them with bloodshot eyes. He sharpened his knife.

A girl suddenly burst into the dining room from the music room. "Run! Get out—get to the exit! He's in the house somewhere!" she screamed.

"Yes, he is. He's right here," the master of the house said. He reached for her and dragged her to him. She screamed again, trying to wrench herself free. He smiled.

He took one of the knives he had been sharpening.

And he slit her throat.

SARAH DIDN'T KNOW what had gotten into Davey; he was usually the most polite person in the world. He'd been taught the importance of *please* and *thank you*.

But he was almost pushing.

And he knew their radio station tickets gave them VIP status.

Light sword held before him, he made his way to one of the actors herding the line. "VIP, please!" he told her.

"Uh, sure. Watch out for that thing!" She started to lead them up the line, toward the house. As she did so, there was a scream, and one of the actors came bursting out the front door.

She was dressed as a French maid—a vampire or zombie French maid, Sarah thought.

She stumbled out of the entry and onto the porch, grabbing for one of the columns. Blood was dripping down her arms and over her shirt—she appeared to have a number of stab wounds.

"Don't!" she shouted. "Don't… He's a killer!"

Applause broke out in the line. But then someone else burst out of the house—a ghoul dressed in an Edwardian jacket.

He crashed down, a pool of blood forming right on the porch.

More applause broke out.

"No, no, that's not supposed to happen," the zombie leading Sarah up the line murmured.

Davey burst by her; he was headed to the house, his light saber before him.

"Davey!" Sarah shrieked. Something was wrong; something was truly wrong. They needed to stay out, needed to find out if this was an excellent piece of play-acting or…

Or what?

Imaginary creatures came to life and started killing people? Actors went crazy en masse and started knifing the populace? Whatever was going on, it seemed insane!

The sensation that crawled over Sarah then was nothing short of absolute terror—but Davey was ahead of her.

With his Martian Gamma Sword.

He was charging toward the house.

Davey! She had to follow him, stop him and get him away—no matter what!

TYLER COULD HEAR nothing but diabolical laughter.

And screaming—terrified shrieks!

Suzie hopped on a chair and grabbed a serving platter for defense.

The master of the house turned toward them, dropping the body of the girl whose throat he had slit. It fell with a flat thud.

Sean squeaked out a sound that was nearly a scream.

Hannah grabbed Sean, thrusting him between her and the big man with the massive knife.

"Back up, back up, back up!" Tyler said.

Hannah did so. Sean turned to flee.

The master of the house went for Sean. He picked him up by the neck.

"No! Stop, stop it!" Tyler shouted.

This couldn't be happening.

"This isn't funny. It isn't right!"

The character didn't seem to hear Tyler. And Tyler had no choice. He leaped forward, shoving Hannah away, and tried to wrest Sean from the killer. He grabbed Sean's arm and pulled.

"No!" Suzie shrieked.

Tyler looked up.

The master of the house was approaching her with the massive knife, dragging Sean along with him. Then he turned. He came swinging toward Tyler, still dragging Sean. Tyler held on to his friend and jerked hard; Sean came free and they staggered back—Hannah, Sean and himself—until they crashed into the table.

Hannah began shrieking in earnest. As she did so, Tyler became aware of the tinny scent of blood.

Real blood.

And he looked around the table and he knew.

They were people. Real people. And they were dead. Really dead.

"No!" Suzie shrieked.

She slammed her serving platter at the master of the house.

He just laughed.

And raised his carving knife.

DAVEY RACED ACROSS the porch, pushing aside the bleeding maid and hopping over the body of the man in the Edwardian dress.

Sarah had no choice but to follow.

He burst through into a mudroom. There were bloody handprints all over it.

Some were fake—stage blood.

Some were real—human blood.

She could tell by the smell that some of the blood was real.

Davey rushed through to the foyer, his Martian Gamma Sword leading the way. But there was no one there. He threw open another door.

"Davey, stop! Please, Davey, something is going wrong. Something is…"

They were in a music room; it was empty—other than for a bloody body stretched across a floral sofa.

"Davey!" Sarah shrieked. "No, no, please…"

She started to whirl around. There were holograms everywhere. A child in black with a headless doll appeared.

And then a hanged man, the noose still around his neck. All kinds of ghouls and creatures and evil beings began to appear in the room and then disappear.

"Davey, please, we've got to get out. Davey!"

She gripped his arm as the terrifying images swirled around them.

"Not real," Davey said. "Sarah, they're not real."

He was moving on—and she heard screams again. Terrified screams...

He went through a black hazy curtain and they were in the dining room.

And there were Tyler, Hannah... Sean and Suzie... It appeared that they were all being attacked by...a creature, by someone or something. They had fallen back and were struggling to rise from the dining table, where there were...

Oh, God, corpses, real corpses. Dead people, all around the table. Suzie and Hannah were yelling and screaming, and Tyler was reaching out, but the carving knife was coming down and it was going to sink into Tyler's chest at any minute!

She heard a terrible scream—high-pitched and full of fear and horror. And she realized it was coming from her...

And she had drawn the attention of the...

Man. It was a real man.

An actor gone insane? What the hell?

No, no, no, no. It was impossible. It was Halloween. It had to be a prank, an elaborate show...

The man was real.

Absolutely real.

He was tall and big and had long scraggly white hair and he might have played a maniacal killer in a slasher movie.

Except this wasn't a movie.

And he was coming at her.

He opened his mouth and smiled, and she saw his fangs. Long fangs that seemed to drip with something red...stage blood...

Real blood.

She screamed again.

It sounded as if it was coming from someone else, but it was not. It was coming from her.

Tyler struggled up from the table. He slipped.

He was slipping in blood.

"No, no, no!" Sarah screamed.

And then Davey stepped up. He thrust her back with his arm and stepped before her, his cheap little plastic sword at the ready.

"Leave her!" Davey shouted, his voice filled with command.

The man laughed...

And Davey struck him. Struck him hard, with all his strength.

The man went flying back. He slammed into the wall, and the impact sent him flying forward once again.

He tripped on a dead girl's leg...

And crashed down on the table.

Right on top of Tyler and Sean and Hannah, who had already been slammed down there. It was too much weight. The table broke with an awful groaning and splintering sound.

Shards and pieces flew everywhere as what remained of the table totally upended.

Tyler let out a cry of fear and fury and gripped the man's shoulders, shoving him off with all the force of a high school quarterback.

To Sarah's astonishment, the man, balanced for a matter of seconds, staring furiously at Davey—and then he fell hard. And didn't move again. She saw that he'd fallen on a broken and jagged leg of the table.

The splintered shaft was sticking straight through his chest.

Tyler got up and hunkered down by the man carefully, using one of the plates off the table as a shield.

"Dead," he said incredulously. He looked up at the others. "He's dead… He fell on the broken table leg there and…oh, God, it's bad."

"Out of here! It's evil!" Davey commanded. "It's still evil."

They were all shaking so badly no one seemed able to move. Davey reached for Hannah's arm and pulled her up. "Out!" he commanded.

And she ran. Suzie followed her, and then Sean, and then Tyler met Sarah's eyes and took her hand, and they raced out, as well, followed by Davey—who was still carefully wielding his plastic sword.

They heard sirens; police and security and EMTs were spilling onto the grounds.

The medics were struggling, trying to find the injured *people* among the props and corpses and demons and clowns.

When the group of friends reached a grassy spot, Sarah fell to the ground, shaking. She looked up at Davey, still not beginning to comprehend how he had known…

Or even *what* it was he had known.

"I told you—that house is evil," he said. "I told you— my dad. He taught me to watch. He stays with me and tells me to watch."

IT HAD BEEN the unthinkable—or easily thinkable, really, in the midst of all that went on at a horror-themed attraction at Halloween.

Archibald Lemming and another inmate had escaped from state prison two weeks earlier. They had gotten out through the infirmary—even though he had been in maximum security. News of the breakout had been harried and spotty, and most people assumed the embarrassment suffered by those who had let them escape had mandated that the information about it be kept secret.

Archibald Lemming had been incarcerated at the Clinton Correction Facility for killing four people—with a carving knife. The man had been incredibly sick. He'd somehow managed to consume some of the blood in their bodies—*as if he'd been a damned vampire.* He'd escaped with a fellow inmate, another killer who was adept with a knife and liked to play in blood—Perry Knowlton. Apparently, however, Lemming had turned on the man. Knowlton's body had been found burned to little more than cinders in the crematorium at an abandoned veterinary hospital just outside the massive walls of the prison.

Sarah knew all that, of course, because it was on the news. And because, after the attack at Cemetery Mansion, the cops came to talk to her and Davey several times. One of them was a very old detective named Mark Holiday. He was gentle. His partner, Bob Green, was younger and persistent, but when his questions threatened to upset Davey, Sarah learned she could be very fierce herself. The police photographer, Alex Morrison—a nice guy, with the forensic unit—came with the detectives. He showed them pictures that caused them to relive the event—and remember it bit by bit. The photographer was young, like Bob Green. He tried to make things easier, too, by explaining all that he could.

"Archibald Lemming! They found his stash in prison. Idiot kept 'history' books. Right—they were on the Countess Bathory, the Hungarian broad who killed young women to bathe in their blood. The man was beyond depraved," one of the cops had said that night when he'd met with the kids. He'd been shaking, just as they had been.

People were stunned and angry—furious. If there had been better information on the escape, lives might have been saved. Before the confrontation with Davey and his friends, the man had killed ten people and seriously injured many more. He'd managed to escape at a time when it was perfect to practice his horror upon others— Halloween. He had dressed up and slipped into the park as one of the actors.

But many survived who might have died that night. They had lived because of Davey.

It did something to them all. Maybe they were in shock. Maybe denial. Guilt over being the ones who made it out. And confusion over what it meant, now that the normal lives ahead of them seemed all the more precious.

Sarah was with her cousin and her aunt when Tyler came to say goodbye.

He was leaving the school, going into a military academy and joining the navy as soon as he could.

Sarah was stunned. But in an odd way, she understood. She knew she had closed in on herself. Maybe they all had, and needed to do so in order to process that they were alive—and it was all right for them to go on.

She, Tyler and their friends had survived. And it was too hard to be together. Too hard to be reminded what the haunted house had looked like with all the dead bodies and the blood and things so horrible they almost couldn't be believed.

So she merely nodded when he told her he was leaving. She barely even kissed him goodbye, although there was a long moment when they looked at each other, and even *this*—losing one another—was something they both accepted, and shared, and understood.

Sarah gave up cheerleading and transferred to a private school herself, somewhere that hadn't lost any students in the Cemetery Mansion massacre.

When college rolled around, she decided on Columbia and majored in creative writing, veering away from anything that had to do with mystery or horror. She chose a pseudonym and started out in romance.

However, romance eluded her. She was haunted by the past.

And by memories of Tyler.

She turned to science fiction.

Giant bugs on the moon didn't scare her.

Except…

Every once in a while, she would pause, stare out the window and remember she was alive because of Davey and his Martian Gamma Sword.

Still, by the time she was twenty-seven, she was doing well. She had her own apartment on Reed Street. For holidays she headed out to LA—her parents had moved there as soon as her dad had retired from his job as an investment banker. Of course, they always tried to get her to join them with a permanent move, but she was a New Yorker and she loved the city. Sometimes she guest-lectured at Columbia or NYU. Upon occasion, she dated. Nothing seemed to work very well. But she was okay. She had college friends, and since she'd worked her way through school waitressing at an Irish pub, she still went in to help out at Finnegan's on Broadway now and then. The Finnegan family were great friends—especially Kieran, who happened to be a psychologist who frequently worked with criminals. He always seemed to know when Sarah wanted to talk a little about what she'd been through—and when she didn't.

It wasn't the happiness she had envisioned for herself before the night at the Halloween attraction.

But it was okay.

She hadn't seen Tyler—or any of her old friends—for over a decade.

Sarah had been living in the present.

And then she heard about the murder of Hannah Levine.

Like it or not, the past came crashing down on her.

And with it, Tyler Grant reentered her life.

Chapter One

"Tyler!"

Davey Cray greeted Tyler with a smile like no other. He stepped forward instantly, no hesitance after ten years—just a greeting fueled by pure love.

It was as if he had expected him. Maybe he had.

Tyler hugged Davey in return, a wealth of emotions flooding through him.

"I knew you'd come. I knew you'd come!" Davey said. "My mom said you were busy, you didn't live here anymore. You work in Boston. But I knew you would come." His smile faded. "You came for Hannah." Davey looked perplexed. "Hannah wasn't always very nice. And I watched the news. She wasn't doing good things. But... poor Hannah. Poor Hannah."

Yes, poor Hannah. She'd disappeared after leaving a bar near Times Square.

Her torso and limbs had turned up on a bank of the Hudson River.

Her head had come up just downriver about a half mile. She had been savagely cut to ribbons, much like the victims ten years past.

According to the news, Hannah had become a bartender, and then a stripper—and then a cocaine addict.

Had that already been in the cards for her? Or had her life been twisted on that horrible night?

"Poor Hannah, yes. Nobody deserves to have their life stolen," Tyler assured Davey. "Nobody," he repeated firmly. "Had you—seen her?"

Davey shook his head gravely. "My mom doesn't let me go to strip clubs!" he said, almost in a whisper. Then he smiled again. "Tyler, I have a girlfriend. She has Down syndrome like me."

"Well, wow! That's cool. Got a picture?"

Davey did. He pulled out his wallet. He showed Tyler a picture of a lovely young girl with a smile as magnificent as his, short brown hair and big brown eyes.

"She's a looker!" Tyler said.

"Megan. Her name is Megan." Davey grinned happily.

"That's wonderful."

"Sarah set me up on the right kind of page on the internet. It really is cool."

"I'll bet it is! Leave it to Sarah."

"She loves me. And, you know, she loves you, too."

"Of course. We all love each other."

By that time, Renee Cray had made it to the door. She was a tall, thin, blonde woman in her late forties, with big brown eyes just like Davey's. "Tyler!" she exclaimed.

And then she, too, threw her arms around him, as if he was the lost black sheep of the family being welcomed back into the fold.

Maybe he was.

"Tyler! How wonderful to see you! We knew, of course, that you'd joined the navy. And I know Sarah had heard you're living in Boston, working there as some kind of a consultant. Police consultant? PI? Something like that?"

"Exactly like that," he told her.

Renee continued to stare at him. "You're here…because of Hannah Levine, right? But…what can you do? What can anyone do? Is it horrible to say I'm glad her parents died in a car accident years ago? But what…" Her voice trailed off, and then she straightened. "Where are my manners? Come in, come in—you know the way, of course!"

He entered the parlor; Renee and Davey lived in a charming little two-story house in Brooklyn that offered a real yard and a porch with several rocking chairs. Renee was a buyer for a major retail chain and was able to keep up a very nice home on her own salary. Since the death of her husband, she had never done much more than work—and care for Davey. Tyler doubted she had changed. She was, in his opinion, a wonderful mother, never making Davey too dependent and never becoming codependent herself.

"Sit, sit," Renee told him. "Davey, get Tyler some tea, will you, please? You still like iced tea, right?"

"Still love it," Tyler assured her.

When her son was gone, Renee leaned forward. "Oh, Tyler! It's been so hard to listen to the news. I mean, bad things happen all the time. It's just that…you all escaped such a terrible thing, and now Hannah. Of course, her lifestyle…but then again, no one asks to be murdered… They haven't given out many details. We don't know if she was raped and murdered, but she was…decapitated. Beheaded. Just like—"

She broke off again, shaking her head. "It's like it's the same killer—as if he came back. Oh, I'll never forget that night! Hearing what had happened, trying to find Davey, trying to find you children… Oh, Tyler! Hannah now…it's just too sad!"

"It's not the same killer," Tyler said quietly. "I saw Archibald Lemming die. I saw him with a wooden table leg sticking straight through him. He did not miraculously get up and come back to kill again. Hannah had demons she dealt with, but they were in the way she looked at life. It's tragic, because no one should ever die like that. And," he reflected softly, "she was our friend. We were all friends back then. We haven't seen each other in a while, but...we were friends. We knew her."

Renee nodded, still visibly shaken.

Maybe they hadn't seen Hannah in a long time, but she had still been one of them.

"Tyler, I guess it's been in the media everywhere, but...you weren't that close with Hannah, were you? Had you talked to her? How did you come to be here?"

He smiled grimly.

Sarah. Sarah was why he had come. He thought back, hardly twelve hours earlier, when he had heard from her. He had received the text message from an unknown number.

Hi Tyler. It's Sarah. Have you seen the news?

Yes, of course he'd seen the news.

And he'd been saddened and shocked. He'd been there the night of one of the most gruesome spree killings in American history, and then he'd gone on to war. Not much compared to the atrocities one could see in battle. Between the two, he was a fairly hardened man.

But...their old friend Hannah had been brutally murdered. And even if her life had taken a turn for the worse lately—which the media was playing up—neither she, nor any victim, should ever have to suffer such horrors.

While Tyler hadn't seen Sarah in a decade, the second he received the missive from her, it felt as if lightning bolts tore straight through his middle and out through every extremity.

They said time healed all wounds. He wasn't so sure. He never really understood why he'd done what he'd done himself, except that, in the midst of the trauma and turmoil that had swept around them that night in a long-gone October, Sarah had still seemed to push him away. She always said she was fine, absolutely fine. That she needed to worry about Davey.

She had rejected Tyler's help—just as she had refused to understand he'd been willing to make Davey his responsibility, just as much as Davey was Sarah's responsibility.

They'd all had to deal with what had happened, with what they had witnessed.

Tyler had always wanted her to know he loved Davey, and he never minded responsibility, and he didn't give a damn about anyone else's thoughts or opinions on the matter. They had to allow Davey a certain freedom. When they were with him, they both needed to be responsible. That was sharing life, and it was certainly no burden to Tyler.

But Sarah had shut down; she had found excuses not to see him.

And he'd had to leave.

Maybe, after that, pride had taken hold. She had never tried to reach him.

And so he had never tried to get in touch with her.

But now...

Now Sarah had reached out to him.

He'd kept up with information about her, of course. Easy enough; she kept a professional platform going.

He liked to think she had followed him, as well. Not that he was as forthcoming about where he was and what he was doing. He had become a licensed investigator and consultant. Most of his work had been with the Boston Police Department; some had been with the FBI.

He knew she hadn't gone far. Her parents had rented out their Brooklyn home and moved to California. Sarah was living in Manhattan. She'd found a successful career writing fiction—he'd bought her books, naturally. Her early romances reminded him of the two of them; they'd been so young when they'd been together, so idealistic. They'd believed in humanity and the world and that all good things were possible.

Her sci-fi novels were fun—filled with cool creatures, "aliens" who seemed to parallel real life, and bits of sound science.

Part of why he'd never tried to contact her again had been pride, yes. Part of his efforts had actually been almost noble—her life looked good; he didn't want to ruin it.

But now…

Yes, he'd seen the news. Hannah Levine had been murdered. The reporters had not dealt gently with the victim because of her lifestyle. They hadn't known her. Hadn't known how poor she'd grown up, and that she had lost both parents tragically to an accident on the FDR. They did mention, briefly, that she'd survived the night of horror long ago.

As if reading his mind, Renee said, "They're almost acting as if she deserved it, Tyler! Deserved it, because of the way she lived. I'm wishing I had tried harder. Oh, look! If she hadn't been an 'escort,' this wouldn't have happened to her. I feel terrible. I mean, who ever really understands what makes us tick? Not even shrinks! Because…well, poor child, poor child! She never had much—that father of hers was a blowhard, but he was her dad. Both dead, no help…and she was a beautiful little thing. She was probably a very good stripper."

That almost made Tyler smile. "Probably," he agreed. "And yes, she was beautiful. Have the police let anything else out yet?"

"We know what you know. Her body was found… and then a few hours later, her head was found. First, we heard about the body in the river. Then we heard that it was Hannah."

The front door opened and closed. Tyler felt that same streak of electricity tear through him; he knew Sarah was there.

Renee frowned. "Sarah must be here."

"I'm sorry. I should have said right off the bat that she was meeting me here," Tyler said. "That's why…why I came. She didn't tell you?"

"No, but…that's great. You've been talking to Sarah!" Renee clapped her hands together, appearing ecstatic.

"We've exchanged two sentences, Renee," he said quietly. "Sorry, four sentences, really. 'Did you hear the news?' 'Yes.' 'Will you come and meet me at Aunt Renee's?' And then, 'Yes, I'll come right away.'"

Renee just nodded. Davey was coming back in the room, bearing glasses of iced tea. "Sarah is here," Renee said.

Davey nodded gravely. "Of course she is."

Tyler watched as she walked into the parlor. Sarah. Whom he hadn't seen in a decade. She hadn't changed at all. She had changed incredibly. There was nothing of the child left in her. Her facial lines had sharpened into exquisite detail. She had matured naturally and beautifully, all the soft edges of extreme youth falling away to leave an elegantly cast blue-eyed beauty there, as if a picture had come into sharp focus. She was wearing her hair at shoulder length; it had darkened a little, into a deep sun-touched honey color.

He stood. She was staring at him in turn.

Seeing what kind of a difference a decade made.

"Hey," he said softly.

"Hey!" she replied.

They were both awkward, to say the least. She started to move forward quickly—the natural inclination to hug someone you held dear and hadn't seen in a long time.

He did the same.

She stopped.

He stopped.

Then they both smiled, and laughed, and she stepped forward into his arms.

It was impossible, of course. Impossible that they had really known what the depths of love could be when they hadn't even been eighteen. Then he'd felt as if he'd known, right from the first time he'd seen her at school, that he loved her. Would always love her.

That no one could compare.

And now, holding her again, he knew why nothing had ever worked for him. He'd met so many women—lots of them bright, beautiful and wonderful—and yet nothing had ever become more than brief moments of enjoyment, of gentle caring, and never this...connection.

Sarah had called on him because a friend had been murdered, and he was the only one who could really understand just what it was like. This didn't change anything; whether he loved her or not, she would still be determined to push him away when it came to relying on him, sharing with him...

Back then, she hadn't even wanted him near.

They drew apart. It felt as if the clean scent of her shampoo and the delicate, haunting allure of her fragrance lingered, a sweet and poignant memory all around him.

"You are here," she said. "Thanks. I know this is crazy, but… Hannah. To have survived what happened that October, and then…have this happen. I understand you're in some kind of law enforcement."

"No. Private investigator. That's why I'm not so sure how I can really be of help here."

"Private investigators get to—investigate, right?" Sarah asked.

"Why don't you two sit down?" Renee suggested.

"Sit, sit. Have tea!" Davey said happily.

Once again, Tyler sat. For a moment, the room was still, and everyone in it seemed to feel very awkward.

"I'm glad you came," Sarah said. "Not that I really know anything. I belong to a great writers' group that brings us down to the FBI offices once a year for research, but… I really don't know anything. I don't think the FBI is involved. New York police, high-crimes or whatever they call it division… I just— The killing… sounds way too familiar!"

Tyler nodded. "Yeah. Though psychopaths have beheaded and sliced up victims many times, I'm sorry to say. And, of course," he said, pausing then to take a breath, "well, we were there. We saw the killer die back then." He looked over at Davey and smiled tightly, still curious about how Davey had sensed so much of what had gone on. "We were all there. We saw him die. Davey was a hero."

"My dad. My dad was with me," Davey said.

"In all he taught you, and all you learned so well!" Renee said, looking at her son, her soft tone filled with pain for the husband she'd lost.

"The police may already have something," Tyler said.

"When a murder like this occurs, they hold back details from the press. You wouldn't believe the number of crazy people who will call in and confess to something they didn't do, wanting what they see as the credit for such a heinous crime. I have friends in Boston who have friends in New York. Maybe I can help—all depends on whether they want to let me in or not."

"Sarah has friends, too!" Davey said.

Sarah looked at him. "I do?"

"Kieran!"

"I haven't talked to her in a while," Sarah murmured.

"Who is Kieran?" Tyler asked.

"A friend, yes," Sarah said, looking at him. "She and her brothers inherited a very old Irish pub on Broadway—downtown, near Trinity and St. Paul's. The oldest brother manages, Kieran works there sometimes."

"You worked there!" Davey said.

"I did—I worked there through college," Sarah said. "Anyway, Kieran is a psychologist who works with two psychiatrists, Drs. Fuller and Miro. They often work with the police—they're geniuses when it comes to the criminal psyche. And her boyfriend is a special agent with the FBI. So, yes, if I asked for help…"

"That's excellent," Tyler told her. "And it could really help, as far as finding out whatever information there is forthcoming. Other than that… I'm not law enforcement."

"But people hire PIs all the time," Renee said.

"When someone is missing, the family might hire someone. In murder investigations that go cold…"

"We can hire you!" Davey said happily.

"We're not her family," Sarah said.

"That doesn't matter. We were her friends," Davey said. He was quiet a minute and made one of his little frowns. "She was mean to me sometimes, but she was my friend, too. Mostly she was nice to me."

They all fell silent.

"I'll figure something out, and I'll keep you posted. I do have a legal standing as a private investigator, but it's a lot nicer if the police want me involved."

Sarah nodded. Again, they were all quiet.

"So, what's happening in your life, Tyler?" Renee asked. "It's so very long since we saw you. Davey has missed you."

"I know what Tyler has been doing! I follow his page," Davey said. "He dated a model! Pretty girl, Tyler. I think, though, Sarah is prettier. But I saw the pictures of you."

"She's very nice," Tyler said. "She's—in Romania now. Shooting a catalog, or something like that."

"You must miss her," Davey said.

"We were casual friends."

"BFFs. That's friends with benefits," Davey told his mother, certain she wouldn't know.

"Davey!" Renee said. "Please, Tyler came as a favor. Let his private life be private."

Davey had lowered his head. He was chewing on a thumbnail, something he did, if Tyler recalled rightly, when he was nervous—or hiding something.

"You've got to be able to help somehow," Sarah said, as if she hadn't heard any of their exchange. "I'm so frustrated. I feel so worthless. And I feel terrible that I didn't keep up with her. I mean…we were friends once. I don't know what that night did to her. We all dealt with it differently. But…" She paused, inhaling a deep breath. "Sean suggested there was something—"

She broke off again. He knew what she was going to say. In the confusion with police and parents—and the horror that seemed almost worse when it was over and the garish lights were on—both Sean and Hannah had suggested there was something weird about Davey.

That it was downright scary, the way he had known something was really wrong.

"We talked. Davey told me. I think the police understood, but others didn't. My uncle taught Davey to watch people—to have excellent situational awareness, like an operative or a cop. Because people can be so cruel and mean. My uncle wanted Davey to be able to protect himself from that. Davey knew when kids wanted to—to make fun of him. He was good at avoiding such people. He was amazing at looking out for bullies. He saw that man… Archibald Lemming. He'd noticed him earlier. And he'd seen him go into that particular haunted house, and that was how he knew. But…"

"I told them," Davey said, nodding grimly. He brightened. "But they lived!"

"You were a hero," Sarah assured him.

Davey's smile faded and he looked grim. "But now Hannah is dead. And I'm afraid."

"You don't need to be afraid, Davey," Sarah assured him quickly. "You'll never be without one of us."

"Or my girlfriend!" he said brightly. "Megan," he reminded Tyler.

"Trust me, young man. Megan's mom and I will make sure you two aren't in any danger. Someone will be with you," Renee said.

"Can we still kiss and all?" Davey asked.

"We'll look away," Renee promised. She shook her head. "We're trying to keep it real—they have ten-year-old minds in grown-up bodies."

Davey giggled. Then again he looked grim. "It's scary. Sarah has to be with somebody, too."

Sarah smiled and reached over and patted his hand.

"Davey, I won't be out late at night. I won't be anywhere without friends."

"You live alone."

"You could come stay here," Renee said.

"Aunt Renee," Sarah said, "I need to be near the universities. And here's the thing. We know Archibald Lemming is dead. What happened to Hannah is tragic, and one of those horrible events in life that happen to mirror another. I'll be careful. But I'm always careful. I grew up as a New Yorker, remember? I've been savvy and wary a long, long time. Besides…" She paused and looked over at Tyler. "This must be…random. The act of some horrible, twisted thing that parades as a human being. Tyler… Tyler went to war. He knows very bad things happen."

"We followed you when you were deeped," Davey said.

"Deployed," Aunt Renee said.

"We were afraid you wouldn't come back," Davey said.

"Well, I am here, and I will find out what I can to help see that this man who killed Hannah meets a justice of his own, I promise," Tyler said.

He rose. He did need to get checked into his hotel room. And he needed to find out if the people he knew had been able to pull any strings for him.

"You have my number?" Sarah asked him.

He smiled at her curiously. Of course he did. They had been texting.

"Same number, right?"

She shook her head. "Well, it's the same as about five years ago?"

Tyler frowned. "But…you have my number?"

"Has it changed?"

"Never. It's the same one I've been texting you on."

"I—I didn't get a text. Davey told me you were coming."

Davey was up on his feet and running out of the room.

"Get back here!" Sarah commanded.

Davey hadn't quite made the door. He stopped and turned around.

He looked at Sarah.

"He needed to come. Tyler needed to come. I..."

"You pretended to be me," Sarah said. "Davey! You must never do things like that!" she added with dismay.

"Davey, I should cut your texting time with Megan!" Renee said firmly.

Davey sat down, crossing his arms over his chest, his lips set stubbornly. "Tyler is here. He needed to be here." Then he threw his arms out dramatically. "Do what you will!"

"Just don't do it again! Ever!" Sarah said, horrified.

She looked at Tyler. "I'm so sorry. I never would have twisted your arm, made you come here. I mean, it was on national news, you'd hear about it, but..."

"I need to be here," Tyler said softly. "Davey is right. I've got some things to do. I'll be back with you later. We may need help from your friend."

"Kieran," she said. "Kieran Finnegan. And she's living with a man named Craig Frasier. He's—he's great. I don't know if the FBI will be investigating this, but..."

"We'll talk to him."

He wanted to hold her. To pull her to him. But she was already trying to back away. She hadn't done it—hadn't contacted him. Davey had. And Tyler needed to remember that.

"I'll be in touch later tonight," he said.

He didn't hug her goodbye. But as he went to the door, Davey raced to him. "I'm sorry, Tyler. I'm so sorry."

"It's okay, buddy, it's okay. You're right. I need to be here. The police might already have a lead on this madman, okay? But I'll be here."

He nodded to Renee and Sarah, then headed out of the house. He imagined Sarah might follow him, tell him that the years had been wasted for her, too, that she knew, just seeing him again, that...

Didn't happen.

He drove into the city and checked himself—and his car, which was as expensive to park as booking another room!—into his hotel. He had barely reached his suite before his phone rang.

And this time, it was actually Sarah.

"Tyler," she said excitedly. "We're in!"

"What?"

"This makes me feel worse than ever, but... I just got a call from a lawyer. Tyler, Hannah left a will. She has me listed as next of kin. She didn't have much money—barely enough for her funeral," Sarah said softly. "But that means that I can hire you, that it can all be legitimate, right?"

"I can work the case—even work it as if you've hired me. That's not the point. I have to form some relationships, step carefully, keep in with the police. We need everyone working together."

"But I am next of kin. You will stay, you will—"

"I will stay," he promised her softly.

And a moment later, he heard her whisper, "Thank you. Thank you!"

And then...

"Tyler?"

"Yes?"

"I am so sorry. I don't know why... I lost everyone.

I should have been her friend. I really should have been her friend."

He didn't know what to say.

"Time doesn't change things like that. You were her friend. And…you're still my friend, Sarah. I still love you. I will see this through, I promise."

And he hung up before she could say anything else.

Chapter Two

"Survivor's guilt," Kieran Finnegan said softly.

Kieran was a good friend. While the hectic pace of her life—she worked as a psychologist for a pair of psychiatrists who worked frequently with the police, FBI and other law enforcement agencies, *and* helped out at the family pub—often kept her in a whirlwind where she didn't see much of her friends, she was the kind of person who was always there when she was needed.

Sarah had called her that morning.

It was Sunday noon. Hannah's body had been discovered the morning before; last night, Tyler had come to Aunt Renee's house.

And while Finnegan's on Broadway was doing a sound weekend business—they had a traditional roast entrée every Sunday that was very popular—Kieran was sitting down with Sarah. Of course, Finnegan's was in good shape that day as far as staff went, and since Sarah had once worked there, she could probably hop back in to help at any time herself, just as Kieran would do if the need arose.

Kieran had assured Sarah she would be there to spend some time with her, talk to her. As a very good friend would do.

That made Sarah feel all the worse about the lousy friend she had been herself.

"Survivor's guilt?" she repeated, shaking her head. "Honestly, I don't think so. I mean, what happened years ago…all of us survived. We survived because of Davey, though, honestly…some of the guff he had to take afterward! People wanted to know what kind of a medium or seer he was. 'Down Syndrome Boy Sees Evil.'" She was quiet for a minute. "Well, I have to admit, I was young and easily irritated, and Hannah…" She bit her lip and shrugged. "I was annoyed. She liked to have Davey around for the publicity, but then wanted me to leave him home if we were going out for the night or clubbing. She would use him when it seemed he was drawing a lot of attention, and then be irritated if we were spending any real time with him. But now…"

"From what I've gleaned through the media, her murder was brutal," Kieran murmured. "And far too similar to the method of the massacre at the theme park. Here's the thing. You're experiencing terrible guilt because Hannah is dead, and she was your friend—even it was a while ago. You both survived something horribly traumatic. But now she is dead. And you are alive. And all that happened before is rushing back. But, Sarah, you're not guilty of anything. Hannah survived that night—along with your other friends—because of Davey. You felt protective of Davey. That was only right. So quit feeling guilty. Hannah did choose to live a dangerous lifestyle. That doesn't mean what was done to her isn't every bit as horrid and criminal. But she may have put herself in danger. You have done nothing wrong. Of course, you could learn to be a bit more open to the possibility there are good people out there, and good things just might happen—and most of your friends truly love Davey."

Sarah leaned back and picked up her coffee cup, grinning. "Do I have a really big chip on my shoulder? I'm not sure whether I should enter therapy or say ten Hail Marys!"

"Do both!" Kieran suggested with a shrug. She let out a sigh. "Sarah, if you weren't really upset, you wouldn't be human, and I'd have to worry about you. Or rather, you would be a sociopath and I would have to worry about you." She shook her head. "Craig was saying that it was uncanny—the remarkable resemblance to what happened before." She hesitated. "In the actual killing, that is. Archibald Lemming found himself an amazing venue in which to carry out his bloodlust—what better than a haunted house? But it isn't him."

"It could be someone who studied him or knew him."

"Possibly."

"And someone like that doesn't stop, right?" Sarah asked.

"No," Kieran admitted unhappily. "When such a killer isn't caught and the killing stops, it's usually because he's moved on, been incarcerated for another crime or he died. This kind of thing…"

"It's not just someone who wanted Hannah dead?"

"I doubt it. What was done was overkill. Now, overkill can mean just the opposite. You see it with victims who are stabbed or bludgeoned over and over again—their killer was furious with them. Or sometimes, with someone else—and the victim they choose is the substitute for the one they want to kill. But again, remember I'm going from what was in the news. The way that this was done…"

"You think there will be more victims."

Kieran was thoughtful. "Yes—if we're talking a copycat killer who had a fan obsession with Archibald Lemming. I am afraid there will be more victims. Then again, people are clever. Maybe someone had it out for Hannah and wanted her dead specifically. Make it appear there is a psychopath or sociopath on the loose. There have been cases where several people were murdered in order to throw off suspicion when just one was the real target."

"Archibald Lemming was a psychopath, right?"

"Yes, the term applies to someone who is incapable of feeling empathy for another human being. They can be exceptionally charming and fool everyone around them—Ted Bundy, for instance. There are, however, psychopaths who turn their inclinations in a different direction—they become highly successful CEOs or hard-core business executives. They will never feel guilt. A sociopath, on the other hand, reaches his or her state of being through social factors—neglectful parents, bullying, abuse. Some function. They can be very violent, can show extreme bitterness or hatred along with that violence, but they're also capable of feeling guilt and even forming deep attachments to others."

Sarah nodded, listening to Kieran. It was good, she figured, to have a concept of what they might be dealing with.

But dead was dead. Hannah was gone. And it didn't matter if she'd been viciously murdered by one kind of killer or another. It had been brutal.

Kieran smiled at her grimly. "I know what you're thinking. But when hunting a killer, it's helpful to have a concept of what you're looking for in his or her behavior."

"Of course! And thank you!" Sarah said quickly.

"So... Tyler Grant has come back to help?" Kieran asked. "And you were listed as Hannah's next of kin. That's good. It will allow him a lot of leeway."

"The FBI hasn't been asked in yet, right?"

"No, but Craig has a lot of friends with the police."

Kieran was referring to Special Agent Craig Frasier, FBI. They were living together—sometimes at Craig's and sometimes at Kieran's. He had the better space in NYC, so Kieran would eventually give up her apartment, most probably, and move in with him. They were a definite duo; Sarah was sure marriage was somewhere in the future for them, especially since Kieran's brothers—Declan, Kevin and Danny—seemed to accept him already as part of the family.

"Do you think…" Sarah began.

"Yes, I think!" Kieran said, smiling. She inclined her head toward the door. Tyler must have arrived. Sarah found herself inhaling sharply, her muscles tightening and her heart beating erratically.

Why? She wanted him here; she wanted…a solution. Hannah's killer caught and put away for life. She wanted…forgiveness.

Maybe it just seemed that their lives—so easy a decade ago—had come to an abrupt break. It had become a breach, and she wasn't sure things could ever be really right for her if she didn't come to terms with that.

Once upon a time, she had been so in love with him. High school! They'd been so wide-eyed and innocent, and the world had stretched before them, a field of gold.

Kieran stood, waving to him.

"You've met Tyler?" Sarah was surprised. She hadn't known Kieran in high school.

"No," her friend said, shaking her head. "He called about meeting up with Craig. I looked him up after—found some pictures online. Rock solid, so it seems."

Rock solid.

Yes, that had always been Tyler.

"But how…?"

Kieran laughed. "How do you think?"

"Davey!" Sarah said. She wasn't sure whether to be exasperated or proud of her cousin. Devious! No, being devious wasn't really in his nature. Pretty darned clever, though!

Tyler reached the table. Sarah stood, as Kieran had. It was still awkward to see him. He'd grown into a truly striking man with his quarterback's shoulders and lean, hard-muscled physique. There were fleeting seconds when they were near one another that she felt they were complete strangers. Then there were moments when she remembered laughing with him, lying with him, dreaming with him, and she longed to just reach out and touch him, as if she could touch all that had been lost.

He was obviously feeling awkward, too. "Sarah," he said huskily, taking a second to lightly grip her elbow and bend to kiss her cheek—as any friend might do.

That touch...so faraway and yet so familiar!

"Hey, I hear Davey has been at it again," Sarah said. "This is Kieran, of course."

"Of course," Tyler said, shaking her hand.

"Craig should be here any minute. He had to drop by the office," Kieran told him.

"Thanks," Tyler said.

"Coffee? Tea? Something to eat?" Kieran asked. "We are a pub. Our roast is under way."

"I'm sure it's wonderful," Tyler told her, smiling. "I've heard great things about this place—you're listed in all kinds of guidebooks."

"Nice to know."

"I would love coffee."

"I'll see to it. Black?"

"Yep. It's the easiest," he told her.

Kieran smiled pleasantly and went to get a cup of coffee for him.

Tyler looked at Sarah.

"Craig is great. You're going to like him a lot," Sarah said. "I can't believe Davey is making all these connections."

"The kind we should have made ourselves."

Kieran was already heading back with coffee. And she was indicating the old glass-inset, wood-paneled doors to the pub.

Craig had arrived.

He hurried to the high-top table where they'd been sitting. "Hey, kid," he said to Sarah, giving her a quick kiss on the cheek. He looked at Tyler. "Tyler, right? Grant?"

"Tyler Grant. And thank you, Special Agent Frasier."

"Just Craig, please. And sorry," he added, watching Kieran arrive with coffee, "you're going to have to slurp that down. We need to get going. The man on this particular case is a Detective Bob Green. He's a twelve-year homicide vet—he worked the Archibald Lemming case years ago. You might know him when you see him, though he wasn't the one doing the interviews back then, his partner was. He's senior man on his team now. Good guy. We can join him for the autopsy."

"That's great! Thank you," Tyler told him. "I know you have other cases."

"This caught up with me in the midst of a pile of paperwork," Craig told him. "My partner is handling it for me, and my director knows where I am, so it's all good."

"What about the site where Hannah was left?"

"I can take you there." Craig turned to Kieran, slipping an arm around her. "Save us supper, huh?"

"You bet."

The affection between them wasn't anything overt or

in-your-face. It was just that even the way they looked at one another seemed to be intimate.

"Okay, we're on it," Craig said. He turned and headed toward the door. Tyler looked back and nodded a thanks to Kieran. He glanced at Sarah and gave her something of an encouraging smile.

She remembered his words from last night. He would stay on this.

He loved her still.

Friends...

Yes, sometimes friends loved each other forever. Even if they couldn't be together.

AUTOPSY ROOMS COULD be strange places. It was where doctors and scientists studied the dead and did their best to learn from them. The NYC morgue downtown was huge; the body count was almost always high. It wasn't that so many people were murdered; New York had had less than a hundred homicides in the past year—a large number, yes, but considering that it was home to eight million-plus people, and double that number came through almost on a daily basis, it wasn't such a massive amount.

But the homeless who died so sadly in the street came to the morgue, as did anyone who died at home or in hotel rooms, or anywhere else about the city other than with a doctor or in a hospital or directly under a doctor's care and with a known mortal disease.

Autopsy was no small neat room with refrigerated cubicles. Those existed, but for the most part, the place was a zoo comprised of the living and the dead—doctors, techs, photographers, cops, receptionists, computer crews and so on.

The living went about living—joking, taking lunch

breaks, grabbing time to make appointments for themselves, call the cable company or check on the kids.

Detective Bob Green was a man in his late forties or early fifties with a thatch of neatly cut blond hair that was beginning to veer toward white, a slender face and dark almond eyes that contrasted with his pale skin and light hair. "Special Agent Frasier!" he said, greeting Craig.

Then he turned to Tyler.

He had a grave smile and a sturdy handshake. "I remember you," he told him. "I remember you all from the night at the horror park. Do you remember me?"

"Yes, I do. You were with an older detective, Mark Holiday. And a police photographer—I think his name was… Morrison. You were great with us back then, so thank you. It was hard. At first, I remembered little from that night except for the carnage and worrying about my friends," Tyler told him.

"Alex Morrison… He's still with us. So—you headed into the military and became a PI," Green said.

"I did."

"Thought you might become a cop. You were good that night. Composed. You're good in a crisis."

"Glad to hear it," Tyler told him. "Thank you."

"To be honest with you two, the autopsy already took place. But Lance—sorry, Dr. Layton—is waiting with the corpse." He paused, eyeing Tyler again. "You were there when Archibald Lemming killed all those people. We didn't know if…well, this does beat all. Of course, at this time we just have one dead woman—your friend," he added softly. "And it would be great to keep it that way. But… I was there, you were there… See what you think."

He led them into a room where a number of bodies lay on gurneys, covered properly with sheets.

A tall, thin man who reminded Tyler of Doc from *Back*

to the Future stood by one of the gurneys. The ME, Dr. Lance Layton.

The man was waiting patiently for them. He greeted Craig with a smile and a polite nod. And Tyler realized he was curious about him, watching to see how he was handling being in a room with corpses. The doctor didn't extend a hand; he wore gloves, Tyler saw.

"You've seen your share of the dead, I take it?" Layton said.

"Four deployments in the Middle East, sir. Yes, I've seen my share."

Layton nodded and pulled back the sheet.

And what he saw was Hannah. What remained. She'd been such a pretty girl, olive-complexioned and with a bit of a slant to her dark eyes. She'd grown up to be an attractive woman—or she would have been, in life. If she had been alive, her eyes might have narrowed and hardened; she might have looked at the world differently. She hadn't always been the kindest or most sympathetic human being, but she'd never deliberately caused pain. She loved partying; she loved a good time. Beaches and margaritas. She'd gone toward the "dark" side— though she might have been nothing but light, had life not touched her so cruelly.

But not as cruelly as death had.

Her head sat apart from her torso and limbs. They were in different stages of decomposition.

"How was it done?" Tyler asked, and his voice was, to his own ears, thick.

"A knife. I believe she was lucky. Her killer hit the artery first. She would have bled out quickly while he continued—sawing at her."

Beheading a human being—with a knife—wasn't an easy thing to do. Strong executioners with a honed blade

*still had to use formidable strength; English axmen had
been famous for botching the job. With a knife...*

And this was Hannah.

Tyler remembered the last time he had seen her, not
long after the night at the horror attraction. They hadn't
talked about it the way they might have. The pictures of
the dead in the "dining room" had been all too fresh in
their heads. She had been quiet and grim, as they all had
been, with the police. Each had been asked to give an account of what had happened. They'd been kids, ushered
in and out, with protective parents or stepparents with
them. A silver lining, one of the detectives had said, was
that Archibald Lemming was dead. There wouldn't be a
trial; they wouldn't have to stand witness.

And God help them all—they didn't need another Archibald Lemming on the streets.

Now, here, looking at the body of a young woman who
had been an old friend, he found his memories were vivid
and they were rushing back.

Archibald Lemming had decapitated four young people; the bodies had been seated around the table.

The heads had been upon it.

Tyler looked up at the ME and asked, "Drugs, alcohol? Anything on her, anything that would help explain
how she was taken?"

Layton glanced at Detective Green. Tyler figured
that Layton's loyalty was to the cop first; he'd obviously
worked with Craig Frasier before. Layton wasn't telling
him anything until he knew Green approved his sharing of details.

"Alcohol. And, yes, cocaine. At the rate she was im-
bibing... I'm not sure she'd have been long for this world
as it was. She had been partying, I take it. She was last
seen at a bar in Times Square," the ME told him. He

glanced at Green again, and Tyler realized he must have learned that through the detective.

"It doesn't look like she put up much of a fight, but then again, the state of the body... Being in the water can wash away a host of evidence," Layton continued. "Thankfully, she wasn't in long. Her, uh, body pieces were found at several locations along the river, but we believe they were disposed of at the same site. The current washed her up...the parts...just a bit differently. Since they were separate locations, they were discovered by different people."

"The body was cut up," Tyler noted.

"Yes, but most of the cuts are postmortem. If there is any salvation in this, I think she bled out quickly. The torture inflicted on her after... I don't think she felt. I wish I could say all this with certainty. That's just my educated opinion."

Once again, Tyler remembered the bodies around the table. They had been posed. This could be the same handiwork, as far as the beheadings went. But Hannah hadn't been posed; she'd been thrown in the river.

"It might be a copycat, it might not be," Craig murmured, obviously thinking along the same lines.

"We'll release the body toward the end of the week," Dr. Layton said. "We're holding on just in case..."

Just in case another body or body parts wash up on the riverbank again.

Detective Green, Craig and Tyler thanked him and they left the morgue.

When they were out on the street, Green looked at Tyler curiously again. "Where are you going from here?"

"Site inspections," Craig said.

"We're going to the bar where she was last seen, called

Time and Time Again," Tyler said. "Then we're going along the Hudson—where the parts washed up."

"I don't think the discovery sites will help you," Green said. "Not even the killer could have known just where she'd pop up—or if she'd be taken in by a fisherman or a pleasure cruiser or what. Maybe you'll get something I didn't get at the bar. Good luck with that."

"If we find anything, we'll call immediately," Craig assured him.

Green nodded. "I know you will. Good day, my friends."

He headed off in one direction. Craig and Tyler turned in the other.

"Time and Time Again?" Craig asked.

Tyler nodded.

Time and Time Again. How tragically apropos.

KIERAN DIDN'T WANT Sarah going home. "You shouldn't be alone right now," she told her. "I mean, not with what has happened."

Her words surprised Sarah. She hadn't thought about being in danger herself. "I'm not being judgmental—trust me, not in any way!—but I've never led a lifestyle like Hannah was living. I mean…she was trolling for tricks. She was stripping—and not in a fine gentlemen's club. Not that a fine gentleman can't be a psychopath, right?"

"Charming, well-dressed and handsome to boot," Kieran assured her. "But the murder was so horrible…people are scared. And not just hookers. And if you're not scared, I think you should be. Anyway, wait until the guys get back, at the least. I've talked to Chef. He's saving us all a nice dinner. Until then…"

"I need to be doing something," Sarah said. "I can't just—sit here."

"What do you want to do?"

Sarah hesitated. "Look up what I can find on the past. Find out more about Archibald Lemming. Find out about the prison break. About him and his friend."

"The pub office here is all yours. We have a very nice and well-behaved computer on the desk. No one is making any entries on a Sunday. We'll be busy. Make yourself comfortable."

"Kieran, that's Declan's computer," she said uncomfortably. She knew the Finnegans, and she knew the pub. She had been grateful for such a great place to work when she had been in school.

Declan was the oldest of the Finnegan clan. He had taken on the responsibility of the pub. The others all pitched in, but Kieran's brother Danny was a tour guide and her other brother, Kevin, was an actor. The workload fell to Declan.

Kieran grabbed her hand. Declan, a handsome hunk of a man with broad shoulders, a quick smile and dark red hair, assured her that she was more than welcome to the computer, to his office and the run of the pub if need be.

Sarah found herself led down the hall to the office; Kieran signed on to the computer there.

"Knock yourself out," she told her cheerfully once Sarah was set. "I'll be wherever for the moment. When Craig and Tyler get back, you can tie up, we'll have roast and we'll see you locked in for the night."

Sarah frowned; she didn't want to be afraid. She was a New Yorker! She had never feared the subway, though she did carry pepper spray. If she'd been afraid of every perceived threat, she'd never have made it in the city.

But Kieran was gone. And Sarah didn't know where to begin—other than to key in the name "Archibald Lemming."

His crimes—even his initial crimes—had been horrendous. He'd received the death sentence, but under pressure by right-to-life groups after his sentencing, the death penalty had been altered to "life and ninety-five years." To make sure that he never got out.

But of course, he had gotten out.

Lemming's first known victim had been a kindergarten teacher. She'd been found in her home, her head almost severed from her body. He'd managed to get his second victim's head off. It had been left on a buffet table in the dining room while she'd been seated in her favorite chair. He hadn't discriminated by sex—his third victim had been a man, a plumber, who'd been found with his fingers wrapped around a beer, his torso in a recliner in the living room, his head atop the TV.

Lemming had been interviewed by the police, since he had hired the plumber to do some work in his home. It was also discovered that he'd had a flirtation going with the first victim, who had lived in his building. He'd been let go—there had been no evidence against him. Then the body and head of his landlord had been found—set up much the same as the others. And despite his "charming" protests, he'd been connected to the crimes via DNA—he'd cut himself during the last murder, and his own blood had given him away. He'd been incarcerated, where, according to prison officials, he'd been a model prisoner. Until, with Perry Knowlton—another murderer who used a knife—he'd escaped via the infirmary.

And gone on to kill and kill again in a frenzy in the "haunted" house.

Sarah sat back and breathed for a minute.

This was crazy.

She had seen the man die. He had no children—none known, at any rate. And if he'd had any offspring, it was unlikely that they knew he was their father. He'd been a loner: no wife, no girlfriend. He'd gone to work every day on Wall Street—and he'd killed by night.

She scanned the information on the page again. He was, by pure definition, the perfect psychopath. No emotion whatsoever. No regret. He was cold and brutal. He'd even murdered the man with whom he'd escaped.

Sarah frowned and started reading again.

Yes, she'd seen Archibald Lemming die.

But...

She sat back, still staring at the screen. And to her own amazement, she thought she had a theory.

Chapter Three

Being escorted back to the office by Danny Finnegan, Tyler found himself grateful that Sarah had found such a supportive group of friends.

Just going through the pub, he'd heard people call out to Danny and to one another.

"Regulars?" he asked. "They all know each other?"

Danny, a leaner, slightly younger version of his brother Declan, shrugged and grinned. "Our folks—and theirs before them—wanted it to be a real Irish pub. Well, back in the day, men had a room, and women and families had a separate one, if they were allowed in at all. But hey, progress is a good thing, right? Yeah, we like to be an Irish American *Cheers*, and we want everyone to feel welcome."

"I do," Tyler assured him.

Danny pushed open a door in the long hallway. "Tyler and Craig are back, Sarah!"

She had been very seriously staring at the computer screen and looked up quickly, a question in her eyes.

Tyler wished he could tell her that yes, simply going to the morgue had solved the whole thing.

He prayed that eventually, and sooner rather than later, they would have answers.

It wasn't going to be easy; they had nothing to go on.

"Kieran will have roast out for you all in a few minutes. We've got you at a back booth," Danny said, and left.

Tyler dropped into a chair in front of the desk.

Sarah stared at him. "It was…horrible, wasn't it?" she whispered.

He nodded. "I can't help but remember—we all had such promise."

"But did you learn anything?"

"I'm heading to the bar where she was last seen, Time and Time Again, around eight or so. If they get some of the same clientele nightly, someone might know or remember something." He hesitated a moment. "She wasn't working at the strip club anymore—she hadn't been for about two weeks. From what I understand, it was a pretty decent place. I've heard it's easy for strippers to become involved in drugs—helps them through. But there are a number of clubs run fairly well, professionally—no touching for real, and no drugs. Anyway, Hannah was fired about a week ago. Craig and I dropped by the club after we visited the sites where she was found."

"So…wow. I feel worse and worse."

"Don't. Something happened that night ten years ago. We were incredibly lucky. Thanks to Davey, we weren't killed. But we all changed. We became introverted. And when we got over it, time had passed. This was in no way your fault—you have to know that. You couldn't have stopped what happened in Cemetery Mansion, any more than you could have saved Hannah now. You have to accept that."

"I know."

"The thing is… I do think this is random. The first suspects in a murder are always those closest to the victim. Except in a case like this. There's no one really to look at—her last boyfriend was in Chicago when it happened."

"Random…" Sarah paused and took a breath. "I know this may seem far-fetched, but I have an idea who we're looking for."

Tyler couldn't have been more surprised. "Who?"

"Perry Knowlton!"

He was still for a minute. "Perry Knowlton is dead. Archibald Lemming killed him, too. Police found the ashes in a veterinary clinic before they even caught up with Lemming."

She shook her head firmly. "They never proved it!"

"What do you mean?"

"I've been reading up on Archibald Lemming and Perry Knowlton all day. I've studied every newspaper article, every piece of video. They found a body so badly burned there were no DNA samples—maybe there might have been today, but not back then. They found his prison uniform. They found trinkets he carried. But they never proved without doubt that the bone fragments and ash they discovered were the remains of Perry Knowlton."

Tyler had read up on the killers, too.

And she was right.

Before, Knowlton hadn't been someone to consider. He hadn't made any appearances over the years and had been assumed dead. He was a killer, too. A serial killer. Like his prison buddy, Archibald Lemming, he had loved to kill with knives. He hadn't been known for decapitating his victims, but for slashing them, the kill strokes being at the jugular vein.

"Maybe," Tyler said.

"But how, and where has he been? Those are the things I've been wondering. I mean, he'd be in the system. If he'd been arrested for any crime in the past ten years, his prints would be on record. They'd have known it was him. What? Did he find a distant farm somewhere and hide out for ten years? Kieran said serial killers don't stop, unless they are dead or incarcerated somewhere." She flushed, her beautiful blue eyes wide. "I know I just write science fiction novels, but I am good at research."

"Sarah, your theory is just as sound as anything else we have at the moment, that's for sure," Tyler told her. "I—I don't know. We can look."

There was a tap at the door and Kieran stuck her head in. "Roast!" she said. "You need to keep your strength up if you're going to continue working on this thing. That means actually having a meal. Craig says you're going to the bar later. Nothing to do until then except fuel up!"

"Sounds good to me," Tyler said. He rose. Sarah still had a bit of a shell-shocked look about her. He walked around the desk and reached for her hand. "Let's eat," he said.

"Dinner," she agreed.

She stood. Her palm rested in his. He couldn't believe ten years had passed and it was still incredibly good just to hold her hand.

And then she smiled at him.

And he knew. He'd waited forever to be back with her. He sure as hell hadn't wanted it to be like this... But he had never managed to fall out of love with her. And that was why nothing else in his life had ever been more than a fleeting moment in time, sex between consenting adults, panacea to ease a pain he'd refused to admit existed.

Maybe it was true that there was one person in the world who was simply everything, one person you were meant to love for a lifetime. Still, neither of them had fallen apart; they had created good lives. Responsible lives.

So why had he left?

Because she had pushed him away. And that would never lead to a lifetime of happiness. And, of course, he was still afraid she would push him away again. But at least not in the middle of a murder investigation. Not this one.

"Thank you," she said quietly.

There was something soft in her eyes. Something that made him think of years gone by.

It hurt.

And it was good, too. Oddly good.

"You're welcome," he murmured.

They made their way back down the charmingly paneled old hallway and out to the restaurant section of the pub. As promised, Kieran had a back booth for them, out of the way of the now very busy crowd. Sunday roast was apparently extremely popular.

Although Craig was careful about what he said, Tyler learned the FBI agent had been working on an organized crime case that included bodies found as the result of a rather old-fashioned but very efficient form of retribution murder—they had their feet stuck in concrete and had been dropped in the East River. "My partner, Mike, has been doing some cleanup paperwork for me, but we still have a few arrests to make. I'll be as much help as I can."

"You've opened doors for me. I'm grateful," Tyler said. "And Sarah might have a very good idea for us to pursue."

She hiked her brows in surprise and flushed again. "I hope you're not going to think I have an overactive imagination," she said.

"We definitely think you have an overactive imagination," Kieran told her. "But that's a good thing. It pays. On this, however, what do you think?"

"Tell them," Tyler urged.

And so she did.

Neither Kieran nor her boyfriend looked at her as if she were crazy.

"That's true?" Craig asked. "I remember the case—when Archibald Lemming died here on that table leg. Of course, the entire country talked about it. But I never studied anything on Perry Knowlton. As far as the public was concerned—as far as everyone was concerned, really—the man was dead, a victim of the man he had befriended. Now that is something I can look into for you."

"That would be great."

"Excuse me," Kieran said. "Drinks, anyone?"

They opted for iced tea all around and she disappeared to get it. Another smiling waitress arrived with their plates.

The food was really good.

The conversation became lighter. They learned that Kieran and Craig had met during a diamond heist. Because of Kieran's employers, Dr. Fuller and Dr. Miro, she was able to help Craig with a number of cases—recently one that had involved the deconsecrated old church right behind the pub. "My brother was affected by that one... He'd been in love with a victim," Kieran said softly. "That's Kevin. You haven't met him yet, Tyler. But I'm sure you will!"

Tyler told them he was living on Beacon Hill. He described his daily work. "I take on a lot of missing-children cases," he said. "When I'm lucky, I find them—most often, they're runaways. When they're not... I have a great relationship with the Boston PD, which is very important. I won't work possible-cheating-spouse cases—

too sordid. I have worked murder cases—a number of cold cases. It wasn't always that way, of course, but working the cheating spouse thing just seems nasty—and finding justice for someone feels really good."

"Have you ever considered coming back to New York, Tyler?" Kieran asked.

"It's home. One never knows," he said.

"Boston, New York…so many great cities!" she said. And then she looked at her watch. "Whoa. Well, dinner with you two was great. I wish we were heading to a play or a movie now, but I know you want to stay focused. It's eight o'clock."

"Time to go," Tyler said, rising.

"Are you going with him?" Kieran asked Craig.

"I have to head to the office for at least an hour or so," he replied. "Hey, this man is a good investigator. He'll do fine."

Sarah had risen, as well. "I'm going with you," she said.

"Sarah," Tyler protested. "That's not a great idea."

"I can help."

"How?"

"I can make you look human and sweet—better than looking like a linebacker out to tackle someone!"

TIME AND TIME AGAIN was off Forty-Second Street and the Times Square area, but far enough away from the theater district on Ninth Avenue to just miss most of the theater-going crowd.

It would best be described, Sarah thought, as a *nice* dive bar.

She definitely wanted all her facilities about her, but deeply disappointed the bartender by ordering a soda with lime.

"Don't you want a Ninth Avenue Special, a Dive-Bar Exotic or a Yes, It's Time Again?" he asked her.

He was a young man of maybe twenty-five. Cheerful and flirty.

Sarah was sitting at the bar; Tyler was meeting with the night manager in his office.

"No, thanks. Just the soda water."

"Your friend a cop?" he asked her.

She shook her head, smiling though, and looked around. The place was decorated with old posters that depicted the city during different eras. They helped cover the fact that the bar really needed to be painted.

"No, Tyler isn't a cop."

"But he's in there asking about that girl," the bartender said. He had a neatly trimmed beard and mustache combo, and she wondered if he was a student at one of the city's colleges.

"Yes, he's asking about Hannah Levine," she told him softly.

"I'm Luke," he said, looking down the bar to see if he was needed. He wasn't. He leaned on it. "The cops have already been all over us. She was carrying one of our promo matchboxes—that's how they knew she'd been here." He grimaced. "They have raised lettering—really swank matches for this place, but we get a mixed clientele. We cater to the local music scene."

"Nice," she replied. He was friendly, and she decided she might be able to help the investigation. She could ask questions, too, and maybe in a different way. "Are you from New York?"

"Nope. Akron, Ohio. Loving being here. Don't be deceived by appearances. This is actually a great place. Yes, we have a few lowlifes hanging around. But it's honest work for me and helps pay the bills."

"Hannah was my friend," she said softly.

"Oh?" He seemed surprised. He leaned closer to her. "You don't look like a junkie."

"Hannah wasn't on heroin," she said defensively.

"No, just everything else. She came in here frequently. The owner had barred her for a while, but…people liked her. She just—well, she looked for tricks here, you know."

Sarah winced.

"Hey, I'm so sorry. I guess you hadn't seen her in a while."

"No, I hadn't. But…"

"I can see you care." He straightened and said, "Excuse me," and hurried down the length of the bar, speaking to customers seated on stools along the way. He refilled a few drinks, whispered to someone and then headed back to speak with Sarah.

"I don't know what it was with her!" Luke said. He lowered his voice. "We dated a few times, but then… I found out she was hooking. I…well, that didn't work for me. I want to have a wife I'll grow old with, kids. Hannah said she'd never settle down. But we didn't part badly. We were friends. I tried to help out, give her food—pay her bar tab when she walked out. She was her own worst enemy. Sometimes I thought she was committing slow suicide. Even when she had people trying to help her, she'd laugh them off. She said she loved the danger of hooking, you know?"

Sarah did know. Hannah had wanted to be on the edge—she'd wanted to skydive, ride the fastest coaster, speed on the FDR.

"I don't care what she was doing. What happened shouldn't have happened to her or to anyone!" Sarah said passionately.

"No! Of course not! I didn't mean that. Just that…"

I don't know who she might have met, who could have done such a terrible thing…"

His voice trailed off as he realized he obviously didn't need to remind Sarah what had happened.

"Were you working when she was here?" Sarah asked him.

"I was coming for the late shift. But I was just outside. Coming in."

"And you talked to her?"

He nodded. Sarah thought she saw the glint of tears in his eyes and his voice was husky when he said, "She gave me a big hug and a kiss on the cheek and told me she 'was about to go roll in some dough.' I assumed that meant she had met up with a rich guy willing to pay a nice price. She was so pretty. Even…even with the drugs and alcohol. And nice. No matter what, she had something about her. A core that had some real warmth, you know?"

"I do know," Sarah assured him. She cleared her throat. "Did you tell the police what she said?"

"I wasn't interviewed. I wasn't actually in the bar when she was here, so the manager never called me to talk to the police."

"And you didn't volunteer to help?" Sarah asked.

"Hey. They were trying to paint a picture of her I don't agree with—that she was a druggie whore who got what was coming to her."

"That can't be true. Any sensible, decent person knows that, whatever someone's lifestyle, they don't deserve such a horror 'coming to them.' That can't be—"

She was suddenly interrupted by Tyler's deep voice right behind her. "Whatever made you think the world was filled with sensible and decent people?"

She fell silent. The bartender was looking at Tyler.

Sarah quickly introduced the two. They shook hands as Tyler crawled up on the stool next to Sarah's.

"You're not a cop?" Luke asked him warily.

Tyler shook his head. "I'm a PI, in from Boston. Mainly here because, as I'm sure Sarah told you, Hannah was a friend."

"Pity you guys weren't around when she was still living," he murmured.

"Yes, we're well aware of that," Sarah said.

"Hey," Tyler said. The word wasn't spoken angrily, nor was it shouted. But it was filled with the fact that Sarah could not be blamed—nor could any of them.

"A sick killer is responsible, no one else. When she was a kid, no one could tell Hannah what to do. I sincerely doubt she'd have listened now. But we were her friends," Tyler went on. "And we will see that justice is done for her."

"Okay, okay!" Luke said, hands in the air. "Look, I'm sorry I didn't go bursting into the office and say hey, yeah, I knew Hannah. I don't know who killed her…"

His voice faltered suddenly.

"What is it?" Sarah asked.

"A man."

"A man?" Tyler asked.

Luke nodded. "He was in here several times a couple of weeks ago. I thought that he was watching Hannah. No way out of it, with those cat eyes of hers…bedroom eyes, you know what I mean? Anyway, he was watching her."

"Was he…old, young? Can you describe him?" Tyler asked.

"Well, he was average. He wore a low-brimmed hat all the time—I sure don't know his eye color or anything like that. Narrow face. Wore a coat, too. But then, you know, when it's cold, people don't always take their coats off in bars. Especially this one—the heating system isn't so great."

"Anyone else unusual?" Tyler asked him.

"I'll think…honestly, I'll think about it. But as far as this place goes… I mean, describe unusual. We get all kinds. Some hardworking, partying-on-Friday-nights kind of people. Drug dealers now and then. But Willie— you met Willie, the night manager, right?" he asked, looking at Tyler. "You were just in talking with him, right?"

Tyler nodded.

"He doesn't like drug dealers or junkies. He can usually ferret them out and he's as tall and muscle-bound as you are, dude," he said, glancing quickly at Tyler and then grimacing at Sarah as if they shared a great joke. "I think they hired him because they don't need a bouncer when he's on. Also, he's the owner's cousin. Owner is in Utah, so… But you see, Hannah left here—after that, we don't know."

"I know," Tyler said. "And, listen, the cops on this really are good guys. If I can get them to send a sketch artist down here, do you think you could help us get some kind of an image of the guy in the hat and the coat?"

"I'll go you one better," Luke promised. "Bring your guy down. We'll also post that we need any help—no matter how minute—anyone can give. How's that?" He pointed across the room to a large bulletin board. "Trust me. People will want to help. Kind of like back in the days of Jack the Ripper, you know? People may like to think this guy only went after a prostitute and he won't target them. But this kind of thing…" A shudder shook his whole body. "This is terrifying!"

"Hey, is there actually a bartender in here?" someone shouted from the end of the bar.

"Hang on, there, Hardy! Give your liver a breather! I'm on the way!" Luke said. He nodded to the two of them.

"Did you pay yet?" Tyler asked Sarah.

"No." She scrambled in her tote bag for her wallet, but Tyler had already set a bill on the bar.

"I think I'm supposed to be paying you," she said. "For your services."

He stared at her and smiled slowly. "I was that good, huh?"

She realized just how her words might be taken, and yet of course he was teasing.

Still…

Ten years between them.

She felt the blood rise to her cheeks. She had not blushed this much since…well, since forever.

"I meant I'm next of kin, or so Hannah said. I'm hiring you to find her killer."

He shook his head. "I'm going to find this killer for Hannah. And for all of us," he said.

TYLER HAD BARELY gotten into his hotel room after dropping Sarah off at her place when his phone rang.

"Tyler?"

He was curious the caller had voiced the question, as he always answered his phone with one word, his surname, "Grant."

But despite time and distance, he knew the caller.

"Sean," he said.

"Yeah, it's Sean. Hey, how are you? I know this is out of the blue, but…"

There was fear in Sean's slightly garbled and wandering words.

"I'm here. In New York."

"Because of Hannah?"

"Yes."

"Thank God!" Sean said. "I mean, you were in the military, right? You, uh, know your way around a gun and all that."

"I know my way around a gun and all that," he agreed.

"I'm afraid they're after us," Sean said.

Tyler hesitated. Then asked, "Sean, who are *they*? Everyone thinks what happened to Hannah is horrendous, but why would any 'they' be after all of us?"

"You don't know the latest. Oh, well, it just broke. Maybe you haven't heard."

As Sean spoke, Tyler realized he had another call coming in—from Craig Frasier.

"Excuse me. I'll be right back with you," he told Sean. "Craig?"

"There's been another murder. Body and head left in a park by the FDR. There was ID. Her name was Suzie Cornwall."

Suzie?

Sarah's best friend? God, no.

"Bob Green called me. You can join us at the park. I'll text the address."

He switched the call back over. "Sean, my God, I'm so sorry—"

"Oh, Suzie—our Suzie—is here with me."

"What? Listen, Sean—"

"No, no, I heard on the news. Suzette Cornwall was murdered. But it's not our Suzie. Our Suzie is here, with me. We're married now, you probably know, so she's Suzie Avery. The cops found me—I guess as a Suzie Cornwall's husband, in whatever database. She was Suzie Cornwall, too. But…oh, Lord! Our Suzie is here. She's fine. But that's just it, don't you see? He—or they!—got

Hannah. They're looking for us, Tyler. They're looking for us—the group at Cemetery Mansion that year."

That was crazy. Just crazy. The only person who might want some kind of revenge was Archibald Lemming. And Lemming was dead. Tyler had seen the table leg protrude right through his body.

He'd seen the blood. The ripped and torn flesh, down to the organs and bone. Lemming was not alive. And Tyler had lived with the fact that he was at least partially responsible for that man's death...no matter if he was a murderer the world was better off without.

Perry Knowlton? Was he really out there? Had Archibald Lemming helped him pretend to die—so that he could live?

"Tyler? Help!" Sean said softly.

"All right, listen, Sean. You and Suzie stay close and keep your doors locked. Don't go out tonight. Stay in until I know what's going on. You hear me?"

"I hear you. Loud and clear. Door is locked. But please, don't you see? He killed Hannah Levine. Now he's killed a Suzette Cornwall. We're all supposed to die, Tyler. I don't know why, except that we were there. We were there."

"I'll be in touch. Just stay put. Where are you living now?"

"Brooklyn. Got a little house."

It was too bad Sean wasn't living in a tiny apartment with no windows and one door.

"Windows—check all the windows. Make sure you're secure."

"Got it. You'll call me?"

"As soon as possible. I'm meeting the cops at the site."

He hung up; he didn't have time to waste on the phone. He put a call through to Sarah. Her phone rang a few times, and in those split seconds he felt debilitating panic setting in.

Then she answered.

"Sarah, listen to me. I'm asking Detective Green to get a man out to your aunt's house. Now I do think we're all in danger."

"What? What are you talking about?"

"Have you seen the news?"

"No."

"Okay, it's not the Suzie who was our friend, but a Suzie Cornwall was murdered. I just talked to Sean. They're fine. But I'm going to stop by for you. I need to get you somewhere safe. You can stay at Kieran's with her for now. Craig has been living there, mostly, I guess, so I am assuming it's pretty darned safe. You have to lock yourself in…"

"A woman named Suzie Cornwall was murdered?" she asked.

"Not our Suzie."

"Poor woman. Oh, my God, poor woman!"

"Sarah, listen to me. Don't open your door until you hear my voice!"

"Right, right. I won't," she promised.

"And call Davey and Renee. Tell them to stay put until we figure something out."

Tyler hung up, and then, with his wits more thoroughly about him, he dialed Craig back. Craig let him know that yes, of course Kieran would be happy to have Sarah come stay with her. He should have said something; he had thought it was a given.

Tyler thanked him and headed out. His hotel wasn't far from Sarah's place on Reed Street. It seemed as if the distance had somehow become greater since the last time he drove it.

He left his car in the street, not caring what kind of a fine he might get, and took the steps to her apartment two at a time.

But Sarah was ready to go. She had a little bag with her. She looked at him with wide eyes, shaking her head. "That's too much to be a coincidence, right?"

"It's too close," he agreed.

"My theory... I think it has to be right!" she whispered.

"It may be right. Listen, I'm taking you to—"

"Kieran's. I figured. Where else could you drop me at midnight—or is it 1:00 a.m. yet?"

He just nodded.

Then he told her, "I'll find out more when I see the crime site."

They hurried out to the car and he got her in safely before he jumped back in the driver's seat. When they got to Kieran's place in SoHo, he parked the car in the street again.

"Go on—I'll run in!" Sarah told him.

"Not in this lifetime," he answered, leaving the car and taking her arm.

Kieran lived above a karaoke bar. Someone was warbling out Alice Cooper's "The Man Behind the Mask" as they made their way up.

The singer wasn't so bad. His choice of song seemed grating.

Of course, Sarah knew which unit was Kieran's door. She stopped in front of it.

Tyler reached out to knock.

And then it touched him that they were on the run from an unidentified threat, and he was on his way to go see the corpse of a woman—an innocent victim—who, just earlier today, had surely believed she had years left before her.

Life was fleeting.

He turned, pulled Sarah into his arms and kissed her. It was a hard kiss, hurried and passionate, hotly wet and very sloppy. She was surprised at first, but then she returned his kiss, and when he released her, she looked at him breathlessly, with confusion.

"Tyler—"

"I love you. I've always loved you. And so help me God, we will survive this!"

Kieran's door opened; she'd heard something. She had expected them. Tyler saw one of her brothers was there, as well.

"Danny is going to hang with us," she said.

"Great," Tyler said. "Okay—"

"Don't even say 'lock up.' I'm a New Yorker, and I live with Craig!"

He actually smiled at that. Then he turned and left. No cops had ticketed his car and no tow company had taken it away.

He drove quickly and competently.

He needed to reach the crime scene.

To see everything in situ.

He had to get there.

And, dear lord, how he dreaded getting there, as well.

Chapter Four

Danny Finnegan was really a great guy.

Once upon a time, Sarah and he had almost dated. She'd somehow known that it couldn't be a forever kind of thing between them, so they'd stayed friends.

Danny, she thought, had realized the same thing. They were never going to be friends with benefits, either—it would be just too awkward for them and the entire family. And having the Finnegan family as friends was something special; they'd tacitly known that anything between them—other than great friendship—could destroy it all.

And still she loved him as a friend, as she did Kieran.

If it weren't for the fact that two people had been murdered in a fashion reminiscent of a decade-old massacre, it might have been just a late evening with friends.

Kieran made hot chocolate and set out cookies; Danny diverted Sarah with weird stories about the city. "Believe it or not, this lady kept her son's corpse in the house for years—up in Brooklyn. She didn't kill him—poor guy died young of disease. But she kept him—and the only reason the body was discovered was that she was hospitalized herself. A relative went to get some things for her and…well, the son was down to skeletal remains. I've heard stories about other people keeping corpses, but I know this one is true! The papers all covered it. We're a great state—and so weird. Oh, not in the city, but up in Elmira, John Brown's widow—she being the widow of the John Brown's raid John Brown!—received a head. A skull, really. Another man named John Brown died down in Harpers Ferry, a skull was found and everyone said that it was John Brown's—so they sent it to her."

"Ugh. What did she do?"

"Sent it back, of course!" Danny said.

Sarah smiled, knowing he knew she'd grown up in the city and would be aware of the history of the state, but maybe not all the most bizarre bits and pieces of fact and lore.

"Hey, Cooper Union had the first elevator shaft—not elevator, actually. Otis hadn't come along yet, but when building, Cooper had the basic idea, using a round shaft!"

Sarah laughed. "I think I did hear something about that years ago—NYU students often hung out with Cooper Union people."

Her phone rang. She glanced at the number and was surprised to see that despite a few hardware upgrades over the years, Suzie Cornwall's number was still in her contacts.

She answered quickly. "Suzie?"

"Hey. You okay? I'm sorry. I shouldn't have called. I mean, it was okay—not okay, Lord! I'm sorry, it was not okay, it was terrible, horrible, when Hannah was killed. But…it didn't really terrify me. It saddened me, but it didn't terrify me. Sarah, now he's killed a *Suzie Cornwall*. Oh, my God. That poor woman. She was killed for having my name! I'm so scared, Sarah. So scared. Do you think that… Davey could help?"

Stunned, Sarah stared at the phone. "Suzie, hey, hey, yes, of course I know you're scared. But… Davey is a young man with Down syndrome. He isn't a medium, he isn't magical. That night…he saw Archibald Lemming slinking around. He saw him go into the house. My uncle taught him to be wary. How to really notice things, to watch out for people because, sad as it may be, the world is full of bullies who want to hurt those who are at a disadvantage instead of helping them. He didn't want Davey to fall victim to someone who meant him ill."

"But…he *knew* that night!" Suzie whispered. "Oh, I'm sorry. Sean said this wouldn't make any sense."

"Congratulations, by the way. I 'liked' it when I saw that you two had married, but I figured a zillion other people did, too. You looked beautiful."

"Yes, yes. Thank you. I think I actually saw your 'like.' I should have called or written then, or…you know. Oh, but I've bought all your books!"

"Thanks. I didn't think you were a sci-fi fan."

"I'm not."

"Well, then, thank you very much."

"Oh, but they were good. Oh, Sarah! I'm so scared."

"You're home, right? Tyler told you to go home and stay there and lock in, right?"

"But what do we do in the morning? Sean and I both have jobs. He works down on Wall Street. I'm up by the park at the new department store there—I'm a makeup artist. Sean is a stock broker."

"Maybe, just tomorrow, you shouldn't go in. Maybe they can arrange police protection."

"For the rest of our lives? Sarah, they have to find this maniac."

Both Kieran and Danny could hear Suzie through the phone, she was talking so loudly. Sarah looked at them both, shaking her head.

"No," she said firmly, gazing at Danny and Kieran. "Until they find the killer."

"It's Lemming. It's Archibald Lemming. He's back. He's come back, and he knows we were there. He's going to kill us all."

"It's not Archibald Lemming. We saw him die."

"He's come back—somehow."

"No. It's someone just as sick, using what happened."

"But...how? How is this person finding us?"

"He made a mistake—he didn't find you. Unless this is sheer happenstance and he killed a woman who happened to have the same name, or your maiden name."

"Lemming must be whispering from the grave. He'll keep killing, it wasn't happenstance. He's after me."

"He'll be stopped."

"But what if—"

"Tyler is back in New York," Sarah said simply. "And I know he won't stop."

THE BODY OF the woman was seated on a park bench, hands rested easily in her lap. If she just had a head, it would have appeared she had simply decided to relax a minute and enjoy the beauty of the park.

She'd been wearing a red sweater and jeans. All around the neck area, the sweater was darkened; blood had dried into it.

As Tyler arrived, Craig came forward, telling the officer who was keeping the crowd back that Tyler was with him.

"We're on it now," Craig told him, referring to the FBI. "This morning, with this second kill and the name of the victim, the police chief decided to bring us in, along with every law enforcement agency in the near vicinity. He's a good guy. No jurisdictional bull with him. He wants murders solved."

He'd spoken as they came to the body. Police photographer Alex Morrison was there, snapping pictures quickly. Detective Bob Green was present, too, leaning close to the victim, but not too close. Dr. Lance Layton had been called out; he had already arrived, as well.

Thankfully, none of them looked at Tyler as if he didn't belong, or as if he were an interloper.

"No defensive wounds," Layton said. "But the bastard did saw through her neck with a blade—a serrated blade, so it appears. Might have drugged her first. Pray that he did, the poor thing! Had to have—no one could feel that kind of pain and not react."

"The head?" Craig asked quietly.

"It was left in a kid's swing," Green said. "Doc had it moved—it's in the back of the wagon."

He was referring to Dr. Layton's vehicle. The back door to the van was open, an officer in uniform standing guard before it.

"We'll take a look," Craig said grimly.

They did; the officer knew Craig and gave way.

The head was in a sterile container.

Her hair had a brown base, but had been multicolored in blues and greens and pinks, just as many women were coloring their hair. Though it was difficult to tell from a severed head—all life and vitality gone—it appeared she had been a bit older than their Suzie. Judging from the headless body, she had probably been about the same height and weight.

"How did he get her here?" Tyler wondered aloud. The FDR was just above them. The park was surrounded by apartment buildings, all of which had storefronts at the bottom. It was a typical New York City neighborhood—the park offering some trees and fake grass, but all around it, the congestion of giant buildings and all the trappings needed to house millions of people on an island.

"She was found after dark by some folks who jumped the fence—a babysitter who'd lost her phone here. I don't think the killer thought she'd be found until morning," Craig told Tyler. "The media got hold of it just about the same time as the police, so God knows what pictures are out there. They had her name first—she lived in that building just over there. No ID on her, but our teenage babysitter knew her because they live in the same building. Her name is on the buzzer in the foyer. No night guard or desk clerk in the place. No cameras. The cops are doing a door-to-door now, but...so far, no one saw anything."

"He killed her elsewhere and got her in here fast."

Tyler looked out at the crowd watching the scene. The killer could be there—with the others, watching them all, enjoying the fruit of his labors.

"Crime scene techs are going over the place with a fine-tooth comb," Craig said. "We're hoping to hell the officers or the techs will find something—anything. And," he added grimly, "we're hoping Lance will tell us she was drugged and unconscious before this happened. Press conference first thing, autopsy right after. Until then..."

"I need to be with Sarah," Tyler said. But he paused, looking around the scene. The park, with the shaded benches for moms and dads and babysitters. The colorful playground created for children, with crawl bars, slides and multileveled platforms.

The park was fenced, but the fence was wood and easily scaled.

"Facts we have will be coming through email," Bob Green said, walking over to them. He always seemed to be studying Tyler. Tyler just stared back at him. He supposed he was a curiosity to the detective. He had been there when Archibald Lemming had attacked a group of teenagers in a haunted house. When there had been so much fake blood it had been hard to figure out where the real blood began. "We'll share all information on this immediately, to facilitate working together. This has to be stopped. The mayor called me personally. I have a meeting with my guys and the FBI at the crack of dawn, and we have to be ready for the press conference. We'll have the park roped off for the next week, at least." He lowered his head, letting out a sigh of disgust. "Kids. Little kids come here. The babysitter…she's a student at NYU. All of about twenty. Can you imagine a little one walking in on a sight like that?"

"No one should ever have to walk in on a sight like that," Tyler said.

"Is there…anything you can think of, anything about Lemming, anything at all that might help?" Green asked him.

"Lemming died that night. We don't believe, however, that the man with whom he escaped is dead."

Green frowned. "Ashes and bone fragments and his prison uniform were found. Lemming used Perry Knowlton to escape, then he killed him."

"He's the only man who would really know exactly how Archibald Lemming worked," Tyler said. "And there was no DNA. There sure as hell were no fingerprints. There's no proof the man is dead."

"At my office we're going to work on the concept that he might be alive," Craig said.

Green nodded slowly. "And he's out for…revenge?"

"Possibly."

"Then you're all in danger. You, Sarah, Sean Avery and the other Suzie Cornwall. And Davey Cray," he added softly.

"And Davey," Tyler agreed. "Can you give them protection?"

"I can. And you might be right. Then again, the killer could be anyone. There are sick people out there who fall even more sickly in love with criminals and killers. Especially serial killers. Some of the fan mail those guys get in prison…it's enough to make your hair stand on end. But we need something to work with. Anything."

He was still looking at Tyler, apparently wanting an answer.

"As you said, our lives are in danger. If I had any kind of an idea, I guarantee you, I'd share it."

"There's nothing, nothing from that night…?"

"I remember Archibald Lemming coming at me with a blade. I was in shock. I was terrified for myself and the others. Sick from what I saw. And then Sarah and Davey were there—and I pushed Lemming off us, and we saw Lemming die. We can't look to the past. It isn't him doing these things. But I believe it is someone who knew him."

"Let's get out of here—it's nearly three in the morning," Craig said. "We can think it all out for hours, talk it all out…but there's nothing more we can do here."

There wasn't. The dead woman's torso was being loaded for removal to the morgue; they would, at that point, just get in the way of the officers and techs working. She obviously had been killed elsewhere; she'd been displayed. Not thrown in a river. Displayed.

"Interesting," Tyler said.

"Yep."

"Yep?"

"You're wondering how, if the park was locked, one man got the body over the fence. It's damned unlikely he just waltzed in with the corpse and a head."

"And yet, could two people working together be quite so sick?"

"I guess we need sleep," Craig said. "Clear heads are better."

They had separate cars; they headed to them, both aware they were going back to Kieran's in the Village over the karaoke sushi bar.

Walking down the street, Tyler was aware of the way his Smith and Wesson sat in the holster at the back of his waistband.

Because he couldn't help but wonder if someone was watching.

This was Kieran's neighborhood, not Sarah's. Sarah lived far down south on the island, on Reed Street.

And the killer didn't know everything; after all, he'd murdered the wrong Suzie Cornwall.

Tyler wondered how many other people might have the same names in New York City. None of the group had an unusual name.

Craig had parked ahead of him. He caught up and they walked together. "You think he's had enough for one night?" he asked Tyler.

"Hannah hasn't been dead more than a week—and from what the ME said, she's probably only been dead about five days. Water hides a lot of truths. And now… I don't know. Hard to tell if he's just getting started—if he's been locked up for years, or murdering kittens and puppy dogs for practice."

"I think this person has killed in this manner before," Craig said. "He knows just how hard it is to decapitate someone with a knife. He enjoys the struggle to manage it all, and he's proud of himself for doing it."

"There's got to be something on this guy somewhere."

"Somewhere. Thing is, how do you suddenly do things

so horrible? Where has this guy been? How do we have a repeat of Archibald Lemming now—out of the blue?"

"There is something, somewhere," Tyler said with determination. "We just have to find it."

They had reached the stairs to Kieran's apartment.

The karaoke club had gone quiet; it would be dawn in another few hours.

Kieran answered the door as soon as she heard Craig's voice. "Anything?" she asked anxiously. Danny and Sarah had come to stand behind her. They all looked at Craig and Tyler expectantly.

"A corpse, as grisly as you would expect," Tyler said.

"And her name was... Suzie Cornwall?" Sarah said. "For sure?"

"From everything we understand," Craig said. "Cops are canvassing the neighborhood and the forensic team is busy," he added.

"This one was more like...before, right?" Sarah asked.

Tyler hesitated to share the gory details. "She wasn't tossed. In two pieces. She was in two pieces, but set up for shock value. No haunted house, but an audience of children and young mothers, if she hadn't been found until morning."

"We'll know more then. Kieran, I think we should talk to your fine doctors, Fuller and Miro, tomorrow," Craig said. "There will be a press conference and then we'll go to the autopsy, but after that..."

"Of course," Kieran said.

"Not that you're not brilliant and haven't learned just about everything from them," Craig told her.

"Sure, sure...no charming sweet talk, huh? I was about to pull out our blow-up beds. We all have to get some sleep, even if it's only a few hours. Danny is going to hang in and we've actually got it all covered. I figured

I'd take Sarah and we'd pull a girl thing and claim the bedroom, and then one of you on the sofa and two on the floor—"

"I have a hotel room, and it's under the business name. I don't need to make it more crowded here," Tyler said.

"Oh, but it's so late," Kieran protested. "Or early."

"It's okay. There's no traffic," he insisted.

"I'll go with you," Sarah said.

"What?" He said the word sharply, though he didn't mean to be so abrupt.

It didn't matter. She ignored the tone. "I'll go with you."

"We should have gone to Craig's place—much bigger and nicer," Kieran admitted.

"It's all right, the hotel is great. I'm on the twentieth floor. There's security on at night. And I was in the service. I wake up at just about anything," Tyler said.

Sarah already had her bag. She was coming with him.

"All right. Let us know you get there okay, huh?" Kieran asked.

"Hey, this guy has hit only vulnerable women so far. I'm not vulnerable," Tyler assured her. "But yes, we'll text as soon as we're there."

He'd never agreed Sarah should come. Out in the hall, once Kieran had closed and locked the door, he turned to her. "This isn't a good idea."

"Probably not," she agreed.

"You can just stay with your friend—"

"Too crowded."

"You'd have the bedroom—"

"Look, you'll be leaving again, after all this, I know that. I don't really know what I'm doing, either. But this has happened. We're together now. And I... I know you. Whatever this is, for however long... I'd rather be with you right now. Kieran is great. Craig is great. Neither of them was at Cemetery Mansion."

"We need to be careful, over everything else."

"Yes, I know. But right now I want to be with you. Yes, you left me before. I expect you'll leave again. And that's all right. That's—that's the way it has to be."

He hesitated, ready to open the door to the street. He looked at her and said softly, "No, don't even try to tell me you believe it happened in that order. You left me long before I ever decided I had to go."

He didn't give her a chance to protest. He opened the door and hurried her out to the car.

He wondered if he should think it was wrong, crazy. He knew where this was going.

And he could only be grateful for the moment.

"So, WELCOME TO my temporary castle," Tyler said, opening the door to his room.

It was a slightly nicer hotel room at a middling upscale chain hotel. There was a small sitting area with a sofa Sarah assumed opened up to an extra bed, a large bath and a very inviting, big bed with some kind of an extra-squishy mattress that promised a great night's sleep.

It was barely night anymore and she wasn't really intending to sleep. Not right away.

Tyler locked the door and slid the bolt. Sarah had wandered in and set down the small bag she had packed to head over to Kieran's.

"My favorite chain. I have one of those 'frequent stayer' cards with them."

"You're in hotels often?" Sarah asked.

"I travel around some. Business."

"But not often in New York."

"I avoid New York," he said.

"But you're here now," she said.

He turned, studying her, his hands on his hips. "And you—you're here right now."

She nodded, not sure about her next actions. She had forgotten just how she loved everything about Tyler. Even the way he stood now, curious and confident. Not aggressive—just confident. They'd both had it so easy when they'd been younger. She had known she'd gotten lucky—not just because of his easy laughter, kindness and natural charm. She was lucky because they had found each other. They'd never been the brightest, best or most beautiful; they had just fallen in together when they'd been fifteen and sixteen, when she'd dropped some papers, when they'd both reached down to gather them up and had crashed heads. And then laughed. They were new then—new kids at a new school.

She shrugged off the memory and took a hard look at the man standing before her.

"You said you still loved me."

"I do." He didn't hesitate. "And I believe you love me."

"And that sometimes, love just isn't enough."

"Right. Sometimes love just isn't enough."

"But for tonight…"

"Or today," he said drily, glancing over at the clock on the mantel.

"For now…"

She thought he was going to say something like "Come over here!" Or that he would take the few steps to reach her.

But he didn't. "For now… I really need a shower. I was…there. Anyway, a shower."

He turned away, pulling a small holster from the rear waistband of his jeans and setting it on the little table by the bed. He shed his jacket and shoes. She was still just standing there, and he shrugged and headed on into the bathroom.

He didn't close the door. She wasn't sure whether that meant she was being given an invitation or not.

Sarah quickly slid out of her sweater and jeans, glad he had gone into the shower. She wasn't sure she could have disrobed with anything like sensuality anymore—it had been too long.

Awkward! That was her theme emotion with him now. Once, everything had been so easy. And now...

Naked, she tiptoed toward the bathroom door. The shower was very large. Tyler was standing under the spray, just letting the water rush over him. She knew, of course, what he was feeling. He felt that he smelled of death and decay, and the water would never be cleansing enough. She had felt that way after the night at the Cemetery Mansion. And for a long time afterward.

She opened the shower door and slipped in behind him, encircling his waist with her arms and laying her head against his back.

He turned, pulling her to him, gently lifting her chin and her face. His mouth moved down upon hers, soft and wet and steaming. He touched gently at first, so that she barely knew if the steam and heat was him or a whisper of the water beating all around them. Then the pressure of his kiss became hard, his mouth parted hers and she felt his tongue, and with it, wings of fire crept through her memory and more.

The water sluiced over and around them, deliciously hot and sensual. His hands held her tight against him first, and when it seemed her breasts were all but welded to his chest, she felt his palms slide seductively down her back, his fingers teasing along her spine. He pressed his lips to her shoulder, and her collarbone, and then his eyes rose to hers. The way he looked at her...the past and present rolled into one. They had been so young once.

His eyes were no longer young. And yet she loved everything she saw within them, even if that wisdom meant he would leave her again, and this, this thing between them that was so unique, would be nothing but a memory.

He reached behind him to turn off the water. And he grinned suddenly. "I was thinking of some great, cinematic moments of romance. I should sweep you up, press you against the tile, make mad love to you here and now..."

"Except one of us would slip on the soap and we'd end with broken limbs?" she asked, smiling in turn, a little breathless, surprised she'd been able to speak.

"Something like that," he said. "And we have a dreamy mattress...and, hmm, neither of us has to do the laundry. Let me try this!"

He thrust the shower door open and stepped out, and then surprised her so much she gasped before laughing as he swept her up in his arms. "There's no staircase for me to carry you up dramatically, but..."

"We're soaking!"

"The heat is on—no pun intended—and we'll dry."

And still she smiled. He walked the few steps needed and let her fall into the softness of the bed, and then he came down in turn. He was immediately by her side, half atop her, finding her lips again with his own, his hands skimming over her, touching her with caresses that made her forget everything but a longing for more. They seemed to meld into a kiss again, rolled with the pile of soft covering, and then his lips found hers, left them, moved down the length of her body, hovering here and there over her breasts, then snaking downward. He caressed her thighs with kisses and erotic finger play, and she writhed, twisting to come back around to him, to touch him, press her lips against his skin, taste the cleanliness of his naked flesh, the warmth of him, the fire, the essence...

She saw his eyes again as he came over her and thrust into her. She met his gaze squarely with her own, reaching for him, pulling him ever closer to her. The bed cradled them as they began to rock and twist and writhe together.

She remembered the way they had been...

And it was nothing compared to now. Memory hadn't served so well. He could tease so sensually with the lightest brush and then move hard, and the sensation would be almost unbearable. She was achingly and acutely aware of his body...muscle, bone, every movement. He was leaner and harder than ever; his shoulders had grown broader, his abdomen tighter...he moved with a fluid fury and grace that swept her into moments of sweet oblivion, lifted her, eased her down, lifted her again... and then to a climax that seemed to shatter everything, straight down to her soul.

They lay in silence, just breathing. For a few moments, the sound was loud. It began to ease. She felt the slowing of her heartbeat; she thought that she heard his, too.

She tried to think of something to say. Something... that explained her current emotion. Something deep or profound.

She didn't speak first.

He did.

"Hmm," he said lightly. "I guess I have missed you!"

"Well," she murmured, "I'm ever so glad."

He rolled up then, looking down into her eyes. "You really are beautiful, Sarah. Inside and out, you know."

She shook her head, confused. "Just decent, I hope, like I want to believe most people in the world are."

He rolled over again, plumping up a pillow. "Oh, Sarah. So far above decent! I'd definitely rate you an eleven this evening!"

"On a scale of one to ten?"

"One to twenty."

She hit him with a pillow.

And he laughed and moved over her again, smiling. "On a scale of one to five…an eleven. Maybe a twenty or a hundred…"

He kissed her.

It had been a very, very long time.

They made love again. She thought it was dawn when they finally slept. And it was too bad. They really had so very much to do…

A killer to catch.

More murders to stop…

Including their own.

Chapter Five

Tyler was amazed that he hadn't had to drag himself out, almost crying from exhaustion. But he wasn't tired; he felt that he was wide-awake and sharp—as if some kind of new adrenaline was running through his system, something that changed the world.

Sex.

With Sarah. Different as could be…and sweet and explosive as any memory that he could begin to recall.

Biology, like breathing. Should have been. It just wasn't. Something made people come to other people and, whatever it was, it was strong. Sometimes, it became more. Sometimes it lasted forever. Sometimes it didn't.

He stood in the situation room at the precinct while the facts of the murders were laid out for the dozens of officers, agents and marshals crammed into it. All they really had were the facts that had to do with the murders—they had nothing on suspects, clues or anything at all. Dr. Layton was there, and he explained the cutting off of the heads; even some men Tyler knew to be long-timers looked a little pasty and green as they listened. Lance would be starting the second autopsy today and would soon know more. Bob Green asked Tyler to talk about their theory that Perry Knowlton might still be alive, as they knew for a fact that Archibald Lemming was dead.

Someone asked how the man could have been hiding for years and suddenly come out to commit such heinous acts. At this point, Craig asked Kieran to come forward and offer what insight she could. Tyler saw that Kieran must speak to various groups of law enforcement often; she was prepared and calm.

"As you all know, serial killers only stop when they're forced to stop. A trigger of some kind—death of a loved one, work failure, financial loss, or other traumatic losses usually start a killer off. Sometimes it's just an escalation, and it's sad but true, children who torture animals often grow up to be the next generation's serial killers. Perry Knowlton had been incarcerated for the murders of eight women in upstate New York. He and Archibald Lemming met in prison. For all intents and purposes, it appeared that Archibald killed Perry—it wouldn't have been against his nature, and he killed men and women alike. But the two might have had some kind of honor among killers—Perry Knowlton started the fight that got both men into the medical complex from which they managed to escape."

"But that doesn't answer where he's been all these years," an officer said.

"Possibly locked up."

"Fingerprints!" another agent reminded her.

"He might have been in a hospital or mental facility, or had a physical issue causing him to lie low. Or he might have been killing other places."

"Did you forget the killings at that haunted house years ago?" another officer asked, his tone derisive.

Tyler started to move forward again. He was surprised to see that Sarah had moved up to the front of the crowd, and she looked to Kieran and said, "May I?"

On Kieran's nod, Sarah took a deep breath and spoke.

"I'll never forget that. I was there. With my friends. And we survived because my cousin had been taught to watch people—because people, in general, can be cruel. My uncle taught my cousin to carefully observe his surroundings and the individuals nearby. That night, he saw Archibald Lemming at the theme park before he went into the Cemetery Mansion. Lemming was alone when Davey saw him then—of course, that scenario fits if Knowlton is alive or dead.

"After Hannah Levine was murdered, I started researching everything that happened surrounding the escape. Nothing proves beyond a doubt that Perry Knowlton is dead. Also...there are over two hundred thousand unsolved homicides on the books right now in the US alone. Hannah was found in the water, so he might have been disposing of his victims in a way in which they weren't found."

There was silence around the room. Tyler was pretty sure everyone there was thinking about the one who had gotten away—their one case they couldn't crack. And it wasn't something that made them feel good.

"Thank you!" Detective Green said, moving in. "Now, get out there, officers. This killer is not going to become an 'unknown' statistic!"

"One of the police spokesmen has been briefed on what we do and don't want out for public knowledge," Craig said quietly to Tyler. "He'll handle the press conference. We can get on to the autopsy—and then over to Suzie Cornwall's building. She wasn't working. She was a patient in a clinical trial, quite seriously ill, or so her landlord told the police. The odd thing is..."

"What?" Tyler asked.

"We have a picture of her—when she was living. She really did resemble the photos we've seen of Suzie Cornwall Avery—at first glance, they might have been the same person."

Tyler was quiet for a minute. He hadn't seen Suzie in a very long time, but human nature didn't change. Suzie had always been a good, sweet soul, with a high sense of social responsibility. It wasn't going to make her feel any better, knowing that while a woman had been killed because she happened to have been given the same name at birth, that poor woman had been ill.

The stakes were high; Sarah was right. The killer was out to find those who had been there that fateful night a decade ago at the Cemetery Mansion. The night Archibald Lemming had been killed.

Revenge?

Just a sick mind?

Whichever didn't really matter. They were in danger.

"Sarah...do we bring her?"

"No, I figured she'd be comfortable with Kieran, and I have an agent staying with them at Finnegan's. They'll be fine. Trust me—if this bastard is after Sarah, he'll know by now she's with Kieran. But in my line, if there's a threat, we shoot to kill."

"I'm getting more and more worried about the others. Especially Davey."

Craig looked at him while Sarah and Kieran walked across the room to join them.

"What about this," Craig suggested. "I can have Davey and Renee brought into the city. We have an amazing safe house—easy to guard. It also has escape routes in the event the officers on duty should be killed, automatic alarms in case of a perceived danger... And my boss, Director Egan, is huge on preventing bad things. He'll want them there."

"Really?" Sarah whispered. "That leaves only Sean

and Suzie, and Suzie is so terrified by what happened that she's about ready to be institutionalized!"

"They can be brought there, too. It's big. I think there are actually three separate bedrooms."

"How long can we keep them there—or keep guards on them?" Tyler asked.

"This isn't going to take long," Sarah said softly. "You will catch him soon, or…" She paused and looked at them unhappily. "Or we'll all be dead. All of us who were in the Cemetery Mansion."

IN TYLER'S MIND, Dr. Lance Layton looked more like a mad scientist than ever. His white hair was going everywhere, half of it standing straight up on his head. He was thoughtful and energetic. "I have all kinds of tests going on. Here's the thing—poor lady was not long for the world. Poor thing! She was undergoing a new kind of cancer treatment—meant she didn't lose her hair to chemo. She had liver cancer that had spread just about through her body. Death might have been a mercy, if it hadn't been so…"

He stopped speaking. "Well, small mercy. She wouldn't have been terrified or in pain long, but would have bled out within a matter of seconds. That's something that we can truthfully tell her loved ones."

The woman had been going to die, anyway, a slow, painful death. He hoped that would help Suzie live with herself.

The police photographer, Alex Morrison, was standing by quietly. Layton looked over at him. "You're—you're getting enough?"

"I am. But the head, yes, we need a few more angles on the head."

"Right," Layton said. "Thankfully, the powers that be

are concerned enough on this case to keep everyone on it working together—it's harder when you have different techs and photographers and detectives. Well, I mean, not really for me. Other than that I have to repeat my findings, though some just prefer written reports, anyway, and a written report..."

"I'm not in your way?" Morrison asked.

"No, not at all," Craig assured him.

Morrison nodded to them both and began his work.

"Thank you, Morrison. All right, down to it."

He began to drone on. Tyler listened, mentally discarding the findings that meant nothing to their investigation.

But then Dr. Layton got to the stomach contents. "Here's what's interesting. Now our first victim, Hannah Levine, had eaten hours before her death. Miss Cornwall had eaten far more recently. Both had enjoyed some prime steaks. I don't know how much that helps you, but they may have dined at the same restaurant. I know that the city is laden with steak houses."

"Interesting—a possible lead," Tyler said. "And then again, maybe they just both enjoyed steak."

Morrison, working over by the stainless steel tray that held Suzie Cornwall's head, cleared his throat. "I think I have everything we might possibly need," he said.

He looked a little flushed. Tyler certainly understood. The head no longer really resembled anything human. It hadn't been on display long, but the sun, the elements and bugs—and the violence of being chopped off—had done their share of damage. The flesh was white, red, bruised and swollen.

"Thank you, Morrison," Layton said.

"I'm sure you've been thorough," Craig said, nodding to the photographer. "I know they want to have a decent sketch out by tomorrow. The photos we found of her on social media just aren't very good. If we use them along with the images you have, an artist can come up with something that will work well in the newspapers."

"Right," Morrison said grimly. "They're going to put an image out, correct? Ask for help?"

"That's been the decision, yes," Craig told him.

The photographer nodded at them all and left quickly.

Layton continued his analysis.

They listened awhile longer, looking at the body the whole time. To his credit, even Layton, long accustomed to being the voice of the dead, seemed deeply disturbed by the remains of the murdered woman.

Then it was time to try to find out how, when and where this Suzie had met her killer.

"Oh, lord!" Sarah said.

Kieran, who had been busy with her computer, looked up.

Sarah was at her own laptop, working in Kieran's office at the psychiatric offices of Fuller and Miro. She'd intended to be busy with her current novel, *Revenge of the Martian Waspmen*, but just hadn't been able to concentrate on her distant world.

"What is it?" Kieran asked.

"I finally keyed in the right words that led me to the right sites that led me to more sites. I've found so many unsolved and bizarre murders…"

"Show me!"

Kieran walked around her desk to stand behind Sarah.

Sarah pointed and spoke softly. "This one—up in Sleepy Hollow, and chalked up to it being Sleepy Hollow. 'Headless corpse found in ravine.' Then, here. 'Hudson Valley—help needed in the murder of local bank teller,' and, when you read further, you discover that she was found in two pieces—head on a tree branch, torso in the river. Then here's another in southern Connecticut—'Skull discovered off I-95, no sign of the body.'"

"There are probably more. I'm sure Craig has his tech guy working on it," Kieran mused. She sat again. "The guy's got to be living here somewhere. Somehow. But how? He'd need a credit check to rent an apartment. He'd need to make money somehow. And he'd have to pull all this off—and manage to look like one of the crowd."

"Is that so hard in New York City?" Sarah asked. "I mean, think about it. In New York, whatever you do, don't make eye contact. We walk by dozens of down-and-outers on the streets and in the subway. A few years back, a newspaper writer did an experiment and gave one dollar to each person with a cup or a hat just on the streets. Within a mile radius, she'd given away two hundred dollars. He could have begged on the street. He could have done a dozen things. He could have robbed people—without actually killing them. No lost wallets are ever found. We're a city of tremendous wealth and the American dream, but when that fails…"

"It's a good theory," Kieran said. "We'll talk to Craig. Give me a minute!"

She disappeared and then returned to her office with Drs. Fuller and Miro in tow.

Fuller was maybe fifty, tall and extremely good-looking.

Miro was tiny, older and still attractive, with dark curly hair, a pert little gamine's face and an incredible energy that seemed to emit from her.

"Show them what you just showed me," Kieran said.

And so Sarah did. And when she was done, Fuller said, "I think you've found something. Sad to say, but in history, many people have gotten away with crimes for years. And if these killings are associated, he was careful to commit his murders in different places."

"But all close to the central point—New York City," Miro put in.

"I believe my esteemed partner and I are in agreement on this," Fuller said. "This could all be the work of one man. And," he said, pointing at Sarah's computer screen, "this is old. Dates back almost ten years. This could have been Perry Knowlton's first kill after the massacre in Cemetery Mansion."

Sarah felt a sense of panic welling in her; she wasn't afraid for herself—well, she was, of course—but she was terrified for Davey.

She looked at Kieran. "Can you make sure that my aunt and Davey are safe?"

"Absolutely," Kieran promised. "And I'll tell Craig that my good doctors have weighed in. We need to follow up on your theory. I'm not sure how, but we need to move in that direction."

EVERYONE WAS SAFE, and Sarah was extremely grateful.

"We had a cop at the house, or just outside the house, and of course I brought out coffee," Aunt Renee told Sarah. "I have to admit, I've been trying not to panic. This is…this isn't coincidence. This is terrible. If Hannah was a target, and then…seems they killed the wrong Suzie, but she was a target, and if I was to lose you and Davey, oh, my God, I'd just want to be dead myself. I can't believe this. It isn't fair. Of course, I do know," she added drily, "that life isn't fair, but still, you all survived such terror…"

Sarah gave her a big hug. Then Suzie and Sean hugged Renee, and then Davey, as their FBI guards stood back silently, letting the reunion go on.

A young woman with the leanest body Sarah had ever seen—she wondered if she even had 1 percent body fat!—came forward then. "Pizza is on its way," she said cheerfully. "We don't have any delivery here. An agent always acquires food. The Bureau has control of the entire building, with sham businesses and residences—used as office space, we're careful with taxpayer dollars!—but we want you to be relaxed enough to…well, to exist as normally as possible under the circumstances. I'm Special Agent Lawrence."

She indicated a tall man nearer the door. "That's Special Agent Parton. We're your inside crew for the moment and we work twelve-hour shifts. Our apartments are in this building—we're always on call. Tonight, however, you'll have fresh agents—nice and wide-awake, that is. The doorman and the registrar downstairs are agents, and there are two agents in the hall at all times. If you will all get together and draw up a grocery list, we'll see to getting what you need. The kitchen is there—" she pointed to the left of the front door "—and the central bath is there." She pointed to the right. "One of us will always be at that table by the door, while the other might be with you. In the very unlikely event that every agent between the entry and you is brought down, there is a dumbwaiter in the back that is really an elevator. Naturally, our engineers have worked with it—nothing manual, no pulleys or cranks. You hit a button, the door closes and it takes you down. It can't be opened on the ground level from the outside—it can only be opened from the inside once you're down there. Same button, huge and red. You can't miss it."

"This is wonderful. Thank you!" Sarah said softly.

"Catching the bad guys is our job—along with keep-

ing the good guys alive!" Special Agent Lawrence said.
"Let me show you to your rooms," she added.

The living room or parlor boasted a dual area—a TV
and chair grouping to the right and a little conclave of
chairs to the left. They were led down a hallway.

The bedrooms were sparse, offering just beds and
dressers and small closets.

"The best place I've ever seen!" Aunt Renee said.

"This one? Can I have this one?" Davey asked, looking into one of the rooms.

They were really all the same. There had to be something slightly different for Davey to want it.

There were no windows. No way for a sniper to have
a chance; no way for an outsider to see who was inside.

"Davey, whatever room you want!" Suzie said.

Davey grinned.

"What's special about it?" Sarah asked him.

"The closet is painted blue. 'Haint' blue, like they told
us when my dad took me on a ghost tour in Key West.
Haint blue keeps bad things away."

"Excellent," Sarah told him.

"I'll go next to Davey," Aunt Renee said.

"And we'll be across the hall," Sean agreed. "And
Sarah—"

"I won't be staying. I'm going with Tyler."

Renee protested, "Oh, Sarah! The two of you should
both be here—"

"Try telling a military man he needs extra protection!"
Sarah said lightly. "I swear, we'll be fine."

"You're staying with Tyler?" Sean asked her. "Have
you been seeing each other again? Last I heard, he was
out of the military and living in Boston."

"He came because of Hannah. We'll see this through,"
she said.

She heard Tyler's voice; he had arrived at the safe house. It had, she realized, gotten late. She knew he and Craig had been going to the autopsy and then to interview the building owner and whatever friends—or even acquaintances—they could find of Suzie Cornwall's, to try to trace her steps before she was taken by her killer.

"Excuse me," Sarah murmured and hurried out. He and Craig had arrived together.

She gazed at him anxiously. She didn't ask any questions; they were all in her eyes.

Tyler nodded, looking over her head, and she realized that Special Agent Lawrence, Renee, Davey, Suzie and Sean had all followed her out.

"Suzie," he said softly, "this can't make it better, I know, but the Suzie who was killed was already dying a horrible death."

"What?" she asked.

"Cancer—it had riddled her body."

"Anything else?" Sarah asked.

"We went to her building and to the hospital. No one could tell us anything. She was likable, she kept to herself. She was polite and courteous, and I'm sure we would have all liked her very much. But even her doctor said that the experimental drugs weren't having the desired effect. She was going to die a slow and horrible death."

"Poor woman, to suffer all that, and then…"

"Dr. Layton, the medical examiner, said she died quickly," Tyler said.

They were all silent. It was impossible not to wonder which would be worse—a slow and horrible death as her body decayed around her, or the horror of having her throat slit, her head sawed from her body.

"It's my fault," Suzie whispered.

"No. It's the fault of a sick and wretched killer, and

don't think anything else," Tyler said firmly. Again there was silence. Not even the agents in the room seemed to breathe.

"So," Tyler said. "We think that Perry Knowlton might still be alive. We're going to try to relive that night—together, all of us except for Hannah, of course. Try to remember what we saw in that haunted house—and if any of us might have seen Perry Knowlton."

"Might have seen him?" Sean said, confusion in his voice. "We didn't know what he looked like. Not then. I mean, later, there were pictures of him in the papers and on TV and all, but… I sure as hell didn't see him in Cemetery Mansion."

"Let's go through it. We came through at different times. Let's see what we all remember."

"It will actually be good for you all—from everything I understand from my police shrink friends, including the shrinks Kieran works with," Craig said. "And where is she, by the way?"

"She's with your partner, Mike, at Finnegan's," Special Agent Lawrence said.

"She's not a target, and Mike would die before anyone touched a hair on her head," Craig said. "Shall we?" He indicated the sitting area.

Sean and Suzie, holding hands, chose the little settee. Renee sat on one of the wingback chairs, and Tyler and Craig sat across from them. One chair was left, though there was room on the settee. "Sarah, sit," Davey said. "Sit, please."

She smiled and sat. Davey settled by her side on the floor, curling his legs beneath him.

"Davey," Tyler said, "let's start with you. You knew there was something bad going on. And I'm sorry. I know you've been through this before."

"I saw him. The bad man. Archibald Lemming," Davey said. "But I didn't know his name. My dad warned me about men like him."

"But your dad wasn't with you, whispering in your ear or anything?" Craig asked.

Davey gave him a weary look. "My dad is dead."

"Of course," Craig said, "and I'm so sorry."

"He said he would always be with me in all the good things he taught me," Davey said. "So I watch for bad people. He was bad. I saw him go in Cemetery Mansion."

"And that's why you didn't want to go in," Tyler said. He smiled at Davey. "And you warned us, but we were foolish, and we didn't listen."

"I was okay once I had my Martian Gamma Sword!" Davey said, perking up. He leaned back and looked up at Sarah. "And it was good, right?"

"It was excellent. You were a hero."

"Which is why the bad guy wants to kill me now," Davey said pragmatically.

Sarah set her hand on his shoulder.

Tyler told him, "Don't worry. We will never let that happen. So, Davey and Sarah stayed out, while Suzie, Sean, Hannah and I went in. There were people ahead of us, but the theme park was letting only a few go in at a time, so while there were people ahead and people behind, we were still more or less on our own."

"There were motion-activated animatronic characters everywhere," Suzie said. "I remember that."

"I remember when we were going in, the 'hostess' character stationed there—a French maid, I think—was acting strangely." Tyler went on. "I don't think she knew anything then, but I'm sure she felt as if something was odd. Maybe she was bright enough to have a premonition of some kind—maybe someone was late or early or had gone in or hadn't gone in. She seemed strange. Which, of course, would have been normal, since it was a haunted house."

"I remember that, too," Sean said. "As a high school senior I couldn't admit it, but...yeah, I was scared. But you know, we were part of the football team back then. We couldn't be cowards."

Suzie was nodding. "Honestly? I think—even though we were assholes about Davey not wanting to go in—I think we were a little unnerved from the get-go. Then there was the massive character in the music room. Very tall, and blond. That automaton, or whatever. Scared the hell out of me."

"What?" Sarah asked. "An automaton?"

"You couldn't have missed it," Suzie said. "Seriously, it was tall. Over six feet. It was creepy. Really freaked me out."

Sarah frowned. "You know, we talked to the cops, we talked to each other...and still, sometimes, it's like I remember new things. Maybe even my nightmares, I'm not sure. Honestly, I know we were almost running from the start, but when Davey and I came through, there was no character. There were no figures in the music room. Who could have moved an automaton in that kind of time? Especially a big one?"

Tyler leaned forward. "I remember it clearly—I remember how it scared Suzie horribly. It was definitely there."

"And when Davey and I came through, there was definitely not a character there," Sarah said.

"He was sitting at the piano," Suzie insisted.

"Not when we came through," Sarah said.

"Maybe it..."

"What? Just disappeared?" Sean asked her.

"But—I was so sure it was an automaton! It—it talked to me!" Suzie said. "Oh, my God! He saw me that night. He saw my face clearly. And yet…he killed another woman." Suzie stared at Tyler and Craig hopefully. "Was it possibly accidental? Was she old, was she…different… was she…not like me?"

"I'm sorry, Suzie. She wasn't your twin, but…"

"But he saw me over a decade ago. People change," Suzie said harshly. She sighed. "Okay, fine, so much for that theory. He meant to kill me. To behead me. To saw my head off!"

She started to sob. Sean pulled her close.

"Don't cry, Suzie," Davey said. "He wants to kill all of us. And he's a terrible person. None of it is your fault."

"Poor Hannah…but could it be? Could it really be?" Suzie whispered.

"Him," Davey said somberly.

They all looked at him. He had propped his elbows on his knees, folded his hands and rested his chin upon his knuckles. He looked like an all-seeing wise man.

"Him, the other killer, the bad guy," Davey said. He shook his head. "Yes, I think he was the other bad guy. If you saw him. He was gone when Sarah and I came through. He was gone, because he knew. The one guy— Archibald Lemming. He was meant to die. But his friend, the one everyone thought was dead—he meant to live. He was there that night, but he got away. It would have been easy. Everyone was screaming and running. Yes. It is him, right? He killed Hannah. And he's still out there, right? He's the one who is trying to kill all of us."

There was silence.

Then Tyler told Davey, "But you knew, Davey. You saved us then. And you know now, and so you're going to help us all save ourselves now." He smiled. "Because your dad taught you to be smart. He taught you to know people, which is something we who don't have Down syndrome don't always do."

Davey smiled back at him.

"Mom is good, too. Dad taught her to be a little bit Down syndrome."

Renee smiled and nodded. "Yep. I'm a little bit Down syndrome, thanks to your dad. He was a very good man."

Davey straightened proudly.

Tyler turned and looked at Craig. "I think that must be it—the character who was there, and then wasn't. Archibald Lemming didn't kill Perry Knowlton. I think maybe Lemming had a death wish—but he wanted to go out with a bang. Lemming had some kind of insider info about escaping through the infirmary. They killed personnel to escape, but even then they had to have timing information and all. So, say that Knowlton was the brains behind the escape. And then they found Haunted Hysteria. What a heaven on earth for someone who wanted blood and terror!"

"And all these years," Suzie said, "he's been just watching? Waiting? Is that possible?"

Sarah said softly, "We think he has been busy. Yes, he's been in New York City. This is theory, of course. But we've done some research. We think he's still been murdering people. He just takes little jaunts out of the city to kill."

"Oh, my God!" Suzie said.

"But now," Tyler said, "he's killing here. Right in the city."

"Revenge," Sarah said.

"But…he lived!" Suzie protested.

"Yes, but he might have idolized Lemming. And while he's a killer, and he's been killing, this is different. He's been imitating Lemming, but not making a huge display out of his crimes. But now…who knows? Maybe he was careful, but then saw Hannah on the street or something. Maybe he was just biding his time. But the thing is, now…"

"Now?" Suzie breathed.

Sarah looked at Tyler. "And now we have to have our justice—before he gets his revenge!"

Chapter Six

The safe house wasn't far from Finnegan's, making it simple to leave and head to Broadway and the pub. Kieran had gone there to help out, which she often did when she was anxious and waiting for Craig.

But by the time Sarah and Tyler reached Finnegan's, it had grown quiet and Kieran was back in the office. Declan, Kevin and Danny, Sarah had learned, had become accustomed to having their office turned into a conference room for Craig and Kieran when something other than inventory and payroll needed to be attended to.

An undercover agent, someone who worked with Craig, was sitting at the bar, watching the crowd while sipping a Kaliber, Guinness's entry on the nonalcoholic side of beer.

He greeted them with a friendly nod when they arrived. Declan, behind the bar, cheerfully sent them to the office. Kieran was at the desk.

"Everyone is good—safe?" Kieran asked as they entered and took up chairs in front of the desk.

"Safe and sound," Sarah said. "I'm just so glad Davey is there now. I have a feeling that Perry Knowlton must know Davey was the key to ending everything that night."

"Maybe not," Tyler said. "He didn't try for Davey first."

"No, he went for Hannah, who, sad to say, was an easy target. She wouldn't have recognized him, but maybe he recognized her. And she would have been an easy first mark because...because she would see men. She was working as a hooker," Sarah said sadly.

"And that makes sense—go for the easiest victim first," Kieran said, nodding.

"And we think we have a lead, though where it can take us, I don't know," Tyler said.

Craig went on to explain what they'd discussed.

"And no one really saw him, right? What he really looked like?" asked Kieran.

"I never saw him at all, and neither did Davey. We think he was pretending to be an automaton in the music room. From what they said, he scared Suzie half to death when they went through. But there was no such person— or automaton—by the time Davey and I arrived. He could have run out already—or he could have gone through any one of half a dozen emergency exits."

"But his picture was in the papers, on the web and TV screens, right?" Kieran asked.

"Yes, of course," Tyler said. "I did see him. He was very distinctive. Tall, at least my height. And lean. With a long face with sharp cheekbones and jaw."

"Well, at least not a medium height—someone who blends in with the crowd. But there are a lot of men over six feet in New York City," Craig said.

"Maybe you should be staying at the safe house," Kieran said thoughtfully.

"No," Sarah said.

"Well, Tyler, too—he's one of you," Kieran pointed out.

Tyler shook his head. "I think Sarah and I will be all right. If he comes for one of us, it's going to be when we're alone. He isn't going to come to a hotel room. He doesn't kill with a gun, but with a knife. I have a gun. And it's always best to bring a gun to a knife fight. As long as you're steady, the gun is going to win every time."

"And we should have something to work with soon enough," said Craig. He looked at Sarah and nodded an acknowledgment. "Sarah had it right, we think, from the beginning. We found no less than ten unsolved murders that had to do with total or near decapitation, ranging from Westchester County—Hudson Valley and the Sleepy Hollow area, as Sarah found—to Connecticut and New Jersey. Regional police are sending us everything they have on those killings. We'll be able to go over them tomorrow. But most importantly, our tech department has entered the last known picture of Perry Knowlton into the computer. Tomorrow, we'll be starting off the day with images of what Perry Knowlton might look like now, and we're putting out pictures of Hannah and Suzie. Hopefully, someone might come forward, having seen them somewhere. Our appeal to the public will contain a subtle warning, of course. No one is safe while this man is at work."

"We should call it a night," Kieran said. "And get started again in the morning. I have a court appearance at nine, so I'll be out part of the day. Sarah, you should hang at the safe house during that time."

Sarah knew she probably should. That fear did live within her somewhere.

But she was going to be with Tyler.

She smiled. "I'll be safe," she promised.

Everyone stood. Out in the bar and dining area, they said good-night to Declan, the only one of Kieran's siblings still working.

Tyler and Sarah were silent as they drove to the hotel.

The valet took the car; the hotel lobby was quiet. There was no one in the elevator with them.

"You think we're really safe here?"

"I think I'll shoot first and ask questions later," Tyler said.

She smiled.

"You should think about going to the safe house," he told her quietly. "It's one thing for me to take chances with my life, but... I'm not so sure you should have that kind of faith in me."

"I have ultimate faith in you."

That night, she didn't have to join him in the shower. The door was barely closed, his gun and holster were barely laid by the bed before he had her in his arms, before they were both busy grasping at one another's clothing and dropping it to a pile on the floor. His kisses had become pure fire, heated, demanding, like a liquid blaze that seemed to engulf her limbs and everything in between. She returned his hunger ravenously, anxious to be flush with him, to feel his flesh with every inch of her own, feel the vital life beneath that skin, muscle, bone, heartbeat, breath...

He pressed her down to the bed and made love to her with those hot liquid kisses...all down the length of her body. The world faded away in a sea of pure sensation. She crawled atop him, kissing, touching, loving, as if she would never have enough.

And then they were together, he was in her, and the sensation was so keen she could barely keep from crying out, alerting the world to their whereabouts and exactly what they were doing.

She bit her lip, soaring on a wave of sheer ecstasy. All that lay between them seemed to burst with a show of light before her eyes, a field of stars and color. Then she drifted into the incredibly sweet sensation of climax as it swept over her and shook her with a flow of little shudders and spasms. And then they were still, with the incredible sense of warmth and comfort and ease, her just lying beside him.

She felt she should speak; she didn't want to. They'd been this close once before, when life had been all but Utopia.

But everything had changed. He'd said that she'd left him—but he had been the one to walk away. Move away. Start a completely new life.

He pulled her close to him.

She thought he might speak.

He did not. He just held her, his lips brushing her forehead as they lay there.

She stared into the darkness for a long time, not sleeping.

There was sound. The slightest sound in the hallway.

Tyler was out of bed, his Smith and Wesson in his hands, before she could really register the noise. He went to the door. And then he came back, returning the gun to the side of the bed. Sliding in beside her, he told her, "Two girls in 708 returning from a night at the bar. They're trying to be quiet—kind of surprising one of them hasn't knocked the other over yet!"

She smiled. This time, when he pulled her close, they made love again.

And then she did drift to sleep.

She thought she would dream of sandy beaches, a warm sun and a balmy breeze—and Tyler at her side.

Instead, she dreamed of a tall dark man lurking in the shadows, watching her. She was back in Cemetery Mansion, racing after Davey, trying to stop him. And she was in the music room, with no one else there, and it seemed no matter how fast she ran, she couldn't reach the dining room, couldn't find Davey, couldn't get out. And though she couldn't really see him, she knew that he was there. The tall dark man.

Watching her.

Calculating when it would be her turn.

TYLER HAD NEVER needed much sleep, and he was glad of it. At just about six in the morning, he woke; at his side, Sarah was twisting and turning.

He whispered to her, pulling her closer to him, not wanting to wake her, but not wanting her to suffer through whatever was going on in her dreams—or nightmares. He wanted to ease whatever plagued her, even while he marveled at being with her once again. Her body was so smooth and sleek, curved upon the snow-white sheets. Her hair had always been a sunny shade of gold, and it fell around her like a mantle.

"Sarah," he said gently.

Her eyes opened. For a moment, they were wide and frightened—just for a moment. And then she saw his face, and she smiled and flushed.

"Nightmare," she murmured.

"So I gathered. About?"

"Cemetery Mansion," she said softly. "You know, sometimes it takes me a few minutes to remember what I had for lunch the day before—but I remember everything about that awful night."

"So do I."

"Do you ever...dream?"

"I've had some dreadful nightmares, yeah, for sure."

She sighed. "I'm glad to hear it. I mean—I'm not glad you have nightmares. I'm glad I'm not the only one. I guess that's not really very nice, either!"

"You're human."

She stared at him for a moment, blue eyes still very wide, but her expression grim. "Human. So is this killer. He's human—and he's done these things!"

Tyler was silent a minute. Then he told her, "There's something wrong with people like Archibald Lemming and Perry Knowlton. You know that—you've been around Kieran enough. When they get to such a point, it's a fine distinction between psychopaths or sociopaths— whatever wiring they have in their heads, it's not normal. In a sense, they've lost all their sense of humanity. The normal person is heartsick to hear about an earthquake that killed hundreds, but this killer would want the pictures. He would relish the death and destruction. He would wish that it had been his handiwork."

She shook her head. "I can't feel sorry for him. He's sick, but after what he's done to people…that kind of sickness doesn't draw any sympathy from me. I guess it should, but it doesn't."

"The thing is…even if he were to finish this bit of revenge—"

"You mean, kill all of us."

"Even if he were to finish, he wouldn't stop. It's impossible to know now if he did commit any or all of the unsolved crimes you and the FBI found. It's impossible to know if he was gearing up, practicing for this—or if, in his warped mind, he realized that he should take his desire to kill and turn it into revenge."

"He's got to be stopped!" she whispered.

"He's careful. Hannah was an easy target. He found Suzie Cornwall—the wrong Suzie Cornwall—and lured her off alone easily enough. But now we're onto him. And he'll figure that out. I don't think he intends to take any chances, so we have to keep the others at the safe house and be incredibly alert and aware ourselves."

He heard his phone buzzing—it was time to be up and moving.

He reached for his cell. He wasn't surprised the caller was Craig.

"The pictures are about to go out."

"That's good."

"Yes, but you have to know something."

"What is that?"

He heard a bit of commotion. The next thing he knew, Craig was gone and Kieran was on the phone.

"Tyler! He's been at Finnegan's. This man…this man who appears to be Perry Knowlton…he's been at Finnegan's several times. I'm not there all the time so I don't really know, but… I've seen him! I've seen him at least three times!"

IT WAS EARLY and that meant there was no problem for Declan to open the pub just for friends and family. His siblings along with his fiancée, Mary Kathleen, and Craig, Tyler and Sarah sat around two tables that they'd pushed together, drinking coffee.

Sarah made sure Tyler was introduced to Kevin, Kieran's twin—the one brother he'd not met yet. Kevin couldn't stay long; he was shooting a "Why I Love New York" commercial for the tourist board at ten.

"We shouldn't have asked you to come in," Tyler said. "Nice to meet you—and I'm sorry."

"It's all right. Declan called me as soon as he received the message from Craig with the police computer rendering of Perry Knowlton. I never waited on him, but I know I've seen the bastard in here."

"It's frightening—and interesting. Because if you recognize him, hopefully others will, too," Tyler said.

Craig had printouts of the composite lying on the table. He told them, "Perry Knowlton is forty-three years old now. He started his killing binge at the age of twenty-nine, and was convicted of five murders and incarcerated by the time he was thirty-one."

Tyler picked up the account. "In prison, he met Archibald Lemming, and they probably compared their methods for finding their victims—and for killing them."

"And," Kieran continued, "they would remember their crimes. They were probably thrilled to have someone to tell, trying to one-up each other all the time. They liked to enjoy their memories over and over again—just as others would enjoy talking about their vacation to Italy, or a day at a beautiful beach."

Declan tapped the image of Perry Knowlton that lay on the table. "A few times before—and then less than two weeks ago—he was at the end of the bar. He ordered whiskey, neat. He was polite and even seemed to be charming those around him. Easy, level voice."

"You're sure it was him?" Tyler asked.

"I'd bet a hell of a lot on it," Declan said.

"And I'm damned sure, too," Kevin said.

"He was at a table, maybe a month ago," Mary Kathleen told them all. "And he was quite amicable, very nice, complimented the potato soup and the shepherd's pie."

"I served him when he was hanging around with a number of the regulars," Danny said. "He had them all laughing."

"The all-around guy-next-door," Kieran murmured. "Historically, there have been several truly charismatic serial killers, the poster boy being Ted Bundy. He worked for a suicide crisis center, for God's sake, with Anne

Rule—long before he was infamous for his crimes and she was famous for her books. But he wasn't the only one. I don't know that everyone would have fallen for Charles Manson, but he knew how to collect the young and disenfranchised. Andrew Cunanan—Versace's killer—was supposedly intelligent and affable. Paul John Knowles was known as the 'Casanova Killer.' The list can go on, but…"

"A charming, bright, handsome psychopath," Sarah murmured. "Great."

"But he's been exposed now," Tyler reminded her. "Someone knows him. Someone has seen him and knows his habits."

"Oh, aye, and sure!" Mary Kathleen said. "He likes good shepherd's pie, tips well enough and has lovely laughing green eyes. Ah, but how they must look when—" She broke off, shivering. "Horrible. Don't just shoot him. Skin him alive, saw him to pieces!" she said passionately.

Sarah set her hand on Mary Kathleen's. "But that's what makes the difference between us…" she said. "We wouldn't do those things to another human being. Although I understand completely what you're saying. I was there. The idea that killers find a little torture themselves does have its appeal."

"Do any of you remember the first time you saw him—and the last time?" Tyler asked.

"The first time…" Declan mused.

"Last October!" Mary Kathleen said. "Oh, I do remember—because I had to leave early that day. Me niece was coming over from Dublin. He offered to pay his check quickly."

"That was nearly five months ago," Kieran murmured.

"Do you think he's been looking for Sarah all that time?" Kevin asked.

"How would he have known that she worked here at all?" Declan murmured.

"He might have found her by accident. He might have seen her one day and followed her... It's a huge city, but we all know that sometimes it can be a very small world. And it's easy to discover personal details on social media," Tyler said.

"My address was never out anywhere!" Sarah said firmly.

"Of course not," Declan said. "But you might have written something about the pub. And that brought him here."

"Maybe," she murmured.

"He must have figured out after the first month or so that she wasn't working here anymore," Declan commented flatly. "But..."

Craig's phone rang and he excused himself.

"He thought that she'd come back," Tyler said. "He knew you worked here at some time or another, Sarah. And when was the last time anyone saw him?"

"Like I said," Declan told him. "Ten days to two weeks ago. Sorry I can't be more definite."

"He knows some things, but obviously not enough," Kieran said, looking at Sarah. "He didn't know Suzie wasn't using Cornwall anymore—he didn't know she and Sean Avery were married. He tries to find what he's looking for, but he hasn't the resources he'd surely love to have. That means we've got an edge on him," she added softly.

"Director Egan called," Declan told them. He was, Sarah knew, Craig's direct boss. "He says he'll keep Josh McCormack in here, watching over us and the pub, during opening hours. We are licensed to have a gun, which is behind the bar. But only the family has access."

"Oh! If something were to happen to someone in the pub, or to Finnegan's... I'm so sorry I seem to have brought this on you!" Sarah said.

"You didn't," Declan said. "We're tough. We'll manage, as we always have."

"Sláinte!" Mary Kathleen said, raising her coffee cup.

Smiles went around; coffee mugs were lifted in cheers.

Craig returned to the table. "Tyler, there's been a break in the case. The bartender at Time and Time Again also recognized Perry Knowlton from the composite. I think we should talk to him again."

"Ready when you are," Tyler said, standing. He looked down at Sarah.

"Hell, no," she said. "I'm not staying anywhere. I'm coming with you."

WHEN THEY REACHED the bar in the theater district, Detective Bob Green and his photographer, Alex Morrison, were already there.

Tyler almost ran into Morrison. "Hey, you all made it," the man said, watching him curiously. "There are no security cameras here, so they want pictures of the bar and the entry. Seems our fellow Knowlton liked to hang around here a lot. He flirted with Hannah—sorry, you can talk to the bartender yourselves. I'll get on with it."

He seemed to be taking pictures of all aspects of the bar.

The place was still closed; it was ten thirty and Tyler imagined it opened by eleven or eleven thirty. They needed the time alone with Luke, the bartender.

Luke was already talking to Detective Green, who was seated on one of the bar stools. He saw Sarah coming and smiled and waved—obviously a bit taken with her. That was good; she had said she could be helpful, and though Tyler really wanted her safely far away from the action, she was useful. So far, she'd actually garnered far more info than he had, just by being friendly and curious, and he was supposedly the investigator.

Luke greeted them all and offered them coffee.

For once, Tyler thought he'd been coffee'd out.

"I should have been able to meet you wherever," Luke said. "I don't usually work days, but…the other bartender quit. She saw the picture and she just quit. That guy's been in here lots. He was teasing and flirting with Hannah the night…the night she…the night she was murdered. But can it really be him? He seems really decent. Nice—he tips big, unlike a hell of a lot of people around here. Are you sure that it's him?"

"We're sure we need to find him," Tyler said.

"Have you seen him since Hannah was killed?" Sarah asked.

"Oh, yes."

"Yes?" Tyler asked.

"Hell, he was in here last night! And, I mean, until the news this morning, I had no clue. No clue at all. I was nice, he was nice. Oh, God, he's good-looking, you know. Flirtatious. He talked to so many girls. I just hope…oh, God! I hope none of them turn up dead!"

"We're hoping that, too," Craig said.

Detective Bob Green looked at Craig. "You guys are handling the safe house. We'll see to a watch on this place."

"He won't come back here now," Sarah said.

"Well, he's pretty cocky," Luke said.

Sarah shook his head. "He didn't think that we'd know it was him—but now he knows we're looking for him, thanks to the picture we released to the press. I think he'll lie low for a while. But hey, sure—keep an eye on the bar."

"We don't have a hell of a lot else," Green said.

"She's right, though."

Tyler swung around. It was the photographer, Alex, who had spoken, and he was now coming up to join them. He flushed and said, "Hey, I'm with the forensic unit—civilian. Not a cop. But I've taken a hell of a lot of photos, and…well, here. Here's some of what I got at the park the other day. The park where Suzie Cornwall was found. If you look…"

He held his camera forward, twisting it around so that they could gather close and see the images right-side up.

"We're looking at the body of Suzie Cornwall in situ," Green said.

"Yes, yes, but I just realized what else I have here— studying it all. Let me enlarge it for you… Look at the people," Alex said. He clicked a side button; the image honed in on the crowd, growing larger.

And there he was.

Perry Knowlton, aged just as the computer suggested he would age.

Tall, with a headful of blond hair. Lean face, rugged chin, broad, high brow. Lean, long physique. Tall, yes, standing next to a rabbi with a tall hat—and a guy who looked like a lumberjack. He almost blended in with the crowd.

"He does come back to the scene of the crime," Sarah murmured.

"He's been everywhere!" Alex murmured. "He's been here. God knows, the man might have been in the city since the Cemetery Mansion massacre."

"You remember the massacre?" Sarah asked him.

"Anyone who was in the city at the time remembers it," Detective Green said.

"Some more than others," Tyler said, studying Alex. "Were you at the theme park?"

"Yeah. Oh, yeah, I was already there—when I was called in to work for the local unit that night! I was still so raw—I'd made it into the academy, but one time when I was sitting around sketching to pass the time, a colleague told me they were short in the forensic department. My curiosity was tweaked, and I figured I could always come back and finish the academy. I never did, but…anyway. I wasn't making any kind of big bucks, if you know what I mean, so I was moonlighting, too. Working part-time for the amusement company. That night, I was working as a float—you know, I was sent wherever they were missing an employee or actor. That night I was a ticket taker, not far from where the Cemetery Mansion had been erected. I can't believe I was there—that I might have seen the creepy bastard go running by me—as he escaped. I just remember the blood and the screams and the people who were so terrified, running, running, running…" He stopped, shaking his head. "Hell, I'd give my eyeteeth to help in catching this bastard, so anything—anything at all I can do to help, I'm there. I'm going to go back over the pictures we took of the crime scene when we found Hannah Levine…you know, um, both places where they found her…head and torso."

"Interesting," Tyler said. "Maybe you can find some kind of a distinguishing something about him that will give us a clue as to where he's been living—he has to be in the city somewhere."

"He wears black in these pictures," Alex commented. "A black coat."

"He wears a black coat when he's in here, too," said

Luke. He cleared his throat. "Do you think he will come back here? I mean, I should be okay, right? He's going after women."

Alex Morrison was flicking through his digital pictures. Tyler reached for the camera.

He'd just recently been taking shots of the place. The large, etched mirror behind the bar; the old wooden stools; the rather shabby booths out on the floor; and the tables there. He had taken pictures of the tables inside and of the outside of the establishment.

A large canopy awning hung down over the front of the building, though it hadn't become a warm enough spring yet for patrons to want to sit outside. Or even have a window open.

But Alex Morrison had taken pictures outside, of the streets leading east and west of the bar. He had caught other buildings in his shots.

And he'd caught a number of pedestrians.

Tyler studied the pictures. He felt Sarah's hand on his shoulder; she was looking over at them, as well.

Mostly, it appeared to be Manhattan's daily business crowd—rushing here, there, trying to get to work on time.

People were in line at the coffee shop toward the corner.

A woman had paused to adjust her shoe.

Tyler glanced up at Alex Morrison. He was probably just in his early to midthirties now.

Tyler vaguely remembered him as the photographer back then, but they hadn't had any real contact at the time. But Morrison had been decent, straightforward, yet gentle due to their ages.

However, not as brave or passionate as he seemed to be now.

His photos were good. He had an eye for focus and detail.

"Touch here, and you can enlarge wherever you want," Alex told them.

"Thanks."

"Go back a few," Sarah said. "There's a really great long shot. It brings in the street, going toward the Times Square area."

Tyler flicked back.

And at first, he saw nothing unusual.

No details at all. And then he paused.

There was a woman in the road. The street wasn't closed to traffic, but she was jaywalking and in the middle of the road as cars went by her.

All around her, neon lights blazed—even in the morning.

The pictures hadn't been taken an hour ago. Some had just been taken as Alex had entered the bar.

Tyler touched the screen as Alex had shown him. The image enlarged.

She was wearing a white dress, white coat and low white pumps. She had a bobbed platinum haircut—like Marilyn Monroe.

He could see that, compared to other people walking in the vicinity, she was tall. Really tall.

"She…" Green murmured.

"Oh, Lord!" Sarah said.

"What is it?" Alex Morrison asked them, frowning as he turned the viewing screen back toward himself.

"She is a he," Tyler said quietly. "She is Perry Knowlton. When did you snap that?"

"That's…that's one of the last images I took—maybe ten minutes ago."

Tyler was up and heading out before the others could blink.

No.

She was a he, and the "he" was Perry Knowlton.

And he was out there, close.

Closer than they had ever imagined.

Chapter Seven

Sarah sat tensely on her bar stool.

Tyler had raced out; Craig rose, but hesitated.

"Go on—one of us should go, too, and hell, you're younger than I am, if you're going to be running around!" Detective Green said. "I'll stick here. Alex is with me."

Then Craig was out the door.

"He won't be there anymore," Alex said dismally.

"It hasn't been much time. And he's a tall man in drag. They have a chance at finding him," Detective Green said.

Alex shrugged; it was apparent he sincerely doubted that.

"He's picked up new talents," Sarah said.

"What do you mean?" Alex asked.

"I've been reading a lot about him. Loner. Had an alcoholic, abusive father, but I really wonder what that might have meant. He was very young when he was apparently discovered cutting up little creatures in the park. And then…"

"So, what new habit?" Alex asked.

She smiled. "I guess he learned at Cemetery Mansion about costumes. There was nothing in his earlier history about him dressing up to perform any of his atrocities—

or even to go and view the fruit of his labor. Nothing about wearing women's clothes."

As she spoke, her phone rang. It was Tyler. Her heart leaped with a bit of hope that he'd called to tell her they'd taken Perry Knowlton down.

Really, too much to hope.

"He's not on the street, but we're not ready to give up," he said. "I'm going to ask Detective Green to get you to the safe house. You can spend a little time with Davey and everyone."

She bit her lip. She didn't really want to go; she liked working with him and Craig—questioning people, listening.

But she couldn't keep Detective Green sitting here all day on a bar stool.

And she knew it was unsafe for her to stay alone.

"Sarah, is that all right?"

"Of course," she said. She handed the phone to Bob Green.

She heard Tyler's voice speaking, and then Green told him, "I'm going to get some men on the street, as well, but…we know now Perry Knowlton is capable of being a changeling. He could be anything and anywhere by now."

Sarah could hear Tyler's answer. "But that's just it— we are aware now. That makes a difference."

"I'll see Sarah to the safe house. More officers will be out immediately—I'll join the manhunt when I've made sure Sarah is with the others."

He hung up and handed the phone back to her. "I'll get you there now, in my car."

"You're going to leave already?" Luke asked, looking unnerved. "Someone needs to be… Am I safe?"

"He's on the run. He won't come back here," Green replied.

Luke swallowed. He looked at Sarah and said, "Um, come visit some other time, huh? We're not usually such a bad place. I'm…"

The detective had already risen. Luke was actually looking a little ashen, and Green clamped a hand on his shoulder. "You're okay. I will have a patrolman on his way here. You're going to be okay."

PERRY KNOWLTON WAS tall and blond and had ice-cold dark green eyes.

Which really meant nothing now. Eye color could easily be changed with contacts. Hair color was as mercurial as the tide.

He couldn't change his height.

They started where Alex Morrison's digital images had last shown him.

Craig took the right side of the street.

Tyler took the left.

He entered a popular chain dress store. A number of shoppers were about, but he quickly saw the cashier's booth toward the middle front of the store.

"I'm looking for a woman, very tall, platinum hair, in a white dress," he told the young clerk. "Have you seen her?"

"Oh, yes! Your friend came in just a few minutes ago. She's trying on maxi dresses. I helped her find a size."

Tyler smiled. "She's still here?"

"Dressing rooms are at the back."

"Thanks!"

Tyler hurried to the rear of the store. There was a row of fitting rooms, five in all. Only one was in use; he looked at the foot-long gap at the bottom of the doors.

Someone was standing in a pool of white.

The white dress?

He drew his gun and kicked open the door.

A middle-aged woman, quite tall, with a fine-featured face, stared at him in shock.

"I'm so sorry. Oh, Lord, I'm so sorry—I'm after a killer," he said. Hell. That sounded lame; he was just so damned desperate to catch Perry Knowlton.

He was so damned close.

Now he might well be close to a lawsuit.

"I'm so sorry, honestly."

She smiled at him. "Sure, honey. But hey, you're the best excitement I've had in some time. I guess that was a gun in your pocket! Hi—I'm Myrna!"

THE FBI SAFE HOUSE was really pretty incredible. Entering was like going into one of the hundreds of skyscrapers in the city. They had to check in at the door; the girl at the desk appeared to be a clerk. She was, of course, an agent.

And Sarah was aware that the man reading the paper in the lobby was an agent, as well.

They were given permission to go up. Bob Green paused to have a conversation with the agents on duty at the door. There was complete local-federal trust on this case with those involved, but there was still a conversation.

Aunt Renee was in the kitchen; she'd invited their FBI guardians to her very special French toast brunch that morning, and she was busy cooking away when Sarah arrived. "All done soon! Suzie and Sean are going to join us." She smiled lamely. "It's not so bad here," she said softly. "I wish you were hiding out with us, but... I do understand. As long as you're careful. Davey... Davey is in his room. He's doing okay. He understands."

"Of course he understands," Sarah said. She smiled. "He usually does. He plays us when he chooses!"

"I guess so," Renee said softly. "Sometimes, I wonder if I'm overprotective. But the thing is, there are cruel people in this world. Well, as we know, there are heinous crazy killers, but… I mean in general. Grade school children can be especially unkind, making fun of anyone who is even a little bit different. And there are adults… they may not even be bad people, but…they don't know how to manage. Honestly, sometimes neighbors will walk on the other side of the street if they see me coming with Davey. I need to let some of the good in. Odd thing to realize when you're hiding from a killer, huh?"

Renee smiled ruefully at her. Sarah bit her lip lightly and nodded.

She was overprotective of Davey, too. And, yes, the world could be cruel—besides sadistic killers. But it wasn't a bad thing to protect those you loved.

Maybe it was just bad to assume others didn't love them equally.

"I'll go see how he's doing," Sarah said.

"He loves you, you know."

"And I love him."

"He loves Tyler, too."

"And I know that Tyler loves him."

Renee nodded. "Tyler does love him. He really does."

"Breakfast smells divine," she said. "Is it still breakfast?"

"Brunch!" Renee said.

"Yes, brunch sounds great. There's enough?"

"You know me. There's enough to feed a small army!"

Sarah left her aunt and headed to the room Davey had chosen. She tapped on the door and he told her to come in.

He was sitting cross-legged on the bed, with his computer.

He looked up at her. "I miss my girlfriend!"

"Of course you do. She's a sweetie. But I'll bet she understands."

He nodded. Then he said, "No, not really." He shrugged. "Her mama doesn't even want me talking to her now. Maybe…"

"It will be all right. You called Tyler in, and my friends, Kieran and her boyfriend, FBI Special Agent Frasier—they're all working on it. It's going to be okay."

"It will be okay," Davey said with certainty. He reached behind his back. "I still have my Martian Gamma Sword!"

"Of course. You made it okay once."

He nodded. "You just have to know."

"We didn't see him, Davey. The others saw him. Perry Knowlton, I mean."

"But he knows. I'm so sorry he hurt Hannah. And the other woman."

Sarah was sure no one had described the grisly murders to Davey. Of course, there were TVs just about everywhere.

And Davey loved his computer.

"No more haunted houses," Davey said.

"No. Definitely not."

"Bad people use whatever they can."

"That's true, Davey." Sarah kissed his cheek. "We can all learn from you!" she said softly. "You have that Martian Gamma Sword ready. You just never know."

"You just never know," he agreed.

"What are you doing on the computer? Have you been able to talk to Megan through My Special Friends or any other site?"

He nodded, a silly little smile teasing his face. "Yeah, I talk to Megan. I love Megan."

"I'm very happy for you."

"It's forever kind of love," he said sagely.

"That's nice."

"Like Tyler," he said.

"Oh, Davey. I know...what you did was very manipulative, and yet..."

He grinned. "I think that's better than devious!"

"Well, anyway, it's good that Tyler is here. For now. But please don't count on forever, okay?"

But Davey shook his head. "Forever," he said.

"I think I'm going to go and see if I can help your mom. I got here in time for brunch. Cool, huh? You like being here, right?"

"I'm okay," he said.

He was looking at his screen again. She didn't know if he was trying to communicate with his girlfriend or if he was studying movies—looking up actors and directors.

At the doorway she paused, glancing back at him. "Tell Megan I said hi, okay?"

"I will. I'm not talking to Megan right now."

"What are you doing?"

He looked up at her, a strange expression on his face.

It wasn't mean. Davey didn't have a mean bone in his body, and in a thousand years he would never purposely hurt anyone.

"Davey?"

He smiled then, his charming little smile. "Research!" he told her.

"On?"

"On...whatever I find!"

"Ah. Well, breakfast—I mean brunch!—soon."

She left him and headed out to help her aunt. She wondered, even then, if she shouldn't check out just what he was researching on his computer.

IF HE'D BEEN going to burst in on someone other than the killer he was trying to catch, Tyler had at least chosen the right person.

Myrna was Myrna Simpson, and it just happened that she was the wife of retired police lieutenant August Simpson. While Tyler had awkwardly tried to explain himself, she waved a hand. "Please, don't. I'm fine. No big deal."

"Thank you!" he told her and turned to walk away.

"I believe I know who you're after!" she said. "Tall woman—actually an inch or so taller than me. Very blonde. A drag queen? Or…just someone in costume?"

"Someone in costume, we believe."

"Too bad. He'd make a great drag queen," Myrna said. "He bought some things. I saw a few of them, but the clerk can probably give you a real list."

"The clerk said he was still in the dressing room."

"Two clerks are working. Mindy and Fiona. Come on."

It turned out he'd spoken to Mindy. Fiona hadn't been at the desk. She was then, though, a woman older than Mindy and the manager on duty.

She was suspicious at first. Tyler gave her his ID, but she remained skeptical, even with Myrna Simpson trying to help out.

Luckily, Craig Frasier walked in. His FBI identification made Fiona much more agreeable.

She gave them a list of the purchases made by Perry Knowlton.

"Is she here often?" Tyler asked.

"Often enough, I guess. Every couple of weeks," Mindy said.

When they finished, Tyler thanked Myrna again. "You really had no reason to trust me, but you did."

She laughed. "I told you. I've been married to a cop—now retired—for thirty-three years. I learned a lot about sizing up people with first impressions. Though, to be honest, I mistook your man, Perry Knowlton, for someone with a few issues—not a serial killer. If I see him anywhere, I'll be in touch."

IN THE KITCHEN of the safe house, Aunt Renee had just about finished her special French toast.

"Want to set the table?" she asked Sarah.

After she set places, Sarah headed over to Special Agents Lawrence and Parton, who were by the door, diligently on guard.

"Brunch!" she told them.

"I'll stay. You eat first," Parton told Lawrence.

"You sure?"

"Just make sure you leave me some!" He glanced at his watch, then looked up and grinned at Sarah. "Sorry. We've been on a long shift. Reinforcements are coming in an hour or so."

"You've been great—and you must have my aunt's special French toast. It's really the best!"

She went to get Davey, Suzie and Sean from their rooms.

Of everyone, Suzie was looking the worst for wear. Frazzled.

"I'm just hoping I have a job when we get out of all this," she said. Then she winced. "Of course, I'm hoping to have a life first, and then a job."

Sean was dealing with it better. "I'm seeing it as a very strange vacation. She's usually too tired for sex!" he whispered to Sarah.

"Sean!"

"I'm trying to get a lot of sex in!"

"Sean!" Suzie repeated in horror.

"Oh, come on…hey, I'll bet you Sarah is getting a little, too!"

"French toast, at the moment!" Sarah said. She turned to head out; Suzie and Sean followed her.

They gathered around the table. Special Agent Lawrence said they were free to address her by her first name—Winona. She was a ten-year vet with the force, they learned as they passed eggs, French toast and bacon around the table.

"Agent Parton—Cody—is a newbie, really. He's been with us about a year and a half. Thankfully, there's a constant stream of recruits. It's a busy world, you know."

So it seemed, Sarah thought.

"Tell me about your books," Winona Lawrence said, looking at her. "I admit to being a sci-fi geek!"

"She's working on alien bugs now!" Davey said excitedly.

He explained. Sarah was glad he was doing the talking when her phone rang. It was Tyler.

"You okay?"

"Everything is good here," she said. And she added, "The agents are great."

"Some are more personable than others, so Craig has told me. That makes them good at different things. Anyway, I'll be a while. I wanted to make sure you were okay. We've found out Perry Knowlton has most probably dressed as a woman often. We have a list of his most recent purchases."

"But you weren't able to find him?"

"No." He hesitated. "There's some kind of a new lead. We don't really know what. Craig's director just called and asked him to come in. We have the image of Knowlton's latest appearance out with a number of patrol officers. They're still looking. I'll call back in when I know more."

"Okay, great. I'm fine here," Sarah assured him.

She hung up. Conversation had stopped. Everyone was looking at her.

"We're getting close, I believe!"

There was silence.

Then Special Agent Lawrence said, "Well! I can't wait to read your latest novel, Sarah! You have a wonderful fan club here."

Sarah smiled. And wished she could remember what they'd been talking about before Tyler's call.

She couldn't.

It didn't matter. She realized it was going to be a very long afternoon.

"DIRECTOR EGAN DIDN'T mention what arrived?" Tyler asked Craig.

"I just got a message from his assistant—come in as soon as possible," Craig said.

Tyler thought he could have stayed on the streets, searching, but he didn't think Knowlton was going to allow himself to be found that easily.

He was out there, though. And he was a chameleon. That made the situation even more frightening than before.

He'd made the decision to come with Craig. The FBI just might have something that could lead them to Perry Knowlton. The man had no known address. According to all official records, he didn't exist. He'd died a decade ago.

But he was breathing and in the flesh—and killing people—whether he was dead on record or not.

They reached the FBI offices and went through the security check required by everyone, agents included, and then headed up to the director's office. Egan's assistant sent them in.

Egan was on the phone, but he hung up, seeing that they'd arrived.

"We've had a message from the killer," he said. "It literally arrived ten minutes ago."

"We've received hundreds of messages from hundreds of 'killers,'" Craig said wearily. He looked at Tyler. "You'd be amazed by the number of people who want to say they're killers, or to confess to crimes they didn't commit."

"I think this one is real," Egan said. He glanced at Tyler. "It was actually addressed to you, as well as this office."

"And?" Tyler said.

"Apparently, Perry Knowlton wants to be a poet, too," Egan said. He tapped a paper that lay on his desk and slipped on his reading glasses. "Don't worry—this is a copy. The real deal is with forensics. Anyway, 'Six little children, perfect and dear, wanting the scare of their lives. One little boy, smarter than the rest, apparently felt like the hives. They went into the house, they cried there was a louse, and one fine man was gone. But now they pay the price today…six little children. One of them dead. Soon the rest will be covered in red.'"

"Six little children. Well, we weren't exactly little, but in a way, we were still children," Tyler said. "But he makes no mention of having killed the wrong Suzie Cornwall."

"He might not want to admit that he made a mistake," Craig said.

"Sounds like it might be legit," Egan said. "Naturally, we're testing everything, finding out about the paper and the typeface and all…and what came with it."

"What came with it?" Tyler asked.

"A C-1, I understand," Egan said. "According to doctors, there are seven cervical spine bones in a human being. The C-1 vertebra is closest to the skull. We received one—and we believe it might well have belonged to Hannah Levine. When a victim has been beheaded, the neck bones may well be crushed or... We're comparing DNA. But I do believe that we'll discover it belonged to Hannah."

"So now he's taunting the police. But we just put the images of Perry Knowlton out today—how did he know so quickly that we know who he is?" Craig wondered aloud.

"This arrived via bike messenger. I've emailed you the address for the service. I'll need you to look into it. You should get going," Egan said.

"Yes, sir. We need to inform Detective Green..." Craig said.

"Already done," Egan assured him.

They left the office.

THE MESSENGER SERVICE'S office was just north of Trinity Church, on Cedar Street.

The clerk behind the desk was pale. He was young and uncertain, with a pockmarked face and shaggy brown hair. "I know... I talked to a man from the FBI. I... I have a log, of course. I—I, oh, God! He didn't really say anything—just that the FBI had to know about a package! Was it a bomb? Did we handle a bomb?"

"It wasn't a bomb," Craig said. "What we need to know is who gave you the package to deliver?"

"Um..." The clerk fumbled with a roster on the counter. "Jacob Marley. He paid cash. It was a man...an old man, hunched over, crackling voice. Told me he didn't believe in those newfangled credit card things. He believed in cold, hard cash."

The clerk looked up at them. "Um, we still take cash."

"You're the one who received the package here?" Tyler asked.

"Yes, sir. Er, I should really see your credentials."

Craig flipped out his badge. The clerk swallowed hard.

"It was a transaction like dozens of others. People do still use cash. I mean every day, people use cash!"

"Did you notice where the man went?" Craig asked. "Or where he came from?"

The clerk shook his head. "It was a busy morning. But…there's a subway station just down the street." He tried to smile. "Don't think he'd use a newfangled thing like a car, huh? Then again… I don't know. But he didn't look like the kind of guy who'd be driving a car around the city. How old is the subway?" he wondered.

"Built in 1904," Tyler said briefly, wondering how he remembered the exact year. He'd actually seen a documentary on it, he recalled, and then impatiently pushed the history lesson aside. "But he was here not long ago, right?"

"About an hour ago…yeah!" He suddenly seemed proud of himself. "I have it on the roster!"

Craig started to say more; Tyler touched him on the shoulder.

"The subway," Tyler murmured. "There's no other way. He was just up by the theater district, and while we were going crazy running around and checking out the clothing store, he was on the subway headed here, changing his appearance. He left the package. And then he—then, hell, he went back to wherever it is he comes from."

"He's been in New York City a long time," Craig mused. "He knows the system."

"I'll bet that he more than knows it. Craig, long shot here, but he's had plenty of time to study it. I was watching a program on the roots of the subway and the progression through the years. We know he can leap quickly and know where he's going." Tyler paused and took a deep breath. "Long shot, like I said. I can't help but think that he really knows the subway and the history of it—knows it like the back of his hand. There are so many abandoned stations. We know that the homeless often find them in winter. Do you think it's possible he's living underground somewhere?"

Craig listened and then nodded slowly. "Underground New York. We just had a case that involved the deconsecrated church right behind Finnegan's. Yeah, the subway."

"We know that people do make use of the empty space—warm, and out of snow and sleet and all in winter. An abandoned station—that might even be lost to the history books?" Tyler suggested.

"Surely, in ten years, the man has needed to bathe. Needed running water. A way to eat and drink and sleep and—survive," Craig said.

Tyler shrugged. "I know I'm speculating, but it does work. Okay. My mom told me that once, when I was a kid and we were traveling on vacation, we wound up in Gettysburg and couldn't get a hotel room. So she and my dad parked the car in the lot of a big chain hotel—so we could slip in and use the bathrooms in the morning. Maybe our guy is doing the same thing. Not from a parking lot, but an abandoned station somewhere near several hotels...places he could slip in to use the facilities. Maybe hotels with gyms that have showers—he's evidently good at changing his image constantly. Wouldn't be hard for such a con to snatch a key and learn the identity of a paying guest."

"Possible," Craig said. "Hey, we went on theory. Theory has proved true. We'll head back to the office. In fact…" He pulled out his phone. "Mike should be in. I'll have him get started, pulling up all the spec sheets we'll need."

"Sounds good," Tyler said, and then he was quiet.

"What?" Craig asked, clicking off after speaking with his partner.

"That poem…it still bothers me."

"Because it was bad? Because it mentioned Davey and Sarah and the others?"

Tyler shook his head. "Because it didn't mention the Suzie Cornwall who is dead. He said 'one.' Made it sound as if he just killed one."

"Maybe he doesn't consider a mistake to be one of his kills."

"Maybe. Still…" Tyler shrugged. "You know, I can't help but want this bastard dead. By the same token, I want him alive. I want him answering questions."

"Well, we have to find him if we're going to take him in," Craig said pragmatically, "dead or alive."

SARAH WAS RESTLESS and didn't want to stay at the safe house any longer.

She wanted to be doing something.

Of course, she knew she'd be stupid to head out.

She did the dishes and played a Guess the Hollywood Star game with Davey—knowing full well he'd beat her soundly, and fairly.

Then Tyler called to bring her up to date—it seemed Perry Knowlton had sent a message and a bone to the FBI offices, taunting them.

She was glad when Kieran arrived with her brother Kevin. Due to Kieran's connections, she and Kevin had been given special dispensation to visit.

They sat together in one of the little chair groupings in

the living room area. Craig, of course, had informed Kieran what was going on, and she and Kevin had come to tell Sarah about one of the recent cases they had wound up working on—or rather, that Craig had worked on, and which had involved them. It had revolved around the deconsecrated church and a killer who'd left his victims "perfect" in death.

"The point is, he liked the underground." Kieran paused and looked at her brother. "He killed a young actress Kevin had been seeing."

"I'm lucky I was never charged with the murder," he said grimly.

"I think they're right. I think it's the only solution. This guy has been hiding underground and taking advantage of his obsession with dressing up and—so it seems—his ability to borrow other identities," Kieran said.

"It makes sense." Sarah added, "Tyler said they were going to find a place near hotels—somewhere he could use facilities when he needed them. He's probably a very adept thief—the kind who steals small-time and therefore is never apprehended."

"Quite possibly. Anyway, we think they're on the right track," Kieran said.

Tyler called again then. Sarah hastily told Kieran and Kevin it was him.

"They're at an abandoned station not far from here," she said when she'd hung up. "But so far nothing."

"They'll keep looking," Kieran assured her. "People have the images and they know."

Next, Craig called Kieran. Sarah saw her wince.

"What?" she asked when Kieran clicked off.

"Well, they're getting calls and leads," she said.

"That's good, right?"

"Yes, except it's hard to winnow through them. Apparently, someone even called in about Craig and Tyler. They're phoning in about every man over six feet in the city of New York!"

"Oh!" Sarah said.

"Don't worry, they'll keep working."

Davey peeked his head out. "Want to play a game?" he asked.

"Davey," Sarah murmured uncomfortably. "They're probably busy..."

"We'd love to play a game!" Kieran said.

And so they all played.

For once, Sarah won.

Davey was her teammate.

THE DAY WAS long and hard.

When eight o'clock came around, Tyler and Craig decided to wrap it up and start again in the morning.

They didn't want to be obvious about what they were doing; they didn't want Perry Knowlton to know they were actively searching underground for him.

They'd been provided with a really good map of the defunct stations—those that had existed years ago and were not in use now.

They needed more, Tyler thought. More to go on.

But shortly after eight, they returned to the safe house.

Sarah looked at Tyler anxiously. So did the others.

"We'll be starting up again in the morning," he assured them all. "We did take a step forward today. Another step tomorrow. We will catch the bastard."

He once again tried to get Sarah to stay at the safe house.

She absolutely refused.

He was, on the one hand, very glad.

Because there was nothing like getting back to the hotel room with her. There was nothing like apologizing, telling her he'd been underground, digging around in tunnels.

And then having her join him in the shower. Hot water sluicing over her breasts, her naked body next to his...

Touching, caressing.

Feeling her make love to him in return.

Falling hot and wet and breathless on the clean sheets in the cool air...

Being together, laughing, talking, not talking, being breathless...

Feeling the release of a tremendous climax.

And lying next to her as the little tremors of aftermath swept through him, allowing a sweet relief and tremendous satiation.

He loved her.

He always would.

And she loved him, too.

He just wondered if being so much in love could be enough.

Love was supposed to conquer all. But not if she pushed him away.

He'd think about that later.

The day had been long, but the night could be very sweet.

He allowed his fingers to play over the curve of her back, caress the soft, sleek flesh and then fall lower again, teasing...

She let out a soft, sweet sigh.

"What are you thinking?" he asked her quietly.

"I'm not thinking," she said.

He didn't press it. He just held her. And they lay silently together once again.

A bit later, she moved against him. She teased along his spine with her tongue. Her fingertips were like a breath over his flesh. Her arms wound around him, and he curled toward her and she continued to tease and play and seduce.

They made love again.

And then held one another.

He should have had nightmares. He did not. He slept deeply, sweetly.

And then his alarm went off.

It was morning again. Perry Knowlton was still out there.

And God alone might guess what he would do next.

Chapter Eight

"I wish I could go with you," Sarah told Tyler.

He hesitated. They were showered and dressed, ready to leave.

"I can be helpful—hey, the bartender at Time and Time Again liked me better than you."

He had to smile at that. "Yeah, so…most guys out there are going to like you better than me. And, yes, you have proved helpful."

He wasn't lying. She had been very useful. That didn't change the fact that her being in danger could compromise his—or Craig's—ability to work.

"You're just better at the safe house!" he told her gently.

"Time goes so slowly," she said. She brightened. "But actually, there were a few minutes yesterday when I almost had fun. Kieran and Kevin were by—we played one of Davey's games with him. It was great. Kevin acted out half of his clues for Kieran. We were laughing. I was so surprised they were willing to play."

"Why?"

"Well, they're busy, of course. They don't really have time to play Davey's games."

He was silent. There it was. Her insistence that only she could really be happy to play a silly game with Davey.

"What?" she murmured, sensing the change in him.

"You can be really full of yourself, you know."

She frowned, stepping away. "What?"

"Never mind. Let me get you to the safe house."

He stepped out; she followed, still frowning. "Tyler?"

"Let's go."

He got her out of the room and down to the car. Once they were in traffic, however, she pressed the point.

"What are you talking about?"

"Never mind. Now isn't the time to worry about it."

"When should I worry about it? When we're either dead or you're back in Boston?"

He stayed silent; traffic was heavy. She waited. When they reached the area of the safe house, she pushed again.

"Tyler, tell me what you're talking about."

"Davey," he said simply. "Who do you think you are, really? Other people like Davey, love Davey, and enjoy his company."

"I—I…" Sarah stuttered.

He saw one of the agents—Special Agent Lawrence—in front of the building. She waved at him, hurrying around to the driver's side of the car. "I'll take it for you—you can see Sarah safely up. It will be there…" She pointed to a garage entrance down the street. "Agent Frasier will be by for you in about ten minutes."

"Okay, thanks," Tyler said, getting out of the car. He walked around, but Sarah was already out and walking in ahead of him.

The agent at the desk nodded to them.

Sarah was moving fast; she got into the elevator first. He had to put his arm out to keep the door open.

He stepped in. She was staring straight ahead. He wasn't sure if she was furious or in shock.

"I told you it wasn't really the time."

She didn't reply. The elevator door opened on their

floor. She hurried ahead. At the door she stopped and turned and looked at him. "You're not being fair! Davey is like love personified. He doesn't have a mean bone in his body. Of course people…most people…love him!"

"Then let him enjoy them without you feeling you need to be a buffer."

"I—I don't!"

"You do. You push everyone away."

The door opened. Special Agent Preston was there. "Hey. Did you see Winona? She went down to take the car."

"Yes, we met her."

"Craig is on his way."

"I'm going right down," Tyler said.

Sarah was still staring at him. Now she looked really confused. And worried. Maybe she hadn't realized how overprotective she was—and how much she had doubted other people. Him.

"Go in!" he told her.

He started back toward the elevator. Sarah gasped suddenly, and he spun around—ready to draw on Special Agent Preston.

But the FBI agent just looked puzzled. And Sarah was suddenly running toward him. "Tyler!"

"Sarah, we can talk later," he said softly.

"No, no, no! Nothing to do with us…with Davey. The poem—the poem Perry Knowlton wrote. It was about Hannah, right—not Suzie Cornwall."

"It seemed to be about Hannah." He paused, frowning, wondering what she was thinking.

He'd memorized the poem, and spoke softly, repeating the words. "'Six little children, perfect and dear, wanting the scare of their lives. One little boy, smarter than the rest, apparently felt like the hives. They went into the house, they cried there was a louse, and one fine man was gone. But now they pay the price today…six little children. One of them dead. Soon the rest will be covered in red.'"

"Hannah. We know—from Luke, the bartender—that Perry Knowlton hung around the bar near Times Square. And he went to a dress shop there semiregularly… He seemed to watch Hannah easily enough. Maybe he ran into her by chance one time. He was able to become a woman quickly. And then get to the subway to gather and then deliver the package. Tyler, you need to be looking for something underground not far from the bar and the shop."

He smiled at her slowly. "That would make sense. You've got it, I think. Although…"

"What?"

"I didn't really see anything in that area. He was a regular at the bar, yes, so we looked, but… We'll have to look again."

"But you will look?" Sarah asked.

"Yes, of course."

He gave her a little salute. Then he continued on to the elevator.

"I WONDER WHAT we're costing the taxpayers," Suzie said dismally. She had just flicked the television off. They had seen the artist's sketch of Perry Knowlton one time too many.

Along with pictures of Suzie Cornwall.

The young woman had been ill, and the artist's rendering had allowed that to show.

But Suzie had turned white every time a picture of her came across the screen.

Sarah leaned forward. "Suzie, stop blaming yourself.

He's killed before. If we don't get him now, he'll kill again."

Special Agent Lawrence heard them talking and came forward, just a bit hesitantly. "Please! I know you won't stop, but you have to try to. It's not your fault, Suzie. It's not your parents' fault for naming you, or your dad for having that surname. It's the fault of a sick and pathetic and deplorable criminal mind. You have to accept that. If you don't, you will make yourself crazy."

"If I live to go crazy," Suzie muttered.

"You will live," Winona said, solid determination in her voice. She smiled, and then shrugged, sighing. "Okay, maybe I look a little worn, because I am. I need some sleep. But don't worry. We have replacements coming. Hey, Parton, who is coming on next?" she called.

Cody Parton was at the desk by the door. "Guzman and Walsh, so I've been told," he called.

"Ah, Walsh is a new guy. Guzman has been around forever and knows the ropes. Trust me, you'll be safe!" she said.

She smiled and walked away.

"People can say anything. I can even know it's true. But I can't help it. If that young woman's name hadn't been Suzie Cornwall, she'd be alive now," Suzie told Sarah softly.

"Maybe something worse was in store for her," Sarah said.

Suzie shrugged. "I wish I could think of something productive to do. It hasn't been that long, but I feel as if we've been cooped up forever."

Sean poked his head out of their bedroom. "Hey, guys, wanna watch a movie?" He shrugged. "They have all the movies we could possibly want. Reciprocation...or the cable company sucking up to the Feds, not sure which!"

"I guess so," Suzie said. "A comedy! Sarah, you coming?"

Sarah smiled. "No, I think I'll sit here and…plot."

"Alien bugs, huh? You're going to sit there and go crazy thinking," Suzie said.

Sarah offered her a weak smile. "Am I overprotective of Davey?" she asked.

Suzie hesitated. "Oh, Sarah! Sad to say, I haven't been around you that much lately, so I don't know if you are or not."

"Did I…in high school, was I overprotective?"

"Yes. Sometimes you had the right to be. We weren't cruel kids, but we could be careless. But…"

"But?"

"You really didn't have to be with Tyler and me. And others, of course. Davey has to make a few mistakes on his own, but he's smart. He can handle it. Your uncle did teach him to watch out for the bad guys."

Suzie grimaced and went on into the room with Sean. Sarah sighed, sitting there, torn between thinking about her own mistakes and the fact that they were hunting for a killer.

"You doing okay?" Winona walked back over to her.

She nodded. "Fine, thanks. It just seems…seems like this is taking a very long time."

"This? Long? I was with the Organized Crime Unit for a while—oh, my God! We gathered info for months and months and…um, but this is different."

Sarah smiled.

It wasn't all that different.

It could take time. A lot of time.

"I'm going off in a bit. Can you think of anything I can do for you?" Winona asked.

Sarah liked the woman, really liked her. She smiled and shook her head.

"When do we see you again?"

"Two days. I'll be back on for the next three after that, twelve hours a day!"

"No offense, but I hope we're not here that long. Though you've been very nice."

Winona smiled. "You guys have been easy. I think your aunt and Davey are watching a movie, too. I'll check on everyone before I leave. The new agents are due here soon. Fresh agents. You know what I mean! Replacements!"

Sarah nodded and let her go, leaning back. She closed her eyes, wishing she could sleep, wishing Tyler was there, wishing...

Just wishing that she wasn't so tense, and so alone, wondering if she had pushed people away...

If only she hadn't been so young, so afraid and so unsure. Unable to believe not only in Davey, but in herself.

THEY WERE BELOW the giant high-rises, great pillars of concrete, stone and steel that rose into the sky.

Once upon a time, the subway stop had been called the South Playwright Station. Back then, there had been no movies, and the station had actually been part of the Interborough Rapid Transit Company—one of the predecessors of the modern system.

In those days, the theater district had reigned supreme—there had been no movies. There had not been giant IMAX screens, 3-D, tablets, notepads, computers or any other such devices.

People had flocked here as one of the theater stations. Then a part of the subway had collapsed, and it had been closed off.

One of the city's engineers accompanied Craig and Tyler down to the station. The access was tricky; they had to bend over and crawl half of it. Broken brick lay with beautiful old tile; the station name was still mostly visible, all in tile that was now covered with the dust of decades that had passed without the station being used. The walls were covered in colorful but menacing graffiti from intrepid urban explorers and vandals. Tracks were intermittent, here and there.

The three men used high-powered flashlights as they went, moving cautiously.

"I don't know," Tyler murmured. "This seems a likely location, but how the hell could a tall man come and go, in all manner and mode of dress?"

"There could be another access," the engineer told them. "One that isn't on the maps. I did some digging. I believe there were a few entries in some of the old buildings—in the foyers or on the corners."

"Maybe," Craig said. "I don't think there's anything here, though."

"Wait, let's not head up yet. I think…there's something ahead," Tyler said.

"A door off to the side?" Craig murmured.

There was a door ahead, they discovered. An old maintenance door.

The three of them quickened their pace.

THE NEW CREW was coming on.

Agent Winona Lawrence impulsively gave Sarah a hug. "We really should move like professional machinery, but…come on, I want you to meet the new guys. One of them I've never met—the guy we were expecting called in sick. Oh, and you're going to have another female agent coming in tomorrow. Her name is Lucinda Rivera. She's super. You'll like her, too. But for now..."

The new agents were at the door. Guzman was older—maybe fifty. He had graying hair and heavy jowls, but a good smile when he met Sarah.

The other agent was younger—forty or forty-five, tall, with close-cropped dark hair, a large nose and dark eyes. She wondered if she had met him before, maybe with Kieran and Craig.

"Walsh called in sick," he told them. "I'm Adler. Jimmy Adler. Nice to meet you, Sarah."

"All right, then. We're out of here. Sleep!" Lawrence said.

"A beer!" Parton admitted.

"Parton," Guzman said softly.

"Hey..."

Sarah laughed. "Enjoy your beer, Special Agent Parton." He grinned. "Just say 'Goodbye, Cody!'"

"Goodbye, Cody!" she repeated.

Guzman took up a position by the door after locking it. "You can take the desk," he told Alder.

"Sure thing." The other agent complied.

They weren't going to be as friendly or as easygoing as Lawrence and Parton, Sarah decided. She went back to her chair in the little living room grouping. There were magazines on a table by the sofa. She picked up a *National Geographic* and started leafing through it. There was an article about a new discovery of underground tombs and mummies in the Sahara Desert. She tried to concentrate on the piece, loving the concept of extraterrestrials possibly creating some of the great works in Ancient Egypt. Aliens arriving on Earth thousands of years ago could lead to some great sci-fi ideas.

The agents were making occasional small talk with each other, but Sarah wasn't paying attention. She could block them out. Well, she could tell herself she was concentrating all she wanted.

All she could really do was sit tensely, wishing that Tyler would call.

She had been there awhile when she heard one of the doors click open slightly, and she looked up; Suzie was at her bedroom door, looking troubled.

Sean was right behind her. He beckoned to Sarah.

She went to the door and started to speak, but Sean caught her arm and whisked her in. "You have to talk Suzie down. She's having daydreams, nightmares."

"You weren't there!" she whispered to Sarah.

"I'm confused. I wasn't where?"

"You weren't with us when we first went into Cemetery Mansion. He talked to me…he talked. The thing in the room…the thing we think now might have been Perry Knowlton. He beckoned to me. He spoke… I told myself he was a robot, an automaton, whatever. I was so scared…"

"She's dreaming that she hears his voice," Sean said.

Sarah wasn't sure what, but something suddenly went off inside her.

Instinct?

Like an alarm bell louder than could be imagined.

"We've got to get out," she said. "Now. And fast. Move—move toward that dumbwaiter-slash-elevator they showed us on the first day. Move now. Fast, and silently. I'm getting Davey and my aunt Renee. Go. Go now."

They'd been expecting Agent Walsh.

Walsh had "called in sick."

Maybe she was crazy—maybe she and Suzie were both cabin-crazy, paranoid—justly so, but paranoid.

Maybe.

But maybe not.

THEY MOVED AS quickly as they dared over the rubble and through the dust they raised, to the door at the side of the tunnel.

"Careful," the engineer warned. "You guys want to make it, to keep on searching, right?" he asked cheerfully. "Of course, we could do this for days!"

"Let's hope not," Craig said.

The engineer shrugged. "It's okay by me. I like you guys!"

"Thanks," Tyler said.

Maybe they *were* wrong.

And maybe they were right, but they weren't looking in the right place. Besides tunnels, as Kieran had pointed out to Sarah, streets had been built on top of streets in New York City. Not to mention—as the Finnegan family had all known from a previous case—there were underground tombs scattered about, as well.

But logically, Tyler didn't think Perry Knowlton had been living in a tomb. Unless there was such a thing with easy access to the city streets.

Yet even as they reached the door, he couldn't help but remember the poem Knowlton had written and sent to the police with a bit of neck bone.

Six little children, perfect and dear, wanting the scare of their lives. One little boy, smarter than the rest, apparently felt like the hives. They went into the house, they cried there was a louse, and one fine man was gone. But now they pay the price today...six little children. One of them dead. Soon the rest will be covered in red.

He hadn't realized he'd spoken aloud. Craig stopped walking; Tyler nearly plowed into him.

"Poem still bothering you?" Craig asked. The engineer walked ahead of them.

"I don't know—I just think he would want to gloat over having killed two women so viciously," Tyler said.

"He is in revenge mode."

"Yes. Still, wouldn't he taunt us by saying, hey, and look what I did while I was trying to get the right people?"

"We need to catch him. Then we'll know."

"Wow, this is weird!" the engineer called back to them.

"What's that?"

"Door opens easy as if it had been greased yesterday!" And then he added a horrified "Holy crap!"

Tyler ran forward, Craig right with him.

The door opened to a little room lit by an electric lantern—a very modern electric lantern. There were boxes everywhere, an ice chest, Sterno…a mattress, pillows, blankets.

And in the middle of the floor, a man.

Stripped down to his underwear.

Blood streaked across his temple from a gaping head wound.

Craig was instantly down by his side. "Walsh, just met him the other day. He's got a pulse, slight… I'm pretty sure he was left for dead… His suit is…gone."

"You, sir! Stay with this man," Craig said. He was already trying his cell—and swearing when there was no signal.

"We've got to get to the safe house, have to send a warning. We have to get there!" Tyler said.

He wasn't sure he'd ever felt such a cold and deadly fear.

He was ready to rush back and crawl through the opening, ready to run all the way down Broadway. He was desperate to reach Sarah.

"There!" the engineer cried. "There's your entrance!"

And there it was. Across the little room was another door. Tyler rushed to it and threw it open. Stairs led up, and he took them to another door, then a hallway that twisted and turned.

At the end of the next hallway was a door that led to the foyer of a 1930s building. He burst out of it, with Craig behind him. He heard Craig dialing 9-1-1 for the man in the tunnel.

Tyler tried Sarah's number.

There was no answer.

DAVEY WAS PAYING ATTENTION. He wasn't watching his movie; he was at the door, ready when Sarah slipped across the hall as quietly as possible to open it. He brought a finger to his lips.

"What is it?" Renee asked.

"Shh, shh, shh, Davey is right!" Sarah told her. "Come with me. We have to get out of here."

"Get out of here?" Renee said, puzzled. "But we have FBI guards—"

"I think they've been compromised. If I'm wrong... we'll come right back up. But we're going to take the emergency exit. We have to get to the elevator—the escape dumbwaiter we were shown."

"Sarah, what has happened?"

"Nothing—yet. But please believe me—"

"I have my Martian Gamma Sword!" Davey said. And he did. He produced it, showing them that he was ready to fight.

"Please, I could be wrong, but if not, hurrying may be essential. Please, Aunt Renee!"

Renee still didn't appear to be happy. She looked out the door, down the hall to the living area.

Guzman and Adler seemed to be doing their jobs.

"Please!" Sarah said.

"Mom. Come!" Davey said. He looked at Sarah and said, "You know my mom. Really, sometimes she's a little Down syndrome, too. She concentrates, and you have to shake her up. You know that."

"Now!" Sarah said firmly.

She took her aunt's hand and led the way out. Renee grabbed Davey's arm. They headed silently out of the room and down the hall toward the little enclave where the dumbwaiter/elevator waited.

Of course, they'd never tried it.

Aunt Renee whispered that concern. "What if it doesn't work? What if five of us don't fit? What if the agents are furious?"

She'd barely voiced the question before they heard a thump.

Sarah stared back toward the door to the apartment.

Adler was standing over Guzman.

He still held the muzzle of an FBI Glock in his hand; he'd used the handle to cream the agent on the head.

"Go!" Sarah screamed as the man turned to look at them.

They ran.

"Hurry!" Sean beckoned from inside the elevator.

Sarah was still looking back as she ran. The others plowed into the elevator.

She stared right at the man. The thing. The monster the others had seen that night long ago—but she and Davey had not.

Because he'd already been out of the haunted house. Maybe he'd known that his fellow murderer was on a suicidal spree.

Now he looked right at her.

And he smiled.

He aimed the gun at her.

"Sarah!" Davey shouted.

She jumped into the contraption; they were on top of one another, like rats.

Sean hit the giant red Close Door button.

A shot went off.

The door shut just in time.

They heard the bullet strike...

"His voice! Oh, God, I knew that voice!" Suzie sobbed.

Yes! Thank God she had!

The elevator sped toward the ground floor, and Sarah prayed they could get out and get free and find help...

He didn't have just a knife anymore. Maybe, recently, he'd had a gun along with him as well for his murders. Maybe that was how he'd forced his victims to their murder sites.

Maybe...

"Oh, God, he's coming for us all!" Suzie cried.

ALL THE OFFICIAL cars and all the official power in the world couldn't really move New York City traffic.

Up and out of the tunnel, Tyler and Craig didn't even try it.

On the street level, Craig was able to reach Dispatch to request help; officers would be on the way.

But so would they—via the subway.

Miraculously, they were able to hit an express.

And off the subway, they ran.

Bursting into the foyer of the safe house, Tyler stopped at last.

The desk clerk was on his feet, hurrying toward them. "Agents are up there," he said. "Guzman was down. That man came in with Guzman...he had credentials. There was no reason to suspect... He walked right in. Right by me and the backup. I'm here, but everyone else is out there, on the street. We have people going through the rooms, but…"

"But what?" Tyler roared. He realized that Craig had spoken at the same time.

"They got out, the witnesses… We don't know exactly where now—they didn't come this way. They sensed something was wrong somehow, but…they're out on the street. We have men out there, but—"

Tyler didn't give a damn just how many men might be out on the street. He turned, followed by Craig.

"Hey!" the agent called to them. "Hey, this is important!"

Tyler barely paused.

"He's armed! He has a service Glock. He doesn't just have a knife—"

As the clerk spoke, they heard the explosive sound of a gun being fired.

SARAH HAD REMEMBERED the door would open only from their side—and only when she pushed the button.

She did so. They'd come out in an alley. If they didn't move quickly, they'd be trapped.

"Run! Go!" she commanded.

They tumbled out and began running. The good thing for them was the main door to the building was around the corner; Knowlton had to leave the building that way—his only choice. That gave them precious seconds to get out of the alley, get somewhere…hide!

She had Davey's hand. He was not the most agile person she knew; he wasn't necessarily fast when he ran. She was desperate to find a hiding place before they were seen.

"Davey!" Her aunt cried her son's name with anguish.

Sarah knew that she hated being even one second away from him when there was danger.

She paused, but her aunt, panting, looked at her desperately. "Take him! Take him, keep him safe!"

Sarah nodded. She tightened her grip on his hand and ran on.

Luckily, the street was thronging with people. She kept screaming for help.

They moved out of the way.

Some pulled out cell phones—she hoped they were dialing 9-1-1.

Gasping for air, Sarah soon felt she was reaching her limit.

Trinity was ahead of her.

She had Davey; she had to pray Aunt Renee and Sean and Suzie would run faster than she could with Davey. They could truly get away, would find a shop, a restaurant, anything! Duck in...

She was on the street, ready to run into the Trinity graveyard, when she heard someone shouting at her. She turned.

It was a police officer in uniform.

She drew Davey behind her. "He's after us! The killer is after us—Knowlton, the man who beheaded the two women...he's after us!"

"Now, now, miss!" the officer said. "Miss, I'm not sure what your problem is, but you're just going to have to try to calm down."

"My problem is that a killer is after us!"

"Is this some kind of a crazy game?" the cop demanded.

"No, dammit! Sorry, sorry, Officer, please, I'm begging you—listen to me. There is a killer—"

She broke off. The man who had claimed to be Special

Agent Adler—and was, beyond a doubt, Perry Knowlton—was now casually strolling toward them.

"Get over the fence. Hide in the graves!" she whispered to Davey.

"I won't leave you!" Davey said stubbornly.

"Do it!" she snapped.

To her relief, for once, he obeyed her.

And it was all right; Knowlton was just staring at her. Smiling still.

"Special Agent Adler, Officer, FBI," Knowlton said, ever so briefly flashing a badge. "And that woman is a dangerous psychopath!"

"He's going to shoot me," she told the police officer calmly.

"No, no, miss. He's FBI. Now, I don't know the truth here, but he'll talk to you and—"

Knowlton took aim and fired.

Sarah gasped as the officer went down before her. He was screaming in agony.

Not dead.

Knowlton might be good with a knife—he wasn't that great with a gun.

Sarah was dimly aware of the sound of dozens of screams; people were shouting, running, clearing the street.

And then Knowlton was looking right at her. He was a few feet away from her.

His stolen gun was aimed at her.

"You don't want to shoot me," she told him quietly.

He paused and smiled, clearly amused.

"I don't?"

"You don't like guns. You use them only to scare and bully people—when you have to. This may be the first time you're really using one."

"Sorry—I used guns we stole off the guards when Archie and I escaped."

"Still, you're not very good with a gun. You're much more adept with a knife. And I'm assuming you have one. You like to torture your victims, and that's much better accomplished with a knife."

"Don't worry—I'm carrying a knife. And," he added softly, "when I finish with you, I will find that cousin of yours. Oh, I read the papers, I saw the news! He was the hero, huh? Let's see if he dies like a hero. Oh, dear! Look around. A graveyard. How fitting!"

He smiled. Whether he liked a gun or not, he still had the Glock aimed at her.

"Drop it!" she heard someone say.

She smiled with relief. Sanity! Someone who realized that Knowlton wasn't the law—that he was a killer.

Someone…

Her turn to know a voice.

"Drop it!"

Knowlton stared at her. Smiled. Took careful aim— and then spun around to shoot at whoever was behind him.

A gun went off.

For a moment, it felt as if time had been suspended. As if the world had frozen—it was all a special effect in a movie, because, dear Lord, this couldn't be real. The killer, there, posed before her…

And then he fell.

She looked past him, her knees wobbling, something inside her desperately fighting to keep her standing, to keep her from passing out.

There, past the prone body of Perry Knowlton, was Tyler.

She stared at him for a moment.

And then she ran, and he was ready to take her into his arms. She knew she wasn't shot; she wasn't sure about him.

"Tyler, Tyler…"

"I'm fine. I'm fine, I'm fine," he assured her, holding her, smoothing back her hair. "Are you…?"

"Fine. I'm fine. He aimed at you, Tyler, he aimed at you. He—"

"I'm okay. We're okay," he said firmly.

She was aware that Craig was with them then, briefly checking on the two of them, then hurrying forward to hunker down by the body of the fallen killer.

Others were moving in.

Davey had crawled back over the fence. He raced to them.

Tyler pulled him close, as well.

"Group hug!" Davey said.

Sarah drew back, looking anxiously at Tyler. "Aunt Renee, Suzie, Sean…?"

"They're all right. They went into a clothing store. They're good. We're all alive. All of us… Guzman and Walsh are being rushed to the hospital, and—"

Sirens suddenly screamed.

Chaos seemed to be erupting with a flow of agents and police, crime scene tape—a flurry of activity.

But none of it mattered.

She was being held in Tyler's arms. And anything could happen around her. They had survived again. And this time…

She wouldn't just survive. She would live.

Chapter Nine

Sarah and Kieran Finnegan helped serve the table.

The pub wasn't so terribly busy. It was Wednesday afternoon and the after-work crowd had yet to come in.

Sarah hadn't worked in the pub for years, but Kieran seemed to know that helping with the simple task of supplying wine, beers—regular and nonalcoholic—and a Shirley Temple for Davey was busywork, and sometimes it helped.

They should have all been more relaxed.

Knowlton had been dead now for several days. All the paperwork was done. There had been a dozen interviews with all manner of law enforcement, and then with major broadcasters and newspaper journalists. The Perry Knowlton story was still holding reign over the internet, TV, and papers and magazines everywhere.

That day, however, had not been about Perry Knowlton for Sarah and her friends.

That afternoon, they had gathered to bury Hannah Levine. There had been tears of sorrow and regret; friendship was a terrible thing to lose. And as they'd gathered at the grave after services, Sarah was pretty sure they were all looking back over the years and wondering how the killings at Cemetery Mansion had cost so many their lives—and left behind survivors who were emotionally crippled. There was no way out of wondering how they had let Hannah down. Each individual alive was responsible for his or her own life—they knew that. But they also knew human relationships were priceless and, for most, essential for living.

Sarah had been named as Hannah's next of kin. She arranged for a really beautiful nondenominational ceremony. Hannah's dad had been Jewish, her mom a Methodist, but Sarah wasn't sure Hannah had adhered to either religion. Or any.

But she had been left in charge. And Sarah wanted very much to believe in God and goodness and a higher power. She thought the service was not religious, but spiritual. She guessed Hannah would have liked it.

After the funeral and burial, they gathered at Finnegan's. And just as they had felt lost before, they were all trying to tie up the last little skeins of confusion in their own minds.

"I wonder… I mean, when you were trying to find Knowlton, find out if he could be alive…you found so many other victims. How will…how will you make all that go together?" Sean asked, sipping his beer.

"Agents in my office will do what they can to find out what happened where and when," Craig said. "Most forensic work does take time. We were incredibly lucky— beyond lucky, considering Knowlton's sudden surge toward suicide in his determination to kill you all—that we did make the right calculations in following his movements."

"And we're lucky Sarah got us out!" Suzie said, lifting her glass of white wine to Sarah.

"You knew his voice. After ten years, you recognized his voice," she answered.

"And Davey was ready to move quickly!" Sean said.

"To Davey—our hero!" Tyler said.

They all lifted their glasses to Davey. He smiled and lifted his Shirley Temple. "To best friends forever!" he said, and then grinned. "And to Megan. I get to see my girlfriend tomorrow!"

Everyone laughed. He passed a picture of Megan around. They all assured him she was a pretty girl, and she was.

There was a stretch of silence around the table, and then Tyler spoke.

"I really wish we could have taken him alive," he said. "There was a lot we could have learned from him. I still want to know how the hell he broke in to the playground to be able to display the poor woman he killed, thinking she was our Suzie."

"I do, too," Craig said. "But since he was aiming at your heart, you had no choice but to fire. You know, he would have shot you—and then Sarah. And then he'd have gone for Davey and killed anyone else in his way—until he was stopped. Our agents are still in the hospital. Guzman might be out in a day or two. Luckily, Knowlton didn't really know how to kill someone with a knock on the head. Walsh—the fellow we found in the subway tunnel—will be another week or so. But his prognosis is good. Then there's the cop he shot on the street—he'll be in the hospital for a few weeks. Needs several surgeries. So, Tyler, yeah, you shot and killed him. You saved your own life—and probably others."

Sarah made a mental note to visit the agents and the police officer in the hospital. She hadn't done so yet.

"How did he find us?" Suzie wondered.

"He wasn't just good at hiding," Tyler said. "He excelled at being a people watcher. He was excellent at observation, something he learned—according to earlier notes we recently dug back up from the horror park murders—from the man he admired and all but worshipped, Archibald Lemming. The guards had said that Lemming loved to hold court—and Knowlton loved to listen and learn. Patience, Lemming had taught him, was a virtue. So Knowlton discovered the safe house—by lurking around in any number of his disguises and maybe by following one of us. He watched, and he found an agent he could take by surprise. He was adept at so many things, and he was able to bide his time and wait."

"And," Craig said, "we found out that he stole his 'Adler' FBI identification three years ago. The man did know how to wait and bide his time. He took Special Agent Walsh down for his plain blue suit—and to keep him from showing up at work. He called in sick on Walsh's phone, left him to die in the tunnel—after stealing his gun. Once you all escaped him and he was out on the street, I think he decided he'd kill until he was killed himself—but of course, we were the focus of the rage he's had brewing for the last decade."

They talked awhile longer; they enjoyed shepherd's pie.

Then Suzie and Sean prepared to leave, hugging everyone.

"We need to keep in touch this time," Suzie said. "I think… I think we're relieved and grateful—and sad. But…"

"But we will keep in touch—I've missed you, Suzie. Yes, we will be haunted by what happened to Hannah. But we'll stay friends this time. And I think it will help," Sarah assured her, hugging her tightly in return.

Sean shook hands with Tyler, then the two embraced. "Hey, Boston isn't that far, my friend. We have to all keep in touch," he said.

Tyler nodded. "Yes. Of course."

Sarah noted he didn't refute the fact that Boston wasn't far.

Her heart sank a little. He was returning to his old life; she would be returning to hers.

She thought of the nights they'd been together since Knowlton had died. They had been intense.

They hadn't talked yet. Not really talked. They had made plans for Hannah's funeral. They had answered any last-minute questions they could for the police and the FBI.

It had been easier just to be together.

Davey got up from the table. He was anxious to leave; Renee was taking him for a haircut so he could look his best when he saw Megan.

"I got a girlfriend!" he reminded them all.

Soon after, Tyler smiled at Sarah and asked her softly if she was ready to go.

She nodded.

They weren't staying at the hotel any longer. They went to her apartment on Reed Street.

When the door was closed, he pulled her into his arms and very tenderly kissed her lips.

And suddenly, all the things she wanted to say came tumbling out of her mouth. "I'm so sorry. I don't know why. I think I was always afraid…maybe I didn't want to be hurt myself, and so I tried to make sure Davey wasn't hurt. It seemed to be a way to cope. There are bad people out there…or sometimes, just rude and unkind people. I haven't been… I've been… I just knew how some people felt some of the time, and I love my aunt and Davey and my family, and… I…there was really no excuse. I never meant to push you away. I just didn't want others to feel they had to take on my responsibility—"

His finger fell on her lips. "Some people want part of your responsibility."

"Oh, I know that! And I should have had faith in Davey being sweet and wonderful in his own right, I just…"

To her astonishment, Tyler slipped down to his knees. He looked up at her, eyes bright, and pulled a small box from his pocket. He flicked it open, offering it to her.

"Sarah, I've loved you forever. I've loved you when I was with you and when I wasn't with you. When I was away, you interfered with everything I would try to do, because I could never get you out of my memory…my heart, my soul. Sarah, we've wasted a decade of life, and life, as we all know, is precious. So…will you marry me?"

She was speechless, and then she fell to her knees in turn and began to kiss him. And they both started to shed their clothing, there on the hardwood at the entry to the apartment. When they were halfway stripped, he suddenly laughed, stood and pulled her up. "Let's not celebrate with bruises!" he said. She laughed, too, and she was in his arms again.

Making love had always been amazing. That afternoon…

Every touch, breath and intimacy seemed deeper, more sensual, more erotic. More climatic.

He stroked her back. Rolled and kissed her shoulder.

"Hmm. I think we celebrated. But you haven't actually said yes!"

"Yes! Yes…yes…"

She punctuated every yes with a kiss.

"I can go anywhere. I mean, we are New Yorkers, but Boston is a great city," she said breathlessly. "I can and will go anywhere in the world with you. We can have a big wedding, we can elope, we can do anything at all.

None of it matters to me, except being with you, waking up with you, going to sleep with you…" She stopped, then straddled him with a grin. "My Lord! I could write romance again. Giant bugs—and romance!"

He laughed. He pulled her to him, and they talked and talked, and made love again.

No big wedding. They weren't going to wait that long. A small ceremony at Finnegan's, applauded by whomever might be there, with just Kieran and Craig and Suzie and Sean—and, of course, their families, including—very especially—Davey and Aunt Renee.

Sometime that night, very late that night, they finally slept.

SARAH FELT THAT she was walking on air. She'd called Kieran, who was at work at the offices of Fuller and Miro, but she could meet for lunch.

Relief was an amazing thing. Or maybe it was happiness. So much time wasted, and yet maybe not wasted. She and Tyler had both grown through the years.

And now…

Now they were together. And she was going to marry him. It wasn't even that marriage mattered so much to her—that she would wake up every morning next to Tyler did. That wherever they went, whatever they did, she could go to sleep with him at night.

She'd loved him as long as she could remember.

And now…

The morning had been good. She had worked on her latest manuscript; an Egyptian connection, not through Mars, but through a distant planet much like Earth. The people had been advanced, kind and intelligent, and very much like human beings. A war with a nearby hostile planet had kept them away, and a shift in the galaxies had closed the wormhole they had used to reach Earth. But archeologist and mathematician Riley Maxwell had been with an expedition that had found a tablet, and the tablet had told them about the "newcomers," the "gods," who had come down from space and taught them building and water usage. Soon after her discovery, she was visited by a newcomer to their group, Hank McMillan, and he had been just as anxious to destroy all that she had discovered. And as they worked together and came under attack by a group with strange and devastating weapons, she'd begun to fall in love…all the while discovering Hank was an ancient alien, trying to close all the doors before the still hostile and warlike tribe arrived to devastate Earth…

Of course, they solved it all and lived happily ever after. Her outline was complete!

At eleven thirty, she left her apartment, smiling as she headed toward Broadway to walk down to Finnegan's.

Her steps were light.

She forgot all about the fact that New Yorkers supposedly didn't make eye contact.

She smiled and, yes, people smiled back.

It was a beautiful day, chilly, but with a bright sun high in the sky.

She was surprised when a police car pulled up by the corner ahead of her. She heard her name being called and, frowning, she hurried forward.

Happiness could be its own enemy. She was immediately afraid something had happened to Tyler. Or that something was wrong somewhere. Davey! Her aunt!

She rushed over to the car. Alex Morrison was at the wheel, and he was smiling.

"Hey, I'm glad I found you so easily!"

"You were looking for me? You could have called."

"Well, this just all came about. Hop in. I'll take you to Tyler."

"Oh. Is he all right?" she asked anxiously.

"He's fine, he's fine. We're working on putting some pieces together. With other events, you know?" he said somberly. "Anyway, come on, I'll get you to him and Craig."

"I have a lunch date with Kieran. I'll just give her a call."

"No need. We'll pick up Tyler and Craig and head to Finnegan's." He grimaced. "I can park anywhere with this car, you know."

"Sure. Okay." She walked around and slid into the passenger's seat and grinned at Alex. "You know, I've never ridden in a patrol car!" she said. "I'll give Tyler a call and then let Kieran know that we might be a few minutes late."

"Oh, that won't be necessary!" he said, reaching over. She thought he was going for the radio.

He wasn't.

He made a sudden movement and backhanded her so hard that her head spun, then crashed into the door frame. Stars went reeling before her eyes.

Shadows and darkness descended over her, but she fought it.

Not now. Even as she felt her consciousness slipping away, she struck out.

"Damn you, tough girl, huh!"

Before he could hit her again, she scratched him. Hard. And as the darkness claimed her from his second blow, she knew that, at the very least, she'd drawn blood.

TYLER WAS BACK in Craig's office at the FBI. The Bureau's analysts had pulled up a number of murders, facts and figures, and they were still going over them. Victims had families. And, Tyler had discovered, not knowing what had happened to a loved one was torture for most families. "Closure" was almost a cliché. And yet it was something very real and necessary.

He was frowning when Craig asked him, "What? What now? There's something you don't like."

"There's something niggling me about that damned poem. I wanted to take Knowlton alive."

"Yeah, well, better that *you're* alive," Craig reminded him. "But… I do see what you mean. Knowlton claimed Hannah. She was dumped in the river."

"And Suzie Cornwall was left in a park."

"He could have been working on his methods. What he did wasn't easy—getting himself and a body over the fence. Setting the body up. The head—in a swing."

"Have they found any kin for her?" Tyler asked.

"No, but she had friends. Only, her friends didn't really seem to have much of anything. No one has offered a burial. Instead of the potter's field on this one, I thought the four of us might want to chip in quietly and bury her."

"Works for me," Tyler said.

He was quiet again. Then he quoted, "'But now they pay the price today…six little children. One of them dead. Soon the rest will be covered in red.'"

"I admit it bothers me, too."

"But I shot and killed him. So we'll never know."

"Is it possible for us to look through the photographs again?"

"Of course."

Craig left the office. Reports lay on the desk. Tyler started going over them again.

DNA.

The little vertebra Knowlton had sent to the FBI with

his poem had proved to belong to Hannah Levine, not Suzie Cornwall.

That bothered Tyler as much as the poem. If the bone had just belonged to Suzie Cornwall...

He started reading the autopsy reports again. So much was so similar. Except...

Hannah had alcohol and drugs in her system. Suzie...

She'd had her medication. Dr. Langley believed her throat had been slit, prior to her head being removed.

Hannah...

Hard to tell, with the way her head and torso had been found, washed up from the river.

He drummed his fingers on the table. No usable forensics had been found at the park. It was almost as if whoever had done the crime had studied books on how the police found killers, on what little bits of blood and biological trace could give them away.

Craig walked back into his office. "I got what I could. I called over to Detective Green, asking if Morrison could make sure we had everything, but Alex Morrison called in sick today. He's not there to help me get everything, but at this point, I do think I have it all."

Tyler looked at Craig, listening to the words. And suddenly, he was up and on his feet, not even sure why, thoughts jumbling in his mind.

Alex Morrison had been at the theme park the night Archibald Lemming had killed so many in Cemetery Mansion.

He'd started out in the academy and had gone into forensics.

He knew what was going on with the police—and the FBI.

"We need to find him," Tyler said. "We need to find Alex Morrison."

SARAH CAME TO very slowly.

She wasn't at all sure of where she was. Somewhere deep and dank... It had a smell of mold and age and... earth.

She tried to move; she was tied up, she realized. Fixed to a chair. Her ankles were bound, her arms had been pulled behind her and her wrists secured.

Her head pounded. Her arms hurt. She ached all over. The world was horribly askew. She had to blink and blink.

Reality overwhelmed her. She was a prisoner. And it was perfectly clear. Knowlton hadn't committed all the murders. They had known something wasn't right. Alex Morrison had been a living, breathing, functioning psychopath all the time. So helpful! So helpful as he used everything they had learned, so helpful as he ever so subtly turned them toward Perry Knowlton.

A functioning psychopath? Maybe Kieran could explain such a thing...

She tried to move.

She realized she could struggle, but the best she could ever do would be tip the chair over.

Panic seized her. There was barely any light. She heard a strange droning sound, like a piece of machinery moving...

She grew accustomed to the dim light. Blinking, she saw that, ten feet from her, Alex Morrison was busy at some kind of a machine. She realized, nearly passing out again, it was some kind of a knife sharpener. Battery operated, certainly, but...

Did it matter how the hell it was operated? He was sharpening his knife. To slit her throat, and then decapitate her.

This was where he had killed Suzie Cornwall. He'd

made the mistake—not Knowlton. He'd killed her here, then he'd used a patrol car to dump her body. Easy enough. People seldom questioned a patrol car in a neighborhood, or an officer checking out a fence, or a park, or—

He turned.

"Ah, awake, I see! Oh, Sarah. I could have been nice and seen to it that I dispatched you before…well, you know. Before. But then again, your kind deserves to feel some pain!"

"My kind?"

She wished Kieran was with her. Kieran might know how to talk to such a man. A functioning psychopath.

But Kieran wasn't here. Sarah had to think as her friend might—as any desperate person might think! Think to talk, think to survive—until help could come!

But how and why would help come? No one knew where she was. Everyone thought all the danger was over. No one knew…

There was no chance of help!

And still she had to hang on. While there was breath, she had once heard, there was hope.

And everything suddenly lay before her. Tyler, their future life together that they had managed to deny one another years ago…

"What is my kind, Alex?" she asked again.

He looked at her, leaning against the shoddy portable picnic table that held his knife sharpener.

"Cheerleader!" he said.

"What?"

"Cheerleader. You know your kind!"

"Oh, my God, Alex. I haven't been a cheerleader in over a decade."

"You were a cheerleader then."

"When?"

"Oh, come on, Sarah, give me a break! That night…
at Cemetery Mansion. You were a cheerleader. Oh, yes.
You had your football-playing hunk with you and your
retard cousin."

"Don't you dare use that word around me!"

"Whatever."

"Oh, you idiot! That's why people suffer so much in
this life—that's the reason Tyler and I haven't been together. How dare you! Davey is an incredible human
being. But I didn't believe Tyler really saw that—*because
of people like you, you asshole!*"

She was startled to realize her rage had apparently
touched him.

"Okay, okay, well, maybe you're right about Davey.
I mean…from what I understand, it was somehow him
who managed to bring about the fall of Archibald Lemming. A brilliant man like Lemming."

"A brilliant psychopath and killer, you mean. Not so
brilliant, was he? He's dead. And Perry Knowlton, well,
what an idiot!"

"Ah, but you aren't seeing *my* genius. Knowlton got
sloppy. He got sloppy—because he was afraid I would
strike again before he could. He wanted so badly to kill
you all himself! Not to mention it was useful to me for
everyone to suspect him. I overheard that bit about their
stomach contents—steak. Oh, I loved it! What a cool
clue to lead nowhere—the women just both liked steak.
I wished that Tyler had gone a little crazier on the hunt
for a steak house, but still! So gratifying. I did such a
good job. I followed Knowlton, and I learned from watching. I learned my lessons well. And I was a step ahead."

"You're an ass. You killed the wrong Suzie Cornwall."

His eyes narrowed. "Well, I won't kill the wrong Sarah Hampton, will I?" he asked her.

"How did you get your victim over the fence?" she demanded.

He laughed. "Databases! I found a way to get a key. I opened the lock. I walked in with her leaned against me, like someone who needed assistance—maybe lost something like a cell phone, you know? I just looked like a city worker, a peon. It wasn't so hard. In fact, it was exciting. I had her body leaned against me, her head in a cooler, and I opened the lock and just walked on in. Then…fun. Setting her up. Locking the gates again. Exhilarating! It was great."

Sarah forced a smile. "They will know it's you. You've gotten away with a lot. Let me see…the night at Cemetery Mansion. You thought you wanted to be a cop—that would be a way to see murder and horrible things… and get paid for it! You were in forensics and you were called to the scene. And you saw exactly how gruesome all the blood and guts and gore could be."

"I admired Archibald Lemming to no end," he agreed. "Even as I took pictures of his cold, dead body."

"And you knew Perry Knowlton was still alive."

"I watched him leave the park."

"And you spent the next years trying to find him. Did you?"

"I did, about a month ago. But I never let on. I just watched. And after he killed Hannah…well, I thought I'd help him along. I have access to all kinds of information. I wanted to give him all the precious scoop I could get my hands on. Then maybe we could become partners. But hey…he ignored me. Ignored me! But now the police and your precious FBI friends are all patting themselves on the back. They think they're all in the clear.

Well, I've got you—and before they find you, I'll have your darling Davey, too!"

"Davey is too smart for you," she said. "He was too smart for Archibald Lemming, and for Perry Knowlton—and he'll be too smart for you!"

Alex Morrison smiled. "You try to protect him—well, you would have. Too bad I didn't have you around…before. Oh, but you wouldn't have helped me. The cheerleaders laughed at me. The football players…well, I spent some time stuffed in a locker. Oh, and I had my head stuck in a toilet. And you know what my folks did when it happened? My mother put my head in the toilet, yelling at me to stand up. And my old man—you know what he did? He beat me with a belt—told me a man would handle himself. Well, I'm handling myself now. I'm ridding the world of cheerleaders and football players and popular people who stuff others in lockers. I mean, come on, seriously—they all need to go, right?"

"Can it be this easy?" Craig asked.

Tyler wasn't thinking anything was easy. Sarah wouldn't answer her phone.

She was supposed to have met Kieran.

She hadn't.

Alex Morrison was nowhere to be found.

Craig hadn't tried to placate Tyler. He'd never suggested Sarah was all right somewhere, that she'd just forgotten her phone. That she was an adult and had just gotten busy.

There was no lie to believe in, and they hadn't tried to invent one. Time was everything; they didn't have much.

They had to find Sarah.

But Craig was right. They'd easily used the system to find the patrol car Morrison had been using.

And now they were using GPS on his phone.

Tyler was functioning. Get in the car, move, walk, use his mind…

Find Sarah, find Sarah…

But all the while, he was fighting terror again, that almost overwhelming terror he'd felt when they'd realized Perry Knowlton had taken down an FBI agent and was heading to the safe house.

Did Alex Morrison really believe he could get away with this? Would it matter, would anything matter, if he managed to kill Sarah?

"He's here, right on this spot," Craig said, frustrated. "We've got the old subway map, but I can't find anywhere that's an entry." He paused, looking around the street.

Tyler did the same; he stared at the map again. He scanned the buildings intently.

At the corner was an old stone apartment block. There was a grate, a vent from the massive subway system and underground city below.

It was New York. There were grates in sidewalks everywhere.

But the building appeared to have gone up in the early 1900s.

Right about the same time as the subway.

And the facade had never been changed.

He didn't speak; he rushed ahead of Craig and bent to pull on the grate. It seemed too tight. Craig reached past him, helping him twist the metal.

It gave.

There was a short leap down to an empty little room.

But as his eyes adjusted, Tyler saw an old wooden door.

And the door opened to a flight of ancient, worn stairs.

He and Craig looked at one another.

Tacitly silent, they started down.

At least Tyler prayed that he was silent. To him, his heart seemed to be beating loudly in an agonized staccato.

ALEX MORRISON CAME and hunkered down before Sarah, studying his well-honed knife and then looking at her with a satisfied smile.

"I guess I did want to torture you in a way. I mean, I spent days with my head in a toilet due to a cheerleader."

"I never did anything to anyone, Alex. I just liked cheerleading—I was good at gymnastics. And Tyler was never cruel to anyone in his life. He worked with a lot of the kids who weren't so good, on his own time. He got the coaches to have special days and special races... You're so wrong! Yes, people can be cruel. Kids can be cruel. We all know that, and to most of us, it's deplorable. I didn't have enough faith in people. But you...you're just a truly sad and pathetic case! Kill me. Do it. But it will never end what you feel. It won't help the hatred and rancor that fester constantly within you!"

As she finished speaking, she heard something.

She wasn't sure what.

Rats?

And then she saw. She didn't know how. It seemed impossible.

Tyler was there. Tyler and Craig. They had somehow known, had somehow found her...

Tyler made a motion to tell her to keep talking.

And she realized her position. Tyler was there, yes. And Craig. But Alex Morrison was in front of her. All but touching her. And he had his freshly honed, razor-sharp carving knife in his hands.

"You're wrong!" Alex was saying. "You're wrong.

Every time I kill, I feel a little better. I feel I've sent one of you bitches or bastards on to a just reward!"

"You really should have gotten to spend a lot more time with Kieran Finnegan. She's a psychologist, not a psychiatrist—though her bosses are psychiatrists. She could explain to you that no, you were never going to feel better. I don't really get all of it—I majored in English and mass communication—but there are sociopaths and there are psychopaths. I believe, by the definitions I've heard, you might be the first. I'm not all that sure."

He moved the knife, waving it in an S through the air.

"She could help you."

"I don't want to be helped."

Sarah had never thought it was possible for such large men to move with such silent ease.

But Tyler and Craig had moved across the floor. Tyler was almost at her side. Craig was slightly behind Alex and to his left.

"Alex—"

"Hmm. Maybe I'm...oh, I don't know. But you know, Sarah, I think that if we'd been in high school together, you wouldn't have made fun of me. I think I will be merciful. I was merciful with Suzie. I wasn't so good to that bitchy runaway up in Sleepy Hollow. I sawed at her neck while she was alive. You—I'm going to see to it you bleed out quickly, quickly, quickly!"

"Hey, you!" Tyler called.

Stunned, Morrison swung around. He had his knife out and slashing, but it never made contact. Tyler slammed his arm down on Morrison's so hard and fast the knife went flying and the man screamed in pain.

Craig dived for the chair, spinning Sarah around, then cutting the ropes.

Sarah saw Alex Morrison was on his knees, staring up at Tyler with pure hatred.

His arm dangled at his side.

"I didn't shoot him, Craig," Tyler said. "Maybe we can get something out of him."

"After he's locked up," Craig said.

Sarah could hear sirens again.

Broken arm or not, Craig Frasier was seeing to it that Alex Morrison was handcuffed.

And Sarah was back in Tyler's arms.

"It's over," he told her as she broke into sobs. "It's truly over."

And she knew it was.

Only the nightmares would remain, and if she could wake from them in Tyler's arms, eventually, they would be over, too.

IT WAS A strange honeymoon, Tyler thought, but a great one.

The wedding, just as they had planned, took place at Finnegan's. They'd spent a few days alone in the Poconos, and now…

Sarah had needed to see Davey, and Tyler understood. Best of all was that Sarah believed he understood.

And so…

Buzzers were ringing. Bells were chiming. Neon lights were flashing.

There really was nowhere like Vegas.

And it was great; the actual "honeymoon" part of their extended honeymoon had been personal and intimate and amazing.

And now…

Sean and Suzie had joined them. They were seeing shows, going to music events, hanging out at the hotel's stunning pool. And at night...well, they were making love in their exquisite room.

Ever since the day Tyler had rescued Sarah from Morrison, they'd planned their lives, and were living them to the fullest.

He was coming back to New York. He was going to move his investigations office there.

He could consult with police, or the FBI, since now he had some useful and friendly connections.

And Sarah would keep writing.

She was really much better than ever, she assured him. He had given her that—a greater passion for her work!

It was their last night in Vegas. Tomorrow, they'd head back and get on with their regular lives. Somehow, to Tyler, those words held a touch of magic. Real magic. They'd weathered so much.

They would continue to weather what the future might bring.

They were playing slots at the moment, because Davey loved them so much and could spend hours at a machine with a twenty-dollar bill.

Tyler was pretty sure that Davey's greatest pleasure was hitting the call button for the waitress, smiling broadly when a pretty woman brought him a Shirley Temple and then grinning toward Tyler or Sarah so that one of them would tip her.

Tyler was watching Davey when Sarah finished playing at a silly cow slot machine that said, "Moo!" every few minutes. He reached out a hand, pulling her over to sit on his lap at the stool where he'd found a place to perch.

She leaned against him. They didn't speak.

Life...

It was full of relationships. Cruel parenting had helped

shape Alex Morrison. A brutal lack of empathy and lack of friendship had helped put the nails in the coffin of his psyche.

Tyler knew he'd been lucky.

He'd had a great family. And so had Sarah. And now, so close, they both had Aunt Renee and Davey.

Love was an amazing thing. There could never be too much love for many people in one's life.

And, of course, there was that one special love. Some people were lucky enough to know it when they had a chance to hold it, and hold it fast.

A forever kind of love.

Sarah was smiling at him.

He smiled back.

And it was evident, of course, but he whispered the words.

"I love you," he said.

"And I love you," she whispered back.

Davey had risen. He threw his arms around the both of them. "And I love you!" he said. "Come on, we gotta go up! Gotta get home tomorrow. I have a girlfriend, you know."

Laughing, they rose. It was time to go up to their rooms.

Tyler thought there was nothing wrong at all with a last night with Sarah in that exquisite bed!

* * * * *

Author Note

Many years ago, at a conference, I met a woman who was to become one of my best friends. She's brilliant, funny, artistic and kind. We were young, our children were young and our entire families became best friends—which we are to this day.

Connie's youngest is Josh, who has Down syndrome. He's an amazing young man. He loves the movies and everything about them, and can beat you, hands down, in any movie trivia game. He has all kinds of savvy that you might not expect. He's also a working actor, which is no easy feat. He, like his mom, is kind; there is not a mean bone in his body. I cherish his friendship and his love.

Once upon a time, I had him with me and several members of our two families at a theme park set up as a haunted attraction as Halloween approached. And while he wanted to go into one of the horror houses, Josh was afraid.

I am very easily scared myself. Truly—an absolute easy-mark coward. Therefore, it was quite simple for me to cheerfully say that I would wait with Josh while the others went through the haunted house. But Josh saw a kiosk with some really great light-up toy swords. So we bought one, and then Josh was ready! Being brave and protective, he went ahead of me, and into the fray we charged! (Well, walked in slowly and carefully. I was—and am!—still an incredible coward!)

Actors and animatronics were everywhere.

And I couldn't help but wonder what would happen if just one little part of it all was real.

Thus this story, *Out of the Darkness*, was born!

I hope you enjoy it.

Sincerely,
Heather Graham

*Turn the page for a special first look
at the next thrilling romantic suspense
in the*
NEW YORK CONFIDENTIAL *series
from* New York Times *bestselling author
Heather Graham,*

A DANGEROUS GAME,

*available March 13, 2018,
from MIRA Books.*

Chapter 1

"Kieran, Kieran Finnegan, right?" the woman asked.

She was wrapped in a black trench coat, wore a black scarf that nearly encapsulated her face and held a dark, blanketed bundle against her chest as if it was the greatest treasure in the world.

Kieran wasn't sure when the woman had come in; the offices of psychiatrists Fuller and Miro were closed for the day, the doctors were gone and Kieran had been just about to leave herself. The receptionist, Jake, usually locked the office door on his way out, but, apparently, tonight he had neglected to do so. Then again, Jake might have already left when Kieran's last patient had exited a little while ago.

Whether Jake had been gone or he had forgotten to lock up, the door had been left open.

And so, this woman accosted Kieran in the reception area of the office just as she was on her way out.

"I am Kieran, but I'm so sorry, I'm the therapist, not one of the doctors. Actually, we are closed for the day. You'll need to come back. Both the doctors are wonderful, and I'm sure they'll be happy to see you another time."

And this woman certainly looked like she needed help.

Her eyes were huge and as dark as the clothing she was wearing as she stared at Kieran with a look of despair.

"All right, let me see what I can do. You seem distraught," Kieran said, and winced—wow. Stating the obvious. "I can get you to a hospital. I can call for help—"

"No! No!" The woman suddenly thrust the bundle she'd held so closely into Kieran's arms. "Here!"

Kieran instinctively accepted it. Reflex? She wasn't sure why.

It began to cry. And writhe. *Of course.* The bundle was a baby.

"Ma'am, please—hey!" Kieran protested.

The woman had turned and was fleeing out the door.

"Wait! Hey!" Kieran cried. She reached immediately for the phone, hoping that she'd be in time to reach the building's security desk.

Ralph Miller answered the phone at the lobby desk. "Hey, pretty girl, what are you still doing at work? I've got a few hours to go, and then I am out of here. I hear that the Danny Boys are playing at Finnegan's tonight. Can't believe your brother snagged them. I would have thought that you'd have gotten out early—"

"Ralph, listen, please! There's a woman who was just up here. She ran out. Can you stop her from leaving the building?"

The baby wailed in earnest.

"What?"

"There's a woman in black—"

"In black, yeah. She just left."

"Stop her, catch her! Now."

"I can't hear you, Kieran. I hear a baby crying. A baby! Whose baby is it?"

"Ralph! Get out in the street and get that woman!"

"What?"

"Go catch that woman!"

"Gotcha! I'm gone."

She hung up, then quickly dialed 9-1-1.

Emergency services probably couldn't move quickly enough to help, since the woman was already on the run.

She was running on the busy streets of New York City, where rush hour meant a swarm of humanity in which one could get completely lost. But Kieran still explained her situation and where she was. The operator was efficient; cops would quickly be out. Child services would arrive.

But no matter. The woman would get away.

Kieran tried to hold and rock and soothe the baby while dialing Craig Frasier.

If you were living with an FBI agent, it made sense to call him under such circumstances, especially since he—like Ralph—would want to know why she was working so late when the Danny Boys would be playing at Finnegan's. To Craig, like Ralph, it was still a somewhat normal night—and a Friday night! A nice, normal Friday night—something that was very nice to enjoy, given their chosen professions.

"Hey, Kieran," Craig said. "Are you already at the pub?"

She apparently wasn't good at rocking and soothing and trying to talk on the phone. The baby was still crying. Loudly.

"No, I—"

"Whose kid is that? I can't hear a word you're saying!"

"I'm still at work! Can you come over here now, please?"

"Uh—yeah, sure."

Kieran hung up the phone. She didn't know what Ralph was doing; she didn't know where the police were. She glanced down at the baby as she hurried from the office, ready to hit the streets herself. How old was the tiny creature? It was so small!

Yet it had strong lungs!

Was the woman in black the mother?

She had looked older. Perhaps fifty. Too old for an infant.

Ralph wasn't at the desk; Kieran heard sirens, but, as yet, no police had arrived.

Bursting out onto the New York City street in rush hour, she looked right and left. There, far down the block, she thought she saw the woman.

"Hey!" Kieran shouted.

Despite the pulsing throng of humanity between them, the woman heard her. She turned.

There was something different about her now.

The way she moved. The way she looked; the expression on her face.

And she didn't try to run. She just stared at Kieran, and then seemed to stagger toward her.

Kieran clutched the screaming infant close to her breast and thrust her way through the people; luckily, she was a New Yorker, and she knew how to push through a crowd when necessary.

The woman was still staggering forward. Kieran was closing the gap.

"Listen, I'll help you, I'll help the baby! It's all right…"

It wasn't in any way all right.

The woman lurched forward, as if she would fall into Kieran's arms if Kieran had just been close enough.

She wasn't.

The woman fell face-first down on the sidewalk.

That was when Kieran saw the knife protruding from the woman's back and the rivulets of blood suddenly forming all around her and joining together to create a crimson pool.

* * *

Babies tended to be adorable—and this baby was especially so. In fact, Kieran wasn't sure she'd ever seen an ugly baby, but she had been assured by friends that they did exist.

This little girl, though, had a headful of auburn ringlets and huge blue eyes. Kieran had heard that all babies had blue eyes, but she didn't know if that was true or not. Sadly, she just didn't know a lot about babies; she was one in a family of four children herself, yes, but she and her twin brother, Kevin, were a couple years younger than their older brother and one year older than their younger brother.

Actually, this beautiful baby looked as if she could fit right in with their family. Each one of the Finnegan siblings had red hair and blue or green or blue-green eyes.

"They say it's the Irish," she said softly to the little one in her arms. "But I don't think that you're Irish!"

Talking to the baby made sense at the moment; FBI Special Agent Craig Frasier, the love of her life and often partner in crime—solving crime, not committing it—had arrived shortly after the police. The medical examiner had come for the body of the murdered woman and—while waiting for child services—Kieran was holding the baby, back up in the offices of Fuller and Miro.

Drs. Fuller and Miro worked with the police and other law enforcement. While not with the FBI, they were profilers and consultants for the New York office. The Bureau's behavioral-science teams were in DC, and while they could be called in, the city police and FBI often used local help in trying to get a step ahead of a criminal, or in working with criminals and witnesses when psychological assessments were needed or sometimes when a child or a distressed person simply needed to be able to speak to someone who asked the right questions and put them at ease. Kieran did a number of those assessments before reporting to the doctors, and she worked with victims of domestic abuse and both parents and children when they wound up within the child welfare system—such as a teenager who had been assaulted by her own father, or a senior who was recovering from gunshot wounds inflicted by his wife. Or Kieran's last patient today, Besa Goga. Besa was a sad case, abused for years when she'd first immigrated to the country, and now quick to strike out. Besa Goga was in court-ordered therapy because she'd bitten a man from the cable company. Kieran had only been seeing her a few weeks.

But the office didn't always work with the police department, FBI or other such agencies. They also handled other cases that fell their way through happenstance or other circumstances—like the recovering alcoholic who was also a politician and doing very well with Dr. Fuller.

Kieran had called her bosses to let them know what had happened. Both had said they'd come in immediately.

She had assured them that they must not; the police were dealing with the murder, and child services was coming for the baby.

Dr. Fuller—who had looks as dreamy as any TV physician—was at an event with his equally beautiful wife and their six-year-old.

Dr. Miro was giving a keynote speech at a conference in southern New Jersey.

Kieran had convinced them both that she was fine, that it was just strange and scary. The poor murdered woman hadn't been scary; she had touched Kieran's heart. She had needed help so badly.

But she had called Kieran by name!

And that made Kieran wonder.

She sat out in the waiting area of the offices—right where the woman had come up to her, right where the baby had been thrust into her arms. She thought that the baby was bound to cry soon. That was what babies did. They were hungry or wet or had gas or… She just really didn't have much experience. And she had no clue as to the child's age! But with little else to do—and probably in a bit of shock herself, despite the fact that she'd now thrown herself into the crime-fighting ring for a few years—she talked to the baby. She made soothing noises, discussed her own uncertainty with a cheerful voice and made a few faces.

She could swear that the baby smiled.

Did babies smile at that age?

She knew that some people—experienced parents, grandparents and so on—claimed babies did not smile until a certain age.

This one, she was certain, smiled. She waved her little fists in the air; she grinned toothlessly.

She even cooed.

"Hey!" Craig had come back up to the offices after checking out the scene on the street.

He nodded to the policeman at the door. Since Kieran had no idea what was going on, and since a woman who had been looking for her had just been stabbed to death, having a policeman standing guard was very reassuring.

She looked up at Craig, hopeful. Though, of course, she doubted that he or the police or anyone—other than the killer—knew who had just stabbed the poor woman, or why.

"You okay?" he asked her.

"I'm fine. I was handed the baby. I don't think anyone was after me for any reason at all, but…oh, Lord! Craig, you don't think it is my fault, do you? I mean, if I hadn't chased after her—"

"Kieran," he said, hunkering down by her. "No." His voice was firm and—as usual—filled with confidence and authority. Craig had been a special agent with the FBI for a good decade. He always seemed to exude a comfortable assurance and strength—things she had to admit she loved about him. Well, along with rock-hard abs, a solid six-three frame and the fact that the phrase "tall, dark and handsome" might have been conceived just for him. He had hazel eyes that were like marble, seemed to see far too much and…well, in her mind, they were just beautiful.

"It was all so fast…" Kieran murmured.

Craig adjusted the blanket around the baby. Kieran thought she cooed and smiled for him, too, but, of course, it was hard to tell.

Smile, gas. Who knew?

"Kieran, that woman was trying to save this child. She brought her to you. You aren't to blame in any way. I have a feeling that she was very heroic—and that she gave her life for the child. She might have stolen the baby from some kind of terrible situation. I don't know. None of us can even begin to figure out what might have gone down yet. But I believe the minute she took the baby away from whoever had it before, her hours were numbered." He was quiet for a moment and looked up at her. "This isn't going to be an FBI case, you know. Whoever your visitor was, she was murdered on the streets of New York. It's an NYPD matter."

"Did you talk to Ralph downstairs?" she asked anxiously. "He should have been on the desk—and you're supposed to sign in to enter this building." So it was with most large office buildings in the city. It had been ever since 9/11.

"Yes, of course, I spoke with him, the police spoke with him… He was a mess. He thinks it's all his fault. UPS was here with a large shipment for the computer-tech firm on the eighteenth floor. He thinks she slipped by him when he ran over to help the courier with the elevator," Craig said.

"I can imagine he's upset. Did he ever get out of here? He was planning on seeing the Danny Boys play tonight, too."

"I don't think he went to see the band," Craig said. "The cops let him go about an hour or so ago now."

"Ah," Kieran murmured.

What an end to the week. Ralph Miller was a Monday-to-Friday, regular-hours kind of guy. He looked forward to his Friday nights; he loved music, especially Irish rock bands. He must have been really upset to realize a murder had taken place somewhere just down the street from his front door.

The murder of a woman who had slipped by him.

A woman who had left a baby in Kieran's arms.

A baby. Alone, in her arms.

"Craig, I just… I wish I understood. And I'm not sure about the officer handling the case—"

"Kieran, no matter how long we all work in this, murder is hard to understand. That officer needed everything you could give him."

"I know that. I've spoken with him. He wants me to think. He wants me to figure out why the woman singled me out. He's more worried about that than the baby!" Kieran said indignantly.

"He's a detective, Kieran. Asking you questions is

what he's supposed to do—you know that. *Can* you think of anything?" Craig asked her.

Kieran shook her head. "She probably knew about this office. And it's easy enough to find out all our names."

"Maybe, and then…"

"And then what?"

Craig smiled at her. During the diamond-heist case—when they had first met—she had saved a girl from falling onto the subway tracks when a train was coming. When a reporter had caught up with Kieran, she had impatiently said, "Anyone would lend a helping hand."

For quite some time after, she'd been a city heroine.

So she had a feeling she knew what he was going to say.

"Maybe they saw you on TV."

"That was a long time ago."

"Some people have long memories."

There was a tap at the door, and the officer who had been standing guard opened it to a stocky woman with a round face and gentle, angelic smile. She was in a uniform, and Kieran quickly realized that she was from child services.

"Hi, I'm Sandy Cleveland," the woman told her. "Child—"

"Services, yes, of course!" Kieran said.

She realized that she didn't want to hand over the baby. She didn't have a "thing" for babies—her driving goal in life had never been to get married and have children. She did want them somewhere along the line. But not now. She knew that, eventually, yes, she wanted to marry Craig. She was truly, deeply, kind-of-even-madly in love with him.

But not now. Maybe in a year. They hadn't even discussed it yet.

She didn't fawn over babies at family picnics, and she was happy for her friends who were pregnant or parents, and she got along fine with kids—little ones and big ones.

But she wasn't in any way *obsessed*.

But here, now, in the office, holding the precious little bundle, who had so recently been tenderly held by a woman who was now *dead* with a knife in her back, Kieran was suddenly loath to give her up. And not that it didn't appear the woman from child services was just about perfect for her job. No one could fake a face that held that much empathy.

"It's okay," Sandy Cleveland said very softly. "I swear she'll be okay with me. And don't worry, we take great care of little ones at my office. I won't just dump her in a crib and let her cry. She'll be okay. It's my job—I'm very good at it," she added, as if completely aware of every bit of mixed emotion that was racing through Kieran's heart and mind. She smiled and added, "Miss Finnegan, the street below is thronging with police officers—and reporters. The chief of police is already involved in this situation. This little one will not just have the watchdogs of child services looking over her, but a guardian from the police force, as well. She's going to be fine. I personally promise you that she'll be fine."

"I'm sure—I'm sure you're good," Kieran said. She smiled at Sandy Cleveland.

"That means you have to give her the baby," Craig said, but she thought he understood, too, somehow.

"Yes, yes, of course," Kieran murmured.

And she handed over the baby.

It was so damned hard to do!

"Miss Cleveland, can you tell me about how old she is?" Kieran asked.

"I think about six weeks by her motor function. And,

please, just call me Sandy," the woman told her. "Her eyes are following you—and when you speak, that's a real smile. It's usually between about six weeks and three months when they really smile, and I think this is a lovely and smart girl. Don't worry! I'll get a smile from her, too, I promise."

The baby did seem to be settling down in Sandy Cleveland's arms.

Craig set an arm around Kieran's shoulders.

"Sandy, I'm with the FBI. Craig Frasier. You won't mind if we check in on this little one?"

"Of course not!" Sandy assured them. She shook her head sadly. "I hear that the woman who handed her to you was murdered. There's no ID on her. I'm just hoping we can find out who this little one is. She's in good shape, though. Someone has been caring for her. Yes! You're so sweet!" She said the last to the baby, wrinkling her nose and making a face—and drawing a sound that wasn't quite laughter, but darned close to it. "Hopefully, she has a mom or other relatives somewhere. And if not..." She hesitated, studying Kieran and Craig. "Well, if not—a precious little infant like this? People will be jockeying to adopt her. Anyway, let me get her out of here and away from...from what happened." She held the baby adeptly while using her left hand to dig into her pocket and produce her cards. "Call me anytime," she told them. "I may not answer, but I will get back to you if you leave me a message."

Then she was gone. The cop who had been watching over Kieran went outside.

She and Craig were alone.

Kieran still felt shell-shocked.

"Kieran, hey!" Craig hunkered down by her again as she sank down into one of the comfortably upholstered chairs in the waiting room. He looked at her worriedly. "The cops are good—you know that."

"Craig, you have to be in on this. That detective—"

"Lance. Lance Kendall. Kieran, really, he's all right. He's doing all the right things."

"Yeah! All the right things—grilling me!"

"All right, I will speak with Egan about it tomorrow, how's that?"

She nodded. "Thank you. Get one of your joint task forces going—at least maybe you can participate?"

"Sure." He hesitated. "I guess… Um, well."

There was a tap at the door. They both looked up. Craig stood.

A man walked in. It wasn't the first officer who had arrived at the scene—it was the detective who had arrived while others were setting up crime scene tape around parameters, handling the rush-hour crowd around the body and urging her to get the baby back up to her offices—out of the street.

He was a tall, well-built African American man. About six feet even, short brown hair, light brown eyes and features put together correctly. He was around forty-five, she thought. He wasn't warm and cuddly, but neither was he rude.

"Detective Kendall," Craig said. "Have you wrapped up at the scene for the evening?"

"Yes—a few techs are still down there, but there's nothing more I can accomplish here. Unless you can help. Miss Finnegan—nothing? You can't think of anything?"

"I have no idea why this lady chose me," Kieran said. "None."

"And you've never seen the woman before?" Kendall asked.

"Never."

"Nor the baby?"

Did he think that the infant paid social calls on people, hung out at the pub or requested help from psychiatrists or a psychologist?

"No," she managed evenly. "I've never seen the infant before. I've never seen the woman before."

"All right, then." He suddenly softened, becoming a little warmer. "You must be really shaken. I understand that, and I'm sorry. For now, I don't have anything else. But, of course, I'm sure you know we may need to question you again."

"I'm not leaving town," she said drily.

He wasn't amused.

Kieran continued, "And, of course, I've spoken with both Dr. Fuller and Dr. Miro. I've told them all that I could, and they will be trying to think of any reason—other than who they are and what they do—that the woman might have come here."

"I've spoken with Drs. Fuller and Miro, too," Detective Kendall told her grimly. "And I'm sure we'll speak again."

"I'm sure," Kieran murmured.

"Good night, Special Agent Frasier, Miss Finnegan," the detective said. "You're both—uh, free to go."

He left them. Craig pulled Kieran around and into his arms, looking down into her eyes. "We are free. There's nothing else to do tonight. You want to go home?"

"I know that we both really wanted to see the band play tonight," she told him. "I'm sorry."

"Kieran, it's not your fault—I'm sure you didn't plan for a woman to thrust a baby into your arms and then run downstairs and be stabbed to death."

"It's driving me crazy, Craig! We don't know who she was... We don't have a name for her, we don't know about the baby. I think she was too old to be the mom, but I'm not really sure. And if not…she was trying to save the baby, not hurt it. But who would hurt a baby?"

"I don't know. Let's get on home, shall we?"

"We can still go to the pub. Maybe catch the last of the Danny Boys?" she said.

"You know you don't want to go anywhere."

Kieran hesitated. "Not true. I do want to go some-where. I'm starving—and I'm not sure what we've got to eat at the apartment."

"Yep. We've been staying at yours—if there is food at mine, I'm certain we don't want to eat it."

"Then we'll go to the pub," she said quietly.

Kieran hadn't realized just how late it had grown until she and Craig walked out of the building. New York City policemen were still busy on the street, many of them just managing crowd control; the body of the murdered woman was gone, but crime scene workers were still put-ting the pieces together of what might and might not be a clue on the busy street.

They were in midtown, with giant conglomerates mixed with smaller boutiques and shops. Most of the shops were closed and the hour too late for business, but people still walked quickly along the sidewalks, slowing down curiously to watch the police and try to see what had happened. Kieran looked up while Craig spoke with a young policewoman for a moment; her brother had once warned her that she looked up too often—that she looked like a tourist.

But she loved even the rooftops, the skyline. Old sky-scrapers with ornate molding at the roof sat alongside new giants that towered above them in glass, chrome and steel. And then again, right in the midst of the twentieth-and twenty-first-century buildings, there would be a charming throwback to the 1800s.

From a nearby Chinese restaurant, a tempting aroma laced the air.

Even over murder.

The cops generally knew Craig; he was polite to all of them, as well. They nodded an acknowledgment to Kieran. She'd worked with the police often enough herself.

"Is Detective McBride going to be on the case?" Kieran asked hopefully. They'd worked with McBride before, not even a year ago, and he had been an amazing ally.

Doctors Fuller and Miro worked with city detectives regularly, and—nine out of ten—they were great. Every once in a while, as in any job, there was a total jerk in the mix. Mainly they were professionals, and good at their work, and Kieran knew it. Some were more personable than others. Homicide detectives could be very cut-and-dried. McBride had told her once that homicide, while horrible, was also easier than dealing with other crimes. The victims couldn't complain about the way he was working. Of course, the victims had relatives. That was hard.

She had come to really like McBride.

In this case, a baby was involved. A woman had died trying to save that baby, Kieran was certain. So she felt they needed the best.

Craig looked at her quizzically. "You know that that there are thousands of detectives in the city, a decent percentage of that in Homicide—and even a decent percentage in Major Case."

"Actually, when you break it all down…"

"I don't know who will be working the case—probably more than one detective. But, for right now, it is Lance

Kendall. And he's all right, Kieran. He's good. He was doing all the right things," he added quietly. He looked as if he was going to say something more. He didn't.

He took her hand in his. She held on, letting the warmth of his touch comfort her as they walked down the street. "Hey, remember. I'm an agent. You work with psychiatrists who spend most of their time on criminal cases. It's a life we've chosen, and we've talked about it. This will be just another case—whatever level of involvement we have with it. You can't let it take over—or neither one of us will be sane."

She nodded. He was right. There were other cases where they found themselves on the fringe; and, frankly, every day of Craig's life had to do with criminal activity in the city of New York. They'd already worked on cases of cruel and brutal murders. This was another. And there was always something that seemed to make it better—at least for the survivors—when a killer was brought to justice.

She couldn't obsess. She knew it.

But this one felt personal!

"Yep," she spoke blithely and smiled.

"You're cool?" He didn't believe her, she could tell; it seemed he didn't know whether to push it or not.

But he was right about one thing. There was nothing for them to do right now except try to get their minds around what had happened—and let it go enough to get on with life.

Even figure out how to step back in order to step forward again.

"Yep. I'm fine. Let's get food," Kieran said.

"Sounds good. Thankfully, we always know where to go!"

APPALACHIAN PREY

DEBBIE HERBERT

This book is dedicated to Maxine Brooks,
one of the best readers ever!

And, as always, to my husband, Tim; my dad,
J. W. Gainey; and my sons, Byron and Jacob.

Chapter One

Moonshine again...seriously?

Hidden caches had turned up everywhere in her father's cabin. No surprise there. Lilah snatched two plastic jugs from the back utility room and marched to the kitchen, intent on pouring the illegal hooch down the drain. Corn liquor had destroyed her parents' marriage and her dad's liver. Would have killed him, too, if he hadn't been murdered a week ago.

Unexpected tears blurred her vision as she unscrewed the lid on one of the jugs and poured the liquid poison into the chipped enamel sink. Not that she and Dad had been all that close in recent years, but still, the man had been her father. Lilah tipped the jug. *Glug, glug, glug...*a hundred dollars' worth gone. Could have bought a used college textbook with that money.

She blinked and gazed out the open window. The cabin was nestled in the foothills, with rolling mountains standing sentinel in all directions like a green fortress. A deceptive beauty, as though the price for living in such a visual feast meant being taxed with rampant poverty and violence. Dad's death was the latest evidence of that.

Whoever said you can't go home again was dead wrong. After a mere week, Lilah felt like she'd never left Lavender Mountain. Memories washed over her, most of them unpleasant—her parents' screaming matches, brutally cold nights where they'd all huddled in front of the fireplace. But it hadn't been *all* bad. Some days, wandering the woods with her older siblings, Jimmy and Darla, had been magical.

A faint scrape of boots on leaves and pine straw jarred her senses. Someone approached.

Lilah stilled, picturing in her mind's eye the open front door and windows. Had the murderer returned? She fought the instinct to flee to the back bedroom and lock herself in. Probably just one of Dad's old customers who hadn't gotten the word yet.

Quickly, she raced across the rugged pine floorboards to the den. Through the battered screen door emerged the silhouette of a tall bearded man dressed in denim overalls. What mountain had he just climbed down from? Lilah sprinted to the door and latched the rusty lock into place. A joke of a defense. She reached for the weapon always propped by the door frame, and her right hand curled around the barrel of the twelve-gauge shotgun, its metal smooth, familiar and comfortable.

And loaded.

"What you want?" she called out in her fiercest voice.

The man didn't appear the least bit intimidated as he shuffled forward, his foot on the first porch step. "I got bizness with Chauncey Tedder."

"Guess you could say my dad's out of business," she said, sliding the shotgun next to her hip.

He climbed the second step. One more and he would be within six feet of where she stood. He swayed and squinted, peering into the room. Lilah was painfully aware he could see straight into the little kitchenette.

"Looks to me like you got some 'shine in there," he boomed. "Go git me a jug afore I get really riled."

She didn't aim to find out what the stranger was like

"really riled." This place was well out of range for anyone to hear if she screamed, and Dad was shot not far from the cabin. Lilah unhitched the lock and kicked open the screen door. She drew the shotgun up to shoulder level, finger twitching at the trigger. "I repeat—this place is closed for business. I'd appreciate you spreading the word."

"Whoa, little missy." He threw up his hands and backed away. "Don't mean ya no harm."

He tripped on the step and took a tumble. *Oomph.*

Chagrined, Lilah bit her lip and lowered the shotgun. "You okay there?"

He rose, brushing dirt off his overalls. "I reckon. You sure are a touchy thing. Best be gettin' on my way." With one last sorrowful glance at the jugs on the kitchen counter, he ambled away, gingerly limping on his right foot.

What the hell.

She returned inside, retrieved the full jug she hadn't yet dumped out, and stepped out onto the porch. "Hey," she yelled. "Come on back, you can have a jug."

He shot her a wary look, clearly suspicious of her change of heart. But in the end, the pull of the moonshine outweighed his reservation, and he returned.

Lilah set the jug down at the bottom of the stairs and scampered back to the door.

"Same price as always?" the man asked, carefully pulling out a wad of dollar bills from his side pocket.

"It's on the house. Just don't come back, ya hear? This is the last of it." Unless she found more while cleaning out the cabin. No telling how many bottles were tucked away in nooks and crannies.

A grin split his weathered face as he tucked the money away. "Thank you kindly, ma'am."

He picked up the jug and gave a quick nod before walking across the yard. A sheriff's cruiser rounded the bend in the road and turned into her dirt driveway. The man momentarily froze at the sight, and then took off running to the nearby tree line—more like hobbling with his injured foot—but almost quick enough to get out of sight. *Couldn't have hurt too bad*, she mused.

The cruiser came to an abrupt halt, and a man started to climb out.

Lilah's heart skittered, even faster than when the stranger had suddenly appeared at her door minutes ago. Could it be…

Oh, yes, it most definitely was.

Harlan Sampson. The man who'd quickly won her heart three months ago and then had dumped her twice as fast after a week of fun and games. Her left hand involuntarily fluttered over her stomach, and Lilah hastily jerked it away.

"Well, looky here," Harlan drawled, eyeing the man carting his haul off into the woods. He faced her and pushed the dark sunshades up on his head, revealing the startling beryl-blue eyes that had enthralled her on her last ill-fated visit, which—*damn it*—still sent her heart pounding into overdrive. He walked toward her. "Looks like I finally caught a Tedder point-blank in the act of distributing illegal whiskey."

"Wrong. I wasn't selling. I was giving. Ain't no money exchanged hands here." Inwardly, Lilah winced at the slip into the local vernacular. It had been twelve years since she'd called Lavender Mountain home, but in times of high emotion—and now definitely counted—she lapsed back into the lingo.

"So you say."

She pinched her lips together. "What brings you here?"

"Came to pay my respects, see how you're getting on."

Weeks ago, she would have flung herself on Harlan at those words. But not now. "I'm jim-dandy," she replied, lifting her chin a fraction. "I saw you at Dad's funeral. No need to come over."

"I believe I owe you an apology."

"Forget it." There was no way she'd admit how much his silence had hurt.

His eyes smoldered, and he slowly climbed the porch steps, close enough now to make her breath hitch. "I can't forget it. And I can't forget you."

EVEN GLARING AT HIM, shotgun by her side, Lilah Faye Tedder was a hell of a sight. Harlan drank it in—the long blond hair that tumbled past her shoulders, the elfin delicate face with the determined chin, the slight womanly curves of her body. He had tried to wipe away the memory of her, but with one glance, the old familiar pull returned. He nodded at the firearm. "Mind putting that thing away? Hard to talk to an angry woman holding a shotgun."

A smile ghosted across her face before the hardened set returned to her chin. "You said what you came to say. Apology accepted."

"C'mon, Lilah. Let's talk."

She hesitated, then shrugged. "Suit yourself."

With that, Lilah spun on her heel and entered the cabin. Not much of an invitation, but he'd hardly expected her to welcome him with open arms. The place smelled as clean and as fresh as the pine breeze that blew through the open windows, but with a touch of lemon cleaner. It already had the stale antiseptic look of a bare shell of a dwelling. No knickknacks or frivolities, just an old sofa and a couple of chairs.

"I see you've been hard at work." He'd been here before. Chauncey's old place had been filled with junk when he was alive.

"It's all set for the realtor to list as soon the reading of the will is over. After that, I'll head on home."

Probably for the best, at least for his career. According to Sheriff J.D. Bentley, associating with any Tedder wouldn't reflect well on him or the office. His boss planned on retiring soon and understood that he had ambitions to run and take over the top law enforcement job in the county. And as such, J.D. had driven home the point that he had no chance of winning the sheriff's election if he was a known associate of the outlaw family.

Personally, Harlan couldn't care less about the piddly amounts of money some moonshiners made. No, what disturbed him were the rumors that Lilah's family had turned to the new Appalachian cash crop of growing marijuana.

Following her lead, he took a seat in one of the old chairs that remained. "No reason to hurry home, is there? Now that school's out, I thought you would be free for the summer."

She leveled him with a glacial stare. "That was the original plan. Things changed."

Ouch. Yeah, he caught her barb. Last time she had been home, they'd planned on her returning to Lavender Mountain this summer so they could see each other regularly.

"Sorry about your dad. Must be hard—"

"Any news on who shot him?" Her voice was sharp and cold.

"Not yet," he admitted. "But we're working on it."

"I bet."

This wasn't the same Lilah from March, the woman with the ready smile, the soft eyes and the gentle voice. But she had every reason to be bitter, especially with him.

"We're working 'round the clock. No leads have panned out yet, but we're interviewing his friends and—" he hesitated a beat "—known associates."

"Meaning y'all suspect this was related to his moon-shining."

If only it were that simple. He hedged. "The theory is it revolved around his illegal activities, yes. You and Darla already said he had no enemies or problems with others that you know of."

Silver eyes clouded in pain. "It makes no sense. Why would anyone shoot Dad? It's not like he made a fortune." Her neck turned a fraction toward the back of the cabin.

"Maybe an irate customer?" he suggested.

"Doubt it. Most were regulars." Again, her eyes darted to the rear of the cabin as she folded her arms at her waist.

"Okay, what's going on?" he asked sharply.

Her eyes widened. "I don't know what you're talking about. Nothing's going on."

He strode past her, down the narrow hallway and peeked inside the two bedrooms at the end. One was completely empty, nothing suspicious there. The other housed only a double bed and a dresser. A lacy pale yellow nightgown was draped across a plaid bedcover. An image of Lilah in that nightgown flashed through his mind, and he gritted his teeth at the wave of loss that churned his gut.

"What do you think you're doing?" She followed close behind him, her bare feet padding on the old wood flooring. "You have no right to search my place."

"It's not yours until you can show me the deed has been transferred to you in writing." He crossed the room and glanced cursorily inside the small bathroom with the old-fashioned iron claw-foot bathtub. Nothing out of place there, either.

"Mind telling me what you're looking for?"

He felt a tad foolish for wondering if an unwelcome visitor might have forced his way in and held her hostage.

"Well?" she demanded.

"I'm not sure. But you kept looking back this way, as if something was worrying you."

A flush stained her cheeks. "You're imagining things."

This was getting him nowhere. He changed tactics. "Lilah, I want to help. If there's a problem, tell me. I can't leave you alone out here if there's the slightest possibility you're in danger."

"Why do you care?" she scoffed. "Go on and leave me—again. It's what you do best."

Her words slammed into him like bullets. He'd hurt her. Bad. "I'm sorry," he said, shuffling his feet. "I should have at least tried to explain."

"No explanation needed. I can guess what happened. As soon as your family and friends caught wind of you seeing a Tedder, they jumped all over you. Go on, admit it."

Heat rushed up the back of his neck. She'd pretty much nailed their reaction. He could have borne their objections, but...

"And then your boss piled on, too. Right? Wouldn't look good for the apparent heir in the upcoming sheriff's election to be sleeping around with a lowlife like me."

The accusation in her eyes stung, but not as much as the truth of her words. Yes, he was ambitious. But it wasn't the money and the power he craved—it was the chance to make a difference. This little corner in the Appalachian foothills had always garnered more than its share of hardship and tumult. And somehow, the situation kept going downhill. Elmore County was rife with drug trafficking, ancient feuds and an isolation that led many to a life of crime, believing the laws didn't apply in this neck of the woods.

"I won't deny any of that," he said slowly. "J.D. had a long talk with me. Basically said that if I continued seeing you, he wouldn't endorse me as his replacement."

"And your career means more to you than I do. Fine.

But you could have talked to me instead of giving me the silent treatment."

"You're right. And I regret that."

Harlan regretted a lot of things. He should never have listened to J.D. or anyone else. He should have defended Lilah. He should have never let her slip away.

He was an ass.

Harlan shook his head. No, he'd done the right thing. The people in this county needed him. No point in throwing his career away because of one magical week. But that one week together during her spring break from work and school had been an unbelievable whirlwind of passion and emotion. And then, he'd slipped out of her life without a single word, even after all the plans they'd made for the summer. He raised a hand to touch her, to cup her face in his palms, to tell her he was sorry.

Lilah stepped back, lips curled in a bitter smile. "Don't even think about it, Harlan Sampson. We're done."

Abruptly, he dropped the hand by his side. He'd lost the right to touch Lilah ever again.

"Message received." He took a deep breath and straightened his spine. "But I still don't like leaving you alone out here. Can't you get a room in town until you've finished your business?"

"No."

She turned and headed down the hallway, leaving him no choice but to follow. Lilah opened the front door wide and waved a hand in dismissal. "Goodbye, Harlan."

He nodded, but as he brushed past Lilah, he couldn't resist placing a hand on her shoulder. "I'm sorry for everything. And for your loss. Your dad might have been on the other side of the law, but he was a decent man. I liked him, and he didn't deserve what happened. I'll do everything I can to find who shot him."

The anger and hostility fled, and her lips trembled the slightest bit. "Thank you," she whispered.

"Is there anything I can do for you?"

She shook her head.

"If you think of something, you have my number."

Before she could object, he planted a light kiss on her cheek and stepped out onto the porch. The sun was sinking low in the green mountains, casting a coral and purple hue on the clouds. Damn, he hated leaving her with night approaching.

"Wait. There *is* one thing you can do."

He swung around, eager to help. "Name it."

Lilah lingered in the doorway, rubbing her arm. "I—I found some money today while I was cleaning up the place. In light of what happened to Dad, well, it makes me nervous. It's too late for me to go to the bank, but maybe you could keep it safe for me tonight? I'll come pick it up in the morning and deposit it."

"No problem."

He returned to the inside of her cabin. How crafty of Chauncey to keep a hidden stash of dough. He hoped for Lilah's sake that it was at least a thousand dollars or so. She could use the cash. Working as a teacher's aide and going to college didn't leave her much in the way of money.

"I told Darla 'bout finding a wad of cash up under the mattress, and she wanted us to go on and split it, but I told her it didn't sit right with me. That much money should be reported."

He gave an indulgent smile. "No one would be the wiser if you didn't turn it in. There's no need to worry. I agree with Darla, just keep the money."

"But it's a lot of money. I'll need to talk to the bank manager. Don't they investigate if you deposit more than ten thousand dollars at a time?"

The *hell*. "Excuse me? How much money are we talking about?"

"About thirty thousand."

Thirty. Thousand. Dollars. Ill-gotten dollars, no doubt. The rumors must be true. Chauncey, and probably his partner-in-crime brother as well, had graduated from moonshine to marijuana—or even harder drugs.

"Get it," he said tightly. Small wonder the Tedder reputation stank.

And she'd planned on sleeping on that load of cash tonight? Some folks 'round these parts would kill for thirty grand. Even if Lilah knew how to use that shotgun, she'd have been putting herself in jeopardy staying here overnight with that much money. If anyone else knew about it, she could have ended up with bullets riddling her body—the same fate as her father.

She scampered away, seemingly eager to be rid of the cash. Hard to believe, but at some level, Lilah must still trust him. Damn, he would have to tell J.D. about this. No way he could just let her waltz into a bank and get flagged as a possible drug dealer.

He sat on the sofa and ran a hand through his hair. "What the hell did you get mixed up in, Chauncey?" he muttered under his breath. He kicked back on the cushions and sighed.

Sure was taking her a long time. Harlan drummed his fingers on the wooden arm of the old couch, waiting.

And waiting.

"Everything all right, Lilah?" he called out.

She staggered back into the den, face pale and fiddling with the gold cross chain around her neck.

He stood, dread prickling his scalp. "What's wrong?"

She drew an unsteady breath. "The money…it's gone."

Chapter Two

Gone.

Harlan rubbed his temples and sat back down on the sofa. He pointed to the rocker, and Lilah settled across from him. How to tell her?

"Was your dad in the habit of keeping large amounts of money around the cabin?" he finally asked.

"No." She clasped her hands in her lap. "At least, not that I'm aware of."

"Any idea how he might have come into this money?"

Her lips pinched together. "No."

"Moonshining can be pretty profitable for a few folks."

The muscles in her jaw worked, and she lifted a hand and waved it in the air. "Not for us. Does this look like a mansion or something? If Dad made much money at it, he sure didn't believe in spreading the wealth."

Harlan knew her financial struggle. She'd been working for six years as a teacher's aide, paying for college tuition and books as she could on her salary.

"Sure, he wasn't known for having an extravagant lifestyle," Harlan agreed. "But you told me yourself that he acted different when you visited in March."

"Lots of shady characters hanging around. A younger crowd, people I'd never seen before." She sighed and stared down at her hands. "Lots of long talks with Uncle Thad, too. Whenever I entered the room, they would stop talking. But that wasn't so unusual. In the past, they would come up with some pretty harebrained get-rich schemes that never worked. Part of the reason Mom cut out years ago."

Lilah lifted her head and faced him dead on. "But you already know most of this. I confided a lot to you when—" she hesitated a heartbeat "—when we were seeing each other."

Seeing each other. Images of her flashed through his mind—Lilah lying on his bed, her hair spread against the sheets, the play of moonlight on her skin, the feel of her hand gliding down his abs and lower still... Best not to dwell on that. He cleared his throat.

"Can't help wondering if your dad might have changed his, er, business model. He wouldn't be the first to switch from moonshine to marijuana. That's where the real money is these days."

Gray eyes flashed. "You asking if Dad was a dope dealer? No way."

There was no kind way to have her face the possibility. Might as well be honest. "There's been rumors. We know for a fact that there's a huge drug-running operation that passes through our mountains. We just haven't been able to make a major bust yet."

"Rumors?" She stood and paced, temper sparking in her clipped movements. "Figures. Anything criminal happening in Elmore County and people are going to bring up Dad's name. It's so unfair. He never hurt anybody. And he never sold liquor to the teenagers that came around. Said moonshine was a grown man's drink."

Harlan bit the inside of his mouth to keep from blurting his thoughts. He'd liked Chauncey, but Lilah had either forgotten her dad's more violent tendencies or she'd shoved them to the back of her mind. She hadn't been especially close to her dad, but his death was so recent, so fresh in her heart, and Chauncey *was* her father, after all.

"I'm not judging him," Harlan said, treading lightly. "He had plenty of good qualities—a loyal friend, always minded his own business and generous to a fault. But he had a dark side, too. Chauncey spent many a night as a guest of the Elmore County jail for assault."

She shrugged. "Drunken bar fights."

Fierce fights that had resulted in serious injuries to the unlucky, foolhardy men who crossed him. But he let that pass without comment. "You've never seen anything else suspicious?"

"I know what pot plants look like. If I'd seen any on our property, I'd have reported it. Take a look around for yourself if you don't believe me."

"Your father didn't have to be growing it in his fields to participate. He could have managed an indoor operation."

"I don't know anything about that." Lilah crossed her arms.

If she had a fault, it was stubbornness. She'd come by it honestly as Chauncey Tedder's daughter. That man refused to live life on anyone else's terms and abided by his own creed of what constituted right and wrong—the law be damned. Truth be told, many mountain folk felt the same.

"If you find anything incriminating while you're staying here, I hope you'll tell me."

"Outlaws keeping a step ahead of the law up here?" she quipped. "Imagine that."

Were they ever. Every drug raid ended the same—a dead end with no evidence or suspects in sight. "This is serious, Lilah. Drug operations bring in a dangerous criminal element. They aren't like your dad."

She sobered. "Which is why Dad would never have been a part of that. *Never.*"

He raised his hands, palms out. "Okay, okay. I just can't help worrying about you staying out here alone."

"I won't be here long. There's no reason to stay now that…you know." She let her words trail off.

Now that their relationship was over.

Again, it hung heavy in the air between them, weighing on his shoulders like a thick blanket. "When?"

"Soon," she answered dismissively.

He'd lost the right to question her more closely about her comings and goings. None of his business.

"I'm sorry," he said. "Sorry for—"

"Forget it." She thrust out her chin. "I have."

Had she? Had Lilah really moved on? Because he sure as hell hadn't. "Why don't you stay with Darla while you're here? The next guy coming along to buy 'shine might not be as nice as the one that just skedaddled off your property."

He caught the slight tightness at the edge of her eyes. "She's busy with Ed and her kids. We'd get on each other's nerves after a while, anyway."

"Too bad Jimmy couldn't have stayed longer."

"Yeah. He looked so sad when he had to fly back," she said wistfully.

His old friend, her brother, was no longer the free-spirited kid that he used to hang around with in high school— and occasionally get in trouble with. Jimmy's tour in Afghanistan had changed his carefree attitude. At the funeral, and even afterward, he'd been distant and grave. Shell-shocked, some might say.

The loud rumble of a diesel engine roared from the driveway, and Harlan stepped out onto the porch in time to see a large gruff man at the wheel. He sharply turned the truck, and it circled the yard before heading back down the road.

"Your cruiser is running off my dad's business," Lilah said drily.

He rubbed his chin. "Wish I could leave it here overnight."

"I'll be fine. Just go." With that, she turned away.

He'd been dismissed, and there wasn't a damn thing he could do about it. "At least for tonight, call your sister and see if she'll stay out here with you." At the cold snap of her gray eyes, he added, "Please."

"Maybe."

The old oak door shut firmly behind her. Stubborn woman.

A LEATHER CORDED bracelet with a crimson stone, a triple-stranded necklace of multicolored glass and a tarnished silver ring with a fake cameo carving. Lilah laid the jewelry on the kitchen table and examined the pieces. They obviously held little, if any, monetary value, but they'd been carefully wrapped in an embroidered linen handkerchief inside a red silk drawstring pouch. So they'd meant something to somebody at one time.

Curious, she'd called Mom, who'd snorted when asked if they'd once belonged to her. "Anything I wanted from that cabin, which wasn't much, I took with me when I left your dad." She also claimed never to have seen the jewelry. "Might have belonged to Chauncey's mama, but if it did, I never noticed he had them, and he never mentioned it to me. Your dad wasn't exactly the sentimental type, anyway."

Still, Lilah was reluctant to chuck the pieces in the charity box with everything else worth salvaging. If the jewelry had belonged to Granny Tedder, she wanted to keep it.

At the crunch of gravel outside, she peered out the front window. Good, just Darla and Uncle Thad come to call.

She opened the screen door and waved them inside. Uncle Thad hefted Darla's overnight bag from the truck bed as her sister minced her way to the porch in high heels. Lilah suppressed a giggle. Even as a kid, Darla was into playing dress up and acting like a Hollywood ingenue instead of a hillbilly's daughter.

"Thanks for coming over, y'all. Harlan was over earlier and got me all paranoid about staying alone out here."

"Harlan, huh? He's sexy." Darla winked as she entered, leaving a trail of perfume in her wake.

Lilah ignored the comment.

"Got yer shotgun, don't ya?" Uncle Thad bellowed. "Yer safe enough." He huffed and puffed up the porch steps. He was a giant of a man, over six feet tall, and as strong and as broad-boned as an ox.

He always knew just what to say to make her feel better. She hugged him as he entered the cabin.

Darla walked to the kitchen table, hips swaying. When she pulled out a chair and sat, she crossed her legs, exposing a long stretch of thigh. "You've been working hard. I've never seen Dad's place look so tidy. At least not since Mama ran off." She tossed her hair and sighed. "Be a love and make me a cup of coffee. Those kids 'bout ran me ragged today."

Lilah exchanged a quick knowing glance with Uncle Thad, who was dragging the suitcase to the back bedroom. Somehow, everything always centered on Darla and her needs. Feeling guilty, Lilah set about fixing the coffee. After all, her sister was busy with her own home life and didn't have to come babysit a grown fraidy-cat woman.

"What do we have here?" Darla cooed, picking up the multicolored necklace and holding it to the light.

"Found them under Dad's mattress. Any idea who they belong to?"

"No, but it's mine now." Darla clasped the necklace around her neck and preened. "How does it look?"

Gaudy, actually. Lilah measured the coffee and started the machine. "Mmm," she said noncommittally.

Uncle Thad waved from the den. "Gotta hit the road. Momma's waiting dinner on me."

"Tell Aunt Vi I said hey," Lilah called from the kitchen.

Darla put on the bracelet and ring. "Not too shabby, I guess. Whatcha think, Uncle?"

He stopped and stared. "Where'd ya get those baubles?"

"Lilah found them. Do they look pretty on me?"

"Sure, sure. Not that you need adornment." He winked at Lilah. Uncle Thad knew how to flatter his niece.

"You want to keep one, Lilah?" Darla asked.

"Nah, that's okay. They should go to someone who appreciates them."

Uncle Thad left, and Lilah warmed up a large pot of chicken and dumplings and another pot of butter beans. She was suddenly ravenous and exhausted as the aroma kicked in, and she absently stirred the dumplings, thinking of all the things she'd have loved to discuss with Darla. Hidden matters of the heart. But there was a layer of reserve between them. It seemed sometimes as if Darla resented her. Lilah had left Lavender Mountain years ago, finished her high school degree, and would soon graduate college with her teacher's certificate, whereas Darla had never left, never finished her schooling and had pretty much been forced into marriage when she'd gotten pregnant at sixteen.

Lilah set their plates on the table and sat across from her. "I know the kids keep you busy, but aren't they fun, too? I mean, you like being a mother, don't you?"

Darla shrugged. "It has its moments, I suppose. But it's lots of work. More than I realized it would be."

"But satisfying, right?"

"Sure," she said carelessly, lifting her little finger as she sipped her coffee.

Well, that hadn't been particularly enlightening or encouraging. What had she expected? Lilah ate, savoring the homemade food. As soon as her stomach was sated, lethargy crept in like a drug. She blinked, surveying the dirty dishes with dread. All she wanted was to crawl into bed and snuggle under the covers.

"Hey, kid." Darla's hand closed over hers. "You look beat. I'll wash the dishes."

"You will?" She couldn't keep the surprise out of her voice.

"Of course. You go on to bed."

Beat didn't even begin to cover how exhausted she felt. For the first time since she was a little kid, Lilah had begun taking afternoon naps. "I'll take you up on that offer," she said.

Darla slipped off the leather bracelet and clasped it around Lilah's wrist. "And you keep this. Stand up for yourself now and then, girl."

Unexpected tears gathered in her eyes, and she blinked them back. Every once in a blue moon, Darla surprised her. Nodding, she got up from the table and went to the bedroom. Without bothering to change into her nightgown, she slipped between the covers and fell into the black abyss of sleep.

COLD.

Lilah rubbed the goose bumps on her arm. Wind rustled through the pines and whooshed into the cabin. Darla must have opened a window, she surmised, clambering out of bed.

The scrape of a heavy boot on the wooden floor brought

her to an abrupt halt. The back of her neck prickled. Another step creaked in the hallway, and her mind raced. The shotgun was by the front door, so that was of no use. She hesitated, torn between locking her door or opening her bedroom window and hightailing it into the dark night.

But she couldn't leave Darla alone to face the menace.

Lilah unplugged the lamp on her nightstand and wrapped her hand around the base like a club. Not much of a weapon, but it was better than nothing. She stepped into the hallway and flattened herself against the wall, letting her eyes adjust to the dark.

Moonbeams cast a silvery glow in the den, and the shadows shifted, forming the silhouette of a man in black. He wasn't aware of her presence and crept from the rocking chair to the coffee table, picking up magazines and searching for...something. Did others know about the large amount of cash her father had stockpiled in the cabin? This could get ugly, deadly even. Maybe someone who'd been searching for the money had murdered her dad. Damn it, Harlan was right to warn her away from this place. Darla spending the night calmed her fears, but unless her sister was packing heat, she was of no help.

Lilah peeled herself away from the wall and stepped into the hallway to warn Darla of the danger. At the slight sound, the man straightened and spun around.

He had no face. Where eyes and nose and mouth should have been, there was nothing but inchoate blackness.

Lilah's pulse pounded furiously in her taut body. It was a nightmare come to life—paralysis rooted her feet to the floor and she could hardly breathe. The scream in her throat choked her lungs, refusing to unloose in the deathly quiet.

Suddenly, the intruder turned and ran for the open window. A piercing cry vibrated her ears and brain. It took several seconds before she realized it was her own voice screaming. She stumbled to the front of the cabin on numb feet and dropped the lamp on the sofa, exchanging porcelain for the cold steel of the shotgun's barrel. A bolt of courage rippled down her spine, and she raced to the window and slammed it shut.

"What the hell is going on?" Darla rushed into the room and flipped on the light switch, revealing her baby doll nightie with its feathered neckline. Her mouth was devoid of the usual red lipstick, but pink sponge curlers dangled loosely in her brown hair. Oddly enough, the scanty attire only made her appear like an adolescent. A vulnerable, confused teenager.

"Somebody broke in. Did you open the window in here before you went to bed?"

"No. Is that how they got in? Did you get a good look at him?"

"He wore a mask."

"Oh, my God. I'm calling Ed to get out here."

"No sense rousing him and your kids out of bed. The man's gone."

"Are you crazy? I'm not staying here."

"We could drive into town and stay at a motel. But I don't relish the thought of going outside to get in the car."

"Call your Harlan. Tell him to get here ASAP."

Her Harlan. She wished he was. Not the mean, stupid Harlan who'd dumped her but the old Harlan who couldn't keep his hands off her and whose kisses had made her feel wild and cherished. She lifted her chin. "No. I won't bother him."

"Bother him? Isn't responding to break-ins, like, his *job*?"

She could call someone else in the sheriff's office, but Harlan would get word and come immediately. Lilah thought fast. "We could call Uncle Thad."

Darla grumbled. "Okay. But the only reason I'm not calling Ed is 'cause I don't wanna put my kids in danger."

"I'll make the call while you get dressed."

Darla sped to the bedroom, mumbling under her breath—something about the crazy gene in their family, Lilah thought.

Lilah grabbed the cell phone and punched in her uncle's number with her left hand, still clutching the gun in her right. She turned off the overhead light and stood by the window. Was he out there in the darkness, waiting for another night, another opportunity?

She would never feel safe here again. Maybe Harlan was right. Maybe Dad had gotten mixed up in some new dangerous scheme. A new gamble, a new adventure—one that had cost him his life. Who knew what desperate secrets lived in another's heart? She had to think about her own future, her own sad secret.

As soon as she'd settled her dad's affairs, she would leave Lavender Mountain.

Chapter Three

This was going to kill Darla.

She'd put off bringing up the matter of the missing money, imagining Darla's furious reaction at the news. For the past couple of days, she'd stayed tied up with all the paperwork concerning the robbery and fixing up Dad's old place. Darla was much too busy to be bothered. Okay, that wasn't entirely true or fair—she'd been avoiding this scene with her sister.

Tired as she was from the drama and all her duties, Lilah couldn't up and leave the mountain without letting her sister know the money was gone. She sped down Dark Corners Road to the homestead where Darla, Ed and their three children lived. Her sister would be devastated about the stolen money. If only she'd just let her have it that morning like Darla had begged. And she could kiss good-bye that sisterly chat she'd planned on. After the news, Darla would be in no mood to offer advice and comfort over the matter that had weighed on Lilah for weeks. It wasn't like there'd been much chance of Darla being supportive, anyway, if she was being honest with herself.

At the last sharp bend before hitting town, she pulled into Darla and Ed's gravel driveway. An unfamiliar red pickup truck was parked near the side porch. Maybe Ed had traded in his old clunker. She picked her way through a barrage of mangy dogs and mewling cats that barked or hissed their displeasure at the invasion of their territory.

Old toys and broken furniture almost barricaded the doorway, and she impatiently scooted a rusted table out of her path. Through the screen door she heard Darla talking on the phone.

"Yes, I'll hold. But only for a minute. Longer than that and I'll take my business elsewhere," Darla huffed.

Lilah pushed open the door and entered the kitchen where her sister held a tape measure stretched across the lower cabinets. "You back, sir? I want mahogany," Darla said. "Only the best. And I want it pronto."

Lilah blinked. Wow. This was a change. Ed must have been working overtime.

Darla retracted the tape and scribbled on a scrap sheet of paper, her face puckered in concentration.

"New cabinets, huh? Nice."

Her sister snapped her head up, pencil poised. "What are you doing here?"

Not the welcome she'd expected. But then, she and Darla had never been particularly close. The ten-year age difference was large enough so that shortly after their parents' divorce, a pregnant Darla had married Ed while Lilah had moved over a hundred miles away with their mother.

"Well, I'm leaving, and I thought I'd say goodbye first."

Darla colored slightly. "Right. Sorry I couldn't help out more with the estate stuff. Ed Junior's been down with a tummy ache."

"No problem." Lilah shrugged and waited awkwardly.

"I'll just, uh, get off the phone. Want something to drink?"

"Water, thanks." Lilah plopped down on a chair in the den.

The TV blared, although no one was watching it. Where were her nephews?

Darla returned from the kitchen and tossed her a water bottle. "Where are the kids?" Lilah asked.

"I started them in daycare yesterday. I needed more peace and quiet 'round here." She shuddered. "I'm still recovering from that intruder scare."

"Me, too," Lilah admitted. "I meant it when I said I'm not staying. I'll come back when there's papers that need to be signed when the cabin sells, and for the meeting next week in the probate office."

Darla tossed back her hair. "Both stupid formalities. That cabin's not worth much, and I doubt Dad had more than a few hundred dollars in the bank. A complete waste of time."

"But he had thirty thousand dollars lying around the house," she pointed out.

"Dad didn't trust banks. Besides, I bet he was just holding that money for someone."

Lilah suppressed a shudder. If that was true, was that why the intruder had been in the cabin? Would he return?

"Anyway, do you think you could take care of all the paperwork for me?" Lilah asked hesitantly. "I only got involved with everything because Jimmy was overseas and you said you were too busy with the kids to fool with it. Now that they're in daycare…maybe you could take over?"

"You handle it. You always were good with all that complicated kind of stuff."

Irritation flared between her temples. "But I live over a hundred miles from here, and I'm busy, too."

"You?" Darla scoffed. "You don't have other people depending on you to feed them and watch over them. Or a demanding husband. What else do you have to do?"

That about hit her last reserve of patience. "I have a j-o-b. Remember? I also take college classes in whatever spare time I have."

"Pfft." Darla waved a hand dismissively. "Why you wasting time getting a fancy degree…"

But Lilah tuned out her words. Instead, she was mesmerized by the huge diamond flashing on Darla's left hand. "Ed upgraded your wedding ring? It used to be on the small side." Rinky-dink was more like it.

Darla abruptly lowered her hand and crossed her arms, hiding the ring from view.

The new pickup, ordering new cabinets, fancy jewelry. Well, that little mystery was solved.

"It was you!" Lilah stood and pointed her finger. "You're the one who stole the money."

"It wasn't *stealing*. That was Dad's money, and I'm sure he meant for me to have it."

Of all the selfishness Lilah had witnessed over the years with her sister, this was the most outrageous. "All for you, huh? What about me and Jimmy?"

"Jimmy's making plenty of money in the army."

"And me?"

"You're about to become a teacher. You'll be rolling in dough. I need it more than you. I have a family. You don't."

Lilah closed her eyes, thinking of how much thirty thousand dollars would have helped in paying off her college tuition and upgrading from her clinker of a car to something more reliable. Rolling in dough on a teacher's salary? Not hardly.

She drew a long steadying breath. "We'll see what Jimmy thinks about all this when I call him tonight."

"Do you have to tell him?" Darla flushed and bit her lip. "We ain't spent it all yet. I could give you each a few thousand."

She'd never been so angry. Lilah trembled from the injustice. *Careful, careful. Don't say something you'll re-*

gret. "I'll see you later, after I've spoken with Jimmy," she said past numb lips.

"Ah, come on, LayLay," Darla cajoled, using her old childhood nickname. "Don't get all mad on me."

Lilah strode past her, eager to avoid more confrontation. "We'll settle up after I talk to Jimmy. I'll be speaking with Harlan, too. He knows that money was stolen from the cabin. I'm sure he'll want to question you about the theft."

Darla paled. "Now, look here…"

"Save it for the cops," Lilah said, marching out of the house and back to her car. Of all the nerve. Of course, she wasn't going to press charges, but let Darla sweat it a little.

Inside her car, she backed out of the driveway and then paused. Go left or right? Left meant leaving the mountain, right meant having "The Talk" with Harlan. She dreaded it, but her conscience demanded she tell him. Besides, he'd already called, wanting her to sign the missing money report.

Digging deep into her reserves of courage, Lilah turned right.

THE MOMENTARY LULL in the crowded, noisy sheriff's office alerted Harlan that something was off. He glanced up from his paperwork and followed the gaze of his coworkers to the front door.

Ah, yes. Lilah Tedder had that effect on the opposite sex. She turned her head, scanning the room until she zeroed in on where he sat. Her blond hair glowed like a halo under the harsh fluorescent lighting, but her eyes burned like two flames, hot and flickering.

She was no angel.

Lilah beelined to his desk in determined steps. He hoped J.D. wouldn't come out of his office anytime soon this morning and witness them together. She stepped up to his chair.

"So you've already drawn up the report on the money?" she asked, cutting to the chase.

"Yep." Harlan picked up the printed document. "Just need you to sign it."

She sat down next to him and primly placed her purse in her lap. He slid the paper toward her, and she glanced down. "I'm not signing it. There's no longer any need for a report."

"Why? You found it?"

"In a manner of speaking, yes."

He was missing something. People didn't "misplace" thousands of dollars of cash. "That's good. Where was it?"

"I forgot I'd moved it from under the mattress to the bottom dresser drawer."

She was lying, but why? Truth was, he'd been reluctant to write up the report, not wanting to draw unnecessary attention to her newfound wealth. At least not until the money was accounted for and safely deposited in the bank. Besides, her family's name was mud as it was. This report would drag more fodder and speculation about Chauncey's questionable activities.

"Are you sure about this? What's really going on?"

"I'm more worried about intruders than…"

She stopped, obviously flustered about blurting out that tidbit.

"Intruders?" he honed in quickly. "You have any more men showing up to buy moonshine?"

"No. Never mind about that. I'm leaving today, any-way."

"Sure you won't change your mind?" He'd secretly hoped she would hang around long enough for him to try to win her back.

"It's for the best."

"You're scared. Tell me what's going on. Has someone

hurt you or threatened you in any way?" If they had, he'd hunt them down like a dog and make them pay. He lowered his voice and took her hand. "Tell me."

She jerked her hand away. "There's nothing to tell. Forget the report."

"Sure, never mind that I wasted an hour writing this up," he shot back, hurt and annoyed.

Lilah shrugged. "Sorry."

Her tone implied she was anything but sorry.

"For God's sake, Lilah, what the hell is going on here?" He was conscious of his fellow officers glancing their way. He lowered his voice. "First, the missing money, then you hint at an intruder and now you deny anything's wrong?"

"Don't badger me, Harlan Sampson," she said, glaring. "I didn't come here today to talk about the report, anyway. That's not important."

"Not important?" he asked, incredulous. "Are you for real? I demand to know what's going on."

She jumped to her feet, her face flushed and her voice raised. "You have no right to demand anything from me. Never did. I just dropped by to tell you that I'm—I'm…oh, never mind. I won't bother you with the news."

The room was the quietest Harlan had ever witnessed. From deep in the recesses behind their administrative offices, an inmate could be heard cursing in a holding cell.

This wasn't happening. His mind spun in circles. Surely Lilah wasn't about to say she was pregnant, was she? They'd been careful. Except, well, there were a couple of times they'd been too impatient. He felt like he'd fallen down into a deep well and couldn't catch his breath.

Lilah raised her chin and strolled away, her back ramrod stiff. From the corner of his eyes, he caught Sheriff Bentley shaking his head in an I-told-you-so way.

Instead of heading to the front door, she made an abrupt

turn to the right and entered the women's restroom. Jolene Smithers, a fellow officer, rose from behind her desk. "I'll check on her," she said, eyes wide with equal measures of pity and curiosity.

To hell with J.D.

He found his feet and followed Jolene, aware that every eye in the room was upon them. Someone snickered, and the back of his neck flushed with heat.

LILAH PULLED BACK her hair and leaned over the toilet, gagging. A few deep, shuddering breaths later, she straightened, bracing her hands against the stall's cool metal siding.

That'd been close. For a moment back there, she'd been ready to upchuck all over Harlan's carefully prepared report. One that was no longer needed.

"Get yourself together and get the hell out of Dodge," she muttered.

"You all right in there?" a female voice drawled.

Lilah stiffened. "I'm fine," she said in a mind-your-own-business tone.

"Don't sound fine to me."

Lilah waited. Whoever was on the other side of the door wasn't leaving and wasn't entering the neighboring stall. Just what she needed. Why couldn't a girl get a clean break when she needed to beat a hasty exit? Sighing, she pushed open the door and strode to the washbasin, determined to ignore the nosy stranger. From the corner of her eye, she took her in—a tall rangy woman, wearing a brown uniform and a badge.

"Quite a scene out there," the woman commented drily.

Lilah splashed her face and rinsed her mouth out.

"I think Harlan's worried about you."

"Told ya I was fine." She jerked a paper towel from the

dispenser and dried her face and hands before throwing it in the bin.

"You with child?" the woman asked.

Lilah snatched the keys from her pocketbook and marched to the door. Another minute and she would be out of this stifling place.

"Is it Harlan's?"

The nerve. Lilah's eyes snapped to meet the intruder's. She wore no makeup and her auburn hair was pulled back in a careless ponytail. Still, it was easy to see she was a beauty in a tomboyish, no-frills kind of way with a peaches-and-cream complexion and large hazel eyes.

"None of your business..." Lilah glanced at the nameplate pinned below her badge. "Officer Smithers."

"We're all good buddies working here. Family, even. So is it his?"

Lilah pushed past the woman but Jolene Smithers stepped in front of her.

"Following in your sister's footsteps? Guess I should give you some credit, though. At least you managed to finish high school before populating our county with more Tedders."

The *hell*? It may have been years since she'd lived in Lavender Mountain, but Smithers's lip curl of disgust when she said *Tedders* slashed through time. Once again, Lilah was young and facing the taunts of schoolchildren or braving the slights of classmates who never came to her birthday parties. No parent wanted their child hanging out with the likes of Lilah and her family.

"Get out of my way," she said coldly.

"I'm betting it isn't. Good thing we have paternity tests these days. Keeps riffraff like you from tying down a decent man who—no doubt—will insist on doing the right thing. Either marriage or child support for the next eighteen years."

Jolene's words splattered like acid on Lilah's heart. That much was true. Harlan would insist on doing right by her. But what kind of life would that be—knowing she'd unwittingly trapped him into marriage? He couldn't know the truth.

"And what about his career?" Jolene continued. "He'd be the laughing stock of this county, running for sheriff after a shotgun wedding to a Tedder."

She'd had enough. Lilah went around Jolene and flung open the restroom's door before delivering her parting shot as she stepped into the lobby. "It's not his baby. Okay? You happy now?"

Whipping her head back around, she faced a tall uniformed column of stubborn human male.

Harlan.

His feet were planted less than six feet from the doorway and his face was set like carved granite.

How much had he heard? He couldn't have missed her saying the baby wasn't his. Lilah lowered her head and walked quickly to the door. She'd come by to tell him she was pregnant with his child, but maybe it was best this way.

So why was she near tears? If he had ever loved her, that love hadn't been enough to erase the stigma of her name. Believing she was pregnant by another man, so quickly after their own affair had ended, would be proof to him that she was fickle and unworthy.

OUTSIDE, THE GEORGIA sun beat down like a whip on his face. "Lilah. Stop." He placed a hand on her shoulder, and she froze. He stepped in front of her and gazed at her pale face. Now that he had her attention, he hadn't a clue what to say.

"Sorry you heard the news that way," she said flatly. "Didn't want you to wonder if it was yours, though—just in case we ran into each other in the future or you heard something."

"Are you sure?" he asked. This didn't feel right.

"Positive."

Anger churned his gut. There hadn't been anyone else for him since he'd cut off ties with Lilah. How had she moved on so quickly? "Who?" he ground out past numb lips.

Her brows raised and she regarded him blankly.

"Who's the father?"

"Oh. You don't know him. He's not from around here."

She was lying. He was—almost—sure of it.

"Is the baby mine or not? I deserve the truth."

She hesitated. "You deserve a life with a woman you love. You deserve to be sheriff."

"Is that what this is about? Let me decide what I want."

"Do you love me?" she asked abruptly.

His mind drew a blank. Love? He cared for her...*mightily* cared. But love? "I... I'm..."

Her lips trembled, and she pinched them together. "Whatever happened between us is long over. I have to figure things out on my own."

"You shouldn't have to face this alone. What about this...this other man?" His mind whirled at the possibility she was telling the truth. "Will he marry you? Or at least support you?"

She gave a harsh laugh. "The days of shotgun weddings 'round these parts are long over. Plenty of women have been single moms. I can do the same."

A memory pierced him—her dad at the Foxy Lady bar/

motel, hunting down Ed after getting word that Darla was with child. By all witness accounts, Chauncey had stormed into the dive, red-faced and waving a shotgun, searching for the hapless culprit who'd deflowered his eldest daughter. Seeing Ed shirk into the corner, Chauncey had approached and grabbed a fistful of Ed's camouflage jacket. "Congratulations, you're getting married," he'd announced.

Harlan ran a finger over the collar rim of his stiff uniform shirt. Those days of forced marriages weren't entirely over. Chauncey Tedder would be mighty displeased about this situation if he were still alive. He cleared his throat. "But you don't have to raise a child alone if he—"

"Just go back to work, Harlan. This is my problem, not yours." She darted around him, but not quickly enough for him to miss the tears brimming in her eyes.

"Are you going to be okay driving home?" he asked. Damn it, he still cared about her even though he shouldn't.

She didn't bother responding. Instead, she climbed in her car and backed out of the parking space a tad too carelessly. She whipped out of the lot and accelerated onto the highway. Within a minute, the car disappeared in the distance.

It was as if Lilah couldn't wait to be rid of him.

"She gone?" Jolene was suddenly beside him.

"Looks that way."

"It's for the best, Harlan." She ran a hand along his arm. "Time you moved on. If you ever want to talk, I'm here."

He frowned and moved out of her reach. This wasn't Jolene's first hint she wanted something more than friendship.

"Plenty of other fish in the sea." She smiled and practically batted her eyes.

But he had zero interest in his comely coworker. Instead of a tall redhead, his interest was decidedly marked in favor of a certain petite blonde. One who clearly was over him and might even be pregnant with another man's baby.

So why was he so upset? Hadn't that been what he wanted all along—a clean break with Lilah? But he walked away from Jolene and headed back to work weighted with a heaviness that made him feel suddenly ten years older.

Chapter Four

Harlan considered himself lucky. Today would be so busy that thoughts of Lilah would be temporarily relegated to the back burner. Last night had been a tough and fitful sleep—was the baby his or not and why should he care?—but after numerous cups of coffee, he now had enough stamina to get through the day's scheduled raid.

He and five other officers surrounded the abandoned older home. Kudzu crept over the windows like a living, breathing veil. So convenient for anyone hiding illegal drugs. One would expect to see broken windows and doors in a vacated building, but for all its age and the superficial facade of neglect, the front door was bolted shut with a steel chain and padlock and it lacked signs of forced entry anywhere.

Not only that but also dozens of large footsteps had tamped down the overgrown grass and weeds surrounding the house. They'd been there when he and the team had arrived.

He had a good feeling about this one.

Remote homes sprinkled Appalachia, but this place on top of Booze Mountain took the cake. It had taken them a good half an hour of driving up increasingly narrow and bumpy dirt roads to get here.

Sammy Armstrong sidled over and gave him a broad wink. "How's your girlfriend doing?"

Harlan gritted his teeth. If it had been someone other than his old childhood friend teasing him, he would have busted his chops. "Fine," he spat, not inviting further conversation.

Sammy nudged him. "Lilah's more than fine. A real looker. A man could do worse."

J.D. pulled into the lot and exited the cruiser, patting his uniform shirt pocket. "I got the subpoena. Let's do this."

Alvin Lee, a fellow officer, marched up the sagging porch steps with a pair of giant bolt cutters.

Harlan idly swatted at a skeeter that buzzed near his ear and swiped his arm across his sweaty forehead. The heat was brutal, even up here in the mountains.

The chain crashed onto the wooden porch with a clatter nearly as loud as a shotgun blast. Alvin kicked in the door, and Harlan followed him inside the abandoned home.

The stench of stale food pervaded—a toxic mixture of fried bologna and venison. In the center of the main room, the scratched surface of a long table was littered with boxes, string and packing tape. It looked like an assembly line set up. Easy to guess the sort of merchandise packaged here.

He glanced around the mostly ruined interior, and his spirits sank. It looked deserted. Not even a single marijuana plant in sight. So much for his intuition.

Three other officers entered via the back door, and J.D. strolled into the room, thumbs tucked into his belt. "Find any drugs?" he asked hopefully.

Harlan swiped a finger on the fine layer of white powder on the table. Much too white for mere dust. "Probably cocaine residue," he answered, brushing off the powder on his pant legs. "Afraid that's going to be the extent of our find."

"Damn it. Not again." J.D. stalked off to the adjacent kitchen. "Comb the area for leftover receipts, matches—anything left behind that might give us some clue who's been here."

Sammy slammed his fist into his open palm. "What is this? Almost a half dozen raids now in the last year? They're always a step ahead of us." He huffed in frustration. "It's like they know we're coming."

Dread settled in Harlan's gut as he assimilated the words. He didn't want to believe it. They were a small team, and he'd grown up with most of them on the mountain. They were his friends, his colleagues, the people he trusted in dangerous situations.

But the lure of easy money could mess with a person's mind. He'd seen it before. A younger officer, Caleb, had fallen into that trap last year. First, it was turning a blind eye on minor offenses like illegal poker games. Then it progressed to fixing tickets for family and friends. Word spread until it reached a point where everyone believed they could offer a little money in return for a favor, muddying boundaries. Even if he'd wanted to stop taking bribes, Caleb had confessed that if he *hadn't* taken them, someone would have squealed.

Someone always squealed. You could count on that. It held true for inmates as well as the officers who were supposed to enforce the law.

In the end, Caleb had been fired.

Harlan tapped a finger against his lips. Caleb still dated Marla, one of the two dispatchers on the day shift. Did Marla pump him with information on their scheduled raids? Mentally, he made a note to check on that.

J.D.'s cell phone rang, and he tossed it on the kitchen

counter. "Answer that while I help Alvin search the back bedroom."

Harlan picked it up. "Sampson here," he said, opening a drawer and searching its sparse contents as Marla breathlessly reported the latest news.

Another shooting. Another victim dead.

An icy finger of fear shimmied down his spine. Lilah—and their baby—might be in danger.

LILAH RUBBED HER swollen eyes, then riffled through the stack of bills that had collected in her mailbox during her absence. Absentmindedly going up the stairs, she almost ran smack into Luke McCoy at the bottom of the apartment stairwell.

"Whoa there, missy," he said with a laugh. "We missed you while you were gone." She glanced up, and his easy grin melted away. "You all right?"

Lilah gave him a watery smile. "I'm fine."

"You don't look fine. Need a friend? We could talk over breakfast and coffee."

Sure, but she hated to encourage the guy. He'd been asking her out for weeks now, and if she went out with him, he'd make a big deal of it.

"No, really. It was a rough night, but I'm okay."

"Missing your family, I bet," he said knowingly. "Ms. Cranston told me you went home for your father's funeral and stayed awhile to take care of the estate and stuff."

She made a mental note to be more circumspect with her elderly neighbor. "Right," she agreed, clutching at the excuse.

A brown-and-white cop cruiser whipped into a nearby parking spot, and she idly watched as a man got out. He locked the door and turned, rapidly making his way toward them. It couldn't be. A familiar shock of brown hair, a strong jaw and piercing blue eyes… Yes, it was Harlan. What was he doing here? And dressed in his uniform, too?

"I think breakfast is just what you need," Luke continued, unaware of Harlan approaching from behind. "Let me take you out."

Her stomach revolted at the thought of food. "No, thank you."

"Ah, come on—"

"The lady said no," Harlan snapped.

"What are you doing here?" she asked.

His jaw tightened. "We have business to discuss."

Luke held up a hand and shuffled backward. "I'll leave you two alone then."

Well, at least he might not pester her for dates anymore. So at least something good would come of this unexpected meeting with Harlan.

"Is that him?" Harlan asked stiffly.

"What? Oh, you mean… Never mind, it's still none of your business."

"Seemed pretty spineless to me," Harlan observed. "He cut out pretty quick when I came."

"You practically ordered him to leave," she argued. "Besides—"

"Yoo-hoo, officer!" They looked up the stairs, where Ms. Cranston stood in her housecoat. "That was quick. I just called five minutes ago."

"Ma'am, I'm not—"

"I got to puzzling on that stranger hanging around here last night, and the more I thought on it, the more scared I got on account of—"

"Stranger?" Harlan took the stairs two at a time and withdrew a small notebook from his shirt pocket. "When? What did he look like?"

Lilah followed him, trying to quell the butterflies of alarm in her stomach.

"He was medium height, a little on the thin side and dressed all in black. Kept walking back and forth in that hallway there." She pointed to the hall where Lilah's apartment was.

"Did he wear a black ski mask?" Lilah asked, holding her breath.

"No. If he had, I'd a called the police right away."

"Could you describe his face or hair?" Harlan asked.

Ms. Cranston shook her head. "He stayed in the shadows."

Harlan sighed and returned the notepad to his shirt pocket.

"Thing is," Ms. Cranston continued, "another feller came 'round this morning dressed all in black. I leaned out my window and yelled, 'Hey, whatcha doin'?' He took off running to the parking lot without even turning around to see who was talking."

"Did you get a look at the car make and model, or a tag?"

"It was a big dark blue car," she said. "Sorry, I don't know models and such as that."

Harlan nodded. "Thank you, ma'am." He took Lilah's arm and motioned for the stairs.

"Hope you catch him," Ms. Cranston called to their backs. "I don't cotton to strangers roaming around here. Up to no good, I bet."

"We're going to your apartment, and you're going to pack your things," Harlan said in his no-nonsense voice. "We'll talk on the way to Lavender Mountain."

"Won't be any safer there," she muttered. Inside her apartment, she whirled to face him. "You can't just show up and start ordering me around."

His face was as set as she'd ever seen it. "Have a seat."

Something was wrong. *Bad* wrong. Her jellied legs no longer felt strong enough to support her weight, and she sank into the nearest chair, clasping her hands in her lap. "What's happened?"

Harlan ran a hand through his hair and sank to his knees beside her, so close she could feel the heat of his skin and inhale the scent of his woodsy aftershave. "There's no easy way to break this, darlin'."

Who was in trouble or hurt this time? Jimmy? He'd returned to his tour in Afghanistan last week, and Lord knew that he'd been placed in dangerous missions time and again—

"It's Darla," he said gently, placing a large rough hand over hers and squeezing. "She's been murdered."

No. *No, not her sister.* "I just saw her yesterday," she mumbled. How stupid. As if that meant Darla couldn't possibly be dead. Lilah shook off the useless denial. "How…"

"Shot in the back."

Murder again. The air pressed in and her lungs seized. She squeezed in a painful breath and exhaled. "Same as Dad?"

"Yes."

Without thinking, she collapsed onto his broad shoulders, her body shaking uncontrollably. *Not again. Not again.* Harlan shifted into the chair beside her and guided her onto his lap where she felt cradled by his strength. His hands rubbed up and down her back. She focused on his touch—it was all she could grasp to stop the maelstrom of mourning, which threatened to overwhelm her.

First Dad, and now Darla. All in the space of a week.

Lilah snapped her head up, remembering she wasn't alone in her grief. "Those poor kids! And Ed, too."

Harlan brushed away the tears on her cheek. "We've

called Ed's parents, and they're on the way. If need be, they can keep the children at their place while we get to the bottom of this."

"Surely Ed wants them there with him. And I can go over and stay a bit until things settle down. Help him out. He must be devastated."

"You think so?"

"Of course." She cocked her head to the side, digesting the impact of his words. "You don't... I mean... You aren't saying *Ed* killed Darla, are you?"

"We're not ruling anything out. Usually, a killer is someone known intimately by the victim."

She tensed, fighting the sudden shudder that crawled up her spine. "Not in this case. It's the same way my dad was killed, so it must be the same person. And Ed had no beef with Dad."

"That you know of," Harlan corrected.

"Only when he got Darla pregnant in high school. Once they got married, Dad and Ed got along just fine."

"Did your brother-in-law ever work for your dad on the side?"

"Not that I'm aware of. Are you arresting Ed?"

"J.D.'s questioning him now."

She jumped off his lap. "And the kids? I have to get down there. They might need me." Guilt snaked its way through her gut, insidious and slimy. Who was she kidding? Nobody needed her. She and Darla had had a major argument over the stolen money. The last time she'd seen her sister, she'd stormed out of the house, threatening to put the cops on her tail.

Frantically, she grabbed her purse off the table, eager to leave and keep her mind and hands busy instead of dwelling on the news. "I've got to pack a few clothes, and…and…" She blindly stumbled into the coffee table and rubbed her shins.

"I'll drive you." Harlan took her purse and set it on the sofa. "Go ahead and pack. Take your time. There's no rush."

She shook her head. "No. I'll need my own vehicle. I don't want to be dependent on you to drive me everywhere while I'm back."

"Yeah, about that. The easiest thing all around is for you to stay with me. Ed and the kids have his parents to help out, and there's no sense in you wasting money on a motel."

No. He didn't love her, and she wouldn't be a burden to him or anyone else. Lilah thought fast. There was always Uncle Thad and Aunt Vi, but with their eight children, it tended to be a bit noisy and cramped.

"I can stay with my Aunt Ruth who lives about forty miles from here. She has health problems so she'll appreciate my help around the house and my company." She stifled the impulse to cross her fingers behind her back. Ruth was nearly seventy years old and had never married or had children—a quiet woman like her preferred the solitary life. Yes, she'd recently had minor surgery but, truth be told, Ruth was just fine on her own.

His brow furrowed. "She doesn't have anyone else to take care of her? I don't like you working so hard."

"No. Besides, what's it to you?"

His eyes trailed down to her belly. "Somebody needs to look out for you."

Lilah couldn't help it. She blushed.

Harlan quirked a brow. "Since when have you ever been shy with me?"

Yeah, he was right about that. No point in modesty after he knew every inch of her body. Lilah shook off the sudden images of Harlan's intimate kisses. Now wasn't the time for remembering such things.

"I'll need to call the Red Cross again and get word to Jimmy."

"I can do it for you," Harlan volunteered.

"No. I'm family. I should." Lord, she didn't want to, though. Her brother had enough stress without hearing that yet another family member had been murdered.

"We'll do it together. Tonight."

Lilah wavered. It *would* be nice to stay with Harlan. There was nowhere she'd feel more protected. On the other hand, going to his place would stir up the old memories of the time they'd spent together. A happier time when she'd thought they'd be together forever.

Harlan obviously sensed her hesitation and moved in for the kill. "Come on," he said in his husky, sexy voice. "It'll give us an opportunity to talk. I'm still not convinced the baby isn't mine."

The baby. Lilah's hand went to her stomach. She had to consider more than just her own feelings. Harlan could protect her…protect *them*. It didn't mean they were a couple again. And there was no denying that she and all her family were in danger. This was far from over—something deep and rotten and evil lay at the bottom of these two deaths.

It was only a matter of time before the killer struck again.

Who would be next?

Chapter Five

"It's a formality."

Harlan placed his broad hand on the small of her back and guided her into the antiseptic, frigid forensics room located in the bowels of the county hospital.

Lilah's breath came in rapid, shallow bursts. *I can't do this*. She thought of Ed. He was always in the background at family gatherings, a quiet presence and foil to Darla's chatter and dramatics. A seemingly decent guy.

But now, the normally stoic Ed was barely holding himself together. His large hands were trembling by his sides.

I have to be here. It's the last kindness I can do for my sister. Help her family in their time of need.

"It will all be over in a minute," Harlan whispered reassuringly in her ear.

"Right." One quick glance, a thumbs-up to the coroner from Ed and she was out of there.

An older woman in pastel blue scrubs and a white coat nodded at her briskly, but not unkindly. Lilah's gaze dropped to the gurney where a body was draped over with a white sheet. Darla's body. She forced her leaden feet forward and nodded, glad Harlan's hand remained at the base of her spine. Ed groaned and then pinched his lips together in determination. Lilah patted his arm.

At his nod, the woman turned down the sheet with a practiced flick of her wrist.

Red lipstick blazed against pale alabaster skin tinged with a morgue-blue undertone. Dishwater-blond hair fell carelessly over stiff shoulders. The curve of her jaw and cheekbones, the delicate arch of her brows, a certain sculpting of the nose and lips—Lilah could see herself in the family genetics. Thank heavens they had only revealed her face. There was no hint of the violence she'd endured. But if rolled over, Darla's body would have been visibly marred by shotgun pellets.

The sheet was short on the left side and Lilah observed Darla's lifeless hand that peeked out from under the edge of the cover.

"It's her," Ed croaked. "Darla Marie Tedder Stovall."

The woman immediately pulled the sheet back over Darla, covering her face.

Harlan nodded to the technician. "Thank you, ma'am."

"The secretary out front will have you sign a paper confirming the identification. Sorry for your loss."

They were officially dismissed.

Lilah wanted to say goodbye to Darla, say she was sorry that sharp words were the last ones spoken between them. But it was too late. She swallowed the regret and walked out of the cold room, breathing deeply as they headed toward the desk. A young man handed them a clipboard and pen. "Sign here," he said, motioning to the signature line at the bottom of the sheet.

Ed scribbled his name with shaking hands.

"There's freshly brewed coffee," he offered them. "Can I get y'all a cup?"

Ed shook his head and looked up at the ceiling.

"Yes—I mean, no." She sure could use the comfort of

warm caffeinated liquid, but her own needs were secondary for the next few months.

"How about some water?" Harlan asked her, his deep voice rumbling behind her.

"What I really want is to get out of here first."

Harlan nodded. "Thanks, but we're fine," he told the tech, ushering them to the elevator.

Once inside, Harlan pressed the button and they rumbled up to the main floor. Ed exhaled and scrubbed at his face.

She couldn't imagine the pain he must be in. "How are the kids doing this morning?" she said around the burn in her throat.

"Mom's watching them."

The elevator door opened and they emerged into the main lobby. The hustle and bustle seemed miles away from the stillness of the basement morgue. Ed walked out first, eyes blinking. He held out a hand to Lilah. "Thanks for coming in with me. It helped. I could tell Dad didn't want to do it."

She glanced over toward the patient waiting area where Ed's father slowly rose from a vinyl sofa and shuffled their way. "Understandable. Call me if there's anything I can do. Anything."

He nodded and she watched as he and his father exited the building into the beautiful, sun-shining day.

"It should be dark and stormy," she said, lips trembling. "And pouring down rain."

A nagging sense of unease quivered in the dark recesses of her brain, and she rubbed her temples. Something wasn't quite right about the viewing of Darla, other than the obvious.

"Headache?" Harlan asked.

"No. I can't explain it. But I feel like I'm missing some important detail. I looked at Darla and…" Her voice drifted off.

"It's been a shock. I should have insisted Ed do this himself."

"It would have only made things harder for him, and he needs to be strong for his kids. And it wasn't just seeing her dead. It's something else."

"I'll get you that water and we'll be on our way."

Alone, she regarded the preoccupied staff and visitors go about the business of living.

Harlan returned and pressed a bottle of water into her hands. Lilah sipped it tentatively. Not too bad, actually. It erased the lingering chill in her belly. "Maybe this will help me think better."

"Do you need to go back into the examining room?"

"Hope not. Let me sit here a spell and concentrate."

His hand was powerful and comforting as he guided her to an unused waiting room and onto a sofa. "Take your time. If you want, we can come back tomorrow and talk to the forensics doctor if you need to. No rush."

She didn't want to return and she didn't want to see her sister's body again. *Think.* Lilah placed her head in her hands and reviewed the last few minutes as if she were a camera, detached and methodical, scanning the scene to replay it for details. She'd entered the morgue, blinking from the glaring whiteness of the fluorescent lights and the white walls. The technician had unrolled the white sheet, exposing Darla's face, and then she'd glimpsed Darla's left hand where the sheet had exposed her bare fingers curled at the edge of the metal gurney.

"That's it!" Lilah jerked her head up and snapped her fingers. "Darla wasn't wearing any jewelry. Not even her wedding ring."

"She always wore it?"

"Always."

Harlan didn't appear too impressed with her realization. "They might have removed all the jewelry before you saw her."

She hadn't considered that. They'd probably given Ed the wedding ring and the costume jewelry Darla had been wearing from the cabin.

"Why Darla?" she whispered, leaning her head against the cold hard wall. "Maybe Dad was involved in shady business. Even bigger than moonshine. Maybe even Ed and Uncle Thad and my boatload of cousins are as well. But Darla?"

"Women commit crimes, too—not that I'm saying your sister did."

She shook her head adamantly. Darla hadn't been concerned about anything past her own little world of her kids and her home. And she was much too lazy to get involved with work in any shape, form or fashion.

Lilah wanted to bite her tongue at the traitorous thought. Darla had plenty of good qualities like… Well, no need to make an inventory.

What kind of mess had her father dragged them all into? She would never feel safe again until the killer was captured. And now, she had a baby to protect as well.

HARLAN SHIFTED THE suitcases in his hands and glanced longingly at the master bedroom.

"Don't even think about it," Lilah said flatly. "I'll take the spare."

With a sigh, he walked across to the guest bedroom and set the suitcases at the foot of the bed. Things would certainly be less complicated without sex. "You know where the bathroom is. Anything else you need?"

"I'm good."

Her tone was rigid. So much for their brief moments of closeness during the day's crisis. He'd only been someone to lean on temporarily. Not that he blamed Lilah a bit. He deserved nothing but her mistrust after the way he'd disappeared from her life. And, apparently, she'd found another man soon afterward to take his place. Or so she claimed.

Awkwardly, he placed a hand on her tensed shoulder. "Sorry about Darla."

She nodded and averted her face, but not before he saw a well of tears threatening to spill over. "I'll just head to the shower now."

Lilah opened one of the suitcases and haphazardly rummaged, finally pulling out a pair of flowered cotton pajama shorts and a matching pink tank top. "Excuse me."

She brushed against him and headed out of the room and down the hall. The sound of the shower spray teased him. He shut his eyes, stifling a groan. Lilah was naked. In his bathroom. Just down the hall.

What kind of a man was he to be lusting for her body when she'd just learned about her sister's murder? A sex-starved one, he admitted to himself. There'd been no other woman he'd even thought about being with since Lilah had swept into his life that past March. She'd come home to spend time with her ill father. Her days had been spent with Chauncey, but her nights had been shared with him.

Now it was June and she'd returned pregnant. What was he to think?

Rousing from his stupor, Harlan went to his own room and stowed his gun in the chest of drawers before stripping out of his uniform. He pulled on a pair of shorts and sat on the bed, waiting for his turn in the shower. Too bad they couldn't take one together. He recalled a memorable time when they had. Her soft skin had been wet and slippery to his touch, and the needles of water had sprayed on them as they'd kissed, long and hard, hands exploring every inch of naked flesh.

Stop. Going down that particular memory lane tonight would lead to nothing but frustration and insomnia.

He didn't have to wait long for her to finish. Lilah strode past his open door and then paused. Her hair was plastered to her head, and tiny rivulets of water ran down the front of her thin tank top. Her very *revealing* top, which exposed a faint impression of nipples. His groin tightened and his heart thudded. How was he going to survive Lilah staying with him and obey her no-touch rule?

She leaned against the doorjamb, long legs crossed at the ankles and a couple inches of flat midriff exposed.

It wouldn't be flat for much longer.

Lilah slowly rubbed a towel through the ends of her long hair. "Didn't mean to act bitchy a moment ago. It's just…" She took a deep breath, and her cheeks flushed crimson. "I can't forget the way you cut me out of your life."

"Maybe I shouldn't have listened to—"

She waved an arm, dismissing his excuse. "It's done. If you cared so much about what everyone thought, then what we had wasn't as strong as I'd imagined it to be."

He rose to his feet and crossed the room. "You know my reasons. If I could do it over again, change my past decision, perhaps I would."

"Really?" Her gray eyes pierced his soul. "You might have cared about me, once—a little—but winning an election is more important to you than I ever could be. You've spent years dreaming of this opportunity. And I'd only mess it up for you."

"I won't lie. I want it bad. I want the chance to prove I'm not the kind of man my father was."

He hadn't ever revealed very much to her. Only that his dad drank too much and had been absent almost all his life. His mom had suffered a debilitating stroke last year and Harlan seemed to believe that the years of hardship she'd suffered had played a significant role in her compromised health.

"And you can't prove anything if you're associated with someone like me. A low-class Tedder. A woman with an outlaw family." Her mouth twisted. "You want some kindergarten-teaching, Sunday-school-attending, upstanding kind of gal who'll help your campaign and make you appear respectable."

He scratched the back of his neck. "When you put it like that, you make me sound like a hypocritical jerk."

A sad smile tugged at her lips. "No. I understand why winning's so important to you. I can't fault your goal to clean up the county."

The heaviness of the unspoken lay between them like a smothering blanket.

"But?" he asked, quirking a brow.

"You're the right man for the job. Everybody knows it. You have nothing to prove. And a woman like Jolene would be damn near perfect for you."

He recoiled instinctively. "I have no interest in Jolene."

Her eyes softened. "Glad to hear it. She's kind of a bitch."

The scent of soap and shampoo was all Lilah left behind as she entered her own bedroom and softly shut the door.

Harlan rubbed his face. Lilah shook him like no one else. Every word, every gesture, every touch left him broken and hungering for more. Why did he have to fall for her of all people? He lay on his bed and heard Lilah toss and turn in the next room. She should be here, lying beside him. Did she feel it, too? Need and desire tumbled within him like a summer storm.

He heard a small hiccup and bolted upright. Was she crying?

Harlan padded to the closed door and knocked. No answer. Gently, he pushed it open. Lilah lay curled with her knees drawn to her chest, knuckles stuffed in her mouth. Another moan escaped the physical barrier she'd created with her fist.

"Stop," he said gruffly, sitting beside her. The mattress gave under his weight, and her body rolled toward his. She stiffened, and he brushed a strand of damp hair that clung to her face. "Don't cry," he demanded softly. "It's not good for you or the baby."

"The baby," she sniffled. "I still can't get used to the idea."

"Are you sure it isn't mine?" he blurted.

"I'm sure," she muttered, turning her head away from him.

He leaned against the headboard and put an arm around her shoulder. A long silence stretched between them. He kissed the top of her head. "Everything's going to work out," he promised.

"I don't want to talk about it right now."

"Fine. But I'm staying here with you tonight."

Lilah pulled away and sat up. "No. You—"

He put a finger to her lips. "Shh. I just want to hold you. At least until you fall asleep."

"Promise?"

"I promise."

Slowly, she lowered her body and snuggled against him. In almost no time, the rhythmic rise and fall of her chest assured him she'd finally fallen into a deep slumber. He stroked the side of her soft cheek, chasing away a fallen tear.

Regret twisted his gut. Had he done the right thing breaking off their relationship? Every moment he spent with her would make their goodbye so much more difficult. Still, holding her as she slept felt right. Somehow, they'd figure everything out once the immediate danger had passed.

Chapter Six

Lilah pulled her car into her uncle's driveway. If anyone had a clue what kind of new mischief Dad had gotten into before his death, Uncle Thad would know. Hell, he was probably in the thick of any criminal activity. Dad had been the master moonshine blender with the killer recipe, but Uncle Thad had the connections and a natural-born salesman's charisma.

A cloud of red dirt marked her abrupt halt at the entrance to his cabin. Holding her breath through the dust, she marched to the porch and rapped on the door.

Cousin Lavon opened it, scowling. "Since when did you start knocking?" he complained, turning his back to her and plopping down in front of the TV.

Surly guy. Poor Aunt Viola had a house full of adult children with no apparent desire to move out and get a real job.

Vi emerged from the kitchen, wiping her hands on an apron and appearing even more tired and drained than usual. Her faded olive eyes were red-tinged from crying.

"What brings you here?" she asked. "Figured you'd be too upset about poor Darla to come a callin'. You know we'll all be at visitation tonight."

"What?" Lavon jerked his gaze away from the television. "Can't go. I got plans."

"Stop being so disrespectful." Uncle Thad strolled into the den and frowned at his eldest son. "You're going. Six o'clock sharp."

"Yes, sir," Lavon grumbled, clearly unhappy, but unwilling to disobey his father.

Uncle Thad gave her a sympathetic smile as Aunt Viola quietly slipped back into the kitchen. "Tough day for the Tedders, especially you."

Guilt flickered in her belly. She was plum tuckered from crying and had awoken this morning full of resolve to discover what might have caused her father and sister's deaths. Better that than dwelling on sorrow.

"I—I'd like to talk with you, if you have a moment." Unexpected tension twisted her tongue. Fueled by anger and despair, she hadn't thought through how best to broach the subject. And she sure hadn't counted on others being underfoot.

"Of course." He rounded on Lavon. "Leave us alone."

Lavon sprang up from the chair with just enough sass to show his displeasure, but not enough to risk his dad's anger, either.

"Vi, bring us some tea on the porch."

"I can help her with that—" Lilah began.

"No, she doesn't mind."

A little presumptuous of him deciding what his wife did and didn't mind—but what did Lilah know? They were one of the few couples in the family who'd stayed together for decades. She followed him onto the porch where he took a seat and motioned at the rocker next to him.

"What's up?"

Lilah bypassed the rocker and dragged over a chair, sitting directly across from her uncle. His gray eyes flickered at the subtle act of defiance and she suppressed a triumphant smile. Uncle Thad was one of her favorite relatives but it didn't hurt to bring him down a peg or two now and then.

Best to get straight to the point. "Have you had anyone stalk you or break into your house?"

"No." His head snapped back an inch. "You had any more trouble since the night you called me?"

"A neighbor saw a man creeping around my apartment the other night."

His brow creased. "How'd they know he targeted your apartment, specifically?"

"She caught him looking in my window and hanging out by my door."

Disgust curled his lips. "A Peeping Tom."

That hadn't occurred to her. A random coincidence? "Maybe. If there weren't two recent murders in the family, I might not even connect the two incidents."

"Still no proof that they are. The world's full of sick people."

The screen door screeched open and Aunt Vi emerged, carrying a pitcher of sweet tea and two glasses of ice. Thad pulled a silver flask from the pocket of his pants and poured a splash before angling it toward Lilah. "Care for a nip?"

She quirked a brow. He'd never offered before. "No, thanks."

"Might take the edge off your nerves. You appear mighty riled."

"No."

He shrugged and tucked it away. Behind his back, Vi nodded approvingly and slipped back into the house.

"I am shaken," she admitted, picking up her glass and taking a long, cool swallow. "I don't feel safe anywhere."

"Stay here with us. Our house is yours. Always was, always will be."

If it wasn't for the sullen Lavon, she might have been tempted. "No. You have a full house. And if someone's targeting me, I don't want to drag y'all into the mess."

"You're family," he insisted. "Couldn't bear it if something happened to you, too. You'll be safer here than anywhere else. Me, Lavon and two of the younger boys all have guns, and we won't hesitate to use them." He pulled a cigar from his front pocket and struck a lighter.

Normally, she didn't mind his porch smoking, but the scent of burning tar and tobacco had her tasting bile at the back of her throat. Quickly, she washed it down with another sip of sweet tea.

"I'm staying with Harlan Sampson for now."

The stogie almost fell out of his mouth. "Why?"

"For protection."

Uncle Thad narrowed his eyes. "You seeing that fella again?"

"No. It's just a temporary arrangement until things settle down."

"So you say."

"What's that supposed to mean?"

"You and him were hot and heavy a few months ago. I warned you then and I'll warn you now—stay away from government men. They're nothing but trouble."

Lilah started to make a crack about paranoia, then thought better of it. A little paranoia just might keep her alive at the moment. The lace curtains behind Uncle Thad moved a fraction, and she glimpsed Lavon's face at the window. The big sneak. She'd never liked him. He was a few years older than her and was always the bully at school when they were growing up.

"Harlan means well," she said stiffly, wondering how he had turned the tables on her and her decisions. She set the glass on the wicker table. "I came here to ask *you* a few questions."

His mouth puckered at the end of the cigar, and he drew a long puff of smoke, exhaling it into an elaborate chain of smoke rings. "Shoot."

"Harlan suspects you and Dad, maybe even Ed, have been business partners for more than just moonshine." She pushed through her hesitancy. "You're family, and you know I love you, but I need to ask—have y'all ever been involved in drug operations?"

Uncle Thad drew a sharp breath and coughed. "Drugs?" He coughed again and his face reddened under his beard. "I can't believe you'd ask such a thing. Insulting enough you believe me capable of such a crime—but you suspect your own father? A man who's not here to defend his reputation?"

"It's horrible, and I'm sorry. I asked because I can't explain the thirty thousand dollars cash I found hidden under his mattress."

"For all I know, Chauncey had been saving that money for years. Not really all that much for a lifetime of savings, if you ask me."

"So you deny branching out into marijuana and heavier stuff?"

"I won't even dignify that with an answer." He took a long swallow of 'shine-laced tea.

Awful early for indulging. She'd never observed him to be a heavy drinker, unlike her dad, but the recent deaths apparently weighed as heavy on his heart as they did on her own. Still, she had to push.

"I only ask because there's some reason for the killings."

"I loved Chauncey, but my brother was a hothead. He got in a rousing bar fight at least once or twice a month.

You ask me, someone came up there to his cabin to settle a grudge."

"Maybe. But what about Darla? How do you explain that?"

His face darkened and his left hand balled into a fist. "Word is—the cops think it's Ed."

"You can't believe that. He loved her. I was with him when he had to identify Darla's body. The poor guy fell apart."

"Guilt can do that to a man."

"Grief, not guilt." Was she the only one who believed him innocent? "Thought you liked Ed—wasn't he working with you and Dad on the side for extra money?"

Uncle Thad drew another long puff of tobacco. A shuttered expression on his face replaced the simmering anger. Lilah remembered that look well. He and Dad wore it often when someone inquired too closely about their business.

"He didn't do much outside of a few deliveries," Thad grumbled.

"At a significant risk. Sounds like Ed was the one risking the rap for distribution."

He ignored the subtle gibe. "You know it's usually a spouse in these kinds of cases, don't you? Crimes of passion happen all the time."

Lilah set down her glass with an emphatic thud. "You used to preach family loyalty."

"Ed Stovall is an outsider."

"How can you say that? He was married to Darla for years. They have three children."

"He only married her 'cause Chauncey forced the issue."

"It may have started that way, but they stayed together. That should count for something."

Hearing a crunch of tires on gravel, Lilah turned her head and spotted the familiar brown-and-white cruiser pulling in. She groaned inwardly. What was Harlan doing way out here? Checking up on her? She shouldn't have left a note in the kitchen telling him where she was going. Any hope of gaining information from Uncle Thad was lost for the time being.

The car stopped and he exited, his long and slender frame slowly unfolding in the sun's glare. He stared at them from behind dark polarized sunglasses, but she knew by the twitch of a muscle in his jaw that he was seriously annoyed.

Too bad. So was she.

WHAT GOOD WAS it to have Lilah stay at his house for protection if she ran around all over these mountains without an escort?

Not a damn bit.

Harlan slammed the car door and made his way to the porch, working to control his irritation. It's not as if he'd spelled out the danger to Lilah, but surely she had enough sense to realize she'd put herself in a vulnerable position.

Time to be clearer.

With an effort, he twisted his mouth into a humorless smile, climbed the porch steps and extended a hand to Thaddeus Tedder. "Morning."

Thad rose, obvious reluctance in the slow extension of his own hand. "Harlan."

Lilah smiled brightly. "So you got my note. Want a glass of sweet tea?"

She wore a pink sundress and her loose blond waves tumbled about her shoulders. For all the world, she appeared carefree and poised. But he'd held her last night as she'd cried for her sister, and the faint smudge of purple under her eyes belied the strain she'd been under. A strain for which he was partly responsible.

"No, thanks. I'll pass on the tea," he replied.

Thad gestured to a chair. "Lilah tells me she's staying with you for a spell."

He sat down, aware that Thaddeus was far from pleased at the news. "Seemed for the best."

"She can stay with me. It don't look good—her staying at yer place."

He glanced at Lilah. Spots of red dotted her cheeks. What did her uncle know about them? If he wasn't aware of their prior relationship, he would be in a few weeks. Everyone would be. And they were bound to think he was the one who got her pregnant. And perhaps he was.

"Nobody cares these days," she quickly chimed in. "It's only temporary, anyway."

"Ask me, you should put a ring on that girl's finger. Now that Chauncey's passed away, it's my duty to look after her welfare."

Lilah stood and dug her car keys out of her purse. "It's my decision and no one else's." She went to the screen door and called, "Thanks for the tea, Aunt Vi. Catch you later."

Hastily, Harlan said goodbye to Thad and followed Lilah down the porch steps to her car. Even with his long loping strides, he had to hurry to catch up to her.

"We need to talk," he said as she opened the car door.

"Not now. Not here. Shouldn't you be out arresting bad guys or something?"

"Protecting you is part of my job."

"I'm fine. Nothing's going to happen to me in the middle of the day."

She slid in and closed the door, but Harlan leaned in the open window. "Darla was shot in broad daylight."

Lilah flinched and he wanted to kick himself. He opened his mouth to apologize, then snapped it shut. The reminder was for her own good.

"She was alone at her house," Lilah replied. "I'm here with family. There's a difference."

"No one is above suspicion."

Pfft. "Warning received." Lilah inserted the key and turned the motor over.

This wouldn't do. He didn't want to leave her angry and upset. "Wait a sec. I came home for lunch but never ate. Let's call a truce. Want to grab a bite with me?"

Her hand hovered over the ignition. "I *am* hungry," she admitted, a sheepish smile curving her lips.

"Lucille's Barbecue?" It was her favorite. She couldn't say no to that.

"Deal."

He opened her door and gestured at the cruiser. "Come with me. We'll swing by after and pick up your car."

Twenty minutes later, he congratulated himself. Good call on taking her to lunch. Lucille's was bustling with the clatter of plates and silverware and chattering patrons as they placed their order, and an enticing aroma of smoked pork wafted through the country diner. It was plain with red-topped Formica tables and scuffed aluminum chairs, but the barbecue was the best in three counties.

He quirked a brow at Lilah as the waitress walked away, scribbling down their order. "A salad? Who are you?"

"Figured I needed to clean up my act a little for the next few months."

Her smile was thin, and he was struck at how delicate she appeared, how frail. Life had dealt her nothing but hard blows lately.

Elbert Anders and his two brothers approached—mouths and shoulders sloped downward, but their eyes were determined and lit with commiseration. Elbert came to a standstill by their table and his brothers aligned on either side of his large, bulky frame. The mountain men all sported long bushy beards and wore faded denim overalls. Privately, Harlan dubbed them the ZZ Top triplets. "Sorry 'bout Darla," Elbert mumbled. "We'll be payin' our respects tonight."

"Thank you," Lilah whispered.

It was as if Elbert had opened an invisible barrier between them and the diner patrons. Slowly, others drifted over and expressed their condolences. Tedder or not, the folks around here felt sorry for Lilah losing her father and now her sister. Harlan's spine stiffened as J.D. rose from the back and sauntered their way.

"Sorry for your loss," he said to Lilah, slipping Harlan a loaded look.

Her mouth compressed in a thin line, and she gave a stiff nod, turning her chin away a fraction. A subtle rejection.

"Our office is working tirelessly to find the person responsible for Darla's murder."

"Like you did for Dad?"

"It's an open investigation. We'll get to the bottom of it."

"By harassing my brother-in-law?"

J.D. shot him a can't-you-control-your-woman look, and Harlan laid a hand over Lilah's, stifling her drumming fingers. "We have to explore all avenues," he said quietly.

The waitress glided over with a tray and set down their orders. "Eat up, darlin'," she urged Lilah, patting her shoulder. "You lookin' mighty frail."

Lilah flashed a real smile at the waitress and J.D. ambled out the door, pausing at a few tables to shake hands. Ever the politician—an aspect of running for sheriff that Harlan despised. Genuine interest in others was fine, but continual grandstanding was another. But who was he to judge? He'd sacrificed a relationship for the sake of the upcoming election.

"She's right," said Harlan. "You need to eat up. Want a bite of my barbecue sandwich?"

Lilah shook her head and poured dressing over her salad. "Not really all that hungry anymore."

"But—"

"I know. I'm eating for two." She dug into her salad with determination.

"I'll be with you tonight. You won't be by yourself at the viewing."

"I still have family left," she pointed out. "I'm not completely alone."

"Of course," he quickly agreed, realizing he'd been put in his place. "I just don't want you to be out and about without me until we catch this killer."

"Let's get this straight between us right now. I'm only staying with you temporarily. I'm not without resources. We're just friends."

Friends. Ouch.

She jabbed a tomato with her fork. "And you don't have the right to tell me what to do. Especially not after the way you broke things off with me. Got it?"

"Message received loud and clear. Now eat," he commanded.

Her face flushed and thunder gathered in her eyes.

"Um...please?" he mumbled.

"That's better."

Swiftly, he changed topics. "Spoke with the medical examiner today. Darla's personal effects at the time of death only included clothes and shoes. No jewelry."

"Not even her wedding ring?"

"No."

"Could somebody have killed her just for her wedding ring?"

"Unlikely. Seems to me as if the killer wanted to disassociate any connection with Darla. It's personal."

"You mean Ed," she said flatly. "Still not buying it. Aren't crimes of passion committed in the heat of the moment? My sister was shot in the back in her own yard. No face-to-face spur-of-the-moment killing there. Just like it wasn't with Dad."

"I'm not saying your theory about a drug deal gone bad isn't possible. But we have no proof that your family's been involved in that."

"What else could it possibly be?"

"That's what we're trying to find out." He thought of the failed drug raids. The worm of suspicion still wiggled beneath the surface of his mind. Drug operations gone bad were notoriously bloody, and yet there was nothing to tie the murders to that theory. Still, he couldn't discount the drug angle.

But why would anyone stalk Lilah at her apartment? She lived away from Lavender Mountain and had no immediate connection to anyone involved in illegal activities, anymore. Well, she did still have extended family, a couple of uncles and a number of cousins.

Unless the stalking was an isolated incident. A coincidence.

Thing is, he didn't believe in coincidences.

Chapter Seven

Lilah hated funeral homes. Hated the cloying scent of lilies, the whispered conversations, the piped organ music and the people stiffly dressed in their Sunday clothes. And she especially hated open caskets for viewing. She kept her face averted from the front of the room where family and friends paid their last respects. Tomorrow, she would go out to Dad's old cabin, toss daisies into the wind and say her own private goodbyes. Her eyes slid to the clock mounted on the sidewall. A few minutes past the hour. Soon, everyone but Ed and his parents and kids would be gone, and then she could slip out as well.

Ed's parents herded the children down the aisle and Lilah rose to say goodbye. A few more people left the room, until it was only she and Harlan in the pew area and Ed speaking with the funeral home director.

A loud voice erupted from the back corner of the room, and she turned around.

Uncle Thad and Uncle Jasper were having words—heated words, judging by the flush of color on their cheeks and the tense set of their jaws. Her reclusive Uncle Jasper didn't get along well with others. Never had. But an argument now was totally inappropriate. She started toward them, motioning Harlan not to follow, but Uncle Thad beat a hasty exit without a backward glance.

"What was that all about?" she asked Jasper.

He swallowed hard, Adam's apple bobbling up and down his scrawny neck. "Sorry for the unseemly behavior," he said in his reedy formal voice. He pulled at his tie. "How you holding up, LayLay?"

His use of her childhood nickname nearly undid her. "Making it," she responded gruffly. "You and Uncle Thad having words?"

"That's nothing new. Reason why I prefer to keep to myself. Life's easier alone."

"Don't you ever get lonely?" She didn't understand his hermit-like existence. Jasper had never married, had no friends and seemingly no need for much contact with the outside world. He lived alone at the top of Widow's Peak Mountain in a primitive cabin and kept a garden. His wants seemed few and simple.

"Lonely?" He rubbed his chin. "Nah, I'm used to solitude."

"You're doing okay?" she asked uncertainly. They'd never been close—Uncle Jasper didn't allow others to get too close—but his gruff manner had never insulted her. When she'd been a child, he'd once made her a doll fashioned from straw, and she'd appreciated the gesture, even if he'd shoved it in her hands with no comment.

Gray-blue eyes narrowed on his wrinkled face. "Why? You sayin' I look unseemly?"

"No, no," she said hastily. "It's just... You're getting older. I worry something might happen to you all alone up there."

"The Good Lord will take me when he sees fit. You're the one who needs to be careful." His gaze shifted to Darla's casket. "Bad things happening all over again."

Her heart quickened. "Again?"

"There's bad blood in this family, goin' way back. It's poisoned all our lives."

"What do you mean? That we've been unlucky in our share of tragedy?"

He pinned her with a hard stare. "Doomed."

"You're being superstitious," she said, ignoring the goose bumps climbing up her arms. Bad enough spending hours in a room with her sister's body without listening to her uncle's old-fashioned ideas about family curses. Nervously, she fiddled with the leather bracelet on her left wrist. Its crimson stone glittered like a droplet of blood. "There's a reason for Dad and Darla's murders. The police are working on it."

"Tedders ain't got no business cottoning to the police."

Jasper had never been in the moonshine business with the rest of the family, but he evidently still shared their contempt of the law.

"We have to cooperate with them." She drew a deep, steadying breath. "Do you know if Dad and Uncle Thad might have gotten into something dangerous? Like drugs?"

"There's worse things than moonshine and drugs, like a poisoned history. There's a reason I'm so scarred and a hermit. A reason yer dad was an alcoholic and Thad so... controlling. Go away. Move away from the mountain and never come back."

"Not until I find out who's responsible for all this." She owed her family that much. And if someone was after her, she had to discover the killer to save her baby.

He nodded his head at something over her shoulder. "That there yer fella?"

She glanced back to find Harlan ambling his way toward them.

"He's a friend. Now, tell me, what were you and Uncle

Thad arguing about?" she asked once more, hoping he'd open up before Harlan arrived at her side.

"Don't never be alone with Thaddeus," he warned, his lowered voice urgent and intense. "He's dangerous. He and that boy of his, Lavon, ain't to be trusted."

Dangerous? Uncle Thad was a staple in her life. Warm, kind and always generous when money had been short growing up. "Lavon's a bully, but Uncle Thad's no danger. What are you implying?"

But Jasper clamped his thin lips together and stared mutinously at Harlan who'd stepped up beside her.

"Evening, Jasper," Harlan said, holding out his hand.

Uncle Jasper pointedly ignored the proffered handshake. Harlan shrugged and dropped his arm.

Without a word, Jasper turned his back and headed to the door.

"Wait," she called after him. "I'd like to come visit if that's okay. We need to talk more."

Jasper didn't bother facing them as he answered. "I've said all I have to say on the matter."

"Charming as usual," Harlan commented drily. "What's going on?"

She shook her head. "He gets stranger every year. Kept going on about our family being doomed and poisoned."

"Anything else?"

Lilah hesitated. It felt disloyal to repeat what he'd said about Uncle Thad and Lavon. "That's mostly everything. I need to pay him a visit."

"No. You need to stay put at my house until we've uncovered who's responsible for the murders."

"But—"

"No *buts*. It's too dangerous. If you won't think of yourself, think of your baby."

His words vibrated warm and deep in her core. Even

though she'd told him it wasn't his, Harlan still cared about her unborn child. If she wasn't careful, she could lose her heart to him all over again. Lilah lifted her chin.

"I *am* thinking of the baby. We need to solve these crimes. Fast."

"No. *I* need to solve them. You stay out of it. I'm working on it. Trust me." He guided her by the elbow toward the door. "Let's talk about it outside. We'll catch Ed when he's finished his business with the funeral home."

She pushed through the large wooden door. "Sounds to me like the sheriff's office is only out to railroad poor Ed. As for Dad, you've suggested it's probably nothing more than a riled customer or someone he fought with in a bar."

"We're looking at the possible drug angle as well," he said defensively. "Although, every lead seems to turn into a dead end."

Lilah slipped out the door into the night's darkness. A full moon shone, lime green and mysterious. She inhaled the fresh air and hugged her arms over her chest. "I hope you didn't come with me tonight just to try and corner Ed after the visitation and question him about dealing drugs. He's been through the wringer the past few days. Leave him be."

Harlan shook his head. "The man gets a pass tonight. I'm not heartless."

Heartless Harlan. Lilah felt a sad smile tug the edges of her mouth. After what he'd put her through these past few weeks, she'd say the moniker fit. But what he lacked in heart, he made up for with his dogged determination to do the right thing. She would give him that much. Another woman might be satisfied with those crumbs, but she wasn't. Not by a long shot.

"Speaking of being through the wringer, you look pale. You sure you're okay?" he asked, frowning down at her.

"I won't lie, it's been tough," she admitted. "What happened to Dad was horrible, but he was living his last days, dying from cirrhosis. But Darla is…" She stumbled on the words. "Darla was only a few years older than me. And she has left behind three small children."

"I'm going to get to the bottom of this." His voice was gentle but laced with steel. "I promise you that."

A whoosh of stale air, and Ed emerged from the funeral home, shoulders sagging and head down.

"Need a lift home?" Harlan asked.

Ed jerked his head up. "What?" He swiped at his cheeks and coughed. "Oh, no. Thanks. I'm fine."

Lilah's heart pinched at the sight of his grief. She embraced him in a quick hug, but not so brief that she didn't catch the sharp, sour scent of liquor on his breath. Her worry increased. A few drinks to get through this horrid week was one thing, but if this led to an addiction, she feared for her nephews. Those kids needed him sober.

"So sorry, Ed," she said past the catch in her throat.

Harlan's mouth tightened. "You been drinking, by any chance? If so, I'm going to have to insist on driving you home."

"Just a couple before visitation started," he protested, running a hand through his long thick hair. "Unfortunately, the buzz has entirely worn off."

"Walk a straight line for me."

Ed rolled his eyes but obeyed. His large body didn't sway in the least. He walked back to them and then lifted his right knee and balanced easily. "There. I know the cop's whole repertoire. You want to take me to the station and make me take a Breathalyzer test, go ahead."

"That won't be necessary."

Lilah shot Harlan a dark look before turning to Ed. "This might not be the right time to bring this up, but I wanted you to know…" She hesitated. How to bring this up delicately? "If you need any help with funeral expenses, I talked to Jimmy and we'll both chip in what we can."

Ed stuck his hands in his pockets. "That's awful generous, 'specially considering the way we helped ourselves to the money you found in your dad's cabin."

"Forget about it," she said hastily. If only she could erase the memory of her last talk—no argument, call it what it really was—with her sister over the damned money. That was something she'd have to live with the rest of her life.

"That money will more than cover the burial costs. I returned the new truck and cancelled the kitchen makeover."

What a relief her brother-in-law had a sensible head on his shoulders after all. "That sounds like a good plan. Still, I'm here. If you need help with the kids, well, with anything, let me know."

"Did you ever find Darla's wedding ring?" Harlan asked suddenly.

Again, she shot him a warning look. "Really, now's not the time for you—"

"No. Never did," Ed interrupted. "I searched everywhere, too." His sad brown eyes sought hers. "Couldn't even find that new stuff you discovered at your dad's, Lilah. Hope they weren't some kind of family heirlooms."

"Was she wearing the found pieces last time you saw her?" Harlan asked.

The man couldn't seem to help himself when it came to asking questions. She frowned at him.

Ed's brow furrowed. "Might have been. Can't rightly recall."

"It's no big deal," she assured Ed. "Don't you give it another thought. They weren't valuable, and none of us knew where they came from." She held up her right wrist. "And I have this. Darla insisted I keep one of the pieces."

"Good." He shuffled his feet and stole a glance at Harlan. "Guess I'll be moseying on home now, if you don't mind. I'm beat."

"You be careful," she said softly, awkwardly patting his shoulder.

They watched as he climbed into his old truck and drove off.

"Maybe you should tell me more about this jewelry," Harlan said slowly.

She cocked her head to the side. "Like I told Ed, they weren't valuable at all. Just costume jewelry."

"Humor me."

"This bracelet, a cameo ring and a glass beaded necklace."

He took her hand in his and examined the bracelet. The red stone glittered under the moonbeams.

"Told you. Nothing special."

He didn't speak anymore as they got in his cruiser and drove the twisted roads up Lavender Mountain to his place. Lilah laid her head against the cool pane of glass on the passenger side, mind swimming with images of the people who'd come to say their last goodbyes to Darla.

Let this be the end. No more deaths. No more gut-wrenching phone calls, funerals or heartache.

At Harlan's, they silently entered and switched on the lights. What she needed was a nice long shower. In his bathroom, she stripped and stepped into the shower's hot spray. She reached for the shelf that held soap and shampoo and discovered a familiar bottle of pink gardenia bath gel. Her fingers curled around it as a silly grin split her face. *Her* shower gel that she'd left there in March.

Why hadn't Harlan thrown it away? Had he hoped she would return one day? Maybe she was reading too much into it, but the possibility lifted her heart for a moment.

Cleaned and refreshed, Lilah went to bed and slipped under the fresh sheets, waiting on the welcome absolution of sleep.

HER LEGS TWISTED in the bedsheets and she fought for air. Something deep, dark and heavy pressed on her chest as an unknown menace approached that was familiar but suddenly ominous. It slithered toward her paralyzed body, coiled to strike.

"Lilah, Lilah. Baby, you're safe. I'm here."

Her cramped lungs released and she sucked in oxygen. Harlan's hand splayed over her left breast, calming her pounding heart.

"Shh," he murmured. "Go back to sleep."

She sighed and took comfort in his body stretched out behind her. Despite everything, despite her anger and hurt and her best intentions to keep her pride intact…in the night, Harlan was the one she reached for, the man she wanted beside her. She rubbed her face against the hard muscled biceps wrapped around her. Tonight, she wouldn't fight it. Lilah closed her eyes and sank into dreamless oblivion.

Chapter Eight

"I need the file on the old Hilltop Strangler case," Harlan said.

Zelda, a middle-aged administrative staple in the sheriff's office, and near as powerful as J.D., looked up from the payroll spreadsheet numbers she'd been inputting on the computer. She lowered her tortoiseshell bifocals and stared. "That so? Nobody's looked at that in ages. Not that I know of, anyway."

"Doesn't hurt to take a peek at it occasionally," he said noncommittally. No need to get folks stirred up on a wild-goose chase. This quick glance was only a way to satisfy his overactive imagination.

"So you say." Her intelligent gray eyes sharpened but she rose and went to the row of old steel file cabinets. In seconds, she produced a thick manila envelope bulging with yellowed papers.

"Got to appreciate a man who wants to look at the real paperwork and not the scanned reports," she said with a nod.

"Call me old-fashioned." The computer was a huge convenience, but sometimes all the documents weren't scanned and the photographic detail was often blurred. He preferred to study the original black-and-white photos.

He tucked the folder under an arm. "Thanks."

"How's your girlfriend doing?" she asked, amusement spiking her eyes.

Harlan inwardly groaned. She was as bad as the guys. Ever since Lilah's oh-so-public announcement of her pregnancy, the teasing had been unmerciful. Everyone kept pressing him, curious if the baby might really be his after all.

"She's fine," he answered tersely, cutting off the discussion.

Zelda smirked. "Don't forget to invite me to the baby shower."

He beat a hasty retreat back to his office and opened the file, spreading its contents over his desk. The original police reports were typewritten and riddled with smattering blotches of white correction fluid. No convenient delete key twenty-five years ago when these reports were made. He opened the tattered envelope of photographs.

Victim number one, Amzie Billbray. Age thirty-two, white female.

Victim number two, Raylene Rucker. Age twenty-eight, white female.

Both females were described as a "fallen woman"—a polite euphemism back then for a prostitute. Each looked at least a decade older than her real age—gaunt mountain women with bleak eyes and thin joyless lips that tugged down in the corners. No amount of dark lipstick or blush could completely cover that veneer of desperation.

There appeared to be nothing in common between the victims, other than their shared profession. Both of them were strangled after sexual contact. Both of them were found with their faces buried in their pillows. Despite an intense investigation, no one was ever charged. The only clue was that the victims' friends claimed each of the women was wearing a piece of jewelry that was never found. Cheap costume baubles, they'd insisted, certainly nothing valuable or that would lure a robber to attack them.

Still, the police took notice, believing the murderer might have taken the items as trophies. Mementos whereby the killer felt linked to the women he'd killed and took secret pleasure in reliving his violent crime.

The two killings were a few months apart, and then—inexplicably—no more victims were ever found. It was as if the killer had either spent all his rage (highly unlikely), had moved away, gone to jail, or had died.

Harlan flipped through the dozens of photos, most of them of the crime scenes, until he found the one he sought.

One of Raylene's cousins had provided police with a picture of her wearing the missing bracelet. The photographer had cropped the image to Raylene's wrist and had enlarged the photo.

Harlan squinted at it. It was a leather braided bracelet with two small copper discs alongside a small stone. He flipped the photo over and read the handwriting: "brown leather with a garnet chip and two copper discs engraved with the initials *RR*."

His chest squeezed and his fingers went numb. *No.* What were the chances? Had Lilah really found one of the missing pieces to the old killings? Excitement warred with fear for her safety. But if that *was* Raylene's bracelet, then more than likely Chauncey Tedder had been the murderer all along. And he was now dead.

Harlan leaned back in the chair and steepled his fingers, reasoning out the implications. It wasn't as if he'd been close to Lilah's dad, but he'd always rather liked Chauncey. Sure, he'd been a hotheaded ole cuss when drunk, and he'd been involved in making illegal 'shine, but Chauncey had seemed a decent sort of man for all that. Hard to wrap his mind around Chauncey strangling two women.

If it were true, the news would tear Lilah up inside. Damn, she'd been through enough and was pregnant on top of it all. He hoped to God that when he examined her bracelet tonight it wouldn't have those engraved discs. Quickly, he scanned the rest of the report until he found a written description of the other two missing pieces, a glass beaded necklace and a cameo ring. He picked up that page and the bracelet picture to make photocopies to show Lilah.

"What ya up to?"

J.D. strolled into the room and sank his considerable girth into the chair in front of Harlan's desk. Beefy fingers pawed at the old reports.

Of course, Zelda had told him he'd checked out the file. That woman knew where her bread was buttered.

"Just looking over this old case," said Harlan.

"Any particular reason?"

J.D.'s hands fumbled at the pocket of his shirt uniform, then dropped by his side. The sheriff had given up smoking years ago, but still reached for a phantom cigarette when he wanted to settle in for a chat.

"No," Harlan lied. He needed to get his facts straight first and then break the bad news to Lilah if Chauncey ended up being a postmortem suspect. No way he'd let her hear this news secondhand.

"So out of the blue, you decided to comb through it this afternoon? Strange. No one's requested that file in years."

"Keep up with it, do you?"

J.D. shrugged his massive shoulders. "Glanced at the checkout record Zelda keeps when she told me you wanted to review those old murders. Not like you've shown much interest until now. Doubt the murders cross anyone's radars these days. So, naturally, this makes me wonder if there's a reason for your sudden interest."

Harlan supposed that curiosity was a deeply ingrained personality trait in law enforcement work, but J.D.'s questioning made him slightly uncomfortable and defensive. Their professional relationship had cooled since Lilah had returned to Lavender Mountain.

"You should be glad when employees keep up with these old cases."

"Never hurts, never hurts," J.D. mumbled. "Anything new going on?"

"Nope. Same old stuff."

"That Tedder girl got you on your toes? We don't see much of you at Hazel's bar these days."

"Her name's Lilah, and I've been busy, that's all."

"Sure you have." J.D. rose and lumbered to the door. He paused in the doorway. "Just 'cause she got knocked up is no reason to flush your career down the toilet. If a paternity test shows you're the father, agree to pay child support and move on. I think the good citizens of this county would raise their brows at you marrying a Tedder."

Anger sparked up and down his spine, and he rose. "The good citizens of this county can kiss my ass, then."

J.D. sadly shook his head. "See what happens when you lie in bed with a Tedder? Problems. Sometimes you're better off letting sleeping dogs lie." With that parting quip, he disappeared down the hallway.

That was a hell of an attitude for the county's chief law enforcement officer to espouse.

Harlan slapped the Hilltop Strangler paperwork back in the folder, except for the photo and the missing jewelry description. The case might be old, but it was far from cold.

Despite his simmering anger, J.D. did have a point. If Chauncey turned out to be a serial killer, any affiliation with a Tedder would be a death knell on his dream of becoming sheriff. And this county needed him. J.D. had gotten old and lazy and had let things slide.

Harlan only hoped it wasn't too late to turn back crime in Elmore County.

LILAH PULLED THE biscuits out of the oven and inhaled the fresh-bread aroma. No telling what time Harlan would return; his hours were erratic. She'd go ahead and treat herself to a biscuit. She slathered its golden top with butter and groaned with pleasure as she bit into the home-baked goodness. Too bad Harlan didn't keep cans of preserves. She could buy some apples and peaches tomorrow and spend the day canning.

Abruptly, she lowered the biscuit and grimaced. *Don't get too comfy and domesticated here.* This living arrangement was temporary, best to keep that in mind.

The door opened and a familiar set of footsteps sounded from the den.

"Smells good in here." Harlan entered the kitchen and flashed a wan smile.

"What's wrong?"

He dropped the smile. "Am I that obvious?"

"No, but I can read you."

"That's scary," he tried to joke. "It can wait until after dinner."

"Uh-uh, I'll just worry. Tell me now."

"It might not be anything." He came to her side and the usual tingle ran down her skin at his nearness, but instead of embracing her, Harlan lifted her right wrist and twisted the leather band of her bracelet.

"What are you doing?"

"Take it off."

She shrugged. "Okay. You sure are acting weird. It's just something I found—"

"—in your dad's cabin. I remember."

He unhooked the clasp and held the strip of leather up to the overhead light. "Damn it!"

Dread clawed at her gut. "What?"

Lines grooved in his forehead and his eyes were shadowed with pity as he faced her.

"I'm not going to like this news, am I?" asked Lilah.

"Sit down."

He scraped back a kitchen chair and she perched on the edge of the wooden seat, clasping her hands in her lap.

Ping. Her cell phone chirruped from the counter. *Ping.*

Might as well answer. It could be important. Lilah grabbed it and clicked open the text messenger.

Hey, there…everything ok? Where ya been? Miss seeing u 'round here. When are u coming back? Luke.

Should have known. Nice guy, but a pest. She sighed and tossed the phone on the kitchen table.

"Who was it?"

"Luke." His jaw tightened.

"You met him at my apartment complex the morning—" she swallowed "—that Darla died and you came to tell me."

"What does he want?"

Lilah lifted her shoulders. "Said he wondered how I was and why I haven't been home."

"You sure he's only a friend?" he asked, a sharp edge in his voice.

She squirmed and then straightened her back. "We saw each other for a bit after you stopped calling me."

He opened his mouth, no doubt to ask if Luke was the one who had gotten her pregnant. She rushed to cut him off. "Tell me about the bracelet."

Harlan nodded and pointed to the back of one of the

copper disks. "Can you see that? It's engraved with the initials *RR*."

She squinted at the corroded copper and the initials showed faintly. "Okay. Who's this *RR* person?"

"Raylene Rucker. The original owner."

Raylene…the name tickled the far recesses of her memory but she couldn't quite recall where she'd heard it before.

"She was murdered twenty-five years ago along with another woman, Amzie Billbray."

Images flooded her brain—newspaper headlines of the Hilltop Strangler and whispered conversations from her childhood. Lilah scooted back her chair, as if trying to distance herself from any connection so foul. The scrape of chair and tile was as loud as a gunshot. How could such a small strip of leather create such terror? She felt dizzy. Unmoored.

"How… What…?"

"When you told me about the jewelry last night, it rang a bell. Especially since you'd also found such a large cache of hidden money. That, coupled with the fact that your sister's wedding ring and the other two pieces you found also went missing, well, it all added up to a mystery."

He clasped her hands in his and it grounded her swirling emotions.

"I asked myself if there were any patterns to a past crime and realized there were. So…" He released his hands and pulled a couple of slips of paper from his pant pockets. "Take a look."

With trembling hands, she took the papers and looked down. There. Her—no Raylene's—bracelet in black-and-white with the unmistakable damnable engraving. "I can't believe it."

"Read the description of the other two items. Do they also match what you found and gave Darla?"

"A silver cameo ring and a necklace of colored glass beads. Yes."

The paper slipped from her numbed hands and fluttered to the floor like a dead thing. "I don't understand," she whispered.

"We'll get to the bottom of it," he assured her.

Did she want him to? Lilah stood abruptly and began pacing the small kitchen. "Someone put them there," she mumbled, thinking aloud. "That's why an intruder broke into the cabin and stalked me at my apartment. They were looking for them." She whirled and faced Harlan. "Why? Nobody's going to recognize that stuff after all these years. They're in no danger."

"Some killers like to keep a physical connection to their victims, to the memory of the crime."

"That's disgusting." She sat back down and twisted a lock of hair. "And what were they doing in Dad's cabin? Was he hiding them for someone?"

"Could be," Harlan said flatly.

"Why would he do such a thing? I don't get it."

"Unless the killer was someone very close to him. Someone he loved."

"He wasn't all that close to anyone. After Mom left, he became almost as reclusive as Jasper. Never dated, never went out much."

"He still had family. Brothers, cousins, in-laws. Maybe he was covering for one of them."

She shook her head. "I can't see it."

"There's another alternative," he said slowly.

Lilah stared at him, puzzled. "Like maybe the killer saw the abandoned cabin and thought it would be safe to store the jewelry there? But he could've kept them wherever they'd been all this time. No one had ever discovered his hiding place before."

"A highly unlikely scenario. Besides, the killer would want to keep his trophies close by."

She drummed her fingers on the kitchen table. "The killer could have put it there to frame my dad for the murders."

"He have any enemies you know of?"

"Not really. He got in plenty of bar fights but those drunken brawls always seemed to blow over."

"There's other scenarios here."

She tapped an index finger to her lips. "Could be the killer wanted to buy a pint of moonshine and didn't have cash. So he gave the jewelry to Dad as collateral and intended to return on payday."

"No. Highly unlikely. I still say the killer wouldn't have parted with the trophies for any length of time."

"Maybe the moonshine buyer stole the jewelry from the killer."

"If you're going to steal, you'd pick an item a lot more valuable than a handful of costume jewelry."

She threw up her hands. "What's your theory?"

"There's another option you haven't considered." His voice was soft but pregnant with meaning. Blistering eyes pierced through her fog of confusion.

"If you mean what I think you mean, then you're one hundred percent wrong!" She jumped up so fast, her chair crashed to the floor.

"Calm down." Harlan righted the chair and guided her back into it. "At least consider the possibility."

"My dad wouldn't have killed anyone! How could you think that? You...you bastard!"

He regarded her impassively. "I'm a cop. If I see physical evidence, I have to at least consider the obvious conclusion."

"Damn your logic. You knew my dad. He wasn't a murderer." Anger sparked in every synapse of her brain and body. How dare Harlan suggest such a thing!

"Lilah, be reasonable. If you were in my shoes, you'd draw the same conclusion. At least keep an open mind and—"

"No! And don't tell me to calm down." Lord, she hated to be told that. Made her ten times as angry.

"It's not good for you or—"

"Oh, shut up," she snapped. "What if I accused your father or mother of murder? How would you feel?"

"Maybe you wouldn't be so far off the mark," he said enigmatically. His eyes darkened to the blue-blackness of a storm at sea.

"Don't turn this around on me and play your mind games."

"I'm not into playing games. I'm dead serious."

She couldn't deal with a new set of revelations. Not now. Lilah covered her face with her hands, her entire body trembling with shock.

Harlan stroked her scalp and it felt so good, so comforting. But no, he couldn't fling wild accusations and expect his touch to bring her around like a stray dog needy for scraps of affection. She removed her hands from her face.

"Dad was *not* a murderer. I don't care if he's the convenient answer for you. Dig deeper."

"Of course we will. I'm only trying to prepare you for what's to come."

"Who all knows about this?"

"Just the two of us."

"Can we keep it that way?" The moment she asked, Lilah realized the futility of asking Harlan to suppress evidence. She couldn't ask him to jeopardize his career or compromise his principles. "Never mind."

"I am sorry. I'll speak to J.D. first thing in the morning. Maybe we can keep this matter from going public."

A bitter laugh escaped her throat. "No. It'll leak, eventually. And Dad's not here to defend himself. The Tedder name was always mud in these parts, but there's a world of difference between peddling moonshine and murdering prostitutes."

"Your true friends will stand by you."

"I don't have any friends on Lavender Mountain. Between Dad's fighting and liquor business and Darla's promiscuous high school days, I was always looked down on."

"I never realized it was a problem for you. Jimmy always seemed to get on well enough."

"My brother would beat the crap out of anyone who spoke ill of us. It's different for a girl."

He scratched his chin. "Does it really matter what anyone thinks?"

"You're a fine one to say that. You broke up with me because of my family's reputation." And now, *this*. Damn, he must be ready to ditch her once and for all. "Bet you're going to catch hell from J.D. when he hears the latest. He'll demand you kick me out of your house at once. How do you expect to win an election if you live with the woman the townsfolk will call the Hilltop Strangler's daughter?"

"You let me worry about that."

He was right. She had enough on her plate. Wearily, she rose and stumbled toward the hallway.

"Where are you going?" he called after her.

"To bed."

"Without dinner?"

"Not hungry. Besides, I'm still angry. You know my dad didn't do this."

It seemed a mile to her bedroom and she trudged along with leaden legs. Lethargy swept over her body in waves.

At last, she reached the bedroom, lay down in the darkness and curled into herself. All she wanted was the blessed oblivion of sleep.

Dad couldn't have murdered those two women. She'd never seen him lay a hand on Mom, even when they were in the midst of their worst screaming matches. There had to be some reasonable explanation as to why that jewelry had been hidden under his mattress. Chauncey Tedder was not a killer.

Or was he?

She banished the disturbing question, refusing to entertain her mind's dark whisperings.

Chapter Nine

"And that's why I looked at the old Hilltop Strangler case yesterday," Harlan said, shoving the leather bracelet across J.D.'s desk.

The sheriff peered at it through the plastic zip bag in which Harlan had encased it. His, Lilah's and Darla's fingerprints were all over the thing, but maybe the forensic techs could find a useful clue anyway.

"I'll mail it to the lab in Atlanta and have them take a look. With any luck, Chauncey's prints will be on there. Old coot must have been guilty."

"Probably," Harlan admitted. "Guess you'll want a statement from Lilah on where and when she found it? Maybe talk to Chauncey's ex?"

"Sure thing. And don't you worry, I'll do you a favor and keep this whole affair low key. Forensics has a huge backlog. It'll take weeks before they examine the bracelet. We'll wrap up the case after the election in a couple months and announce to the press that the murders have been solved."

J.D.'s casual dismissal of Elmore County's most notorious unsolved crimes caught Harlan off-guard. "Thought you'd be a bit more excited at the big break in the case," he said. "Especially considering the upcoming election.

Don't you want to capitalize on the opportunity for some good press?"

J.D. reached in his pocket for the non-existent cigarette and then folded both hands on the scarred wooden desk. "Way I see it, bringing up the Hillside Strangler case will just remind folks that it took nearly twenty-five years for us to solve." He narrowed his eyes. "I understand you'd like to see a little publicity for what tumbled in your lap, but think how much it would hurt your girlfriend if you expose her father as a murderer."

"I'm well aware of how this affects Lilah."

J.D. winked. "Then we'll keep this under our hats for now. Besides, I'll feel better about retirement knowing you're the next sheriff. I only hope your association with Lilah doesn't kill your chances. But as much as I disapprove of the Tedder gal, this is the least I can do for you."

Harlan shifted in his seat. It didn't feel right. Owing favors made his skin creepy-crawly. "Don't sit on the press for my sake."

"Why not stay quiet for now? People have assumed the killer either moved away or died. Not like there's a public outcry to find him. Besides, no matter whose prints are on the bracelet, we won't end up with a neat, tidy case. Chauncey's dead, and all we'll really have is an unproven theory."

"But Lilah could still be in danger. If Chauncey wasn't the killer, they're after her."

J.D. waved a hand, casually dismissing his concern. "They were probably after the money in that cabin incident. As for the apartment—could have been anyone or that old lady's imagination. Don't let your misplaced concern for Lilah make you any more foolish. She's caused enough trouble. For now, just sit tight and keep quiet."

For Lilah's sake, he'd go along with it. Not that his opinion mattered. J.D. did what J.D. wanted to do. Although he'd felt the same way last night about Chauncey's guilt, now he wasn't so sure. He would investigate on his own. Have a talk with that Luke McCoy and Ed.

His cell phone rang and a message flashed on its screen. Peaceful Paths Nursing Home. His stomach flipped. Now what? Had his mother taken a turn for the worse? He glanced at his desk calendar and winced.

Today would have been her thirty-fifth wedding anniversary—if Dad had bothered to hang around, that is. But he'd left the marriage, and his only child, long ago. Still, even though his mom's mind had been in a fog since her stroke and the onset of early dementia, she seemed to possess an eerie sense of this anniversary date. Last year, she'd gone into a crying funk for days, and the year before that, she'd had a series of panic attacks.

He answered the call. "Harlan Sampson speaking."

J.D.'s brows lifted as he talked to the nurse for a minute and hung up.

"Anything wrong?" he asked.

"It's Mom. Nurse says she's been weepy and asking for me."

"Poor woman. Go see her. We can hold down the fort."

"You sure?"

"Absolutely. You've accrued plenty of overtime. Take it."

Harlan stood and dug the car keys from his pants pocket. While he was in that area, might as well pay a visit to Luke McCoy and check him out. Maybe even talk to that old lady again and see if she'd seen any other unusual activity at Lilah's apartment complex.

LILAH LEFT THE sheriff's office disappointed and alone. She'd wanted to apologize to Harlan for getting so upset with him last night. Only natural that he'd pointed out the possibility of her dad's guilt. After a good night's sleep, and all morning for reflection, she'd gotten past the initial shock and her knee-jerk response to defend her dad.

She still found it hard to believe but conceded she had to consider it. And, in a way, if it were true, then she was safe. The money and jewelry were gone and she had nothing of value to anybody. Last night had been agony but today she felt ten pounds lighter. If she and the baby were truly safe, that was what mattered most. She'd never take that for granted again.

Inside her car, she punched in Aunt Vi's number on a sudden whim. She didn't want to eat lunch alone, and it would be good for Viola to get out of the house and have someone wait on *her* for a change.

It took some convincing. Vi claimed she was too busy, but Lilah at least persuaded her aunt to let her pick up some deli sandwiches in town and bring them to the house where they could eat together on the front porch. "It'll be like a picnic," she promised.

Within thirty minutes, she arrived at their house and she pulled two bacon, lettuce and cheese sandwiches from a paper bag and set them on a table. Aunt Viola supplied a bag of chips and sweet tea.

"House seems quiet," Lilah commented. "Where is everybody?"

"The kids are scattered about doing their own thing. Thad's out on a liquor run. He's having to do Ed's job now that the police are watching Ed so close. Did you know they've named him a person of interest in Darla's killing?"

Lilah sat down and unwrapped the wax packing on her sandwich. "Harlan told me. I can't believe he did it, though, can you?"

"No. But how well do we really ever know a person?

Even our own family members? We all have our own mysteries and a shadowed side of the soul that's secret."

She stared at her aunt. "Wow. Does that apply to you as well? Can't imagine you having any kind of a dark side."

"Still waters run deep." She flashed a rare smile. "Your uncle can be a tad overbearing at times, so no, I'm not a self-sacrificing Pollyanna every moment of the day and night."

"Thank God. You had me worried," Lilah said with a laugh.

Viola sipped her tea. "How long you planning on staying on Lavender Mountain?"

"I'm actually thinking of leaving. Soon—like tomorrow, maybe. There's nothing to keep me here. Not now."

Her aunt patted her hand. "You've been through more than you should have to at your young age. Especially being with child."

Lilah almost choked on her sandwich. Had she heard about the scene at the sheriff's office? "How did you guess?"

"A certain glow." Viola shrugged and smiled softly. "Are you happy about it?"

"I am now. Wasn't so sure at first. I mean, the circumstances aren't ideal."

"Harlan going to do the right thing by ya?"

"What makes you so sure it's his?"

"I see the way y'all look at each other."

Lilah cocked her head to the side. "You think he cares about me?"

"I'm certain of it."

For the first time in days, a warm glow spread through her body. If it was falsely based on an older woman's delusion, so be it. She could use a little cheer in her life.

"You'll need a strong man's protection if you're going to stay 'round here. Someone like Harlan."

"Again—I might be leaving here. Even if I did decide to stay, I don't need a man to take care of me. And if the Strangler case is solved, I have nothing to fear."

Viola's eyes widened. "Solved? What are you talking about?"

Damn. She'd let that slip. But Harlan didn't say to keep it secret. "The cops have a major break in the case. They…" She drew a deep breath. "They think Dad was the killer."

"Chauncey?" She leaned back in her chair and ran a hand over her forehead. "Nothing should surprise me anymore when it comes to this family."

"We've had our share of tragedy, that's for sure."

"Your dad, like Thad and Jasper, had his demons. No wonder, with the father they had…" She bit her lip and stared out at the piney tree line on the side of the house.

"Grandpa Ernie?" She knew little about him. He'd died in a hunting accident before she was even born. "What about him?"

Vi's eyes were bright with tears. "You can't repeat this to anyone. I mean it."

"I won't. Go on."

"Ernest Tedder was a cruel man. He abused his three boys. And look how it turned out."

Lilah closed her eyes at the jolt of pain to think of their suffering. "Really bad?"

"The worst. Mental, physical and—damn his soul— sexual."

Lilah covered her ears with her hands, as if she could block the words already spoken. "Horrible. No wonder Dad turned to drink."

"And Jasper a recluse, and Thad—well, Thad is Thad."

Her uncle could be a little controlling, but to Lilah he seemed the most normal of the three brothers.

"And there's more," Aunt Vi continued.

Lilah wasn't sure she wanted to hear it, but better to face the problem than always wonder and imagine the unknown. "Okay, tell me."

"That hunting accident that killed Ernest...well, that was no accident."

Oh, no. Not another murder. "Please don't tell me Dad killed his own father."

"No. But you see, he isn't the only killer in the family." Viola picked at the frayed edges of her paper napkin. "Might be best if you leave town. The sooner, the better."

"But why? You implied earlier that I should marry Harlan. He's not leaving Lavender Mountain. Not ever."

Viola retreated into her shell and stuffed the wrappers and napkins in the paper sack. "Feels like there's always danger brewing in these hills. Have to admire Harlan's determination to crack down on crime if he's elected."

"He will be. Unless his association with me brings down his popularity."

"You're a fine young lady. He's lucky to have you."

Her aunt's words were balm to her troubled heart. Lilah gave her a swift hug. A twitch at the curtains caught her eye. Lavon glared through the glass pane, the smoldering anger in his eyes hot enough to scorch. Had he heard their conversation?

As always, even the barest contact with Lavon left her feeling like she needed to go home and shower. All during the drive winding down the mountain, her knuckles were white from clenching the steering wheel and her teeth ground together. All she wanted to do tonight was eat, bathe and veg out in front of the television watching romantic comedies.

Only a quarter-mile from Harlan's place she rounded the curve where a side embankment allowed vehicles to pull over for a scenic view. On impulse, she pulled in and turned off the engine. If Harlan were beside her, he'd tell her to chill. Annoying as he could be sometimes, she kind of liked the concern. She climbed out of the car, walked to the guardrail and looked—really looked—at the panoramic view.

Too often, she took the beauty of the Appalachians for granted. A thousand shades of green dotted a turquoise sky. From here, the wild Chattooga River, which served as the border between Georgia and South Carolina, appeared as a thin line of waterfalls cascading down rocky ledges and mountain draws. Its mad foaming rush to the gorges almost made her dizzy. Lilah took long slow breaths, grounding herself with the earth's energy.

A day at a time. That's how she would survive this. Yesterday's and today's sorrows didn't sentence her to a lifetime of misery. For her sake, and her child's sake, she'd take these stolen moments of peace and build happiness.

Feeling better, Lilah's gaze shifted from the distant mountain ridge back to the county road. There was a flash of sun on metal, and she did a double take. Through a slight clearing, a narrow patch of dirt road was visible. Sheriff Bentley leaned against his cruiser and Uncle Thad stepped out of his truck, pulling a wad of bills from his wallet.

Uncle Thad was supposed to be a hundred miles away in Boonesville making a big 'shine delivery. Or so he'd told Aunt Viola.

Was the sheriff a customer? She was afraid to move, afraid to draw attention to her presence. The low murmur of their voices drifted on the wind, but she couldn't discern the words. They didn't sound angry or look agitated as they conversed for a few minutes. The sheriff tucked the proffered money from Thad into his uniform shirt pocket and pressed a small envelope into her uncle's hands. Thad grinned as if he'd won the lottery and returned to his truck.

No gallon jugs of liquor exchanged.

She stood motionless, hardly daring to breathe, as the men drove off in their respective vehicles, and was relieved as they headed down the mountain instead of passing by her at the scenic overview. If they'd glimpsed her, they hadn't given any indication. Slowly, Lilah returned to her car. Her hands trembled slightly as she started the engine.

She'd never liked J.D. Bentley, and the feeling appeared to be mutual. Harlan admitted the sheriff had warned him off her. But if J.D. was so contemptuous of the Tedder name, why conduct secret business with Uncle Thad? Her best guess was that she'd witnessed a payoff to keep mum on the illegal moonshine operation. But what had J.D. given Thad in return?

Whatever had just transpired, it was probably best she didn't know. *Forget you saw it.* Chastising herself for being overly cautious, Lilah waited several minutes before pulling back out onto the road and heading down the mountain.

HARLAN ARRIVED HOME LATE, as drained as if he'd run a marathon instead of sitting for hours at the nursing home by his mom's bedside. Nothing peaceful for either of them at the Peaceful Paths facility. Between his presence and a dose of medication, they'd gotten through the hard day together.

Damn his father. Oh, the doctors wouldn't pinpoint his mom's ill health as the result of enduring his dad's abuse for years coupled with her hard work to scrape by an existence for the two of them. They would only admit stress might have been a "contributing factor."

But he knew the truth.

His house was cheerily lit and Lilah was stretched out on the sofa in front of the television set. Blond hair shadowed her face like a veil, and he sucked in his breath. He could *so* get used to this. Lilah and a baby.

But if it wasn't *his* baby…what then? Could he live with that? Would the biological father insist on being a part of Lilah's life?

Harlan entered the front door as quietly as possible, but Lilah still jerked to a sitting position and regarded him with bleary eyes.

"How's your mom?" she asked.

"Better."

She quirked a brow but didn't press for details. Good. He didn't want to talk about it, anyway. His gaze drifted down the vee of her cleavage. The impression of her nipples was plain through her thin cotton T-shirt. No bra. Was it his imagination, or were her breasts a tiny bit larger and more rounded already? His fingers twitched at his side. He wanted so badly to cup them and pull Lilah against him. She was so damn gorgeous and sexy, the only bright spot in this dark day.

"Harlan."

Her voice was husky and he swiftly raised his gaze to her face. She stepped toward him and wrapped her arms around his waist.

It was more than he'd dared hope for. He drew her to him and squeezed her petite frame against him. Close enough that she had to feel his need rubbing against her core.

Lilah moaned and pressed her hips into his arousal.

Harlan cupped her heart-shaped face in his palms and stared into gray eyes that darkened with a passion that met his own. He remembered that expression well. "Lilah?" he asked, her name harsh on his lips.

In answer, she took his hand and led him down the hallway to his bedroom.

He was out of his clothes by the time they reached the bed. His body ached as he watched Lilah lift the shirt over her head and swiftly shrug out of her jeans and panties.

She was so beautiful standing in the moonlight pouring through the window. How had he ever turned her away? He must have been out of his mind. Out of habit, he pulled open the drawer of his nightstand for a condom.

"A little late for that," she said with a breathy laugh.

"Right."

He didn't want even the thinnest barrier between the most intimate parts of their bodies. Harlan went to her, ran his hands over her breasts—definitely larger—and the soft mound of her abdomen.

"I've missed you," he said simply. "There's been nobody else."

A beat of silence hung in the air and his brain roared like thunder. This must mean she'd been with another. Which meant the baby very well might be another man's. Or was this where she expected him to say he loved her? His tongue lay thick, heavy and unmoving in his mouth. He cleared his throat.

Feathered kisses trailed along his jaw. "You don't have to say a word," she whispered.

With that, Harlan laid her on his bed and gently kissed her forehead. "You won't be sorry, Lilah. I promise to take care of you. If you'll let me."

She pulled him against her. "Sometimes, Harlan, you talk too much."

Chapter Ten

Go or stay? Tell Harlan the truth or not?

Lilah gathered her hair into a bun at the top of her head, grabbed the water bottle and checked her cell phone. She shook her head in disgust—the battery was only at 12 percent. Probably no reception up here, anyway. She tossed it on the passenger seat and locked the car. Nothing like a walk in the woods to clear her mind and make a decision.

Only twenty yards into the Mossy Creek Trail and her jumbled emotions had lightened. The scent of cypress and pine invigorated and heightened her senses. The occasional sounds of cars passing by eventually faded and a heavy silence engulfed her, like being wrapped in a giant green cocoon.

Lilah continued on and memories of Harlan's touch last night absorbed her thoughts. It had been wild and magical—better than ever. No problem between them when it came to sex. He'd walked into the house yesterday evening and she'd instantly recognized the pain behind his smile. The one he always wore after visiting his mother. She'd gone to him at once, willing to ease his misery, no matter the cost to herself. Making love to Harlan had felt natural and right and she could no longer hide from the truth.

She still loved him.

Which left her with a decision to make. Stay and try

to win his love—or leave to protect her heart and pride? The problem was, besides her own happiness, she had to consider what was best for their baby.

On she walked, sweat soaking her T-shirt as she weighed her options. The path stooped downward and a hint of running water freshened the air. Another quarter mile and she'd be at one of Dad's old stills by Mossy Creek. She glanced at the sky uneasily. Couldn't tarry too long or the path would be dark when she headed back.

A barely discernible glint of copper shimmered in the dying light, peeking out between leaves of dense mountain laurel and a patch of witch-hobble. If she hadn't known the location of her dad's still, it would have gone unnoticed. Lilah went to the brush and peeled back a limb.

Sheets of copper bonded together formed a boiler large enough to hold two hundred gallons of corn mash. Behind it was the thumper barrel, which caught the distilled alcohol as it evaporated under the heat. The clear liquid would then travel through a worm and be released out the money piece spigot where Dad used to bottle it up into gallon jugs.

Curious, Lilah knocked her fist against the steel drum. You never knew when someone in the family would take a notion to reuse one of their many old stills. It always paid for them to keep shifting from one site to another. It kept the long arm of the law guessing. But as she'd suspected, this one gave only a hollow echo. Empty.

For the first time since her dad's death, Lilah wondered if Uncle Thad would continue on with the business. Even if he did, there was the possibility he'd lose a large portion of his customer base. Dad had been the one with the special touch for cooking up the best-tasting moonshine. Uncle Thad could mix the same ingredients of rye, barley, sugar water, yeast and wheat bran, all in the same proportions as Dad, but it didn't taste the same.

"Gots to watch it close all the time," Dad would say. "Then you gotta keep the right temperature in place, use only the freshest ingredients, know when the mash has fermented just right and then you gots to aerate it and test yer brew."

Much to Uncle Thad's chagrin, if the liquor didn't meet Dad's high standards, he would refuse to bottle and sell it. But that attention to quality had garnered them a broad and loyal customer base over the years.

She bent to untie her shoes and a gunshot ripped the air directly above her body. Shotgun pellets tore into the bark of a nearby pine and splinters cascaded like rain.

Run.

The animal instinct to flee spiked adrenaline through her body like an electrical storm. She ran blindly, with no thought of direction, only mindful to keep her body low and be less of a target. The sound of her own breath was heavy. So loud, she feared it could be heard within a mile radius.

Brambles and vines cut into her legs and arms as she trampled off the main path. A small price to pay for cover. She didn't dare look back or stop to hear if anyone approached. Another shotgun blast exploded and she ran faster. The tip of her right foot caught under a tree root and Lilah tumbled forward, jaw and nose slapping the ground. She scrambled to her feet and kept running, spitting out mouthfuls of blood—expecting any moment for a pellet to rip into her backside.

Only her breath and the pounding blood in her ears sounded for a long stretch. Was the shooter still pursuing? It felt like a knife was plunged into her left side and she leaned against a wide oak, her breathing jagged and painful.

A long shrill whistle pierced the woods.

That was no bird.

Painful or not, she had to keep going. Lilah forced her leaden legs to move forward and gasped when she came upon the mouth of a familiar cave. She hesitated, debating the wisdom of seeking shelter within its stone walls.

Another raucous whistle materialized from the opposite direction of the first one. She had to do something. Trotting in a low crouch, she broke for the cave and plunged into its darkness.

Its familiar musky scent greeted her, a reminder of childhood afternoons when she, Jimmy and Darla had played here. They'd named it Hideout Hideaway and had pretended they were pirates. The only booty they'd ever found, though, had been twenty-pound bags of grain and sugar. Jimmy had explained they were for making hooch. The cave had served as an outdoor kitchen pantry of sorts.

Lilah pressed her hands on the damp walls, making her way deep into the cave's recesses, until she reached the back wall.

There was no exit.

She sank to the ground and held her side, trying to breathe shallow and avoid the slicing pain. Had they seen her? Time crawled by while she waited to be discovered. Seconds—or perhaps minutes?—later, bass rumbles vibrated from beyond the mouth of the cave. Two male voices.

The rumble increased as they drew closer. She drew her knees into her chest and stared at the narrow entrance, which offered a view of blooming laurel and a thick clump of pine trees.

Footsteps pulsated from above—they were so close. Did they know about the cave? From their position, it would only appear to be a clump of stone.

"Where'd she go?" one of the men asked.

Lilah stuffed her knuckles in her mouth, afraid of making a sound.

"No clue."

Hold on. That voice had a familiar ring. She tried to process where she'd heard it before.

"Any idea who that woman was?"

The other man hesitated. "Maybe. Might have been one of my cousins."

Cousins? Her mind whisked as fast as a kitchen beater on high speed.

"Damn, kid. You a coldhearted one shootin' at kin."

"Kin or not, they ain't got no business 'round here."

"I reckon you scared her off, no harm done." The man paused a heartbeat. "That's all you were doin' right? Scaring her?"

"Right," the familiar voice answered.

He lied. Lilah could tell it by the flat, hard inflection of his voice.

"Let's head on back, be getting dark soon."

A shotgun blast unexpectedly erupted and Lilah clamped her hands over her ears.

The men laughed.

"If you can hear me, take warning," the man shouted. "Stay away from here and mind yer own business."

Would she ever.

Mercifully, the footsteps resumed, heading away.

Whew. She leaned her head against the cool damp stone and waited for her thrumming heart to settle. Had Dad and Uncle Thad always kept someone on guard near their still? Strange how she'd never associated the moonshine operation with violence. Yes, it was illegal and yes, the state sent tobacco, alcohol and firearm agents scouring the mountains once every few years, but it had never crossed her mind that protecting the still meant shooting anyone who stumbled across it.

Her mouth tightened in anger. Uncle Thad be damned. Soon as she got back to Harlan's, she'd report the location and have this still—and the others—shut down once and for all. Those old monsters of welded copper and steel had caused enough pain in the family. No point in some wandering, innocent tourist being killed over that metal apparatus someday.

Might have been one of my cousins one of the men had stated.

She had a good many second and third cousins scattered over the county, but Lilah's mind leaped to her first cousin. Lavon.

Definitely Lavon. They'd never gotten along—but did he really hate her enough to want her dead? She recalled the cold, hard set to his eyes when she'd caught him eavesdropping on her conversation with Uncle Thad.

She rose to leave the cave, but her legs shook too bad to support her weight. Anger melted, leaving a crippling paralysis in its wake. Lilah sank back down onto the damp ground. A little more time to rest and get herself together, then she would head home. Must have run faster and farther than she'd thought. No matter how many deep breaths she tried to take, her lungs demanded more oxygen. And her heart issued its own brutal demand, a rapid and incessant pumping.

Calm down. This would pass. A few more minutes...

...Only it didn't pass. Surely, she was too young for a heart attack. The baby. Had she damaged her unborn child? *Don't go there.* Yet, the worry festered and the more she tried to dismiss it, the more it loomed. Lilah placed one hand on her heart and the other on her stomach, willing mind and body to slow down. *We're safe*, she repeated like a mantra.

A bit of the tension eased. It was working. Lilah gingerly sank down and rested her entire body on the slab of stone. Closing her eyes, she melded into the darkness and the protection of the cave's thick unyielding walls. Just a little rest before she left its shelter. A little more time to quiet her heart, revive her legs and let Lavon and the other guy move out of the area.

WHERE WAS SHE?

Harlan paced the den and tried to ring her cell phone for the hundredth time, but there was no answer. He walked through the house again, checking tables and counters for a note. Lilah knew he would worry if she was unaccounted for.

Something was wrong. Outside, the shadows had darkened and deepened to the point they were almost indistinguishable in the evening's landscape.

He wasn't taking any chances. What good was it working in law enforcement if you couldn't pull a few strings? Quickly, he dialed the county dispatcher and set up an APB for Lilah's car. Next, he called the landlord of her apartment building in case she'd returned there.

His stomach took a dive. Had she left him for good? Yes, they'd made love last night, and it had been amazing, but he hadn't said the words she'd needed to hear. Maybe she'd finally had enough—had grown weary waiting on him to get his act together.

He couldn't sit in this empty house and imagine worst-case scenarios involving Lilah. Harlan hightailed it to the cruiser and kept the police scanner on as he sped to Thaddeus Tedder's place. With any luck, Lilah was visiting kin and the time had slipped away from her. He flipped on the blue siren switch and climbed the mountain.

The moment he pulled into the driveway, disappointment washed over him. Lilah's car was nowhere in sight. He parked on a diagonal just by the porch where Thaddeus, his wife and their eldest son sat. The cherry from Thad's cigar glowed and moths fluttered around the overhead light.

"You seen Lilah?" he asked without preamble, exiting the car.

Thad spoke for the group. "Not today. Why?"

Viola started to rise from her rocking chair. "She in some kind of trouble?"

"Only trouble she's in is from our deputy here," their son joked.

Everyone kept assuming he was the father. If only he could be as certain. Harlan's hands went to his hips and he glared at the guy—Lavon, if he was remembering correctly. Punk kid. The name Lavon Tedder had come up a few times over the years. All minor incidents—a school fight, petty theft, vandalism. Never could pin anything on him, though; kid was as slippery as his dad. How had Lilah risen above this despicable family?

"Lavon!"

Even in the darkness, Viola's red face was evident.

"When you going to do right by Lilah?" Thad smirked, ignoring his son's rude comment. "Although, if you ask me, she can do lots better than a do-good nobody like you. Told her so, too."

Nobody had asked Thad's opinion. Coming here had been a complete waste of time.

"You hear from Lilah, let me know."

"Can't keep tabs on your own woman?" Lavon mocked.

That did it. "What's your problem, kid? Two people in your family are dead and Lilah's unaccounted for."

"He didn't mean nothing by it," Thad said. "She's probably just visiting a friend."

Harlan wished he could believe in a simple explanation. He also wished for a crime free community, prosperity in Appalachia and world peace. But wishing didn't make it so.

"Let's hope that's the case." He returned to the cruiser and got in, ready to pull out, when Viola came to the door and motioned for him to roll down the window.

"Call me when you find her." Her face taut. "Lilah's always been one to hike out in the woods, alone, but she don't need to be running around at night all by herself."

"Under the circumstances, I couldn't agree with you more."

Harlan drove back to the main road. What next? Lilah claimed to have lost touch with old childhood friends, which just left family. She hadn't gone to visit Ed or her nephews—he'd already checked. And she wasn't with her elderly aunt—he'd called there, too. Which only left Jasper Tedder. The old coot would be even less happy to see him than Thad, not that it mattered.

Darkness seeped in by degrees as he climbed to the top of Lavender Mountain, and with it a heavy blanket of dread weighed on his heart. He had to find Lilah soon. What if she were out in the woods and had turned her ankle—or something worse? Over ten years as a deputy sheriff had provided too many horrific examples of tragic accidents and crimes.

His cruiser headlights pierced the ramshackle building Jasper called home. It was slapped together from sheets of pressed wood and sported a rusty tin roof—one stiff wind away from annihilation. The porch was haphazardly strewn with an ironing board, an old school desk, boxes and plastic bins. Harlan parked and got out of the vehicle.

Jasper stalked out the front door waving his arms. "My peppers!"

Huh? Harlan scanned the premises.

"You run over my pepper plants."

Harlan looked back and, sure enough, he'd driven over a couple. "Sorry, sir. I'll come back out later this week with new plants."

Jasper rubbed at his beard. "I reckon that'll be all right then. See that you do."

"Yes, sir. I came to ask if you'd heard from Lilah today."

White scraggly eyebrows lifted. "She don't come to call very often. Why you asking?"

"It's late and getting dark. She usually lets me know if she won't be home for dinner."

"Well, now don't you paint a nice cozy picture. Fact is, son, you're living in sin with my niece. You can pretty it up any way you please but facts is facts. The Lord don't—"

"If you don't mind, sir. Have you seen Lilah or not?"

"Not today. Maybe she's come to her senses and gone back to her own place like a nice respectable young lady. Back in my day, we didn't cotton to this foolishness of make-believe marriages and such. Far as I'm concerned, y'all are playing house."

He'd been lectured enough today. "The point is—Lilah might be in danger."

The walkie-talkie belted by his hip crackled and the dispatcher's voice sounded: *Navy blue compact car located. License plate ALA34892. Registered owner listed as Lilah Tedder. Found by entrance to Mossy Creek Trail. Vehicle is unoccupied.*

Damn. Adrenaline flushed his body. What was she

doing there? Something bad had happened to her, he just knew it, had felt it all along. Harlan rushed to his car.

"She really in danger?" Jasper sprinted to the passenger's side and climbed in. "I'm going with you. I know that area like the back of my hand."

Harlan hit the gas and turned on the blue light. Mossy Creek had once been a popular path leading to the main Appalachian Trial but he hadn't walked it since he was a teenager.

"Why are you so familiar with this trail?" he asked Jasper. He doubted Lilah's uncle would be much help, but engaging in conversation would help keep the turmoil at bay.

"I have my reasons. Enough said."

Harlan gritted his teeth. Jasper could be maddening. Stubborn as all get-out. If he didn't want to volunteer information, nothing could pry it loose. But right now, he didn't much care how Jasper came to know that neck of the woods as long as he proved helpful.

He pressed the redial number for Lilah's phone on the off-chance she'd called, but he got the same empty ring and the same voice-mail message. In disgust, he dropped it in the console.

Jasper picked it up, palming the phone as if it were an alien object dropped from outer space. "How you work this thing?"

"Now's not a good time for me to bring you into the twenty-first century," he said, rounding a curve a little too fast and fishtailing back into his own lane.

"I'm gonna git us some help. Walk me through the process."

Every law enforcement officer in the county would be there, but if Lilah was lost or hurt in the woods, every person on patrol mattered.

"Press the button on the side and then touch the phone receiver icon."

"Icon?"

"Little picture on the screen."

Harlan slowed down. He couldn't afford an accident along the way.

"Now what?" Jasper asked.

"Press the dial pad option." At Jasper's perplexed expression, Harlan sighed and pulled off to the side of the road. "Just give it to me. What's the number?"

"Don't have to git huffy."

Jasper rattled off the number and Harlan punched it out before returning the phone to him. A ring echoed over the Bluetooth radio connection as he pulled back onto the road.

"Hello," a gruff voice answered.

"Thad? Git out to Mossy Creek Trail and bring anyone you can find for a search-and-rescue."

Jasper spoke loudly, the phone held close to his ear, and Harlan didn't bother explaining that was unnecessary.

"Lilah's car's stranded out there. Our gal's missing."

They arrived at the scene within ten minutes. Three police cars and a state trooper vehicle were already there. Bile rose in his throat at the sight of officers shining their flashlights inside Lilah's abandoned car. Was she in the car and possibly hurt?

Harlan slammed on his brakes, inches from a parked cop car, and hurried over. "What's happening?"

J.D. placed a hand on his shoulder. "No sign of any blood or a struggle. With any luck, she just went for a walk and got lost. We'll find her."

"She left her phone in the car." Officer Alvin Lee honed his flashlight on the passenger's seat where Lilah's phone lay.

"We've got to find her—organize a search," Harlan said.

"We're on it." The nearby state trooper stepped over

and held out a hand. "Harlan Sampson? Trooper Davis. Understand the subject is your girlfriend?"

"Correct." Harlan absently shook his hand.

"Called for a helicopter search-and-rescue mission. In light of the recent murders, approval shouldn't be a problem."

"Thank you." Finally, a piece of good news.

More cars arrived and the night filled with the sounds of people shouting commands and the crackle of static and disembodied voices from police scanners. Blue lights strobed over the scene while officers donned headlamp gear and dug out first-aid kits. Most were no strangers to these missions. Tourists got lost, or hikers on the Appalachian Trail sustained injuries and failed to report to their next checkpoint, alarming their next of kin. He'd always felt compassion for the waiting, worried families, never imagining he'd live through this particular agony himself.

Sammy clamped a hand on his shoulder. "Hang in there, buddy. Lilah's a mountain girl, born and raised. She'll be fine."

"I'm going with you."

Sammy thrust a headlamp, a whistle on a chain and a compass at him. "Figured as much." He looked past Harlan's shoulders and whistled. "Take a look at this."

People streamed from dozens of parked cars. Jasper rounded them together with the help of a cop as they organized a search.

For the first time in the past two frustrating hours, Harlan's throat closed up and he blinked hard. That's what he loved about Lavender Mountain. That's what made this place home. Everyone came together in times of need—without question and without complaint. He recalled nights when he and his mom—for days in a row—were down to nothing but grits for dinner. Some kind anonymous neighbors would leave them a basket of fresh-baked food or a casserole dish warm from their oven.

Harlan strapped on the headlamp, placed the whistle chain around his neck and joined his fellow officers at the head of the trail. Six-by-six, they entered and walked in a horizontal line, their combined lights illuminating the forest like a blazing wall.

They would find her, alive and well. He refused to accept any other possibility.

I'm coming for you, Lilah. Hang on.

Chapter Eleven

A storm of turbulence thundered through the mountain. Lilah was startled awake, bewildered and fearful. Damp stone, darkness and the metallic tinge of blood in her mouth reminded her of the afternoon's events. But what was that roaring cacophony? From the cave's mouth, a monochromic flash of white beams lit the trees. Faraway voices wafted faintly.

She slowly rose and walked on wobbling legs to the entrance, then leaned against the stone aperture. Ahead, a helicopter drew nearer before circling and hovering almost directly above. She blinked, adjusting from the cave's darkness and silence to the piercing light and noise.

They were looking for *her*. She'd been part of search-and-rescue missions before, although never at night. And she'd certainly never been the objective of one.

"Here," she called. But her voice was weak, certainly not audible over the chopper's engine.

A ray of light from above shone directly on her body and she blinked and waved her arms.

"Lilah!"

She distinctly heard her name and turned her head to the right.

Harlan ran toward her, his eyes frantic. "Are you hurt? You're bleeding."

Without waiting for an answer, he picked her up and cradled her against his broad chest, which she buried her face in, shutting out the commotion. She inhaled the scent of clean linen blended with a woodsy note, savoring the comfort and strength of Harlan's presence.

Now she had the answer she'd been seeking when she'd entered the forest hours ago. No way was she leaving this man or this mountain. He deserved to know the truth. He was the father of her child and she loved and trusted him. She'd never stopped loving him, even when he'd withdrawn his affection after her spring break was over.

"We'll get you to a hospital right away," he vowed, stroking her hair. "What happened? Did somebody hurt you or did you just take a tumble?"

Before she could answer, Jasper ran up to them. "Lay-Lay, you okay little girl?"

"I'm fine now."

The harsh lines of her uncle's face relaxed. "Had a hunch you'd head out to this cave when they found your car at the trail entrance. You always did love to play in it when you were a kid. You and Jimmy and Darla, too."

Ah, so that's how they knew where to search. "Thank you, Uncle Jasper."

They were quickly surrounded by others. Spontaneous cheers erupted from the volunteers. Lilah recognized Sammy and Alvin as they pushed their way over.

"What happened, Lilah?" Sammy asked.

She shot Harlan an uneasy glance. "I came out for a walk and two men took shots at me. Sounded like a shotgun. I ran to the cave and hid."

Harlan's arms and chest tightened, hardening against her body.

Alvin gave a low whistle. "Why would they shoot at you?"

Her eyes slid involuntarily to Jasper and he gave the slightest shake of his head, as if asking her to keep quiet. He always called moonshine the "devil's brew," but family was family and they stuck together.

"Who were the bastards?" Harlan's face was pinched and his question clipped. "That's what I need to know."

"I—I can't say for sure. I never saw them, just heard their voices later, outside the cave." Hell, she hated to tell him this next part. "I waited a long time before trying to leave, but my heart was racing and I was exhausted from running. I lay down to rest and then—" she waved an arm at the chaos. "—then I woke to the sound of the chopper."

"You didn't recognize the voices?"

Of course, Harlan cut right to the heart of the matter. She hesitated, unwilling to implicate Lavon in front of everyone. Could she really be one hundred percent positive it was him without having seen his face? If it wasn't Lavon, she'd do him a great disservice by casting blame. And her family would be furious.

"Maybe," she conceded, lowering her voice so only Harlan could hear. "I'll tell you later. All right?"

He looked as if he wanted to argue, but relented when she cupped his jaw in her palms. "Please, I'm tired. I just want to go home. Okay? We can talk there—alone."

Sammy interrupted. "Any injuries other than your split lip? Do you need to go to the hospital?"

"No. No hospital."

Harlan frowned. "Can you walk?"

Lilah spied the sheriff striding toward them with his usual air of impatience, his features stern and implacable. He didn't appear glad to see her one whit. Probably angry she'd created such a stir and cost the good taxpayers' money and time.

"Yes, I can walk." She wiggled out of his arms and stood. "Let's get outta here."

J.D. pulled out his walkie-talkie and informed the helicopter pilot that the mission was accomplished and the person found didn't need a hospital emergency escort. He eyed her with his usual faint air of condescension. "Why were you out walking so late in this area?" he asked in a you-should-know-better tone.

"Didn't know that was a crime." He prickled her temper. But the truth was, she felt guilty. She didn't want to think about how much it cost for a chopper search.

"No crime. Seems strange, though. Girl like you should know the dangers of roaming the forest at night."

"It wasn't dark when I started," she snapped. "And how was I supposed to know I'd get shot at?"

"You saying someone shot at you?" His tone held just a tinge of disbelief.

"Why would I lie?"

Harlan jumped in the fray, squeezing her hand before addressing his boss. "It's late and we're all tired. You'll have a full statement from Lilah in the morning, J.D."

"See that I do."

HARLAN GENTLY DABBED a washcloth at the gash on Lilah's mouth, relieved to find the cut was superficial and didn't even need stitches. Had to hurt like hell, though. Who had done this to her? He tamped down the anger. That could wait. For now, he wanted to take care of Lilah and ease her mind. She stood before him in the shower, the bubbles from her bath gel enticingly covering her rosy skin.

Harlan groaned inwardly at the temptation. Tonight was hardly the time to make love. "Go ahead and get under the spigot so I can wash your hair."

"I'm okay. Could have done this myself," she grumbled but, nevertheless, stepped into the tub of steaming water.

"Thanks for humoring me."

He squirted a dollop of shampoo in his palm and began kneading it into her hair. The feel of the lather in her long blond hair and the flowery smell created a tender sense of intimacy.

"Have to admit this feels like heaven," she said breathily, eyes closed.

Good. This also gave him a chance to more thoroughly check out her naked body for other signs of injury. So far, only scraped knees. His stomach lurched at the thought of how horrible it could have been. If he'd lost Lilah... No, best not to go there.

He rinsed her hair and wrapped a towel around her head. She stepped out of the tub and he gently dried her off. As always, the sight of her naked body was arousing, but tonight it was also tempered with a deep tenderness.

"I'm sorry to be so much trouble." She blinked back tears. "I got everybody riled up tonight, especially J.D."

He followed her into the bedroom where she pulled on a pink nightgown and plopped on the bed.

"Screw J.D. Everyone else was concerned about your safety, not angry."

"He's not wrong. It was stupid to go out there so late in the afternoon. Although, in my defense, I got so spent after running that I couldn't hike back to the car. Plus, it's weird. Inside the cave, even once I knew they were gone, my heart started racing. No matter how much I rested, it felt like I couldn't breathe."

"Might have been a panic attack."

"That makes me sound like a weakling—a hysterical female." Lilah removed the towel from her head and starting working a comb through her long locks.

"No way. You were attacked in the woods and were alone and pregnant. Would have been a wonder if you hadn't panicked. Nobody is judging you for anything. As for being in the woods, you couldn't have known two psychos were roaming about. Speaking of which—it's time to tell me everything."

She sighed. "Right. Remember, it's all just supposition, though, as far as the shooters. That's why I didn't mention it in front of everybody. Darla, Jimmy and I used to play in that cave as kids because it was near one of Dad's old stills. While he worked, we entertained ourselves there. The second I heard the shotgun blast, I instinctively ran to it. While I was hiding, I heard two men talking on the ground above me."

His jaw tightened. "What did they say? Any idea who they were?"

"One asked the other if he'd only shot to scare me away and the other man said he had, but I think he lied. And the worst part is...the man that lied? It might have been my cousin Lavon."

He'd get the truth out of Lavon in the morning—no matter what it took. "I wouldn't put it past that guy. But why would he shoot at you?"

"Maybe he did it to protect the still location? Or maybe just out of plain meanness?"

"You said it was an old still, so that seems unlikely. Unless they're using it again?"

She winced at a tangle in her hair and set the comb on the nightstand. "No. I checked underneath and there haven't been any recent fires lit for cooking moonshine."

Harlan rose and went to the window, gazing at the dark sky. To think she'd been alone and vulnerable out there made his gut clench. Damn if he wouldn't get to the bottom of this first thing in the morning. He'd have Lavon spilling his guts before noon.

"The Tedders *are* trouble. Except for you," he quickly amended. "They wanted to hurt—or scare you—for a reason. I aim to find out why."

"But I could be wrong about Lavon," she added hastily. "I didn't see him so I can't swear in a court of law he was the one. What if I'm wrong? Much as I dislike him, I don't want him locked up on a false charge. And Uncle Thad and Aunt Vi would never forgive me, either."

"You've been through enough without worrying about their feelings."

She bit her lip. "Lavon will be really angry. Whether he's innocent or not."

"I won't let him get to you."

"You can't protect me twenty-four seven."

"Can we at least agree that, until everything settles down, you don't go anywhere alone?"

"I won't go walking alone in the woods again. Probably ever."

She hadn't exactly agreed to his terms, but he couldn't keep her under lock and key, either. "At least promise me that if you leave the house while I'm at work, you'll let me know where you're going?"

"Agreed." She flashed the first real smile he'd seen from her today. "See? I can be reasonable."

Whew. He sat beside her on the bed and ran a hand through his hair. He couldn't be worrying about her safety when he needed a clear head to ponder the possibilities of what was behind the shooting. He'd question Lavon, then go back out to the old still and the cave to look around. Those men were guarding something. If not moonshine, was it drugs? His heart beat faster, the way it did when he was onto something. That area was perfect—off the beaten path but close enough to a main road for easy access to transportation.

"Did you see anything suspicious in that cave?"

"I didn't look. There's several narrow passages in the back, but I've always avoided them. Bats, you know. Why? You think there's something hidden?"

"Could be."

Lilah grinned. "We always knew there was hidden treasure in there."

"I call it contraband, if it's what I suspect it is. I'll know in the morning."

"Drugs? Could be. I want to go with you tomorrow."

"No way. This will be official police work. We can't let civilians come along."

"Please? I think it would help me to go back there in daylight. I'll go crazy just sitting around your home all day."

"J.D. would raise hell."

"So don't tell him. That man's a crook. How can you stand to work for him?"

"I realize you don't like him and I can't blame you. But come on—a crook?"

"I can't prove it, but yeah, I have my suspicions."

He regarded her evenly. J.D. could be an ass. Could her dislike for him be coloring her opinion of his integrity? "Go on. Why?"

"Just the other day I saw Uncle Thad give a him a large roll of money. They were pulled over to the side of the road in an area overgrown with trees and brush—an area sheltered from public view."

Harlan frowned. "Maybe J.D. bought something from him?"

"The only thing I saw exchange hands was my uncle

handing him money and then J.D. slipped him an envelope."

That didn't sound good. A local sheriff receiving money from a known moonshiner? Still, he had to be fair. "I'll ask J.D. about it. He might have bought a large-ticket item from Thad and then your uncle gave him a receipt. Something explainable."

"More likely J.D.'s on the take to turn a blind eye."

If his boss was accepting money to keep quiet about moonshining, what was to keep him from doing the same with illegal drug operations? Could he be the one tipping off the distributors before a raid? If he was, they had a real mess on their hands.

Lilah's mouth twisted. "Can you leave my name out of it when you ask J.D. about the money? He's already unhappy with me. Makes me uneasy to tick off the sheriff."

"Don't worry," he admonished, wanting her to relax and have a good night's rest after her ordeal. Everything else could wait until morning. "All's well. You have the sheriff's deputy wrapped around your little finger."

"Do I?" she asked wistfully, cocking her head to the side.

"How can you not know that?" he asked roughly. He'd opened his home to her, despite the fact it was probably the worst thing in the world for him career-wise.

Her lips tugged at the corners and she held up both hands, ticking off the reasons why on her fingers. "One: because you've never told me you loved me. Two: because I'm bad news for your dream job. And three: because I'm pregnant."

All true. And yet, he couldn't deny that she sent his emotions on a tailspin like no other woman had ever done.

"I love you, Harlan," she said simply. Her eyes shone like pewter.

"I—I care about you." He closed his eyes and tried to order his jumbled thoughts. Could he make this work? Marry a Tedder—one possibly pregnant by another man of all things—and still win the election?

But even if he became the next sheriff, without Lilah by his side, it would be a hollow victory. He was confused, yes, but he knew one thing: he wanted her here with him. To protect her from any harm. Forever.

Only one way to do that. He slid down the mattress and planted one knee on the floor.

"Marry me, Lilah."

She sucked in air and a hand flew to her chest. "But…" She glanced down at her belly.

"I don't care who the father is. I mean, yes, I care, but even if the baby's not mine, I want you, Lilah. What do you say?"

In less than a heartbeat, she was in his arms, her fingers raking his hair, pulling him toward her in a kiss. Her mouth was urgent and pliant against his. The press of her body and the smell of her skin mixed with the soap and the shampoo were like a drug. He could never get enough of Lilah. Not ever. Their bodies sank onto the bed and he leaned on his elbows, taking in the sight of her flushed with passion.

"I take it that's a *yes*?"

A THOUSAND TIMES YES.

In answer, she kissed him again and wiggled her hips against his erection. He might not be able to say the words yet, but he loved her. Whatever messed up hell his dad had put him through growing up, Harlan had a great capacity for love. He'd just proved it by asking her to marry him when he believed her pregnant by another. One day, he would recognize his feelings for what they truly were.

His mouth captured one of her nipples and he suckled while one hand traveled up her inner thigh, hot and demanding. She gasped as one of his fingers entered her core and began moving in and out. He knew just where to touch, where to press and how hard. Lilah broke away and quickly helped him tug out of his jeans. He was as ready as she was and he thrust inside her, the tension building between them in a familiar intimate storm. She came first, and then she floated back down, watching the tense lines of his face and the darkening of his eyes as he reached his own climax.

He rolled off her and she snuggled against his side. Together, their labored breathing relaxed to normal. Lilah traced the strong plane of his jaw and cheekbones.

Now was the time.

"Harlan?" she began tentatively, suddenly nervous.

In response, he took her hand and kissed her fingers, his gaze intense.

"I have something to tell you."

"Go on."

"The baby's yours," she whispered.

He didn't move, other than the widening of his eyes.

She'd expected more. A smile, a hug…something. "Is that okay?" she asked nervously.

Harlan eased back and propped up on his elbows, studying her.

She bit her lip. "There hasn't been anyone else for me, either. I didn't want to tell you earlier because, well, I didn't want you to feel like you had to marry me."

"You lied to me." His voice was hard and unbending. "All this time. You left me wondering. Do you have any idea what it's been like?"

Oh, hell. She'd ruined everything. "I'm sorry. Can we—maybe start over again?"

Harlan was out of the bed in a heartbeat, picking up his tossed clothes in angry swiping movements. She'd never seen him like this before, as if he couldn't even bear to look at her.

"Just wipe the slate clean, huh?" he snapped. "Forget you lied to me?"

She sat up, gathering the bedsheet over her breasts. "I'm willing if you are."

He glared at her. "I bet."

Her own temper rose. "You haven't exactly been blameless yourself. You broke off with me because you didn't think I was good enough for you."

"Not true."

His face flushed, whether from anger or guilt she couldn't say.

"It *is* true," she insisted. "You as much as admitted it the other day."

"My qualm wasn't with you, it was with your family."

"Same thing."

He walked out.

Lilah hugged her knees to her chest, feeling as disoriented as when she'd been lost in the woods. To go from the happiest moment of her life to the silent aftermath of a fight left her shaken.

It's going to be okay, she promised herself. He just needs to cool off a bit and come to grips with the news. After all, she'd had weeks to come to terms with the situation. By morning, this may well have blown over.

Chapter Twelve

It hadn't blown over.

Breakfast had been civil, but decidedly cool. He'd left for work and returned home a couple of hours later, offering to take her to the cave with him. A peace offering, she'd hoped. But on the drive out, Harlan looked about as solemn as she'd ever seen. Maybe coming along to the cave wasn't such a hot idea. "You want another cup of coffee?" she asked, holding up the thermos like an olive branch.

"No more caffeine. I just want to throttle your cousin Lavon. That's all."

At least he was directing his ire elsewhere. "I always feel that way about him. I take it you talked to him this morning?"

"Tried to. He denied shooting at you. Claimed he was nowhere near the cave yesterday."

Doubts assailed her mind. Had she been wrong? She'd been distraught last night. Maybe her dislike of Lavon had tainted her judgment. "Let it go, then. I can't prove it and there's a chance I'm wrong."

"I'm not letting it go. No way. Told Lavon I was keeping an eye on him and if he ever came at you again that… Well, never mind the details. At least I managed to shake up his smug expression a little near the end. Said he was telling his dad that I'd harassed him." Harlan snorted. "As if I'm scared of Thaddeus Tedder."

She wished she'd kept her mouth shut about her suspicions. Now things would be all awkward with Aunt Vi and Uncle Thad. Lilah sighed and looked out the car window for the rest of the drive.

"Sure you want to go back out there?" Harlan pulled off the road at the Mossy Creek Trail entrance.

"Positive."

Anything was better than sitting around fretting. She'd give her aunt and uncle a few days to simmer down about this mess and then pay them a visit. She unbuckled her seat belt and stepped out of the cruiser.

A few strewn cigarette butts and some tossed plastic cups near the trail opening were a reminder of last night's ordeal. Lilah took a deep breath and headed into the woods. She was damn lucky to be alive and walking this same path.

Harlan stepped beside her, his expression still somber. He seemed so…remote and official, wearing his stiff brown uniform. Unapproachable, even.

She forced some cheer into her voice. "This might be fun. Who knows what we'll find in that cave? Jimmy, Darla and me were convinced it held treasure."

"When you were still old enough to believe in the Tooth Fairy and Santa Claus?" A trace of a smile hovered on his lips.

"Not just any old treasure. Pirate's treasure—gold, swords, doubloons."

"Those were some crazy lost pirates if they wandered from shore all the way to the North Georgia Mountains."

Nothing seemed impossible when they had been little. Her throat closed shut remembering Darla's face when she'd found a necklace Jimmy had planted for her in the cave. She'd squealed in excitement, dancing a jig and laughing. She always had liked pretty baubles. A shame she hadn't owned more of them in her short life.

Lilah fanned her face. It was warming up quick. How could Harlan stand walking around in that hot uniform?

"Oh, there's the old still down in the draw if you want to take a look at it," she said, pointing at the location.

"Might as well."

They walked down to the creek and she led him to it, fighting back a bit of guilt. If her father could see her now… But he was dead. Maybe exposing all their dirty family secrets would lead to finding his and Darla's killer.

Harlan bent down and picked up the plastic water bottle. "This yours?"

"Yeah. I stopped to tie my shoelaces when I heard the first shot. Forgot all about the water and hightailed it that way." She pointed eastward.

"Doesn't the main trail take you to the cave?"

"I was in a bit of a hurry," she said drily.

"Of course. I want to retrace your steps, though. You don't need to go through these brambles. I can meet you at the cave."

"No way," she said with a snort. "I'm not walking there alone."

"Fine, you can help me. Keep your eyes peeled for shotgun shells. Which way did you run after you dropped the bottle?"

She pointed straight ahead and he walked forward, with Lilah in tow. Nearly a hundred feet later, he retrieved a plastic casing from the ground. "Here's one of them."

"Will it do you any good?"

"Some. We can check the firing ping marks on the shotgun shell's primer for microscopic identification—see if it matches a particular shotgun."

"That's the best news I've heard all day." Now they were getting somewhere.

"Don't get too excited. All it can really do, legally, is exclude certain guns."

Her shoulders sagged. "Then what good is it?"

"We can get a search warrant for Lavon's guns and run a ballistics test. If the firing pin markings match up, then I'd say we have our first circumstantial evidence pointing to your cousin. Not that we can arrest him without other proof."

"At least we're headed in the right direction."

Through a thick layer of pine needles, her right foot stepped on something hard. Lilah bent and brushed away the needles, picking up another shell. The plastic casing sent tremors up her arm and made her heart skitter. How close had she come to serious injury or death—a couple feet? A few inches? She placed her hands over her stomach.

"You okay?"

Harlan came up behind her and wrapped his arms around her waist, his palms covering her fingers. There, together, their hands lay entwined against her belly where their unborn child grew. Peace washed over her and with it, last night's sorrow. Lilah squeezed her eyes shut and soaked in the sacred intimacy of the moment. She and their baby were safe. Harlan might not recognize his own feelings yet, but this was love. As pure as it got. Eventually, he would realize it on his own.

"I'm fine, Harlan." She turned and pressed her face into his chest a moment before stepping away. "Let's get this guy. Both of them. Maybe today will be the first real break in the case."

He held up crossed fingers. "Your optimism's rubbing off. Could be we get lucky and find something else in the cave."

She high-fived him and they picked their way through the shrubs for several minutes. The stone walls of the cave appeared suddenly.

"There it is. Hideout Hideaway."

"Good thing Jasper led us here last night. Even on the main trail, it's not easy to see behind those huge spruce and river birches." Harlan handed her a flashlight. "Ready?"

In answer, she turned on the flashlight and walked inside. The drop in temperature felt refreshing, although yesterday evening it had gotten a bit chilly. Thank heavens she hadn't been forced to spend the night here.

"What's this?"

Harlan strode to the west side where faint red markings splattered the wall.

"I can't believe it's still there!" Lilah laughed and shone her flashlight on it. "Take three kids and a can of red paint. We had a blast until Dad collected us to go home." She ran a finger over the faint marks. "There's my initials."

Harlan squinted. "Yeah, I see it now. Cool. But show me those side passages you mentioned."

"You're going to get your uniform all messed up," she warned.

"Doesn't matter."

She led him back to the first passage. "This is the smallest one. You'd have to crawl through it. I never did, but Jimmy went a little ways in it once."

Harlan shone the flashlight. "Hmm. Don't see anything here. Doesn't look promising. I'll come back later with Sammy for this one and bring rope. Where's another one?"

"This one's the largest," she said, taking him farther into the cave's recesses. "It's narrow but tall. We won't even have to stoop to walk to the end of the passage."

Harlan led the way and came to an abrupt halt. "Well, looka here."

He stooped down and she peered over his bent figure. A dozen empty plastic baggies littered the ground.

"Looks like trash to me."

"If it's what I think it is…" He put on a pair of gloves and picked one up. Little crumbles of dried leaf and buds were tucked in the corners.

"Is that—" she began.

"Yup. Marijuana."

He shone the flashlight farther into the rock tunnel. "I see a bigger bundle."

He went over and picked up a book-sized package wrapped in cardboard and bundled in twine.

"Open it," she breathed, skin tingling with anticipation.

"Nope. Going to take this back to work, open it there and get it logged into the chain of evidence."

"So that's why those men shot at me. I got too close to their drugs."

"Must be a big-time operation for them to go to those lengths. I suspect this cave's a temporary holding place until transport. Ideally, you'd store marijuana in a dry room."

He directed the flashlight beam at the wet ground where the mud was imprinted with large footprints. "Bet at the crack of dawn they were in here and removed all they could."

Lilah shuddered, suddenly eager to get away. She'd had enough excitement for one day—for a lifetime, actually.

J.D.'S FACE WAS nearly purple with anger.

"What the hell have you been up to this morning, Harlan? First, I get a call from Thaddeus Tedder threatening legal action against our office for harassing his son, and now you tell me you've been trampling through the woods with a civilian?"

This wasn't what he'd been expecting. Not at all. He didn't think J.D. would be *happy* that he'd struck out on his own this morning, but he *had* found drug evidence they'd been searching for these past couple of years. It wasn't much, but it was a start.

"I was careful. Everything was done by the book. Now that we know what's out there—"

"By the book? Are you kidding me?" J.D. shoved the cardboard bundle away from him. "This is worthless to us now."

"I followed protocol," Harlan said stiffly. "I used gloves, took a couple photos with my cell phone and then bagged the evidence. I'll have it all in my report."

J.D. clutched the edge of his desk, white-knuckled. "Forget the report. I'll head out there myself with the narcotics dogs and a team. Meanwhile, I want you to take a week off work. Effective immediately."

What the hell? Harlan blinked. "I don't want a vacation. I want to work this case."

"At this point, I don't care what you want. That time off wasn't a suggestion, it's an order."

"Why are you doing this?"

"You're letting that woman run you in circles. You're so in lust that you've lost your judgment and any sense of perspective." He shook his head in disgust. "Running all over the mountain accusing people of crimes on nothing but hearsay, then striking out on your own at a crime scene and taking your girlfriend along with you. Take a week off and think about it."

"I don't need to think about." Harlan worked to keep his voice down. J.D. was still his boss after all. "Lavon Tedder is a punk. Look at his juvenile record and—"

"I know who the hell he is. Doesn't mean you can run roughshod over the guy."

"You've got to be kidding me." How many times had he witnessed J.D. doing the same? "We have a witness who's almost certain she heard his voice after an attack."

"*Almost?* Not like your girlfriend actually saw Lavon."

Harlan picked up the baggie with the collected shotgun shells and waved them at J.D. "She was almost killed. You really going to let this slide because Lavon went crying to his daddy? We need to get a subpoena for his guns and run a ballistics test to see if they match the shell casings."

"That won't hold up in a court of law and you know it."

"Doesn't mean we can't start building a circumstantial case. Who knows? Maybe it'll even be enough to scare Lavon into a confession."

"Or maybe your rash actions for swift justice will result in a lawsuit against us as well as charges of tainting the evidence."

Harlan stared, dumbfounded. J.D. had been his mentor, had been grooming him to take over as sheriff and now he treated him like this? He'd done nothing wrong. Harlan's conscience was crystal clear. But there was no point in continuing the discussion.

"And if I refuse to leave work?" Harlan asked.

J.D. stood, hitching up his belt. "Son, you don't want to cross me. Get your ass out of here, think the situation over and we'll talk next week."

Harlan went to the door and then turned. "Why are you so afraid of Thaddeus Tedder?"

"I'm not." J.D. sat down and pulled a stack of papers toward him.

"Has he got some kind of hold over you?" Harlan asked quietly. Maybe Lilah was right. Maybe her uncle did pay J.D. for favors. It could have started years ago if Thaddeus had caught J.D. in a moment of weakness, and then his boss had been sucked into staying on the take.

"If you're in hot water with the Tedders, I can help you," Harlan offered.

J.D. nailed him with a glare. "What makes you say that?"

"You were recently seen accepting money from Thad."

J.D.'s hands slammed on the desk. "That's a damn lie. You got proof?"

"Not yet."

Harlan softly closed the door. Let his boss stew on that one.

Zelda scurried toward him with an empty cardboard box. "Thought you might need to pack up a few things," she said sympathetically, trying to push the box into his hands.

All eyes from the dozen or so cubicles were on him. So they'd heard J.D.'s rant.

He shook his head. "I don't need that box. I'll only be a gone a week. I'm coming back."

At least, he hoped so. No telling what kind of trick J.D. might have up his sleeve. Back in his office, he collected a few odds and ends, preparing to leave.

Wait. Not so fast. Just how crooked was his boss? Last time J.D. had been in his office, he'd disapproved of his reviewing the old Hilltop Strangler case and had taken Lilah's leather bracelet. On a hunch, Harlan looked up the number to the forensics office in Atlanta. If there was to be any progress on the case, he'd have to push it. Wouldn't hurt to prod one of his old friends and see if they could prioritize examining the bracelet. J.D. was already ticked off with him, so why not? He punched in the number and spoke to Doug almost at once. At least luck was with him on this.

But the news he received was a bombshell.

The bracelet had never been sent.

WAIT UNTIL UNCLE JASPER lit his eyes on this. Lilah kept a hand on top of the covered casserole dish as she swung into the potholed slash of dirt that passed for his driveway.

Jasper looked up, frowning, from where he was hoeing the vegetable garden. When he recognized his visitor, he nodded and walked to the house, laying the hoe alongside its exterior wall.

Lilah got out of the vehicle, holding up the covered dish. "A chicken and biscuit cobbler. Your favorite."

"It ain't my birthday. What's the occasion?"

"Just my way of saying thanks. If you hadn't directed the search team to the cave, I might have ended up spending the night in it."

He shrugged it off, as she knew he would. "Anyone would have done the same. That dish will do right nice. I'll slice up some fresh tomatoes and cucumbers to go with it."

"Which reminds me…" She laid the dish on the car's hood and opened the back door. "I told Harlan I was coming so he sent a few pepper plants by me to replace the ones he ran over the other day."

"Man made good on his promise, then."

"You can always count on Harlan." She transferred the plants into his thin weathered hands. He was too lean, she decided. The fattening casserole would do him good. She should start doing this once a week to make sure he put some meat on his bones.

"You go on in. I'm gonna pick us some fresh vegetables and water these here plants. They look a little peaked."

"Don't be too long," she said with a smile. "I'm hungry."

It seemed like she stayed that way these days. Lilah marched up the porch steps, careful not to bump into the crates and other junk her uncle insisted on keeping. She itched to pile it all in the front yard and burn it, but Jasper would never forgive her.

Truthfully, the inside of his place was almost as cluttered. He never threw anything away. Lilah placed the casserole on the table and then went to the den and sat on his old sofa. Dang, if she wasn't all tuckered out from working with Harlan this morning and then cooking. The events from yesterday must have been catching up to her body.

She kicked off her shoes and propped her feet on the coffee table, kicking aside a huge leather tome of some sort. Curious, she picked it up and riffled through it. A bible—should have guessed it. Uncle Jasper was devout, but in a hail-fire-and-brimstone kind of way that made her vaguely uncomfortable. Little slips of delicately aged paper were stuck willy-nilly among the pages of King James script. She took one out and read. "Everyone who hates his brother is a murderer, and you know that no murderer has eternal life present in him." 1 John 3:15.

And another: "Whoever brings ruin on their family will inherit only wind, and the fool will be servant to the wise." Proverbs 11:29.

Well, wasn't that just cheery. Carefully, she tucked the paper slips back into their hidden homes. Whatever her uncle chose to extrapolate from the bible was his own business and reading his notes felt like a violation of his privacy. So instead, Lilah flipped the pages to the middle. Smack dab in the center, a long ancestry tree lay folded accordion-style. Its pages were yellowed and scribbled with Jasper's chicken-scratch handwriting. Generations of Tedders were recorded, but she skipped down to the latest entries. Her spirits took a nosedive at the sight of her dad and sister's dates of death. One day hers would be alongside them.

Enough with the gloomy thoughts. In a few months, her baby's name would be listed as a birth on the family tree and that counted in the blessings column of life.

Her fingers traced over the names of great and great-great grandparents.

Ernest Tedder was a cruel man. Aunt Vi's words popped into her mind and she searched for the man's name. It was easy to spot. Amidst a sea of black and blue ink, his name was recorded in crimson.

"Reading the Family Bible?"

She gasped and glanced up as Jasper stepped through the screen door. "You scared me," she admitted with a slight laugh.

He slanted her an approving nod. "Does my heart proud to see a young'un reading the Holy Bible."

"I was just looking at our family tree," she admitted. "Can I ask you something, Uncle Jasper?"

"Reckon so." He settled cautiously into the chair across from her.

"I heard that your father was…" She hesitated. "A harsh man."

His ruddy face darkened. "Yer daddy tell you that?"

"It doesn't matter where I heard it." She glossed over his question. No sense getting him riled up at Aunt Vi. "Is it true?"

"Wicked." His thin lips clamped shut so tight they were white at the edges. "Despicable. Perverted."

Poor Uncle Jasper. It was obvious he'd suffered.

"Was Dad mistreated, too?" She had to know.

"Not so much. He was the baby. Thad and I were the ones that bore the brunt of his wrath."

He stared into space, apparently lost in painful memories.

"Would it help to talk about it?" she asked gently.

"Nope."

Now or never—she had one last question on the subject. "I heard he died in a hunting accident."

His eyes snapped to her. "What about it?"

"Was it really an accident?"

Silence roared in her ears, heavy and dreadful.

"Some have their suspicions," he answered at last.

With that open-ended response, she did have one more question left. "What do *you* think?"

"Sins of the father repeat from one generation to the next. Beware, Lilah. I'd hate to see anything happen to you."

He stood. "And that's all I have to say on the matter. Ever. Understood?"

When Uncle Jasper made up his mind, that was that.

"Yes, sir."

"Very well. Let's enjoy that meal you prepared."

But all through the midday meal and during the drive home, she replayed his cryptic remarks about the sins of the fathers repeating themselves through the generations.

All the way down to Cousin Lavon, who no doubt picked them up from his father. The gloom-and-doom path led her to even wilder imaginings. Uncle Jasper believed they were cursed. Intellectually, she knew there was no such thing but she couldn't shake the ugly questions and insinuations.

She was a Tedder. And it certainly seemed as if her family was cursed. First, Dad was killed and then Darla met the same fate. Who was next? And by whose hands?

It wasn't until later that evening, when she was drifting to sleep, that what had bothered her most of all that afternoon—that had been niggling in her subconscious for hours—made her sit bolt upright.

Just like Ernest Tedder's entry in the Family Bible, Dad and Darla's names had also been penned in crimson ink.

Chapter Thirteen

"He did *what*?" Lilah asked, nearly dropping the pan of water she had been setting on the stove.

Harlan took a seat at the table and ran a hand through his still-wet-from-the-shower hair. He'd debated not telling her what had happened, but she was bound to find out anyway. Besides, the lie of omission had sat heavily on him last night. He'd stayed out late at the bar with Sammy and Alvin, who'd insisted on buying him a couple of drinks and commiserating with him about his enforced leave of absence. When he'd finally returned home, Lilah had been fast asleep in front of the TV and he'd gently carried her to bed.

He'd reconciled himself to her deception and neither of them had spoken of it again. It was his baby after all and their futures were tied. But their relationship still seemed fragile, and he had to concede his own part in that.

"J.D. put me on administrative leave for a week. I'm not going to work this morning."

"That's so unfair. I shouldn't have insisted on going to the cave with you yesterday—"

"It was my decision," Harlan said firmly. She had enough worries without shouldering blame for his career hiccup. "And it was a culmination of several issues that have been brewing between us."

"Still." She set the pan on the stove and brought him a cup of coffee before sitting across from him at the kitchen table. "I've caused you nothing but trouble since I came home. I should leave."

"Don't you dare." That would be what finally did him in.

"What are you going to do?" she asked. "Return to work next week and hope J.D.'s cooled off?"

"No." He hadn't realized he'd already decided until that very moment. "I won't work for him again. Going back would feel like complicity in his crooked games. I won't be a part of it."

"Now you believe me when I say he's been on the take?"

"Should have from the start."

"If you don't go back, what are you going to do, then?" She hesitated, smoothing her hands over her jeans. "I have a little money saved, plus I might get a portion of that money Dad had socked away."

"I've got money," he said gruffly. "Not a problem."

"And I have health insurance with my job," she continued, eyes clouded with uncertainty. "That should cover most of my childbirth expenses. So I can certainly help there."

The baby. J.D.'s timing was lousy.

"Stop worrying. I'm fine," he said, reasoning out the possibilities. "I have plenty of contacts with other law enforcement agencies. I'll take a temporary position elsewhere and, hopefully, I'll win the sheriff's election."

"Doesn't seem right, though, that J.D.'s such a crook and gets to ride out his time until retirement."

"No free rides."

She cocked her head to the side. "What do you mean?"

"I believe J.D. might be the mole in the sheriff's office.

The one that tips off the drug distributors before every raid that leads to a dead end. And I intend to find out the truth."

"How can you prove it?"

"I'm going to the state and federal people to tell them my suspicions. Convince them to set up a new raid bypassing J.D. and his entire office."

"That would be epic. But there's no telling how many people J.D. has under his influence," she warned. "Could be hard to get anything past him."

"His luck has to run out sometime," Harlan muttered, stirring sugar in his coffee.

She gave a sigh. "Suppose so."

"You don't sound convinced."

"It's just that... I wonder how this will affect my family. I don't want to believe Uncle Thad's involved with a drug ring, but if he is, Aunt Vi and his kids will be devastated at the news." She brought a hand to her mouth. "Oh, no. What about Ed? If he's in it, my nephews will suffer. If Ed goes to prison, they won't have a mother or a father."

He took her hand in his. "Let's agree to handle only one problem at a time. Deal?"

She drew a shaky breath. "Deal."

"How did your afternoon with Jasper go yesterday?" he asked, wanting to distract her from their problems.

"Unnerving."

"Oh?" He leaned back in his chair and sipped his coffee. "Jasper not his usual sociable self?" he joked.

Lilah snickered. "Right. Anyway, we got to talking about his father—my grandfather, Ernest. Jasper. He started going off the deep end talking about the sins of the fathers visited on the children, et cetera. So I asked him about the hunting accident, the one Aunt Vi said wasn't really an accident."

Harlan sat up straighter, pulse racing. "And?"

"He didn't come right out and say it, but he insinuated it wasn't an accident."

"I'll take a look at that old file, see what the official report says."

"Can't do that now can you?"

"I'll get Sammy to scan it and send me an email copy."

He'd also ask Sammy to check the evidence room and see if the leather bracelet was still there. Much as he mistrusted J.D., it was possible he'd locked it in storage and had forgotten about it.

Harlan took one last sip of his coffee and rose. "Let's go out for breakfast. It'll do us both good to get out of here."

"You sure? I've already started cooking."

"Save it for tomorrow."

She shrugged. "Suits me. I'll grab my purse."

That was one of the many things he liked about Lilah. She wasn't some glamour girl who would waste thirty minutes on hair and makeup. In less than five minutes, they were in her car and pulling out of the driveway. She'd insisted on driving, saying after the kind of day he'd suffered, he needed to relax and be chauffeured.

"Where are we going?" she asked, easing onto the county road.

"I could use a steak and—whoa!—slow down around that curve!"

Her compact car whipped around it way too fast for his comfort.

"Harlan—I can't!" Her voice rose several octaves. "The brakes aren't working!"

What the hell? He unbuckled his seat belt, practically crawled into her lap and pressed his left foot on top of hers. The brakes pounded to the floorboard, but the car didn't slow one iota.

They gathered speed as the car plummeted downhill.

Trees flashed by the windows at tornado-level speed. *Damn*. He thought fast, scooting back to the passenger side. "It's okay, Lilah, keep steering. After the next curve, we'll come to a field. Make a sharp right into it when I give you the word."

The Mothershed's cow pasture was fairly level and, with luck, the car would grind to a stop with no harm to Lilah.

They rounded the curve.

"Now!" he yelled.

Lilah jerked the steering wheel to the right. Her car careened on its right side, and then fell back down to the ground on the opposite side with a crash of metal and broken glass. He tried gripping the dashboard, but his body toppled forward and his head hit something hard and unyielding. Pain exploded behind his eyes and then, mercifully, a black abyss of nothingness descended.

LILAH BLINKED. HOW ODD. She was in her car, but it wasn't moving. And she was parked in a field, with not a road in sight. The front windshield was cracked, and through the spider-webbed fissures, a cow chewed a mouthful of grass and stared at her indifferently.

Her hands hurt. Frowning, Lilah looked down and saw they were scratched and bloody. Cuts tattooed their backsides and spread up her wrists and forearms. How had that happened? She turned her head to the side and reality and remembrance slammed into her gut.

The brakes had failed and she'd wrecked. Harlan lay lifeless, and a deep gash on his forehead oozed blood.

He was hurt. Was he...?

"Oh, God, Harlan! Wake up. Please, wake up!"

Lilah leaned over and placed a hand over his heart. It beat.

"Hey, in there? Are y'all hurt?"

Outside, a man and a woman ran to the car. The man struggled, but managed to open the door on her side. Arms lifted her out of the vehicle. "No," she protested. She didn't want to leave Harlan's side. "Help Harlan. Please."

Strong arms placed her carefully on the ground and then the woman loomed overhead, her eyes wide with pity. She pushed a lock of hair from Lilah's face. "We will, sugar. Don't you fret now. We called for help."

In no time, a siren's wail erupted and it seemed people were everywhere. She struggled to get a glimpse of Harlan, finally spotting him being helped onto a stretcher and into a waiting ambulance. EMTs brought one to her and she was lifted and placed in the ambulance beside Harlan.

The shock started to wear off, and self-reproach set in. "What have I done?" she sobbed and turned her head to face Harlan—whose eyes were open.

He reached out a hand and squeezed hers. "You okay?" he asked.

"Yes. But you…" Her throat closed up.

"I'm fine." He managed a slight smile. "Might have a headache a day or two, but no big deal."

She let out a sound that was halfway between a sob and a laugh.

"The baby?" he asked hoarsely. "Everything okay?"

She squeezed his hand this time. "I think so. They can check at the hospital."

Unbidden tears streamed down her cheeks. This was all her fault somehow. It was her car and she'd been driving. "I don't know what happened. The brakes were fine earlier. I promise."

"Don't cry. I believe you. I suspect someone cut the brake line."

"Who? Why?" Damn, she was sick of this nightmare.

"I don't know yet, but I'll find out. I promise you that."

"I want it to stop. I want…" She wanted to leave. Pack up and move as far away from here as soon as possible. Mom had been right to run away all those years ago. Ran and never looked back, never returned. Not even for her ex-husband's funeral.

Lilah laid a hand over her eyes, remembering all the reasons she'd stayed away from Lavender Mountain. There was nothing for her here but heartbreak.

Chapter Fourteen

Lilah lay in the early morning darkness, hands over her belly. She stared out the bedroom window, debating her options and her timing as the sun rose, casting violet and purple splashes on the horizon. Nowhere was as hauntingly beautiful or as deadly as home. No matter how long or how far she roamed, this place was forever rooted in her soul.

The ultrasound had checked out normal—the baby was safe. A small miracle that she intended to honor by taking every precaution possible to avoid danger, no matter the sacrifice. And that meant leaving Lavender Mountain for good, Harlan or no Harlan. Much as she loved him, she couldn't put their child's life in danger.

He tossed in bed beside her, moaning softly. She ran a hand over his back, loving the feel of his smooth lean muscles. Lilah's heart squeezed at the idea of saying goodbye. How dangerous could it be to wait a few days—make sure he was over the worst of the concussion?

No. The longer she waited, the harder it would be. If she was lucky, and if Harlan truly loved her, he'd listen to reason and agree to go with her. Start over somewhere safer and with more opportunity for both of them.

"Harlan?" she whispered.

He rolled over at once and opened his eyes, instantly alert.

"Want me to get you a pain pill?"

He sat halfway up and leaned against a bank of pillows. "No. I need a clear head and have too much to do."

"You're off this week. Remember? Courtesy of J.D. Stay in bed and heal. You've got a nasty concussion."

"That might also be courtesy of J.D."

"Really?" She leaned over him. "It was my car. Seems more likely that whoever did this was after me, not you."

"If they hurt you, they hurt me. Either way, it's a message."

"But what message? And who sent it? None of this makes sense."

"Could have been J.D. trying to warn or silence me. I came too close to finding out the truth about him and shutting down his gravy train."

"Or it could be the Hillside Strangler who believes I have his bracelet and wants it back at any cost," she countered.

Harlan flung off the covers and swung his legs over the side of the bed, pausing to draw a ragged breath.

"You're getting up?"

"I'm calling Lewis Slidell in the state investigator's office. Tell him my suspicions about what's going on up here."

"Think he'll listen?"

He flashed a wan smile. "I see you share the Tedder faith in law enforcement."

"Can hardly blame me for that. Guess while you're handling your business, I'll deal with the insurance company about getting my car fixed. My favorite thing to do," she said with a groan.

Lilah carefully eased out of bed, wincing at the sore muscles in her back and legs.

Harlan frowned. "You're hurting."

"A little. No pain pills for me, though. Not even over-the-counter stuff."

"You stay in bed and I'll bring you breakfast."

"I'm not the one with a concussion." He opened his mouth to protest, and she cut him off. "Let's compromise. We'll make toast and coffee together."

"Deal." He stood, grimacing for a moment before following her slow progress to the kitchen. She flipped on lights in the hallway and the kitchen.

"If you'll start the coffee, I'm going to check the newspaper," he said. "See if there's been any press on the so-called accident."

"You think there will be?"

"I gave a statement to the police. Told them what to look for in the car." He gave a sly grin. "And it's entirely possible that the reporter from the local paper was in hearing range when I said it."

"Nice," she said with an answering smile. "They'll know you're onto them."

She measured out coffee grinds and was about to pour them in the pot when Harlan slammed the door and marched into the kitchen waving the newspaper like a machete. "J.D. sure didn't waste any time kicking me to the curb."

He unfurled the rolled-up paper and handed it to her. *Sheriff J.D. Bentley endorses Officer Alvin Lee in Upcoming Election.*

Lilah's mouth opened in a round *o* of astonishment. "How could he?" She burned with indignation on Harlan's behalf.

He flung the paper in the wastebasket. "If Alvin gets elected, I have a feeling it's just going to be more of the same here in Elmore County. He's a miniature J.D."

She gave a long sigh. "Bet you're sorry now I ever came back here."

"Course not, Lilah. This has nothing to do with you and everything to do with me getting too close to J.D.'s illegal crap."

"You know, this might be a good thing," she said slowly.

"The hell?" Harlan scowled, the stitches in his forehead twisting ominously, looking ready to come undone.

"If you don't run for sheriff—"

"Oh, I'm running," he cut in, the muscles in his jaw twitched.

"Forget the race."

His incredulous gaze almost undermined her courage. "Look, I wasn't going to say anything for a few days. Was going to make sure you were okay first, get a rental car and—"

"I'm fine and you can use my car or we can get you a rental today. So whatever it is, spit it out."

"Fine," she snapped. "That's what I was trying to do."

Harlan folded his arms and sat down at the table. "I have a feeling this is bad news. Go ahead."

The man wasn't going to make this easy. Best to spill it all at once.

"I'm leaving," she announced.

"Leaving…what?" His mulish stance was replaced with a look of confusion.

"This place."

"You're leaving *me*?"

"Lavender Mountain. Not you."

"Same thing."

"It's not. Don't you see? Maybe this was meant to be. We can make a break and leave together. What's to stop us?" Doubt assailed her. "That is…if you still want me."

"I want you," he insisted.

"Really? You once let a scumbag like J.D. ruin everything because of your ambition. Sounds to me like you're doing the same thing again by staying here instead of leaving with me."

"That's not fair. You know why I want to be sheriff."

"How bad do you want that career advancement, Harlan? More than you want me and the baby?"

There she'd said it. What she'd promised herself she would never ever do. She'd just forced Harlan's hand to choose between her and his career.

"Don't back me into a corner."

"Don't tell me what I can and can't do," she retorted. This wasn't how she imagined this discussion going down. If she wanted a calm exchange, it had to start with her. Lilah sat down at the opposite end of the table.

"I was going to wait before I brought this up, but now that it's out, let's see it through. I don't want my baby—"

"*Our* baby."

"Okay, I don't want to raise our baby here. I don't want Lavon anywhere near my—I mean, our—child. I don't want our kid growing up alongside moonshiners, alcoholics and drug dealers."

"Be reasonable, Lilah. Drugs are everywhere."

She ignored that. "I'm going to raise him—or her— somewhere less violent. A town where his name won't be associated with crime. I grew up with that stigma and I don't want our kid to go through the same."

"The kid won't have your name, he'll have mine."

As if that mattered. Everyone knew everyone here, along with everyone's family history. "And I won't let Uncle Thad and my cousins set a poor example of how to live."

"Thought you loved your family."

"I do. But I want better for our child. I won't have one

of mine going through what I've been through with two close family members murdered."

"I'll protect you both."

"You can't. I think the car wreck proved that."

"Don't you see? That's why I want to be sheriff, to end all the liquor and drug running and violence. I can do it, too."

"Good luck with that," she scoffed.

"Have a little faith in me."

"Lavender Mountain has a way of corrupting even the best of folks."

"Not me. You were born and raised here and you turned out just fine."

"Have I?"

"What kind of a dumb question is that?"

Wrong thing to say. He could have said, *I think you're wonderful.* Or, *I love you.* Or better, *Let's go down to the justice of the peace right now and get married.*

But he hadn't, and she had her answer. No matter that she'd gone to college and had managed her life as a decent law-abiding and tax-paying citizen—once a Tedder, always a Tedder. Deep down, Harlan didn't believe she was good enough to be his wife.

Her face flamed. Uncle Jasper was right. This was playing house and she was done with childhood games.

She slowly rose from the table. "I think we're done here."

"What does that mean?" he asked as she sauntered out of the room and down the hall. "We haven't finished talking this out yet."

Lilah went to the bedroom and dragged the suitcase out from under the bed. First, she dumped the contents of her lingerie drawer in it and then opened the second drawer of the dresser.

"You're leaving me? Now?"

"Yes," she answered, not looking at him. "Maybe without me dragging you down, you'll win your precious election."

"Look at me, Lilah."

She lifted her chin and leveled a stare. Harlan leaned against the doorjamb looking strong and as sexy as ever. The stitches on his forehead did nothing to detract from his appeal. If anything, it added a devastating touch of vulnerability.

"So you expect me to drive you to your apartment? Aid and abet you in this mess?" he asked with a cool trace of amusement in his tone. "Seeing as you don't have a car right now."

Oh, yeah. She'd forgotten about that little matter. Lilah cleared her throat, gathering her dignity. "A ride to the rent-a-car place will suffice. But if that's too much trouble, I can call Uncle Jasper."

He strolled over and placed a hand on the small of her back, just above her hips. "Lilah," he said softly. "Don't go."

"Why should I stay?" Lilah's voice was tiny and wobbly, even to her own ears. Even more to her chagrin, she was near tears. She'd cried more these past few weeks than she'd cried in her entire life and it frustrated her. Those pregnancy hormones were doing a real number on her emotions.

"Because I want you," Harlan said. "Hell, because I *need* you. At least stay here until I catch the killer. If not for me, for the baby."

She dropped the T-shirt she'd been folding. "Not fair to spring the baby on me."

"Whatever it takes to get you to stay."

"I should be okay at my apartment."

He quirked a brow. "After your neighbor reported seeing a man creeping around there? Doesn't sound safe to me."

"Oh, *all right*," she conceded ungraciously. "I'll stay, with one stipulation."

"Anything."

"I go back to the spare bedroom."

He sucked in his breath, as if she'd dealt him a low blow. "Why? Still mad at me?"

Not angry—she was hurt. Because Harlan didn't love her. He found her lacking as a suitable wife. Prolonging their affair would only make it harder to bear once it was over. Lilah bit her tongue, though. She wouldn't let him know how much that hurt.

"Damn right, I'm still mad at you," she lied.

He took her hand. "C'mon, time for a truce. We'll eat breakfast and I'll drink my morning cup of coffee. We're both sore from the wreck and grouchy as bears this morning."

She took the olive branch. It would make life easier to be on amicable terms with Harlan for the remainder of her stay.

"I won't say no to a couple pieces of toast."

"Toast? I'm going to make us a *real* breakfast—biscuits, gravy, bacon and eggs. You go on back to bed and I'll wake you when it's ready."

She eyed the bed longingly. "I am tired," she admitted. She'd gotten up too early, still tense over the car wreck. They both could have been killed so easily. She gave an involuntary shudder.

Harlan returned her suitcase under the bed and folded down the bedspread. She slipped back into the warm cotton that smelled of Harlan's masculine scent, and he pulled the sheets over her, tucking her in like a child.

"Sweet dreams, honey," he said, planting a swift kiss on her forehead.

Lilah closed her eyes and curled against the pillows. Small wonder she loved him. But sometimes, love wasn't enough.

Chapter Fifteen

This was going to be awkward.

Harlan tucked the padded envelope under his right arm and squared his shoulders. He had nothing to be ashamed of. Resolutely, he pushed open the door to the sheriff's office and entered.

Sammy rose from his desk at once and came to greet him. "Hey, Harlan. Man, you're gonna be left with an ugly scar on your forehead. Got something for us?"

He followed Sammy into his old office, past the gaze of curious, but still friendly, former coworkers. Only Alvin turned a cold shoulder. No surprise there.

"You sure J.D. is out for the day?" Harlan asked, closing the door.

"Positive. That psychological profile training is scheduled for two days. It'll be late by the time he drives back from Atlanta tomorrow evening." Sammy nodded at the package. "Picked that up from the mechanics?"

"Yep. One cut brake line. Got his expert opinion on that recorded on a signed statement. Said no one else had touched the auto part but him."

"Knew you'd cross your t's and dot your i's," Sammy said. "You always do. Everyone here knows it, too."

"Except Alvin," Harlan muttered. But he appreciated the show of support.

"Alvin's an ass."

"Not going to argue about that. Do you have a copy of the old Ernest Tedder hunting accident?"

Sammy slid a few papers across the desk. "Already printed it out in case J.D. made a bitch move and disabled your computer access. Not much in that old report that I can see. Back then, you basically just had a coroner's report and an officer statement."

Harlan scanned the thin account. Ernest Tedder was shot once in the back with his own rifle. His son Jasper had borrowed the gun to go hunting, and had mistakenly shot Ernest only a quarter mile from their family home early one January morning. Witnesses stated that Jasper, then only sixteen years old, was devastated. The family filed no charges, and the coroner's report stated that Ernest died almost immediately when the lone bullet pierced his heart and lungs.

"Shot in the back just like Chauncey and Darla," Harlan mused aloud.

"You still trying to find a connection between the three Tedder murders?" Sammy asked. "Maybe you could argue the last two are, but you're stretching with this old one."

"Surprised I never heard of this before about Jasper accidentally shooting his father."

"Eh, well, it's ancient history. Poor kid. He must have felt awful. No wonder he grew up to be such a crackpot."

Harlan glanced at the second page of the report and observed that it was signed by Investigating Officer J.D. Bentley. Seemed noteworthy enough that J.D. could have at least mentioned the old case while they searched for Chauncey and Darla's murderer.

"Anything new on the recent Tedder murders?" Harlan asked.

"Not a thing. Alvin's still leaning on Ed, trying to force a confession, but I have my doubts the guy offed his wife."

"Lilah doesn't believe Ed did it, either. I'm inclined to agree."

This was the case that most disturbed him. Chauncey hadn't had much time left in his natural life before it was cut short, and he'd had any number of people angry with him at any given time. But Darla was different. She'd left behind three young sons, and there was no apparent reason someone would want her dead, unless you believed it was the result of a domestic dispute. Hard to believe she had been killed over her wedding ring and a few pieces of costume jewelry.

But they weren't just any old costume jewelry pieces. They specifically belonged to two prior homicide victims murdered over twenty years ago.

There was a connection between all five murders, Harlan felt sure of it. And Lilah could have so easily been the sixth victim. Bile rose at the back of his throat. He couldn't lose her. Even the thought of her leaving Lavender Mountain again made him sick. Somehow, he'd find a way to convince her to stay. For now, he needed to concentrate on keeping her alive.

"Our best hope of solving these cases is if there's a fingerprint on the leather bracelet Lilah found."

Sammy glumly agreed. "But the forensics lab takes forever, and there's probably too many prints on it to get any clear markings."

"That's another reason I came in today," Harlan said. "J.D. never mailed the bracelet to the lab. I need to get it out."

"Why would he sit on it?" Sammy asked, lips curling in disgust. "He knows how hard we've been working to solve this. We've pursued every clue with no luck yet."

"That's about to change."

Sammy leaned forward, eyes lit with anticipation. "What's up?"

"After I have Zelda log the brake-line package into the evidence log, I'm going to personally deliver it, and the leather bracelet, to the lab in Atlanta. I've already called Doug and he's expecting me."

Sammy let out a low whistle. "How do you plan on sneaking past the dragon lady? She keeps that evidence room key under close guard."

"I'll sweet talk her, bribe her—whatever it takes."

"Good luck with that," he said with a snort.

"If all else fails—the woman has to take a bathroom break sometime, right? And I know where she keeps the key."

"J.D. will have a fit when he finds out." Sammy's forehead creased in concern. "You do this and J.D. will make your life hell. That's *if* he doesn't fire you."

"He won't fire me."

"The hell he won't—"

"Because I'm quitting." Harlan lifted a sealed envelope he'd brought in with the brake-line package. "Here's my letter of resignation. Signed, sealed and about to be delivered."

"Oh, man. Don't do that! The election's around the corner and I think you can still win. Everyone knows Alvin's unfit, even if J.D. did endorse his sorry ass."

"I said I'm quitting this job, not that I'm dropping out of the race."

"But... You think that's wise? I mean, given that Lilah's expectin'."

"I've lined up an interview for a temporary job." Harlan hesitated, then decided it wouldn't hurt to tell Sammy his plans. "That's another reason I'm driving to Atlanta.

The guys at the state troopers headquarters have been trying to recruit me for over a year. I called and told them I was available and they wanted to talk to me right away."

Sammy shook his head and ran a hand through his dark close-cropped hair. "I'm glad for you, of course, but you'll sure be missed 'round here. We've worked together a long time."

"Hopefully, I won't be away but a few months." Harlan grinned at his old friend. "And when I return, it will be as your new boss."

"Glad to stay on your good side, then." Sammy cocked his head at the closed door. "Got the feeling old Alvin isn't too happy with me right now, consorting with the enemy as it were."

"Screw Alvin." He rose from his chair. "Now to charm that evidence key out of Zelda's tight-fisted hands."

"Good luck."

"Go back to your desk and steer clear of what I'm about to do. No sense getting yourself in hot water. Far as anyone knows, you and I have just been in here shootin' the breeze."

Sammy rose and shook his hand. "Here's to solving those cases."

Harlan waited a couple of minutes after Sammy left, then picked up his items and headed for Zelda's desk.

She was there, manning the fort as usual. Would have been too much to hope she and J.D. were both gone for the day.

"Hello, gorgeous," he said, taking a seat by her desk. An online crossword puzzle showed on her computer monitor.

"What's a four-letter word for a legendary story?" she asked, not bothering to look up. "Starts with an *m*."

"Myth."

Zelda typed it in and pushed up her bifocals. "Yep,

that'll do it. What are you doing here, Harlan? Boss told you to take off."

"Being the excellent employee I am, I couldn't stay away."

He ignored her snort.

"I'm not staying long. Just want you to enter this package on the evidence log." He laid the bundle on her desk.

Sighing, she opened the front drawer and pulled out a hardbound notebook, riffling through to the current page. "Here you go."

Harlan entered his name, date and time, and type of evidence. Zelda's eyes were slanted toward his entry and he stifled a smile. The indifferent air was an act. She wanted to know everything that went down in the office.

He snapped the notebook shut and handed it back to her.

"Brake line, huh?" Her gray eyes zeroed in on his forehead. "You look awful. Glad you're okay."

"I'm touched." He gave her a wink. "Didn't know you cared."

"That so? What are you buttering me up for?"

He feigned innocence. "I'm not. Why don't you give me the key and I'll put this up while you finish your puzzle."

"I'm the only one who goes in there. You know that."

"Can you make an exception? Just this once?"

Zelda tapped a finger to her lips, considering. "Why you so anxious to do it yourself? Never cared before."

To hell with charm, maybe honesty would do the trick. "I've never had anyone try to kill me before. Would ease my mind to see this package locked up."

"Newspaper said it was Lilah's car that wrecked."

"Would have been more awful if she'd been killed instead of me. Or lost our baby."

Zelda grimaced and a lone tear ran down her cheek.

What was this? He'd seen her examine the goriest crime photos and bloodied weapons with nary a hitch.

"I forgot about the baby," she said hoarsely.

Then he remembered. Over twenty years ago, Zelda's two-year-old grandson had died in a car accident. Even after all these years, she must keep his memory close to the heart. Sometimes he forgot that even the gruffest people in his line of work harbored heartaches just like anyone else. Everyone had vulnerabilities.

Zelda pulled a keychain out of her purse and handed it to him. There was only one key on it. "You do what you have to do." She cleared her throat and turned back to the computer. "Now let me get back to my puzzle."

"Yes ma'am."

He debated touching her arm, but Zelda would probably rather he forget he even witnessed her moment of softness.

Once in the evidence room, he haphazardly tossed the package on the nearest shelf. The real cut brake line from Lilah's car was safely locked up in his own vehicle. He'd pass it on to Doug to check for fingerprints, along with that leather bracelet—if he could find it. When he'd signed Zelda's log, he'd peeked at the other entries, and there was no note of a bracelet.

He went to the shelf marked for the current year and month and scanned it. There was a sealed bag of Chauncey's clothes he'd worn the day he was shot, next to it was a similar bag for Darla's clothes, and a couple of ominous looking tagged knives seized in an assault.

But no bracelet.

He checked again. Then carefully examined other nearby shelves to see if it had been misplaced.

Nothing.

Damn J.D. What had he done with it? Why didn't he want it examined? Despite the humidity in the small cramped room, his skin prickled with uneasiness. Perhaps J.D. was involved in more than covering up moonshine and drug operations. If so, trying to solve these cases would be a bigger challenge than he'd imagined.

Harlan locked up the room and returned to Zelda's desk where a scowling Alvin waited.

"What were you doing in there?" Alvin asked, a waspish edge to his voice.

"Depositing the latest evidence in a case. Who are you to question me?"

Alvin puffed out his chest. "I'm going to be your boss in a few months, unless J.D. fires you first."

"That's not going to happen." Harlan handed Zelda the sealed envelope. "My letter of resignation," he told her. "Effective immediately."

Alvin's jaw slackened for a moment and then he bestowed a smug grin. "Wise decision. Now I suggest you leave. You have no business here."

He pasted a smile on his face. "That's okay. I got what I wanted. Take care, Zelda."

Alvin barely moved enough to get out of his way, and Harlan brushed shoulders with him. He'd never cared much for the guy, but now he'd be impossible to work with.

As he neared the exit, he felt a tap on his shoulder.

"I'll hold on to the letter a few days," Zelda said. "In case you change your mind."

Who knew the dragon lady was such a softie? "I won't, but thanks."

Harlan pushed open the door and walked into sunshine, feeling lighter. This was the right thing to do. Tension had been building between him and J.D. for months and he didn't realize how oppressive it had become until resigning. With any luck, he'd have a new job by the end of the day, and new leads on the murders.

"OUCH." LILAH YANKED her hand back and frowned at the stinging nettles. "I've got something for you," she muttered. "A good vinegar dousing."

She stood and stretched. After the heat of the afternoon sun had passed, she'd decided to get some fresh air. It had felt good to weed Harlan's neglected vegetable patch. Nothing like digging in the dirt to keep her problems at bay. With the exception of the occasional passing vehicle and the sound of the radio from the open living room window, it had been a quiet and productive time.

Lilah started for the house. After soaking the nettles in vinegar, she'd take a nice long bath and then read in bed. Since Harlan was going to grab supper on the road driving back from Atlanta, she'd forego cooking and enjoy a sandwich.

A light flickered. In the deepening twilight, the silhouette of a man walked by the lamp near the couch. Heart clamoring, she climbed down the porch step and flattened her body against the exterior wall. Had he seen her?

The sound of a drawer being jerked open drifted through the screen window. Luckily, he appeared too absorbed in his search to have noticed her. Was he looking for valuables? If so, the thief was plum out of luck. Harlan didn't keep large amounts of cash lying around.

Her mind raced with questions. Who was it? How had he entered the house without her hearing? True, she hadn't locked the doors, but it had seemed like she would have seen or heard something.

Whoever it was, he was way too thin to be Harlan. Besides, she'd have noticed him pulling his car in the driveway.

Lilah swiftly debated her options. Her only set of car keys—along with her cell phone—were on the kitchen counter. Escaping to the car or calling for help was a no-go.

The nearest neighbor was a mile away. Her gaze traveled to the tree line at the side of Harlan's property. She could hide there until either the person left or Harlan returned.

But first, she'd have to take a risk and run across the yard. If he saw her…

But what other choice did she have? Wait here until he found her cowering near the window?

She ran, not daring to look back and see if she'd been discovered.

"Lilah? Are you out there?"

That voice again. The same one from the cave. She hit the tree line and scrabbled behind a large oak. One quick glimpse, she promised herself. Just to know if she'd been followed. Carefully, she peeked around the tree.

Lavon leaned out the window; some slight noise must have alerted him to her presence.

So it *was* her cousin after all. Had Lavon come by to rob them—or did he have a more sinister motive? Perhaps he thought no one was home, that she was out with Harlan or friends.

He was so busted this time.

Seconds later, the front door opened and slammed shut. Lavon ran toward the road and she watched as he jogged around a bend and past her line of vision. He wasn't carrying anything in his hands that she could see. Was he crazy? More important, was he coming back?

A car roared to life, heading in the opposite direction of Harlan's house. Lavon must have parked his car down the road and walked here.

What a creep.

Lilah hightailed it back to the house and locked herself inside. Her breath was ragged and her heart scuttled like a frightened rabbit as she slammed down the open window and walked through all the rooms, ensuring all the other windows were down and locked, too. And she still didn't feel safe. In Harlan's closet, she grabbed the shotgun from the top shelf, pulled back the slide and checked the chamber.

Whew. Loaded.

She returned to the den and opened the desk drawer Lavon had been messing with. A quart-sized bag of marijuana, a small plastic baggie of white, powdered substance and three rolled joints laid inside. Lilah drew back, as if she'd discovered a coiled rattlesnake prepared to strike. These didn't belong to Harlan, no way. Lavon had put them there. Quickly, she opened all the other drawers, but nothing else had been tampered with.

How long had he been in the house before she'd noticed? It couldn't have been too long—she'd gone in for a glass of water about twenty minutes before spotting him. Still, that could have given him time to plant more drugs. Lilah went to the kitchen and opened cabinet drawers. Nothing there.

Just to be safe, she would check the bedrooms and bathrooms, too.

Elliptical beams of white light gashed through the front window, followed immediately by a strobing blue light. The angry crunch of gravel on the driveway sounded as harsh as a million firecrackers exploding.

Lilah went to the window and drew back the curtain an inch. J.D. and Alvin exited the sheriff's cruiser at the same time.

This was a set up.

Lilah picked up the cell phone on the end table, and then set it back down. No time to call Harlan.

She had all of two seconds to consider her limited options.

Decision made, Lilah grabbed the two baggies and the joints, and she ran to the bathroom. With trembling hands, she emptied the joints and the contents of the baggies into the toilet and flushed.

A pounding sounded from the front door. "Open up!" a voice ordered.

Marijuana buds and leaves still floated on top of the toilet water and she flushed again. Should she risk trying to flush the baggies, too, or would the toilet overrun? She'd rather have a plumbing crisis than a go-to-jail crisis, but an overrunning toilet would alert them to what she'd done.

She took the two baggies and quickly rinsed them in the sink, hoping that got rid of all traces.

"Open the door," the voice commanded again.

Lilah swiped at the inside of the wet baggies with a towel. She couldn't just throw them in the trash—too obvious. She flung open the small toiletry cabinet, scanned its contents and then grabbed a box of tampons she'd purchased months ago and left there. Most men seemed to have an unreasonable aversion to female hygiene products, so perhaps stuffing the baggies full of tampons would keep them from examining them too closely.

She placed the baggies in the cabinet and shut the door. A quick glance at the toilet and she drew a deep breath. No residue, but she flushed it again for good measure. There—that was the best she could do. Feeling like a low-class criminal, she went to the front door toting a gun in one hand, cell phone in the other. Quickly, she pressed Harlan's number only to reach his voice mail. She left a terse message. "Get home quick. There's a drug bust and you've been framed."

Lilah jerked open the door.

J.D.'s face was stern, and Lilah involuntarily swallowed hard. Next to him, Alvin mimicked J.D.'s hard set to his mouth. What a pip-squeak.

J.D. thrust a paper at her midsection. "I have a subpoena to search this house for drugs and drug paraphernalia. Move aside, please."

She took a step back and let the paperwork fall to the floor. The sheriff walked in first with Alvin close behind.

"Where's Harlan?" J.D. asked.

"Be home any minute." At least, she hoped so.

"You take the kitchen and I'll start in this room," J.D. said, pointing at Alvin.

From the kitchen, she heard Alvin opening drawers and cabinet doors. J.D. made a pretense of lifting sofa cushions and examining objects on the fireplace mantle. Only a matter of time before he went to the desk that straddled the den and the kitchen. Did Lavon have time to plant anything else? Surely the stuff he'd left was more than enough to get Harlan fired from any job in law enforcement—ever—and maybe even jail time. And he could just forget his dream of becoming sheriff.

Lilah picked up her cell phone and hit *record*.

"What are you doing there?" J.D. barked.

"Recording you. Just to keep everything on the up-and-up."

"Turn it off."

Lilah wasn't sure if she was within her rights to record the search, so she didn't argue. But the minute he turned his back to her, she again hit *record* and turned the cell phone face down on the couch. If she was lucky, maybe she'd at least have an audio recording if something crazy went down.

She watched him, clasping her shaking hands together. So, he and Lavon worked together. No wonder the police never found anything on a drug raid. J.D. made damn sure they were tipped-off. And now he wanted to set Harlan up to be arrested just to get him out of the way?

Her body shook violently, but this time with anger. And

what would they do to her? Claim she was a drug dealer, too? Her gut churned as if a gallon of icy slush rolled inside. What could that mean for her baby if she was arrested? They might not let her keep the child.

Oh, hell no. She would fight them every step of the way.

J.D. lumbered toward the desk.

"Already sure you did a thorough search in this room?"

He swung around. "We can come back later with the narcotics dogs."

"No need. You already know exactly where to search."

"What's that supposed to mean?" J.D.'s eyes narrowed and his angry energy filled the room.

"It means you're about to be disappointed." Probably wasn't the smartest idea challenging J.D., yet she couldn't keep the words bottled. "But go on, search the desk. That's where you've been heading all along."

"How—" He snapped his mouth shut and glowered, face flushed.

Alvin hustled over from the kitchen. "What's that supposed to mean?"

"It means J.D. is one hundred percent positive there are drugs in that top right drawer of the desk."

Alvin glanced back and forth between them. "What am I missing here?"

J.D. swiveled, yanking out all the desk drawers, and then slowly turned to face her. "Go check the back of the house," he ordered Alvin, keeping his eyes trained on Lilah.

Alvin hesitated but obeyed.

"Looks like it's just you and me now," J.D. said darkly. He took a menacing step forward.

Lilah scrambled to her feet. "Alvin! Come help me."

J.D. froze.

Alvin rushed back to the den. "Now what?"

"The woman's getting hysterical, that's all. Find anything?"

"I just got started."

"Let's go. We'll deal with this another time."

Alvin's mouth dropped open. If she wasn't so furious, she might have found it comical. "Why? We haven't even begun a proper search."

Instead of bothering to answer, J.D. strode for the door. Lilah followed the men out, watching as they drove off into the night.

She might have won the battle, but this was far from over.

Chapter Sixteen

Finally, Harlan pulled in the driveway. No Lilah at the door welcoming him home, but at least J.D. wasn't there, either. He'd half-expected to find three or four sheriff's cars at the house with blue lights blazing.

"Lilah?" he called out, stepping through the front door. A small piece of paper was lying on the floor and he picked it up. A subpoena notice to search his premises for illegal substances. Harlan crumpled it in his hands and tossed it on the coffee table.

She emerged from the kitchen, clutching a giant bag of potato chips and a glass of soda. "Present and accounted for. I've been stress eating since they left," she added with a wan smile.

He sat on the sofa and patted the empty space beside him. "How about sharing those with me while you fill me in on everything."

She plopped down beside him. "I was outside weeding the garden until it grew dark. When I started back in the house, I saw Lavon through the window. He was rummaging inside, by the desk. I ran for the woods and waited for him to leave."

Bastard. His scalp prickled, imagining what Lavon might have done if Lilah hadn't spotted him and had walked into the house. "He didn't give chase?"

"No. He ran out the front door and then I heard him start his car down the road. I came back in and found bags of marijuana and cocaine, and a few rolled joints. J.D. arrived and pounded on the door for me to let him in." She gave a dispirited laugh. "So I did what any guilty druggie would do. I flushed it all down the toilet before opening the door. Did I do the right thing?"

"Absolutely. If you hadn't, I'd be in handcuffs right now, waiting for someone to set bail."

"You should have seen J.D.'s face when he searched the desk and nothing was there. At least, in the end, even Alvin looked at J.D. with suspicion."

"The little runt was with him. Shouldn't be surprised, I guess."

She shrugged and took a swallow from her glass. "I suspect Alvin's not totally corrupt. He acted as if he still had a conscience. What are you going to do now? They won't stop. Not until they have you—or me—behind bars."

"Not going to happen." He reached in the chip bag and started munching. "I spilled my guts out today with Lewis Slidell—laid out everything and my suspicions about J.D.'s involvement. He's putting together an emergency law enforcement raid. First thing in the morning, Lavender Mountain will be crawling with state troopers, GBI and FBI agents, and anyone else he can get together. They've wanted a break in this drug ring operation for years."

"It's bigger than that," Lilah said, slapping her hands on her thighs. "I don't care about the drug ring. I want to know who killed Dad and Darla, and why they're coming after me."

"Of course, that's my number one priority." He moved the bag of chips to the coffee table and took her hand. "I believe J.D. knows who the killer is, and he's being paid to keep his mouth shut. He's hindered the investigation of the old Hilltop Strangler cases, as well as your family's recent murders."

Harlan felt a tremor run through her small hand. He ran a finger along the throbbing vein in her wrist, painfully aware of how fragile and precious Lilah's life was. And his baby's, too. Whatever it took, they would solve these crimes and catch the killer.

"Is it possible J.D. is the killer?" she asked.

"I wouldn't rule it out."

"If Alvin hadn't been with him tonight… The way J.D. looked at me when I challenged him… I believe he might have hurt me."

Anger pulsed in his temples, a solar flare of energy and heat that radiated down his spine and pooled in his gut.

"Oh, I almost forgot." She rose, went to the desk and returned with her cell phone. "Not sure this can help you, but I have audio of what went down tonight. J.D. had a conniption fit when I tried to video the search, but I managed to record sound."

He took the phone and transferred the video to his email account. "I'll listen to it tomorrow with Lewis and everyone else. Every bit helps."

"Wish I could see J.D.'s face tomorrow when he comes in to work."

"I'm looking forward to it. Crooked cops are scum. When we get through this investigation, Elmore County will have the cleanest law enforcement staff in Georgia."

Lilah cocked her head to the side, studying him. He couldn't quite fathom the play of emotions in her gray eyes.

"I'm glad. You're going to be the best sheriff we've ever had."

"Lavender Mountain will be safe—a good area to live and raise kids. *Our* kids."

She moved to leave, but he gently tugged her arm, pulling her small body onto his lap. "I promise, it will be—and soon."

There was a gulf between them; the ugly words from yesterday hung in the air. Lilah had distanced herself from him—a lonely abyss he was desperate to bridge. He kissed her full lips, still salty from their shared snack.

Lilah moaned and their tongues met. He couldn't fathom how or why, but Lilah was so sweet and so damn sexy at the same time. He moved his hands under her T-shirt and glided them up the smooth contour of her hips and then the arch of her back.

"Stop."

Lilah scrabbled to her feet and ran a hand through her hair. "Not a good idea," she said in a shaky voice. "Nothing's changed."

"Everything's about to change," he argued.

"I'm still who I am."

"I've never asked you to be anything different." What was she after? He scratched his head. "You're perfect just the way you are."

Pewter-gray eyes nailed him. "Do you love me?"

Did he? His heart quickened at the same moment his tongue stuck to the roof of his mouth. *Go on. Tell her what she wants to hear.* Trouble was, he didn't much believe in love. He'd certainly never witnessed it between his parents.

Harlan stared into Lilah's eyes. She was beautiful, kind—everything a man wanted in a woman. The better question was—what did she see in *him*? He'd brought her nothing but trouble.

She was also going to be the mother of his child and he wanted her in his life, even if the thought of raising a baby scared the bejesus out of him. Not like he'd had a decent example from his own father.

"Time's up. I've got my answer," she said softly, turning away from him.

"Lilah, wait. You know I—" Great. *Now* he'd found his voice?

She never turned. Her footsteps padded down the hallway and then came the firm click of a closed door.

UNIFORMED COPS AND men in suits swarmed the Elmore County sheriff's office. Harlan stepped through the entrance in time to see J.D. exit his office.

"What the hell is going on here?" he bellowed, one hand reaching in his uniform shirt pocket.

Bet he'd pay a pretty penny for a cigar right about now, Harlan thought.

J.D.'s eyes narrowed as he spotted him in the crowd. "You got something to do with this, Sampson?"

"You bet I did."

Lewis slid him a warning look and he bit the inside of his cheek. They'd discussed this beforehand—he was to let Lewis interrogate J.D. while he tackled Lavon Tedder.

Sammy jumped up from his desk and came over. "What's going on?"

"It's time we cleaned house." Harlan shot a meaningful glance at Alvin who sported a sweat stain under his armpits.

"Could have told me this was coming," Sammy said with the slightest note of reproach.

"Sorry. It was put together late yesterday and I was told to keep it under tight wraps."

"Guess I can understand that. No wonder I was told to bring Lavon in this morning."

"He's already here?"

"Interrogation Room B. We've got his dad in Room A. Tom's on his way with Ed Stovall in tow."

"Thanks, Sammy." Harlan briefly clasped his hand and made his way to Room B, eager for a second crack at Lavon. He'd make the jerk break this time.

Zelda rushed over and handed him a large envelope and file. "I've prepared everything they said you'd need."

He opened the envelope, nodding when he saw its contents. "Perfect."

She scurried back to her desk before he had a chance to study her closely. She'd worked with J.D. for many years. What did she think of all this? He would ask later. For now, he had a job to do.

The interrogation room was as minimalistic as a jail cell, housing only a scarred metal table and a few folding chairs. An aggressively bright fluorescent bulb shone down from the ceiling—the better to spotlight the person being questioned.

Lavon was tilted back in the chair so far his head touched the back wall. He had his arms folded in front of him and his perpetual scowl was in place.

"You again," he complained as Harlan walked in and sat across the table.

"Yep. And this time J.D. and your daddy can't bail you out of trouble."

"I don't believe you."

Harlan glanced at his watch. "I imagine J.D. will be in handcuffs within the next thirty minutes."

A bit of the smug attitude melted off Lavon's face. "Liar."

"Why lie about that? You'll see for yourself soon enough. Who knows—you two might wind up in the same jail cell tonight."

"I ain't done nothing," Lavon muttered.

"I have an eyewitness who says different."

"Your girlfriend?" Lavon scoffed. "As if that won't look rigged in court. Besides, it'll be her word against mine."

"Her word will be loads more credible than those from some asshole who at age twenty-nine has an impressive list of petty crimes that have escalated over the last year."

He opened the folder and began reading aloud. "Vandalism, Class C Assault, Theft of Property in the second degree, criminal mischief—"

"Lilah's nothing but a whore, just like Darla was. All the Tedder women are the same. Look at—"

A buzzer went off in his head, as loud as a referee's whistle in an empty gym. Harlan slammed the file on the table and lunged.

"Hey, man—you can't do that," Lavon sputtered.

Harlan curled his fingers around the scooped neck of Lavon's black T-shirt. The guy's hazel eyes were inches from his own. "Never. Ever. Talk about Lilah that way."

Lavon gave a forced laugh. "Okay. Cool it, dude."

Harlan slowly released his grip and calmed his labored breathing. He was here to crack Lavon, not lose control of himself.

"Fine. Let's get on with it. We have an eyewitness placing you inside my house last night about seven o'clock. What do you have to say about that?"

He shrugged. "I was home. You can ask my parents. I'm sure they'll vouch for me."

"Just so you know—officers are there now checking for fingerprints."

"They won't find anything," he answered, chin lifting with confidence.

"You think you're safe because you wore gloves? Think again. They'll comb the place for stray strands of hair, too. Bet you didn't wear a hairnet."

Lavon licked his lips.

"Let's cut to the chase. Lilah saw you by my desk, and ten minutes later J.D. was at the door with a search warrant. Luckily, she got rid of the drugs you'd planted. You tried to set me up. Tell me why."

"I told you I was home last night. I had nothing to do with this."

"I'll tell you why you did it. You're involved up to your neck in distributing drugs and J.D. is in on the cut. Y'all saw I was getting a little too close to suspecting the truth, so you schemed to get me out of the way."

"You can't prove it."

"Oh, we will." Harlan cocked his thumb toward the door. "Did you get a glimpse of what's happening out there?"

"No. What?"

Harlan rose and opened the door. "Let me take you on a little tour."

He stayed close by Lavon's side as they went down the hallway and into the lobby. Lavon's eyes widened as he caught sight of all the men and his gaze shifted toward J.D.'s office. The door was open and J.D. could be seen wiping his forehead as three men peppered him with questions.

The incredulous drop of Lavon's jaw was a thing of beauty. Harlan guided him back to the interrogation room. As soon as they were both seated, he opened the envelope. Best to do this before the guy asked for a lawyer and clammed up.

He shimmied the half a dozen shell casings from the envelope onto the table. They were all in individual baggies.

Lavon's jaw tightened. "What's this?"

"We found these on Mossy Creek Trail. Where you and another man shot at Lilah."

"They ain't mine. Probably left behind by hunters."

"The only thing being hunted was Lilah," Harlan said, wanting to shake Lavon like a rag doll.

"Wasn't me."

"You're lying. Lilah heard you while she hid in a cave."

"That don't mean nothing. Her word against mine."

Harlan flicked the baggie. "These mean something."

"Them casings could have come from any number of folks."

"Doubtful."

Lavon's eyes narrowed to slits. "Ain't no way you can pin 'em on me."

"Actually we can and we will."

"How's that?"

"We're getting a subpoena to confiscate all your guns. After that, we'll run a ballistics test to see if we have a match."

Lavon blinked but quickly regained his belligerent stance. "Can't narrow it down to just my gun. It's a common model lots of folks 'round here might have for hunting."

Guy was fractionally smarter than Harlan had guessed, but some time alone in the interrogation room might make him sweat.

"I'll be back shortly." Harlan put the casings back in the envelope and went out the door. At the end of the hall, Lewis saw him and approached. "How's it going in there?"

"Not the greatest. He's not budging on his statement about having no knowledge of the drug ring."

"Time to shake him up a bit more." Lewis pulled a small baggie from his pants pocket and handed it to him.

Harlan held it to the light and peered. "A few hair strands?"

Lewis grinned. "They belong to Lavon. We managed to get them today while he was waiting to be questioned."

Harlan nodded. "I know just what to do with them." Quickly, he strode back to Room B and turned on his cell phone's video before slapping the new evidence on the table. "Recognize these?"

Lavon lifted his shoulders and then dropped them, feigning indifference. "Nope."

"Look closer."

Lavon sighed and looked again. "Brown hair. So what."

"The same medium brown as yours and the same swirl pattern. *Your* hair. We'll have the lab results soon enough."

Lavon paled. "I want to talk to my dad."

"He's being questioned."

"Then I want to talk to a—"

"How long have you been involved in this drug ring?" Harlan interrupted. He was about to lose Lavon. "Tell me the truth. Cooperate with us and this will go a lot easier on you and your family."

"My dad has nothing to do with this."

Now he was getting somewhere.

"Surely, you can understand my skepticism. He already had the moonshine operation in place. It would be easy for him—and more profitable—to substitute drugs for liquor. Not only that, but also his risks were minimized by having the local sheriff on the take."

"But he didn't." Lavon stood, clenching his fists by his sides. "I didn't need to ask him for a thing. I got involved by myself and started making my own money."

His hazel eyes darkened in horror and a hand flew to his mouth. But it was too late: the self-incriminating words had been spoken.

"Wanted to prove you were your own man, huh? Well, junior, you better start naming names. Do that, and the judge will go easier on you. That, and your young age, should go a long way to shortening your prison term."

"Prison? J.D. promised we'd never get caught." Lavon sat back down and held his head in his hands, his shoulders slumped forward. His back shook, but he didn't make a sound.

Lavon didn't look so tough now. He looked like a young scared kid. Harlan nipped sympathy in the bud. That kid had come too close to hurting Lilah on two separate occasions.

"You going to cooperate?"

He removed his hands from his face. "I want a deal," he said in a hard, flat voice. "And a lawyer. I ain't going to prison."

Harlan stood, slipped his cell phone in his pocket and gathered up the files and the evidence. "Oh, but you are. Yeah, you'll get a sentence reduction for naming the others, but make no mistake, jail time is in your future. I'm going to send a couple of detectives in to talk to you now."

In the hall, he answered Lewis's questioning look with a thumbs-up. "He's ready to name the others."

"Great. This will help break J.D. He's pretty close as it is. I have the feeling he's suspected for a long time that he'd eventually get caught." Lewis shook his head. "And to think he was only a few months away from retirement. Stupid."

"And dangerous." The hair on his arms bristled yet again at the thought of how close he and Lilah had come to being framed. "You going to question Alvin Lee as well?"

"Already did. My impression is that he hasn't committed any crime. He's a weak man that J.D. had just started grooming to be his replacement."

"Okay then. Now we need to focus on the murders. Lavon had no reaction to the trophies I put in front of him. I don't think he's involved with the killings."

Lewis nodded. "I've been watching Ed Stovall's interrogation. He's singing about his limited involvement in the moonshine business, but remains adamant he didn't kill his wife. We'll lay photos of all the murder victims, including his former wife, in front of him to see if we get an unusual reaction. I don't believe we will, though."

"What about Thad?"

"Ed told us where the current still is, and where the liquor's being stored. I've got men out now to seize the illegal moonshine. We'll have a good case to prosecute Thad Tedder for the operation. Most likely, Ed will get off with a fine and probation."

Harlan thought of Ed's three sons. "Glad to hear it. Has Thad been shown the victim photos yet?"

Lewis held up a package. "Got some in here. Let's hand it to Marvin Ashton, the GBI officer who's questioning him. We can watch Thad's reaction from the booth."

Harlan took his place inside the booth with several others watching and listening behind the two-way mirror.

Thad sat across from the officer in the interrogation room that looked identical to the other. And that wasn't all that was alike. Thad's brown curly hair was a touch disheveled, like his son's, and he wore the same smug arrogant look his son either emulated or came by naturally through his daddy's DNA.

"Like I keep telling you, I ain't done nothing wrong and I ain't talking to nobody but the sheriff," Thad said.

"And like I told you, Sheriff Bentley's unavailable. You're going to have to deal with me on the charges of distributing illegal liquor."

"I ain't got to do shit."

"It'll go a lot easier on you, and your son, if you cooperate."

"You leave my boy outta this."

"Too late." Marvin smiled with no humor. "Lavon's already confessed."

"What? But he ain't even—he doesn't—"

"Not involved in your business?" Marvin asked. "Maybe not in the moonshine operation, but he's confessed to a much bigger crime. Drug distribution. He's looking at a long prison sentence."

Thad raised his arms and tugged violently at his hair. "No. He wouldn't… I don't believe you."

"They're typing up his confession now. I can show it to you when it's finished, if you'd like."

"Where's J.D.? I want to talk to him."

Harlan shook his head. Thaddeus's first inclination in seeking help was to ask for J.D. and not an attorney.

"J.D.'s got his own troubles this morning. You didn't notice all the cops swarming the place when they brought you in?"

Thad swiped a hand over his face. "This is going to kill Viola." He shuddered and a sob escaped from his throat. "My boy."

Like father, like son, Harlan thought.

"Not only do we have Lavon's confession. We have Ed Stovall's as well. He's told us everything he knows about what you've been running. Agents are out now taking possession of your still and any liquor stored in your holding place."

Thad smashed a fist on the table. "Damn Ed." A crafty look stole into his eyes. "What I mean is—the man's a liar. He's even suspected of killing his wife. Maybe you ought to look at him a little more closely. If Ed knows so damn much, maybe he's the one who runs the whole shebang."

"And then there's another little matter we haven't covered yet." Marvin pulled a stack of old black-and-white photos out of the envelope and slapped it on the table. "Do you remember these women?"

Thad froze for a moment and then a hand jerked across the table to pick up one of the photos. "What—can I look at these?"

Without waiting for permission, Thad picked up the first photo and held it—a look of almost reverence in his eyes. His Adam's apple twisted in his throat and he swallowed hard.

"Bingo," Harlan whispered. "We've found a killer."

"Yep. Look at that," Lewis said in a low voice. "Even with a cop in the room, he can't help fondling her photo."

"Recognize the woman?" Marvin prodded.

Thad set the photo down with obvious reluctance. "Never seen her before."

"You're lying. C'mon, tell me the truth." Marvin lowered his voice and coaxed Thad as if he were merely a naughty child. "Get it off your chest," he said gently. "You've held a dark secret inside for over two decades. You knew that woman, didn't you? Knew her intimately."

"No. I done told you, I never seen her before."

Martin laid down more photos, spreading them out. "What about your brother Chauncey and your niece Darla?"

Thad jerked his head back, repulsed. "Put them pictures away from me. And I want a lawyer, before I say another word to you or anyone else."

"You're going to need one."

Martin left Thad and stepped into the witness booth. "Sorry guys. He clammed up. What do we do now? Arrest him on the liquor charges?"

"We can after we gather the evidence," Lewis said.

"Damn it," Harlan muttered. "Lilah's no safer today than yesterday. We've gotten nowhere on the murders."

"For now, she's safe. We have an undercover cop doing ride-bys to your house. And we know more than we did coming in," Lewis said. "We have a prime suspect now for the murder cases. We'll bring Thaddeus back in later and book him for running moonshine. Try to shake him out a little more. In the meantime, we'll keep working on J.D. The man knows something about the murders, I'm sure of it."

"That's what I've said all along," Harlan agreed. "J.D. kept insisting that the two recent homicides weren't connected, and then he didn't want me investigating the old murder cases. To top it off, I discovered that our only piece of physical evidence disappeared."

Lewis gestured to the open door. "Ready to try and break him?"

"Absolutely."

Chapter Seventeen

Was she being followed?

Lilah checked the rearview mirror. The black sedan was still behind her, albeit at a comfortable, non-threatening distance. It seemed out of place here—too sleek and pricey for Lavender Mountain. And she was fairly certain it had followed her route for the past couple turns on the county roads.

She gave herself a little shake. Paranoia, much? But to be safe, she'd texted Harlan her destination, as she'd promised to do whenever she left the house. Lilah pulled up to Aunt Vi's place, relieved to note that the sedan drove past the driveway and continued on its way. Lilah got out of the car and glanced at the gray sky that was pregnant with rain. Wind whipped the trees—they were in for a doozy of a summer storm today.

Viola met her at the door, face swollen and puffy. Lilah's heart squeezed. Her aunt seemed to lead an unhappy, fearful kind of life. Today had to be the worst ever, what with the cops picking up her husband and eldest son.

"They've got my Lavon," Aunt Vi sobbed and swiped at her wet cheeks.

Lilah gave her a hug. "I know. I'm so sorry."

Viola clung for a moment and then withdrew, rubbing her hands on her apron. "Come on in the house," she said with great effort. Even in the midst of a family crisis, her aunt's ingrained sense of hospitality peeked through.

Lilah followed her inside. Although it wasn't yet midday, the house was dark and gloomy. The curtains were drawn tight over the windows and the TV set was off. Nothing interrupted the funereal silence. And it was one of the few times Lilah could recall that she'd been here and there was no aroma of a meal being cooked. Aunt Vi almost always had a stew of some sort simmering in the kitchen.

She sat on the sofa and regarded Viola with concern. "I'm glad you called me to come over," she began. "Thought maybe you'd be upset with me after I told Harlan about hearing Lavon that night in the woods."

"I was at first," she said. "Then I had to admit that somehow I'd lost control of my child. When Lavon was young and lost his temper, or did something naughty, I'd hope and pray he'd grow out of it. But he never did. Things only got worse. He kept getting into trouble. And now they suspect he's a—a drug dealer."

The tears spilled again and her body wracked with sobs. Lilah absently placed a hand over her stomach. She couldn't imagine how painful it must be having your child disappoint you in that way.

"I don't know what to say, except that you are a good mother, a good person. None of this is your fault. Lavon's an adult and he makes his own choices."

Oh, but she did fault Uncle Thad. Lavon was following in his dad's footsteps by breaking the law.

Lilah bit her lip, reconsidering. No, she couldn't entirely blame Thad. After all, her dad had broken the law as well, and look how great her brother, Jimmy, had turned out. He'd been awarded all kind of medals for his military service in the Middle East.

"Have you heard anything this morning from Harlan?" Vi asked, taking a handkerchief out of her apron pocket and twisting it in her lap. "Have they arrested Lavon?"

"I haven't heard a thing. I'll tell you right away if I do."

Vi nodded. "I'm not worried so much about Thad. He always seems to escape trouble. But drugs are a whole lot more serious than moonshine. I imagine Thad isn't too worried for himself."

That's what came from having the local sheriff in your back pocket. But Lilah didn't point that out.

Viola rounded her shoulders, sat up stiffly in the chair and pinned her with bloodshot eyes. "Do you really believe it was Lavon that shot at you?"

"I do." No sense lying.

Viola's lips twisted. "I'm sure he meant it as a warning shot. He wouldn't hurt his own cousin."

Her tone was weak, defeated, as if she couldn't muster the strength to believe her own words.

"I hope his intent wasn't to harm me. But we'll never know."

Viola shook her head, pushing back a shock of gray limp hair that had fallen in her eyes. "He's not capable of murder. Guess you might find it hard to believe and think I'm just a blind, biased mama for saying this, but I know Lavon. He's no murderer."

Lilah's chest seized and a roar sounded in her ears. Did Viola know something about Dad and Darla's murders? "Who said anything about murder?" she asked quietly.

"Come now, child, their deaths are here between us like a living presence. Don't you feel it?"

"Wh-what do you mean?"

"I mean that whoever killed them probably knew them. What's that they always say on them TV crime shows? You want a suspect, look at the immediate family."

"If you have information, come on out and say it."

Viola stood abruptly and walked to a window, peeking out from behind the lace curtain. "If I'm wrong, you're going to think I'm the sorriest wife a husband ever had."

"Uncle Thad?" Lilah stood and the room spun. Her breath quickened. "Did he kill them? Why?"

"I don't know for sure that he's the killer. Says he didn't do it, but…he lies to me. All the time. He has other women." She dropped her hold on the curtain and faced Lilah. "You ever hear that about Thad? He has run around on our marriage for years."

Yeah, she'd heard rumors; it was a small town after all. "The murders," Lilah said, redirecting her aunt. "Why would he kill Dad and Darla?"

"I'm not sure about Darla, but Chauncey had been blackmailing him for the past few months."

"Dad wouldn't do—" Lilah stopped abruptly and thumped her forehead with her palm. "The thirty thousand dollars. Is that how he got it?"

"Thad paid him cash every week. Oh, your dad swore it wasn't blackmail—that he just wanted extra money to leave his children."

"That's not blackmail. Sounds to me like he just asked Uncle Thad for help."

"But he told Thad that he'd been shortchanged over the years in the moonshine business. Said he'd done most of the work and had nothing to show for it. Chauncey demanded Thad pay up."

She'd always suspected as much herself. Thad and his family always seemed to have money while her dad had always been broke. "It's still not blackmail unless Dad threatened Uncle Thad in some way."

"Thad claimed he was afraid Chauncey would turn him in, but it wasn't exactly spelled out."

Lilah bit her tongue. It all sounded pretty nebulous in her opinion. Dad would never have turned in his own brother. Besides, he'd get in trouble himself.

"Thad's been worried that if the cops found out, they'd suspect he had a motive to kill Chauncey. When they took him away this morning… Well, I can't help wondering if the cops are questioning him about that."

"Why are you telling me all this?" Lilah asked slowly. "If the cops don't know, you must realize I have to tell them."

"Yeah, I know." Aunt Viola hung her head.

Lilah mulled over the conversation and Vi's strange behavior. "You suspect Thad's the killer."

Silence hung between them like a ticking bomb.

Vi licked her lips. "It's possible," she whispered.

"You have to tell Harlan."

"Accuse my own husband with no proof?"

Vi stared blankly into space for a few heartbeats. "Always thought his tomfoolery was the worst thing that could ever happen to me," she said flatly. "Then Lavon started getting in trouble, and I thought that was the worst. But that wasn't it neither. For weeks, I've harbored suspicion about my own husband, and that was horrible. But, today…"

Lilah's heart thumped like drum. "What is it?"

"I'll show you."

Vi rose and lumbered down the hallway, her steps as heavy as if her shoulders bore the weight of generations of Tedder sins.

Had her uncle really killed her father? And what about Darla? Maybe the killings were unrelated after all.

Viola returned carrying a leather drawstring pouch. "Found this hid behind the bathroom pipes when I reached for the plunger. I wish to God I never had."

She took the pouch and opened its tie with shaking fingers. Could it be shotgun shells? A confession note? Lilah carefully shook out the contents.

The leather bracelet with its crimson stone, the bright beaded necklace Darla had once worn, the tarnished silver ring with the fake cameo carving and yet another ring with a gold band and small diamond solitaire. Where had she seen that ring before?

"Looks like Darla's wedding ring, don't it?" Aunt Vi asked.

Yes. Of course. At least she could be certain now that Ed hadn't done it.

Her uncle was the Hillside Strangler. And he'd also killed his own brother. Lilah's entire body trembled and she couldn't control the shivering. A bone-deep cold settled in her heart. But past the horror of it all, another question remained. "But why did Uncle Thad kill Darla?" Lilah asked. "Could she have stumbled on the truth somehow and so Thad had to kill her, too?"

Vi made a strangled sound in her throat. "Maybe Thad didn't kill nobody."

"What do you mean? Vi, all this jewelry was taken from murder victims. The fact that you found them here, hidden in your house, means—"

"Could have been Lavon. I'm almost one hundred percent certain it's not, but I can't rule it out neither. And *that*, Lilah, is the worst thing ever for a momma to experience."

"You aren't thinking straight. Lavon's too young to have committed those old murders. It has to be…" She started to say *Uncle* but the word died on her lips. She would never refer to him as that again. "It has to be Thad."

"Maybe Thad killed those women. Could be Lavon killed Darla, and maybe your dad, too," Vi pointed out.

"What reason would Lavon have?" She racked her brain.

"Maybe Lavon overheard something and thought my dad was a threat to Thad?"

It still didn't explain Darla, unless Lavon thought Darla knew something incriminating about Thad or their business.

Lilah hurriedly stuffed the jewelry back in the pouch. It made her skin crawl to think of her sister and the other two women who'd been killed. And almost as sickening, it made her cringe to imagine Thad fondling the pieces of jewelry while reveling in the memory of their death at his hands. "I need to take this to Harlan straight away."

Viola's tears started anew. "I hope I done the right thing."

"You did what any decent person would do," Lilah assured her. "Thank you."

"Maybe you can just tell Harlan you came to visit me and found it on your own? Leave my name out of it?"

"I always tell Harlan the truth," she said gently. "But if he sees fit, maybe he can fudge over this part of how I got the jewelry."

"I don't know what's to become of us all now," Aunt Vi said with a moan.

"Hopefully, we'll all be a little safer," she said drily. Lilah felt sorry for her aunt, but her sympathy only went so far. If Viola had come forward earlier, she might not have been almost killed on two occasions now. She'd been lucky that she and the baby and Harlan had escaped unscathed.

"I've got to go." Lilah rose and dug her car keys out of her purse, eager to get to the sheriff's office. An ironic smile ghosted across her lips. All those officers swarming to get to the bottom of the murders today, and here she was going to walk in there with the physical evidence they needed to actually make a case.

She walked to Vi and patted her shoulder. "Do you want

to stay with us a few days? Or I could take you wherever you'd like. Maybe stay with someone until this blows over? I don't want Thad to hurt you."

Vi shook her head. "He don't scare me none. Never has. Not even now."

A car sounded in the driveway, a door opened and shut and then heavy footsteps started up the porch steps. Could Thad be home already? Had to be either him or Lavon.

She glanced at Vi. "Sure you're going to be okay?"

The door flung open with a bang.

"What are you doing here?" Thad asked.

His hair was more disheveled than normal, and his eyes darted back and forth between her and Viola.

"I invited her over," Viola said, lifting her chin a fraction.

"After the way her boyfriend's treated me and our son this morning? Who else is here? Looks like a damn undercover police car's parked in front of the house, too."

He glared at Lilah and she nervously clutched at her purse's shoulder strap. "I'll be going now." She faced Aunt Vi one last time, offering a silent invitation for her to leave as well.

Vi shook her head.

Thad stared at the couch, incredulity written on his face. "What's this?"

He brushed past her and went to the couch.

Sunlight streaming through the open front door cast a spotlight on the diamond solitaire set of Darla's wedding ring. Sparkling prisms of colored light glittered like a beacon, mesmerizing Lilah like a trance.

Thad carefully picked it up and turned to them. "Where are the others?"

The quiet, calm voice frightened her in a way his earlier belligerence had not. She took a step backward.

"Stop," he commanded in that same smooth low tone. "Not another step."

"Leave her alone," Aunt Vi said. "It's over."

He didn't spare his wife a glance. "Where's the rest?"

Lilah spun toward the door and he was beside her in a flash, painfully gripping her forearm.

"Give me my things," he said with a hiss.

"Okay, okay." With her free hand, she dug the pouch out of her purse.

Thad let go of her arm and snatched it up. His body was tense, his focus on the pouch all-absorbing.

Run now.

Lilah scrambled across the den to the back door. A strong pull on her purse ripped into her shoulder and she started tumbling forward. She clutched at the wall with one hand and righted herself.

"Thad, stop it!" Aunt Viola threw herself between Lilah and Thad. She glanced back at Lilah. "Go!"

She didn't need to be told twice.

Chapter Eighteen

"You lost her?" Harlan yelled into the office phone. "How the hell did you manage that? Never mind, I don't want to hear your excuses. When did you last see her and how long ago?"

He checked his cell phone. Lilah had texted him thirty minutes ago she was going to visit her aunt. He should have insisted they hold Thad until Lilah had returned home. So much for trusting another person to keep an eye on her. If anything happened to Lilah, it was on him.

"Is there a problem?" Sammy asked.

"Yeah those agents that were tailing Lilah called. Apparently, she's gone missing. I've got to go."

Sammy grabbed his cruiser keys. "I'll drive. Where to?"

"Thaddeus Tedder's."

They hightailed it to the cruiser. Thunder rumbled in the distance and already a few fat drops started falling. Sammy put on the blue light through town. Once they hit the main county road, he shut it off. "Fill me in on what happened."

"All I know is that Lilah texted me that her aunt had called and wanted her to visit. Lewis assigned an undercover cop to tail Lilah, so I thought all would be fine. But the guy called and said that Thad had returned home and he heard screaming from inside the house. He knocked on the door to investigate, and was told that Lilah had run out the back door and into the woods."

Sammy frowned. "Here we go again. But if the cop's with Thad, she should be safe."

Harlan held on to that thought for the ten minutes it took to arrive at Thad's. He strode up the porch and marched inside, not bothering with a knock.

Thad was sprawled on the sofa, head in his hands, while his wife sat at the far opposite end, as if trying to keep the farthest distance possible. The undercover cop sat across the room. He rose and nodded. "Brian Forney, Georgia Bureau of Investigation."

Harlan dismissed him with a quick nod.

"I'll take a look around out back," Sammy offered, standing in the doorway. "See if Lilah's hiding close by."

"Thanks."

Lilah knew Sammy. If she was near, she'd go to him. Harlan faced Thad. "What happened?" he demanded.

"It's time to do the right thing," Viola said. "Lilah knows the truth and so do I. Might go easier on you if you tell it."

Harlan pinned him with a stare. "Spill it. I need to find Lilah."

"It was me," Thad said, staring down at his feet. He drew a loud, unsteady breath. "I killed them hookers."

"Their names were Raylene Rucker and Amzie Bill-bray," Harlan corrected. "They had names and friends and families."

Forney spoke up. "After all these years, we've captured the Hillside Strangler."

We? The man hadn't done anything except lose Lilah and plop his ass in a chair. But whatever.

"What did you say to Lilah?" Harland continued, focusing on Thad. "Officer Forney heard shouting."

Thad reluctantly lifted his head. "She had my things. I lost my temper."

Harlan's own temper threatened to snap. "Did you—"

"Nah, I didn't lay a hand on her. Vi came between us and made me listen to reason. Lilah ran out the back door—she was scared."

Forney unlocked a pair of handcuffs from his belt and started toward Thad. "I'll handcuff Tedder and take him in."

"I'm not done talking to him yet," Harlan snapped. The officer was champing at the bit to take Thad in and claim he'd had a hand in capturing the murderer. Not that it mattered to him, but he wasn't finished with Thaddeus.

"You confess to killing Raylene and Amzie. What about Chauncey and Darla? Did you kill them as well?"

"Nope. I didn't do it." Thad picked up a leather pouch in his lap and cradled it in one palm. "I couldn't kill my own kin. Takes a special kind of sick to do that."

As if there was much of a distinction. As if Thaddeus had a moral imperative higher than any other murderer. Those kinds of hypocritical rationales were the sort spouted by hard-core inmates from inside a state penitentiary.

"Save it for the judge," Harlan barked. He needed to break Thad now while his wife was encouraging him, and before he got locked up in the county jail and had time to worry about saving his ass from the death penalty.

Yet every second that ticked by, he was aware that Lilah was alone and frightened in the woods. He hoped any moment that she and Sammy would walk through the door.

Viola sniffled and spoke up. "What's going on with Lavon? Is he coming home tonight?"

Poor woman. She was fixin' to have a lifetime of lonely

nights in an empty house. "No. He's confessed to distributing drugs and has been charged."

"He'll be locked up for years," Forney added.

Harlan shot him a warning look. That comment wasn't necessary and did nothing but waste valuable time. "Perhaps you can visit him tomorrow," Harlan said to a sobbing Viola. He turned his attention back to Thaddeus. "What's that in your hands?" Harlan asked.

A spark of nearby lightning lit the room, followed closely by a clap of thunder. Sheets of rain assaulted the walls and windows. Damn it, Lilah was out in this storm.

Thad didn't respond to the storm or the question.

Viola jumped up, her thin body trembling. "Give that damn thing to the cops," she screamed at Thad in a high, shrill wail. "What the hell kind of monster did I marry?"

She snatched the pouch out of Thad's hands. No doubt, the man would have put up a fight if he hadn't been so startled by his wife's uncharacteristic outburst.

Viola thrust it at Harlan. "He's ruined my life and Lavon's life. Our boy thinks the world of his daddy. Wanted to be just like him. But at least Lavon's not a killer."

Harlan opened the pouch. It was all there. All the missing evidence. "How did you get the bracelet back? J.D. give it to you?"

Thad nodded.

The depths of J.D.'s despicable behavior stunned Harlan. He'd suspected his boss of turning a blind eye on the drugs and marijuana trade—but murder? That was a whole new level of low.

Harlan picked up the diamond ring and held it to the light. "Darla's?"

"Yeah, but I didn't kill her. I swear!"

"Then how did you get possession of her wedding ring?"

Thad clamped his mouth shut.

"These are all related," Harlan insisted. "Lilah found the jewelry taken from the strangled women in her dad's cabin. Chauncey was killed. She gave the necklace to Darla, and then Darla was killed. Lilah wore the bracelet for a time—now someone's after Lilah."

"You want to serve time for all the murders?" Forney cut in. "Maybe we can cut a deal for the old murders, but not for two members of your own family."

Damn Forney. The last thing Harlan wanted was for Thad to start thinking about arranging deals. He wanted the name of the second killer. And he wanted it now.

To hell with protocol. Harlan grabbed a fistful of Thaddeus's shirt and hauled him to his feet.

"Who is it?"

LILAH TORE THROUGH the backyard and into the woods without a backward glance. It was like the earlier chase—except this time she knew the face of the killer. And instead of heading down the mountain, this time she'd be fleeing upward.

"Lilah! Get back here!" Thad's voice boomed from behind.

Fat chance.

The familiar pine-strewn path was narrower than she remembered from her childhood days. The needles were slick with rain and mud slushed her sneakers. Her feet sank into the ground that had instantly turned to a sticky, sludgy mess. It slowed her progress and strained her calves, but the good news was that it would be much more difficult for her heavyset uncle to sludge his way through the muck.

She was going to make it—unless he returned to his house and got his gun. She was fit and fast, but she couldn't outrun a bullet.

No, no. Aunt Viola would stop him. *Focus on one step at a time.* That was the way to get through this.

Low-lying branches slapped at her face, chest and arms. Her T-shirt and jeans clung to her body and her teeth chattered. Her right shoe stuck in the mud and she stopped to grab it. Leaning against an oak, she slipped it back on and paused to catch her breath. Not too much farther to go to reach safety.

A burst of thunder roared and she cringed. The danger of getting hit by lightning might be better than the chance of Thad lumbering nearby. Rain continued pouring and she sighed. Time to get moving again.

She crossed a small wooden bridge over a swollen creek and knew she was close. Squinting through the downpour, Lilah spotted the cabin and the welcoming warmth of light from a window. She sprinted to the porch and peered through the foggy glass pane.

Uncle Jasper was seated on the sofa with the family bible open in his lap. A shotgun hung over the fireplace mantel. Here she'd be safe and protected.

It was surprising that he hadn't heard her clumsy stumble onto the porch, but the storm must have drowned out the noise. He enjoyed solitude and met visitors on the porch, usually not inviting them into his inner sanctum.

Lilah rapped at the window. She must be a sight—as wet and as muddy as a stray dog left to fend for itself in the harsh elements.

Jasper dropped the bible and half rose from the sofa, squinting his eyes at her form. Bedraggled as she must have appeared, she was recognizable and the startled consternation in his gray eyes morphed to one of surprise.

He disappeared from view a moment and then the back door screeched open.

"Lilah? What are you doin' out there in the rain? Everything all right?"

"I—I think so."

She wanted nothing more than to throw her arms around her uncle's quarrelsome old neck, but he would have hated that. Lilah took a quick glance over her shoulder. Past Jasper's junky backyard, the tree line to the woods loomed large and foreboding, as though it contained ancient dark secrets and harbored beasts both animal and human.

But no Thad emerged, wielding a gun.

Jasper waved her toward the door. "C'mon in."

She hugged her elbows at the waist and entered as Jasper shut the door from behind.

"I was running from Thad. I was afraid he'd hurt me."

Jasper tugged at his beard, regarding her calmly. "I tried to warn you. He's a dangerous man."

"I didn't know how dangerous. Not until Aunt Vi handed me the jewelry she found. Did you know—"

Jasper walked to the window and drew the curtain closed.

"Did you see him? Is he out there?" she asked breathlessly.

"It's just the two of us."

Her shoulders drooped in relief and she sank down onto the sofa. The cushions were still warm from Jasper's body. Her uncle settled in the rocker across from her.

"He's a murderer, Uncle Jasper. The Hilltop Strangler. He killed those two women and…and I think he might have killed Dad and Darla."

His brows rose. "That so?" he asked, as though she'd commented on the weather.

"You don't believe me?" She waved a hand dismissively. "It's true. There's proof. We've got to call Harlan. Tell him to arrest Thad."

"You haven't already called?"

"No. I left their house without my purse or anything. He wanted to kill me, Uncle Jasper. It was in his eyes. I ran out the back door and Aunt Vi got between us. I ran straight here."

"So you did." He picked up his pipe from the side table, filled it with a pinch of tobacco and proceeded to light it.

"Don't you get it?" she asked, frustrated by his wall of calm. "I was chased through the woods. Thad could be here any moment."

"Not likely. He's too lazy for that."

She shook her head, disappointed and hurt at his lack of concern. She would take care of this herself. "Where's your phone?"

"Ain't working." He drew on the pipe and then exhaled cherry-scented smoke. "Storm must have knocked out the line."

Damn it. Lilah buried her head in her hands and fought against the urge to scream in frustration. Instead, she jumped up. Action was the antidote to get through this ordeal. "We've got to lock the windows and doors."

Luckily, there were only three windows. She latched the front door and eyed the shotgun. "That thing loaded?"

"Always is."

"Good."

She eyed him as he rocked in the chair, puffing away. "Can you close the back window while I get these up front?"

"You ain't got nothing to fear from Thaddeus now."

"You don't understand. Aunt Vi found jewelry he stole from those women he murdered. He'd hidden it behind the bathroom plumbing. He walked in on us and saw that we knew. It made him crazy. He wasn't going to let me take the evidence to Harlan."

"Course not. This is most unfortunate."

"Unfortunate?" Lilah snorted. "I'd say it's a bit more dire than that. Thanks for your concern," she added bitterly.

"You set everything in motion the minute you came back here to Lavender Mountain and found that stuff Chauncey stole." He made a tsking sound. "A shame Thad couldn't have found it first."

"Are you talking about the money? Why does it matter who found it?"

"I ain't talking about the blackmail money."

"Look, I don't know what trash Thad's filled your head with, but Dad didn't blackmail him," she said hotly. She'd had it with everyone putting down her dad, especially when it came to his own brothers. "He knew he was dying and asked Thad to help him out. For us. His kids."

Her throat swelled, threatened to close shut on her. Okay, so taking the money wasn't her dad's finest moment. But he'd done it for Jimmy and Darla, and for *her.* In his own bumbling way, he had wanted to help.

The scent of cherry tobacco made her stomach roil. It clung heavily in the room now that one of the windows was shut. Which reminded her—Lilah strode past him and slammed the back windows shut, too.

"You mind not smoking right now?" she snapped. "I know it's your house, but it's making me nauseous."

Jasper scowled. "It's never bothered you before." His eyes traveled down her body. "You ain't with child are you? I've heard rumors."

Lilah bit her lips. She'd deliberately not said anything to Uncle Jasper, knowing his strict religious bent. But since he'd outright asked… "Yes. I'm pregnant."

"Harlot."

Lilah shook her head. He hadn't really said that—had he?

"You turned out no different than those fallen women Thad killed."

Jasper dropped his pipe in the ashtray and it clanged as loud as a dropped shotgun shell. Burnt ash spilled out of it like bits of molten lava. Lilah couldn't tear her gaze away. She didn't want to look up and see the disgust in Jasper's face.

"I thought you were different from your sister," Jasper continued. "She was always trash. But you—I had hopes you'd turn into a decent, respectable lady." Gone was the detached tone and odd indifference. His voice crackled with condemnation. "Now look at you. Pregnant, unwed and living in sin."

She lifted her chin. "Don't you dare talk about my sister that way. Or me, either. After today, you'll never have to see my face again. Trust me on that."

"No doubt."

The eerie calm had returned, as though he'd slipped back on a mask.

"How about letting me borrow your truck," Lilah said stiffly. She wanted out of the smoky, stuffy room. "I'll see it's returned to you tomorrow."

Jasper bent over, picked the bible up from the floor where he'd dropped it earlier and then rifled his fingers through a jar filled with ink pens. He selected a crimson one and laid it in the middle of the book where their ancestry tree was located.

Crimson.

Ernest, Dad and Darla's names had been scribed in the color of blood.

Lilah took a step backward. "If you'll just give me those truck keys," she said desperately. "I'll go away and never come back. Promise."

"We both know it's too late for that. Poor LayLay. You'll be the hardest one of all."

"I—I don't know what you're talking about." She took another step backward, mind in a whirl. Somehow, she'd stepped into the twilight zone. "Look, just give me the keys—"

"Chauncey was a blackmailer. A man can't treat his family like that. It's wrong."

This was no alternate universe. This was real. If she wanted to survive, for her baby to live, she'd better get it together.

"You're right," she agreed, playing along. "It was wrong. Dad shouldn't have done that."

"I had to kill him. What kind of man threatens to turn his own brother into the police? Chauncey found that jewelry and guessed the truth. Only a matter of time before he ruined everything."

"You knew Thad killed those women?" she asked, breathless.

"From the start."

Jasper stepped past her.

She couldn't help asking. "Why didn't you do something?"

"They were nothing but harlots. An abomination. Still, he shouldn't have killed them. We had an agreement. He wouldn't tell anyone I'd killed Dad, and I'd keep my silence."

He lifted the gun from the mantel and cocked the slide, checking the chamber. "Yep, loaded."

"But killing your father was like—self-defense. Right? He hurt you."

"That's the way I seen it," Jasper agreed. "Shot him cold in the back and claimed it was a hunting accident. Only mistake was that I didn't know Thad was watching."

"So when you found out Thad strangled those women, you couldn't say anything for fear he'd turn you in."

"Exactly."

Lilah backed all the way into the doorway, feeling behind her for the door handle. Where was it?

Jasper gave a crooked smile. "Go on and open the door. We'll take a little walk."

What was she thinking trying to get outside? Better to stay inside. Jasper was crazy—not stupid. If he shot her in the cabin, he would never be able to cover up the crime. "It's—it's raining," she stammered, grasping at straws.

He barked a laugh.

She scooted along the side of the wall, away from the door, not daring to turn her back on Jasper.

"Did you kill Darla, too?"

"Had to. Stupid chit. All over that cheap glass bauble. Thad and I tried to reason with her, offered to get her another necklace in exchange. But she'd taken a shine to it. Or so she'd claimed. Kept asking why it was so important to us, demanding to know why we wanted it. She always was the sassiest little ole thing."

Lilah hoped that the killing had been quick, that Darla hadn't known what was coming. "So y'all argued. Did you force her to hand over her wedding ring?"

"That came afterward. Thad said the missing ring might make it look like a possible robbery."

No, Thad had only wanted to expand his sick collection of tokens. They were both responsible for her sister's death, but she still wanted to know who had pulled the trigger.

"Was it you or Thad that shot Darla?"

"Me. I'm the eldest. The one who cleans up his little brother's mess. 'Sides, Thad's a coward at heart."

"Big words from a man who shoots defenseless women in the back."

The broad side of his free hand smacked her across the face and she fell to the floor. Pain exploded in her right cheek and ears. Lilah hunched up, instinctively shielding her stomach from another blow.

The next landed on her right thigh—a vicious kick.

"Get up," he commanded.

Lilah scanned the room, desperate for a weapon. Her eyes lit on the bible and she crawled to it, picking it up and clutching it to her chest.

"Put that back on the table," he ordered. "You ain't worthy enough to be holdin' it."

"You wouldn't shoot a woman holding a bible, would you?" She inched away from him, needing to get out of striking range.

Jasper swooped down and grabbed a handful of her hair. "Get up now!"

The book fell out of her hands and she rose to her feet, tears blinding her eyes. "Okay, okay. Please stop hurting me."

His grip released a fraction. "And now we take that walk."

He marched her to the door and thrust it open. Her scalp was on fire.

This was it. She was going to lose the baby, lose Harlan, lose her life. In ten minutes, she'd be nothing more than another death her uncle recorded in crimson ink.

Wind swept the rain onto the porch and the sky rumbled. He would force her into the woods now and shoot her in the back like he'd done with Dad and Darla.

"Please," she begged. "Don't shoot me. I won't tell anyone."

"Damn straight you won't."

HARLAN CLIMBED IN the cruiser, adrenaline spiking his body like a bolt of lightning. Lilah had run from the lion's den right into the belly of the beast.

Sammy scrambled onto the seat beside him. "I'll radio for backup," he said. "We'll send a search team to check the woods in case she didn't make it all the way to Jasper's."

He didn't answer. All his attention was on the slick roads. The windshield wipers blasted away sheets of rain, squeaking out a message. *Hur-ry, hur-ry, hur-ry.*

"We can't help Lilah if you get us killed on the roads," Sammy warned. "Should have let me drive again."

"I got this."

"She's going to be okay," Sammy promised.

He had to believe that, had to cling to that bit of faith. Otherwise, he couldn't function.

The tires squealed as he rounded a bend a bit too quick. The cruiser spun wildly in a half circle before he regained control.

"Not so fast," Sammy cautioned.

Easy for him to say. His wife and kid weren't in danger.

Finally, *finally* he arrived at Jasper's.

Two figures were on the porch. Damn this rain. His vision was limited to one-second patches of clarity as the wipers continued their frenzied action. He hit the accelerator and then skidded to a halt at the ramshackle cabin.

His heart jackhammered at the sight of Jasper poking a shotgun at Lilah's back. *No!* He jumped out of the car, pulling the pistol out of his side belt.

"Stop!" he ordered. "Drop the gun, Jasper."

Lilah's gray eyes, turbulent as the storm clouds above, lit on him.

And then, he knew the truth.

He loved her.

Madly. Heartbreakingly, bone-crushingly loved her. Probably always had. How could he have been so stupid for so long? He couldn't lose Lilah. Not now—not ever.

"Let her go!" Harlan ordered. "Set the gun down and put your hands in the air."

Jasper lowered the shotgun to his side, but he grabbed Lilah in a chokehold with his free hand.

"You ain't takin' me alive," he shouted. "And if I go, she goes, too."

Jasper backed up to the door. Bastard was planning to barricade himself in the cabin with Lilah as his hostage.

"Don't do it, Jasper," he warned. "Let her go now or it will only end up worse for you."

"Couldn't be no worse," he huffed, dragging Lilah with him.

Lilah pulled at his arm and kicked his shins, but Jasper's hold didn't loosen.

He couldn't let Jasper get her inside the cabin. Harlan holstered his gun, lunged forward and leaped up onto the porch.

Jasper shoved Lilah to the side and started raising his shotgun.

There was no time to draw his pistol, or get out of Jasper's way so Sammy would have a clear shot at the bastard. Harlan did the only thing he could do. He dove at him, hoping to knock the shotgun out of Jasper's hand before the shot went off.

He didn't make it.

A roar exploded and a tremendous pressure burst on his left shoulder. Lilah's scream echoed in his brain. *The shotgun*. He focused his eyes on it and managed to fall forward, knocking it out of Jasper's hand. It clattered on the wet rotting floorboards of the porch.

"Harlan." Lilah leaned over him, eyes wide in horror. He felt blood ooze from his shoulder. Soon, the pain would set in. For now, shock and adrenaline kept his mind sharp and focused.

"I'm okay," he said with a rasp. "Go get in the car and stay low."

Jasper's footsteps pounded by them. Coward was running away.

Harlan pulled himself to a seated position. He could still shoot with his right hand if Jasper came back toward them.

"Halt, or I'll fire!" Sammy yelled, aiming his pistol at the fleeing Jasper.

Chapter Nineteen

Sammy fired a warning shot in the air, but Jasper kept running—drawing closer to the edge of the woods.

Lilah lifted her chin. *Get in the car, my ass.* Jasper was getting away. The man who had killed her dad and her sister and had almost killed her.

She picked up her uncle's fallen shotgun and steadied it against her right shoulder. With no hesitation, she racked the chamber and took aim through the drenching downpour.

Boom.

Jasper's body twitched in the air and then hurtled to the ground.

Got him.

Dead center through the heart, if she wasn't mistaken. Shot in the back the same way he'd murdered his own kin. Justice could be a bitch sometimes—but not today.

"Good job," Harlan drawled, his voice weak.

Lilah set the gun against the wall and knelt beside him, kissing him soundly on the mouth. "Let's get you to the hospital," she said, helping him to his feet.

Sammy rushed over to them and slid his shoulder under Harlan's right arm. "Lean on me." He tossed Lilah the keys. "Open the back door and start the car."

She caught the keys in the air and turned.

"Hey, Lilah," Sammy called. "Great shot."

"That's my girl," Harlan added.

THE HOSPITAL ROOM was filled with flowers and fruit baskets. A large window on the far wall allowed a view of bright stars glistening over the mountains, as well as a few lights from cabins in the hollows.

Who would have thought a hospital room could be so cozy or so beautiful?

The nurse had finally shooed out the slew of visitors, declaring her patient needed rest. Despite their speedy arrival at the hospital, Harlan had lost a lot of blood. They'd given him a transfusion and were keeping him overnight for observation—much to his disgust.

Lilah lay down on her cot beside the sleeping Harlan, close enough so she could reach out and touch him. He'd claimed not to be tired, but ten minutes after the nurse had run off his guests, the medication had done its job and he'd drifted away. Gently, she ran her fingers over his right hand. She should have been exhausted, but she was wide-awake.

And so damn grateful to be alive and with Harlan.

"Hey, gorgeous," he mumbled. "You're still here. You should go home and rest."

"Hush. I'm exactly where I want to be. With you."

Harlan squeezed her hand and she enjoyed the peaceful silence between them—the sort that is most appreciated after the passing of a storm.

"Can we get it right this time?" Harlan asked, breaking the quiet. "A ring, a wedding—the whole nine yards."

Her mouth curved upward. "You asking me to marry you again?"

"I won't stop until we're properly married," he said.

"I know I can be a pompous ass, and my future's uncertain—"

"It's not," she argued, picking up the silver star badge on the end table. "Lewis Slidell left this for you." She pinned it on his thin cotton hospital-issued gown. "You're the new sheriff in town and quite a catch."

He held her arm. "Doesn't mean we have to stay here. I'm willing to leave Lavender Mountain if that's what you want."

Her breath caught. Being the sheriff was his dream job. "You'd do that for me?"

"I'd do anything to have a chance with you again."

"Is that the medication talking?" she asked with an unsteady laugh.

"Hell, you know I love you, Lilah. My life was never the same once you walked in it." He grimaced. "Only took a life-or-death situation to make me realize the truth. Can you stand to be married to such an idiot?"

Which left the original problem that had destroyed their relationship the first time. "What about your career? Won't being hitched to a Tedder destroy your reputation?"

Harlan winced. "Anyone who knows you realizes that I'm the lucky one." He drew a deep breath. "And if we're getting everything out in the open, there's something you should know. It was never about whether you were good enough for me. I'm the one not good enough for *you*."

"You? You're damn near perfect, Harlan," she argued.

"I've told you about my father. I promise you, I'll do everything in the world not to be like him. I want to be the kind of husband and dad that you and the baby deserve. Here or wherever you want to live."

Damn, she loved this man. And, truth be told, she loved her home. Together, they would raise their children nestled in the same ancient mountains where they and their families had lived. Harlan would make it a safer place; she had absolute faith in him.

She leaned over the hospital cot, kissed him chastely on the forehead and started to pull away. Harlan tugged her with his uninjured arm and she fell on top of him. "Harlan!" She giggled. "We can't. What if the nurse comes back?"

He gave an exaggerated sigh. "Guess I'll have to wait until we get home."

Home with Harlan—that had a nice ring. "Just a few more hours. And then we'll have the rest of our lives together."

* * * * *

LET'S TALK
Romance

For exclusive extracts, competitions
and special offers, find us online:

- **f** facebook.com/millsandboon
- **⊙** @millsandboonuk
- **🐦** @millsandboon

Or get in touch on 0844 844 1351*

For all the latest titles coming soon, visit
millsandboon.co.uk/nextmonth